EVERLIGHT

EVERLIGHT

ECLIPSE BOOK THREE

Lindsay French

Podium

Cover design by Dawn Adams and Aleta Rafton

ISBN: 978-1-0394-9134-2

Published in 2025 by Podium Publishing
www.podiumentertainment.com

Podium

EVERLIGHT

CHAPTER ONE

The eighth summer of our kingdom faded into frigid fall days and dwindling sunlight.

My village sprawled out across the land below me, reaching much further than in the old days. Back then, it was only known as Denstar, home to the stubborn and battle-hungry warriors who escaped Eskel the Ruthless for so long, and not the jewel of a young kingdom as it was now. This place had grown with me and our people into a bustling city of multistory buildings and paved roads. We'd built all of this together from the ruins of an old Skia Hellig, and we lovingly helped it grow each year.

Today I stood atop the stone wall of a tower assembled for me to rule from and marveled at how this felt more like home than any place before it, when eight years ago I never believed myself capable of feeling comfortable in a place like this. In a role like this. But this was my family. This city, this kingdom, these people. I belonged to the Elvadel kingdom from the moment we created it. Heart, body, and soul.

Frigid wind bit my face and the tips of my fingers, the only parts of my body left exposed as the light of summer gave way to a quickly approaching winter. In Skia Hellig, the icy temperatures needed little time to overcome our lands. Darkness consumed more of our sunlight with each passing day. Soon we'd only have a few hours of full sunlight every day.

I slid my left foot along the rock wall and opened my stance, focusing my power on the very tip of my sword. Another gust of wind might have hurled me from the tower if not for how I anchored my body with my power. The pain prickling my cheeks kept me focused as I stared at the blue bead of energy steadily growing smaller. While it looked like such a tiny amount of power, the dense energy could reduce the tower I stood upon to a pile of dust if I released it. The chaos that preceded my ascension to ruler taught me to never stop honing my power, because danger lurked all over Skia Hellig and beyond.

Nash drifted from the wall and floated directly in front of the bead of energy, so close that if I flinched, it might hit him. The fear of unleashing it upon him flashed down my spine, and I recoiled. My energy dissipated.

"I told you before not to do that," I said.

He lifted my sword so the sharp tip found his heart. "Do it again." He wore his dark beard a little longer this time of year. With his hood hiding his curls from view, the golden hue of his eyes popped. "You're still too afraid of your power. Trust yourself. What good is pushing your limits if you're not confident?"

"What if the wind gusts again?"

Rather than speak, he merely held my gaze, silently challenging me.

I clenched my teeth and focused on forming the dense ball of energy again, only this time it wasn't even a fraction as powerful as before.

Nash shrugged. "We'll work on it."

"I don't want to work on it."

"Well, that's the problem with peace, isn't it? You don't have enough enemies to test this out on. Those are the stakes you need."

I shook my head. "The stakes of accidentally mauling my husband if I so much as sneeze?"

"Yeah. Those stakes."

I rolled my eyes and dropped my sword to my side. He eased back onto the tower with me, his side brushing mine. "Have faith, Sharpshooter."

Nash slid his arm around my waist and drew me against himself. He lifted us from the tower, so we floated in the air. My stomach fluttered at the pull of gravity that insisted on dragging me back to the ground. But he held me steady and firm in the gusting wind where we hovered over the village. He'd always held me steady.

"Are you going to try out your new move at the competition?" Nash's breath warmed my temple.

"Great idea. I can accidentally kill our most promising warriors."

The brick buildings and colorful homes grew in size as he lowered us toward the ground. Sometimes I missed our quaint houses that had peeked from the hills like little faces, but we needed more housing than that these days. Paved streets complete with streetlights lined our main roads. Our village had changed so much.

Crowds already gathered at the center of town where we rearranged our community area into the main arena for our annual competition. Vendors sold food and goods from stands, villagers helped to finish setting up tables and benches for seating, and tucked into every spare space were small arenas for competitions.

Markus endlessly mocked the idea of hosting any kind of combat in the center of town rather than in the fields surrounding it, but no one wanted to miss a moment of the action. It made no sense to force the children and elderly into traveling or to erect new areas for cooking and serving food. If our people loved anything as much as fighting, it was eating and drinking. The community area provided us with everything we needed. We could handle fixing any damages we caused.

Markus had also questioned Nash when he originally pushed for a yearly competition back in the first days of the kingdom. My advisor had balked and said we literally had thousands of more important decisions to make. But Nash understood people. That made him a great spy back when Eskel the Ruthless forced him into service, and it made him a great war chief now. People needed community, even warriors. No, especially warriors. And so, this competition came into being the very same year our kingdom had eight long years ago.

I looked forward to it every year.

More than providing our people with community, tradition, and entertainment, the sparring matches challenged our warriors and allowed us to watch for promising young fighters.

Heads lifted in our direction as we neared the ground. Nash's longer legs dangled below mine until his feet touched down on the stone tiles of the makeshift arena. Mine settled right after him, and his palm smoothed over my side briefly before he released me. With all our responsibilities, some days we only managed to have these stolen touches and glances, so we savored each one. The eyes of the kingdom never strayed from us, not for a moment, but we learned how to be alone in the midst of a crowd, even if only for fleeting moments during busy weeks like this.

"Prophet—"

"War Chief—"

No less than a dozen people barked our names at once as everyone crowded us, two advisors tugging us in opposite directions. I glanced back at Nash over my shoulder, catching his gaze. The familiar quirk of his smile filled me with warmth. We both loved the festival, and I knew what he was thinking. Nash couldn't wait until it was our turn in the arena.

"We're running out of lodging." One of Markus's assistants spoke above another who tried to direct my attention elsewhere. "Can we use rooms in the tower for—"

"You know I don't care about that," I said with a sigh.

The advisor who ushered me away nodded subtly toward an elderly woman seated in the front row of the stands. "The grandmother of the chief from the village—"

I waved my hand. "I know." Then, smiling wide, I rushed forward to take both her hands. "Elara. I didn't believe you last year when you told me you'd travel all this way."

Weathered fingers gripped mine. "You must be busy. You don't have to sit with me."

"They can wait a few minutes." I glanced at the small crowd waiting on me and they all shuffled back several steps, averting their eyes.

"Do you ever have time alone?" she asked.

"Only when I hide out on the roof."

She laughed loudly and patted my hand, surely thinking I was joking. Her expression quickly straightened, though, and emotion filled her voice. "I'm just happy I lived to see days like this. I never could have dreamed of this kind of peace."

Her words wound a tight loop around my chest, because the threat of war never receded far from our kingdom, and any peace felt only like a rest between battles. "I just want to hold on to it." I thought I hid the anxiety from my voice well, but the sympathy softening her knowing smile told me she saw plainly how deep that fear ran. I rarely allowed myself to feel it, but it was always there, wasn't it? Always there asking, what if?

Or rather . . .

When?

"Oh, dear." Soft hands smoothed over mine. "Let go of your worries." Her gentle voice drifted over the raw, fearful places within me. "Some peace runs so deep that not even war can crush it. You've done well, child. We're ready for our next dark season, whenever it may come. No one can stop the cycle of war and peace, not even the Prophet Eclipse. We can only nurture that peace that will see us through."

I nodded, trying to imagine feeling that kind of acceptance about the inevitability of suffering when I wanted to believe that if I fought hard enough, I could save the people I loved from pain. Ruling a kingdom taught me this was delusional, and yet I couldn't accept it. "I'll trust you on that."

After I became the new Prophet of the Valley and we founded the Elvadel kingdom, we quickly dealt with all the clear threats we faced. The year of turmoil without a leader after I killed Eskel fueled the people's desperation for unity. The Valley-dwellers had been hungry for power of their own and fought tirelessly to protect our piece of the world. The coalition we amassed to take on Lote and the threat from Elias's world provided us with all the might we needed to secure our land. We fought and we won. But those painful days never left my heart.

Not that the years since then only offered us peace. That couldn't be further from the truth. The Flatlanders battled to reclaim the villages Eskel the Ruthless once stole from them, but those villagers wanted to remain in our kingdom now. We defended them against the Flatlanders in two separate short wars. Plenty of danger still threatened the Valley, but it felt like peace to me after all I'd faced in my life.

I knew, though, that while we'd secured our kingdom, Skia Hellig was not a stable land. What came next? That question stirred fear within me. Any conflict, no matter how minor, could plunge us into war.

I started to say something else to the elderly woman when her attention shifted toward the arena and her eyes lit up. I heard the yell a moment later.

"Finally!" Elsie ran toward me in a full sprint. Sunlight glinted off the silver band wrapped around her thin mess of braids, holding them back from her face. I missed when she wore her curls loose and full, but our little warrior would never allow anything to hinder her in a fight. Rightly so. I'd never allowed my hair to get in the way either.

She bounded over a bench and skidded to a stop right in front of me. Her brand-new armor matched the style of young warriors training for battle, and it made her look too grown-up.

"What took so long?" she asked with her fists on her hips. Then, seeming to remember her manners, she turned toward the woman beside me and dipped her head. "Oh, hello, dear elder."

I let out a heavy sigh. Elsie had offered just enough of a welcome to skirt around being chastised, or so she likely thought. "Introduce yourself properly."

Though the girl smiled politely, I recognized the annoyance in her golden-brown eyes. "I'm Elsie, a junior warrior-in-training."

Warriors-in-training most certainly existed, but not any junior ones. Elsie made that title up for herself, because at thirteen she did not yet qualify for any official training position. I struggled to hold back my smirk.

Elara raised her brows. "Daughter of the great Prophet Eclipse and the fearless War Chief Nash," the woman corrected with an amused smile. "Of High Councilwoman Trish and—"

"That and . . ." Elsie sucked in a deep breath. "Future undefeated War Chief Elsie."

"What a formidable young lady you are. I'm Elara, the mother of Chief Frode, and the grandmother of a young man you may remember. A young warrior in-training named Rylan."

Elsie's stare smoldered at the name. Her shoulders straightened and her hand settled on the handle of her right blade. "Yes, I remember Rylan."

"He's competing today," Elara said.

No one needed to tell Elsie that. After she was defeated by the young man two years older than her in the twin sword competition, she'd talked about little else for weeks afterward. Elsie prided herself as the greatest adolescent twin-sword wielder, though such a thing didn't exist before Nash became war chief.

"I'm sorry you'll have to witness your grandson's defeat," Elsie said.

Elara chuckled lightly. "You should never apologize for your victories. You'll only encourage him to train more."

The girl smiled at this and lowered her head with much more deference this time. "Thank you for your wisdom, elder."

"Now, run off and play," I said.

"You mean train." Elsie's eyes narrowed. "I am not playing, and you know that."

"Sure."

She groaned at my jesting, but she still looped her arms around my neck and whispered in my ear. It occurred to me then that she no longer needed to rise onto her toes to do it. "You better beat Daddy in the first match this year. His ego is getting too big."

I squeezed her arm and kissed her cheek. "You know I will, baby girl. Now go find him and tell him you want me to win."

She grinned and ran off with her twin blades bouncing lightly at her sides.

"I believe I was promised another meeting, too," Elara said.

I looked up at those waiting for me, gauging how antsy they looked. "Will you get him?" I asked one of the men, butterflies filling my belly as they always did when we reunited, no matter how long or short our time of separation might have been.

One of the young men ran off quickly. I didn't have to wait long before I spotted Nash cutting through the crowd. My legs moved on instinct, drawing me closer.

Elsie strode beside him with both hands resting on her swords, but the gleeful smile undercut the tough demeanor she wanted the world to see.

I should have known. Despite only arriving at the festival a short while before, Nash already beat me to it. My heart melted.

His large hands lovingly cupped the small bundle against his chest, the white straps of the carrier tight against his leather armor.

I ran the last few steps until I saw his precious face. "There you are," I said softly.

Tiny feet kicked at the sound of my voice. Honey eyes opened sleepily, searching for me. The baby stirred until his gaze found mine, and then the bright, toothless smile spread over his chunky cheeks.

He saw me.

The pure rush of joy that captured his little body seized my heart so it skipped a beat. I needed to hold him and never let go. I needed it like my lungs needed air.

"Hi, Finn," I whispered and slid my fingers into my son's hair. Nash smoothed his hand over my hip, holding me close while we both looked at our baby. He had his father's eyes, just like Elsie.

And he was ours. We were his.

For right now, for this short time in his life, we were his world. Nash, Elsie, and me. But he'd always be mine.

All this happiness inevitably ushered in that twinge of fear that I'd lose it all, but the warmth filling me, the overwhelming joy and awe pounding in my chest, flooded me so much that the anxiety couldn't dim the happiness. Not right now.

I didn't know how Elara could be right about a peace so steadfast that not even war could break it, but this moment made me believe it might possibly be true.

Only wasn't this peace also as fragile as the four-month-old infant nestled against my husband's chest?

We were so powerful and so fragile. So fully both at the same time.

CHAPTER TWO

Elara shuffled close to us and brushed back Finn's short tufts of hair. "What a beautiful boy. It is a pleasure to meet you."

"This is Finn," Elsie said, apparently minding her manners this time. "He's the future second to our undefeated War Chief Elsie."

Nash smiled wryly. "Is that so?"

"It is so." Elsie raised her chin. "I guess if he wants to be a Prophet, he can be that. No offense, Ma, but I'll be too busy with the warriors to do anything else." She seemed to mull this new thought over. "Prophet Finn. It sounds right."

It did not sound right to me. I could hardly imagine him as a toddler, or a young boy, a teenager. Definitely not as a grown man ruling a kingdom. I didn't want my children to ever carry such weight, but if they wanted it, I would help them seize it for themselves.

A problem for another day, because for now, Finn was tiny and innocent. I kissed his soft forehead, and Nash's gaze found me. Seeing him cradling Finn against himself melted me from the inside out. Every time.

Elsie took Finn's hand and seemed to forget all about her status as a junior warrior-in-training or the stakes of her upcoming matches. She cooed at her baby brother and bounced on her toes when he unleashed that rapturous giggle.

I pressed against Nash and relished the fullness I felt.

Having this baby was by far the scariest thing I'd ever done. In fact, the fear of managing a pregnancy while leading the kingdom paralyzed me for several years after I'd decided I wanted to try for one. The vulnerability for myself and my people felt insurmountable. It required a level of trust in Nash as my husband and war chief that he proved more than deserving of. A trust in all those who lead with me as well. But even though I trusted, I still struggled so much with my fear. Often, I couldn't sleep at night while pregnant, worried that a terrible threat might strike when I went into labor and that we'd lose everything because I wanted to bring this life into the world. Because I dared to do something for myself and my family.

One thought had held me back for so long. Our kingdom and our lives were finally safe and stable. How could I risk that, no matter how much I wanted a baby? Wasn't that foolish and selfish?

At one point, I'd look at Elsie and I'd know in a place that reached much deeper than my fear that my family deserved to live. To expand. To become all we wanted to be. This was what we were fighting for. Life. Our lives and everything that made them worth living. I refused to sacrifice my life or our family to fear, no matter how impossible it felt to overcome.

I clutched Finn and Nash tightly against myself and breathed in the freshness of new life. Fragile, peaceful, frightening, courageous new life. He was worth it. So worth it.

The thoughts tried to wiggle their way into this moment. What if I couldn't give him the time and attention he needed? What if war called me away? What if I died and not only left behind a kingdom and a family, but this brand-new baby who depended on me?

There was no preparing for the worst, so dwelling on it made no sense. While I couldn't erase the anxiety, I refused to freely hand it power over my life. When the thoughts stormed through my mind, I did my best to think about something else.

Right now, I imagined how wonderful it would feel to tuck him in tonight and listen to Nash sing him to sleep with that quiet, baritone voice of his. I looked forward to that every single day.

"Ma." Elsie's giggle reminded me that she was still young when she acted so grown up all the time. "Look."

We enjoyed our time together for a few more minutes before I returned to festival preparations. Within hours, no less than a thousand people converged upon the village, until every inch of the center of town and all the surrounding rooftops filled with onlookers.

Running this kingdom took so much time that I really cherished every single day like this one. When it finally came time to sit beside those I held most dear, it felt like the wings of a thousand butterflies fluttering inside me. Leif and Arn sat in the row behind us with all their kids—I swore they'd adopted every child in the Valley. It was hard to keep track of them all these days. Rune leaned forward to hug me from behind, so tenderhearted no matter how tall and burly he looked now. The gentleness of his spirit defied his warrior's appearance. "Hi, Auntie," he said.

I reached behind myself for him. "Hi, sweet boy."

He smiled at that, though it would have embarrassed Elsie.

Wren plopped down beside him and drew him into a hug. "Where's mine?"

Rune grinned, looking so content as he returned the embrace.

I leaned back, resting against Wren's legs, while Piercey took his place beside her. Our family had grown so much, and I knew this was still only the beginning.

Even though we all lived here together, we struggled to find time to relax like this. Everyone was too busy.

Piercey resigned from the Sacred School seven years ago and left the director position to Val in order to work with Markus as a permanent advisor. My old friend's role continued to grow beyond our small kingdom, though. Piercey wanted to see all of Skia Hellig agree to peace negotiations. His diplomatic work encouraged chatter throughout the peninsula that perhaps we now required a new kind of Prophet. One whom we could trust to judge fairly and facilitate talks between rulers.

Wren served as one of Nash's top commanders, while chiefs from all over the Valley called upon Leif for assistance in training their young warriors. With Nash leading the Valley as war chief, and my role as Prophet, it was a wonder we ever had time to sleep.

So days like this with all of us sitting together with our families felt perfect.

Leif leaned forward, smacking in my ear as he chewed his venison jerky. "Next year, you'll face me, girl."

I shoved him back. "In an eating contest?"

He knocked my arm out of the way so he could tear a fresh piece of meat off, his teeth close to my face. I stabbed my finger into the crook of his arm and hit him with a small zap of power that made him wince.

"Stop it," Arn whispered, tugging Leif back.

I smirked in victory, but Leif raised the jerky again, his threat clear. Only Nash ripped the piece from his hand.

My friend's eyes widened when Nash ate it himself.

"You're lucky you're holding an infant," Leif said.

"Is that your recipe?" Nash asked. "It's very good."

Leif humphed and muttered, barely audible, "I knew I should have ripped your throat out before."

"What was that?" I asked.

Though Nash didn't turn around to see Leif again, he was smirking. And I knew that Leif was too, beneath his scowl.

"Look!" Elsie yanked my sleeve and pointed at the baskets that the volunteers carried to the makeshift stage. She sat on the ground, wedged right between my leg and Nash's, in the place she'd sat every year since she was a little girl. The front row had never been quite close enough for her. "There's more colors this year."

No less than a hundred baskets of powder covered the floor of the makeshift arena, all different shades of color. The unexpected surprise of the festival had been finding more than just the most talented warriors, but also those with other amazing gifts. In Elias's world, they highly valued artists. I hadn't originally intended for the festival to encourage the arts, but that just showed me what the people could accomplish when given the power to do so.

The opening ceremony began as it always did. Four people with power sat together on a bench, their focused stares shifting to the sky.

No one needed to tell the crowd to quiet. An expectant hush settled like winter's first snow over young and old alike. An explosion of red powder burst directly over the area, high in the air, and unfurled in a sheet of shimmering energy. Blue and purple erupted next, forming a hazy triangle. Powder drifted up into the sky, unfurling to paint our stories over the clouds. The quiet broke as gasps peppered the gathering.

While my people watched the display of power, I stole a look at them, at the scarred faces of warriors who fought alongside me tirelessly day after day. At the young, innocent eyes already dreaming of the day they'd join us in battle. I looked at Nash, taking more than a glance, as his fingers stroked Finn's tufts of hair, and his hand held the baby close to his heart. I knew all the memories that tinted his look with the kind of heavy contentment earned through winning impossible wars, the kind born of leading an entire kingdom of warriors through battles that decided whether our children lived or died. The gold and silver sparks now lighting the sky filled his eyes, brightening when Elsie grabbed his knee with a gasp. Explosions popped overhead while waves of rolling light stretched beyond what we could see, coating the sky in a radiant gold, lined with silver veins.

"Daddy!" Elsie whispered it, most definitely not wanting the young warriors-in-training to hear the remnants of childhood in her voice. Remnants that I so cherished.

The kids all squealed and cheered while watching the lights dance above us. Not long ago, Elsie would have joined them. Now she held the excitement in so she was quiet, but she couldn't hide the glee beaming from her face.

Elsie looked exactly as she had at six or seven years old in the early days of the festival when she'd never seen anything like it. Soon, she'd be old enough to officially start training, and not long after, we wouldn't be able to hold her back from battle. And even if her eyes lit this brightly after that, it would never be exactly the same again. It couldn't be. War changed everything.

But today was not that day. I refused to allow it to come into being in my mind before it even happened in real life. I refused to grieve the shadows of future losses still unfathomed and unfathomable.

So I melted against Nash's shoulder. He shifted to wrap his arm around me and pulled me into his warmth.

Finn fussed for a moment, not yet used to the rancor of Skia Hellig. That wouldn't last long.

"Welcome, brothers and sisters," Markus's deep voice belted throughout the crowd, aided by power. He walked into the arena with his long arms raised. "Welcome to our grand celebration, in the glorious eighth year of the Elvadel kingdom. Our great Prophet and war chief welcome you to our home. We are all honored to be here with the mother and father of our kingdom."

Markus loved this part, which worked for me, because I hated doing it. I relaxed with my family while Markus impressed himself—and, in all fairness, the entire kingdom—with his charisma and charm. His eyes found mine as he gave a smile, maybe remembering the early days when he cajoled me into doing the parts of this job I hated with the promise of days like this. I'd been so young then, that I sometimes forgot I was still young now. Every other Prophet was still at least ten years older than me.

Markus's remarks would soon transform into a show of our history as a kingdom, and while everyone else loved this part of the festival, I always cringed. It wasn't because of the pain behind those memories, but because of the way he told the stories. Like they were tales passed on through the genera-tions. It didn't feel like my story. But I supposed it was no longer my story. It was theirs. The people of my kingdom who needed me to be more than any human ever could be.

Still, I twisted with the unpleasant anticipation of watching the rest of the opening remarks.

"Once, the poison of Eskel the Ruthless spread over the entire Valley." As Markus spoke, black powder as dark as obsidian shot up from several baskets and coated the sky like an impenetrable black cloud. Lighter shades of black and gray rose up, mingling until they formed a shadowy figure that held a long spear. Silver power flashed in tiny bolts of lightning.

My people fell silent again, watching the show unfurl above them as Markus narrated our bloody history. The artists blended into the crowd, making it look like the picture created itself. Like they weren't the genius behind their own work. For a moment, the young seemed to buy into the illusion and forget that this wasn't real.

People like me who washed the blood from their armor couldn't forget this was only a show. I bit my cheek.

Nash dipped to whisper in my ear, his lips brushing my skin. "What do I get if I win our matches?"

I scoffed and twisted to glare at him. "Absolutely nothing but scorn. You won't win."

His smirk dragged me through time just the same as if I used my power to travel to our past. The same smirk as the very first day we met. As every time he'd teased me since. "You're adorable when you're mad, though. That's something."

My jaw tightened. "Don't. I won't give you the satisfaction."

He returned his stare to the arena. "Already are."

"Damn it, Nash." Despite my pouting voice, I still nestled back beside him. Nash knew me so well. Knew when I needed him.

But I still couldn't let him get away with winning, so I dug my knuckles into his ribs hard enough that he brushed my hands off. My pettiness only made him smirk again.

"Let me beat you down in peace," I said. "Don't take this from me."

Nash kissed my temple and then nodded. "Alright, I'll let you win."

He knew I never wanted him to let me win. I wanted to defeat him soundly, with no question about who bested who. My fist jabbed his side, stirring the baby.

His eyes widened. "Really?" he whispered.

"Sorry," I mouthed at Finn and took him from Nash's arms. "It's your dad's fault." With Finn curling up against me, the entire world felt right, as if there wasn't a single awful thing happening anywhere right now. His body was so tiny and soft against me. So innocent and perfect.

This time when Nash smiled at me, it was serious and full of life. "I love fighting you during the festival."

Warmth filled my chest. So much warmth, I wasn't even sure how to contain it. "Me, too."

"Be quiet," Elsie whispered. "You're so annoying when you flirt. It's gross."

"You'll make him do it more," I said. "You know your dad can't resist vexing us. He's too much of a child."

"One day," Nash said to Elsie, "you'll love someone so much that you'll start a family—"

"Oh, for the love of the gods." Elsie plugged her ears and closed her eyes.

"—You'll have kids just so you can torture them with how much you love each other."

"You're ruining the ceremony," she whined.

"Then you'll thank me for setting such a good example and preparing you to live a long, joyful life."

"She's not listening anymore," I said.

Elsie trained her stare on the glittering red figures forming an army above us.

Nash held me close as we quieted, held me in place as he had for almost a decade now. I hoped I'd helped hold him in place, too.

Soon, dozens of different colors of powder formed an image of Flare's face, shockingly similar to how she really looked.

"It's time," Nash said.

Elsie continued to watch, her stare fervent.

"Elsie," Nash said with a warning note in his voice.

She groaned and looked down as she withdrew the cloth we made her bring from her pocket, begrudgingly stuffing it in her ears to block out the noise.

We never used to allow Elsie to remain during this part. She and Trish would leave to return to the tower until it was over. But two years ago, Elsie insisted that it was her right to hear our history and to deal with it however she wanted. I couldn't deny that, so we allowed her to stay, as long as she did not watch the part where I died.

I couldn't bear for her to see that in any depiction.

Besides, she was still a child, and it was our job to protect her.

I used to be tempted to look away, but of all the pain that haunted me still, somehow this no longer hurt me. I didn't fear memories of the Prophet killing me at Dr. Henderson's behest, not when I'd lived it so many times. Not when

I returned home beyond what once felt so singular. Plenty of past pain invaded my nightmares and hung heavy in my heart, but killing those two wasn't part of that. So, I wanted my people to see me watch. I wanted them to know that I'd conquered this part of the story. That I could watch her kill me and not even flinch.

As the dark spear of powder plunged into my depicted form, red powder burst and rained down over the crowd.

My brow raised at the new addition this year. "A little crass, isn't it?"

"We can tell them to stop," Nash said, as he did every year.

"It honestly doesn't bother me because it's nothing like it was. It's just kind of silly."

"They love it." Nash tucked a strand of my hair behind my ear. "The Prophet Eclipse gave her life to fight the gods and then stole her body back to save us all. They can't get enough of it."

"It makes it feel like it didn't really happen when it did."

"Shh," Nash whispered. "Legends never feel real. It's your fault for becoming one while you're still alive."

If I really wanted to put a stop to this, I could. Markus would never hurt me by resurrecting the pain of days I'd left behind. But I'd once spent a great deal of effort trying to derail the inevitable transformation of my name into Eclipse and my life into something much more than mine. So, I endured the discomfort every year. Like Nash said, the people loved it.

I tapped Elsie's shoulder when the story turned to the chaotic days after I killed the Prophet so that she could watch the birth of our kingdom. She was right. She did need to know our history, because one day she'd be the one making it. Elsie needed to see our mistakes and not repeat them, and learn from what we did right.

The girl looked enraptured as she watched our life dance through the sky.

"They don't have the full story," Nash said. "You're right." He kissed my jaw while everyone was too distracted by the show to even remember we existed right here in the flesh and not merely as pretty pictures in the sky. "The rest is for us."

I ran my knuckles along the side of his face. "I'd tell the story differently."

"You know too many secrets. You'd anger the gods."

The thought of their security system gripped me with a sudden, paralyzing fear. In the last eight years, there'd been no sighting of him, no reminder of his promise that if we defied the natural order of the gods, he'd kill us. How could we learn to defeat an enemy we'd only seen once? Who could appear at will and finish us with a snap of his fingers?

The same fear darkened Nash's eyes. We said nothing more, only watched the rest of the show while holding each other.

When it finished, the powder fell like rain all over us, bathing us in our own history. Once it cleared from the air, the sun seemed to turn back on and shone brightly upon us.

"So let us begin," Markus shouted. "Bring your mightiest warriors. Let our young test themselves and let our legends remind us all of what we aspire to be." Lifting his hand to me and Nash, Markus grinned. "There's no better way to start than with our most popular tradition." When he raised his fist in the air, all our people screamed and cheered, challenging us to the arena.

Piercey took Finn from me and Wren pinched his round cheek.

"Have fun," my old friend said.

The crowd roared when Nash and I stood. The excitement of facing him pumped through me. Last year, we couldn't have a real match because of the pregnancy. Nash hadn't even wanted to face me, which made me mad enough to fight him for real. He most certainly was not going to swing his sword at me when he worried any wrong move might hurt me or the baby. It drove me crazy.

But this year . . .

This year there was no holding back.

We eyed each other as we walked up to the arena, the people growing louder with each step. Even with the power amplifying Markus's voice, we could barely hear him.

"Our mighty Prophet Eclipse and the fierce War Chief Nash."

CHAPTER THREE

The people chanted the names they'd given us.

I preferred Max the Sharpshooter and Nash the Unknown to Prophet and War Chief, but those names existed now as family names, marks of those who truly knew us.

Nash and I climbed into the arena and kept our stares locked on each other as we walked to Markus. Our people loved this nearly as much as we did. They loved that their war chief could take on their Prophet, when the kingdom considered me invincible. I wasn't. But I couldn't convince any of them of such a truth. That I was human and fallible like the rest of them. Coming back from the dead might have played a role in that. After my ascension to Prophet, stories like that couldn't be kept quiet. While I managed to guard our most important secrets, all of Skia Hellig knew of my greatest exploits within a year's time.

Markus smirked at each of us. "Don't cause too much damage. We're busy enough as it is."

"We can't worry about damages when fighting, Markus." I nodded at the warriors gathered around the arena on benches. Their shields would protect the people and village alike. "That's their job."

He sighed and then lifted the necklaces holding our sealing stones. Nash and I grabbed them eagerly, ready to begin.

I fastened the silver chain around my neck and closed my eyes as I focused upon the clear stone dangling from it. The fire of my power poured out from my body into the necklace until it stung my skin. The stone now glowed red against me.

Piercey and Elias created this incredible device together during one of the rare times the gods allowed them to work together in the other world. It relied upon me using my own energy to bind my power, so no one could ever force me to bind it. The chip at the heart of the stone prevented the slightest leak of power while it was activated. I loved that this enabled me to train and spar with our warriors, regardless of whether they had a neural implant or not.

Nash bound his power in the stone as well, turning it a deep blue. Then he winked at me, already trying to unnerve me. Every year, he won the powerless sword fight against me, and every year I returned the favor once we fought with our power.

And every year it infuriated me that I still couldn't beat him at both.

I narrowed my eyes while he merely smirked in return. He loved to tease me as much as he loved to fight me, and I supposed that was because they were two sides of the same coin. It still bothered me that he won at this, too—the teasing and flirting. He knew I hated losing.

But I did love the look he got in his eye.

Nash's hands settled on his twin blades, looking deceptively relaxed when he was prepared to strike in a fraction of a second. The motion hushed all those watching. Anticipation buzzed inside me.

My own smile broke through my forced frown, and I snapped forward to cover it, not wanting to let him feel satisfied with himself once again. At least not with our swords drawn and a crowd watching.

No matter how many times I saw Nash draw his swords, I never got used to the rapid blur of his blades. How anyone could move so fast without power amazed me.

Our weapons clashed with a hissing promise of more to come. The clang of sword against sword erupted in rapid succession. The people studied the display of swordsmanship eagerly. I couldn't pretend the fascination was for the heavy arc or rapid thrust of my blade, but for how handily their war chief fended off the sword of their invincible Prophet.

I understood. Watching Nash fight mesmerized me, too.

Rolling off my shoulder, I sprang up, forcing him to block low. Then I abandoned the assault to pivot behind him. His blade snapped behind his back, catching my own. I tensed in anticipation for the moment the tide of the match would change, for the strike that signified Nash no longer observed but drove forward on the offense.

There was never any preparing for it.

He turned on his heel, locked onto my eyes, and as quickly as he'd unsheathed those swords, he drove both his blades for my core. I threw all my weight into my blade to defend against the attack and still I barely held him off. In the past, it would have landed me on my ass.

Pride and satisfaction flooded Nash's face when I successfully blocked the powerful attack. He didn't slow down, though. No time to get my bearings. I used both hands to block the next one, my arms shaking and my blade wobbling. He was too strong. Another hit like that would break my defense for sure when I couldn't use my power to fortify myself. And I was certain he'd held back just then.

"We talked about this," I said as we both struck. These weren't real hits, though. Only enough to keep the crowd happy while we talked.

Nash didn't ask what I meant because he knew exactly what he was doing. "I can't help it."

It was hard enough for him to knock me down during a sparring match before the baby, but now that I'd carried our child, I wasn't sure he could bring himself to do it. He'd gotten too used to pampering me last year. The damn man. I needed him to do this. I needed a real match against him.

"Fight me," I demanded. "Don't punish me because you feel guilty that you couldn't endure the pain of pregnancy for me."

He laughed quietly. "I'm not punishing you."

Nash stayed with me every step of the way through the pregnancy, delivery, and recovery. He'd seen every moment of suffering, how hard it was even for someone like me who was accustomed to pain. I really was ready to fight, though. Finn was four months old, and I had worked hard to prepare for this match.

"Are you sure you're okay?" he asked. "Truly recovered?"

"Yes."

He nodded, speaking quietly. "Okay. I'm sorry."

"Not forgiven." But my grin told him the opposite. I threw myself forward and unleashed a series of rapid strikes. I could see Nash wrestling with his instinct, but I trusted him to overcome it and to face me the way we both truly wanted. We loved fighting each other, and I wouldn't allow having a baby to change that.

The muscles in his jaw bunched and a certain hardness came over him. That lethal look quieted his expression.

A wave of exhilaration hit me. Nerves and excitement. The fear that I couldn't win and the determination that I absolutely must.

This time when Nash moved, I instantly knew I wasn't going to stop him. I tried, but the twin swords knocked mine away, leaving me wide open. His knee came for my stomach, and I jumped back as he grazed my tunic. Despite the concern in his eyes, he kept coming for me.

Even though Nash forced me onto my heels, the challenge fueled me. The next time he attacked, I wedged my sword between both of his and twisted my wrist like he'd taught me. It spread his blades just enough for me to slip through and close in on him for a devastating thrust of my blade. One that brought me so close I felt his breath wash over me.

Nash dropped one of his swords to catch my wrist. Knowing I wouldn't be able to free my arm, I let the momentum swing me, so my back landed against his chest. I slammed my palm into the crook of his sword-wielding arm.

When he didn't budge, I threw my head back for his throat, but he released me and sidestepped. Desperate for the advantage, I wheeled around to block him from retrieving his sword. He slid across the ground, scooping it up on the way, and then he was fully armed again.

I groaned with disappointment. He looked surprised and exhilarated. Nash hadn't expected me to get that close.

"Get him, Ma!" Elsie screamed from the sidelines.

My muscles burned as I attacked as rapidly as possible, searching for any opening. Our swords danced until Nash successfully knocked mine to the side with one of his and jabbed for my midsection with the other. I shifted to the right, just evading the attack, and caught his forearm against my side. He was stronger than me and he'd easily break free, but it gave me a precious second to reposition myself.

Instead of ripping his arm away from me, he slipped it behind me and pulled me against his chest. With my sword still forced off to the side by his and his free arm holding me close, we were both left open. Our bodies pressed together so tightly I felt his pounding heartbeat against my chest. It lasted only a second, but Nash brought his mouth to mine and stole a kiss. The heat and softness of his lips warmed me in the cold.

I shoved him back even though my body wanted to lean in for more. "You ass."

He grinned, his gaze skittering down me as he repositioned his swords. "I'm only human, Sharpshooter."

"Don't kiss me when we're fighting," I said.

His sword caught mine and we spoke with only our steel separating our faces. "You love when I kiss you while fighting."

I kicked at him and forced a few inches to open between us. "Not with the whole kingdom watching."

The cocky smirk crawled back onto his face, and he rolled his shoulders, looking far too confident. "Make me apologize, then."

That drew out my own grin. "Oh, I will."

Even more desperate to win, I attacked so ferociously that the steel of our blades cried out as if they were in pain. A loud crack erupted. The top half of my sword flew free and embedded itself in the ground. My eyes widened at the jagged edge of my broken weapon.

I refused to lose because of a broken sword.

Screaming, I ran into Nash so hard that he caught me, seemingly on instinct. Rearing back, I swung my broken sword for him. When he blocked it, the uneven edge caught one of his swords. It spun from his grasp.

We both dove for the sword to retrieve it. I landed on top of him, straining to reach, but he rolled me over to block me from grabbing it.

Nash locked my wrists above my head, nearly wrenching the sword from my grasp. We both breathed hard, coated in sweat despite the cold wind. The feel of his hard chest bearing down against me made me think about how my lips still burned for another kiss.

Never trust a spy in battle. Especially not a charming one.

I rammed my knee into his side and tried to slam my head into his.

Nash shifted to dodge the headbutt, but the hit jostled him enough that I ripped out of his grasp.

We both rolled, jumping to our knees. I landed with my sword already swinging. An armored forearm blocked it. One of Nash's twin blades might have cut into my side, except I caught it with my sheath. My arms trembled with his exertion as his hot, heavy breath fell against my face.

"You got distracted," I said.

He made no apologies, the love of battle and the heat we both felt bright in his stare. "You did, too."

We shoved back from another, on our feet now, swords ready. The people cheered, but I barely heard them. As desperately as I wanted to finally win this first match, I almost wanted to let him kiss me even more.

Instead, I launched forward, but twisted right before striking, coming up on his left side at just the right angle, because I knew every one of his weak spots. Seeing what I was doing, Nash grinned and blocked. He'd barely made the move in time, but that didn't matter. He stopped me and the disappointment stung.

I reared back from another hit when his sword cut against the top of mine and wrenched it from my grasp.

Just like that.

I stared in horror at my fallen blade while he set the tip of his sword against my chest. "I win."

My jaw tightened and anger flashed through me. How could I let him break my sword and then knock it from my grasp? Looking at him, though, a different kind of tension competed with my frustration. Nash looked amazing with the high of the fight shining in his eyes and his chest pumping.

"Good fight," I said.

His stare tore through me. "Incredible fight."

I almost did it. Almost dragged myself up to his lips even though everyone watched. But he beat me in the match, and then he kissed me for the whole kingdom to see. So, I eased in, rising to my toes, drawing him to me, playing his game. As soon as he shifted my way, I popped him in his side.

Nash grunted and uttered a low chuckle, lips close to mine. Eyes still on me. The fight still burning in them. "So petty."

"I warned you." My fingers found the clasp of the necklace and I removed it, feeling the fire of my power pour back through my body. "You brought this on yourself."

His gaze wandered. Quiet enough for only me to hear, he said, "I know I did."

I shook my head at his teasing and brazenness. At his seriousness as well.

"I'm going to win this year," he said, and I thought he really believed it, just as I did in the last match. He unfastened his necklace and threw it to the side.

Of all the things in my life that amazed me—and there were too many count—this stunned me the most. That this man loved me, and I slept beside him every night of my life. That I got to have him. Him.

His eyes glowed with eagerness, bright against his short, dark beard.

I drew in a very long, slow breath and steadied myself. Any enemies out there who wanted to fight me for real right now would do best to run and hide, because I felt like I could instantly eviscerate anyone who tried to take this precious family from me.

"I'm ready to fight," I shouted desperately, earning a laugh from Nash.

CHAPTER FOUR

The warriors raised a powerful shield around the arena to protect everyone who was watching. The light gray dome flickered with energy and slightly blurred the faces of those in the audience.

Nash lifted from the ground and hovered over the sun, so I needed to squint to look at him.

"Already resorting to cheap tricks?" I asked.

"Just catching my breath," he said.

I rolled my eyes. The people loved to see him fly because we knew of no one else able to do this. If not for connecting with Jax, I doubted Nash ever would have figured out flight.

He drifted over me so I could see him without the sun shining in my eyes. "Ready?" he asked.

I answered by raising my palm to him and blasting him with an unseen wave of energy. He dodged in the air and impressed me with his steadiness. Even two years ago, Nash might have careened out of control.

When he first acquired his powers eight years ago, he advanced faster than I thought possible. Piercey believed that the two of us somehow connected with our power or drew upon mine from previous lives. We both possessed an uncanny amount of energy, and Nash was the only person I'd taken through time with me. That day when I'd slipped after he first saw me use my power, I took him back to the eclipse, and I wondered over the last few years if entangling with him like that had unlocked something in him as it had for me.

But I knew with no doubt that Nash could not yet beat me in a competition using power. He must have known the same about me and his twin swords. No one could beat us in such a match, not even each other.

I loved that even more than I hated it.

We fired on each other to warm up with our powers, using shields or dodging to defend ourselves. Nash flew straight down for me, and I teleported out of the way just as his powered punch cracked the stone floor of the arena where I'd been standing.

I reappeared in front of him, already kicking. He blocked with both forearms, but the force of the attack splintered his armor.

He ripped the guards off his arms and threw them to the side.

The people loved seeing us fight with our powers, except I worried about hurting Nash. Without the use of the necklace to bind our energy, I relied upon my own control. Accidentally hurting all those people as a child still haunted me.

Every year that we dueled at the festival, Nash performed considerably better than the previous year with his power. So that actually increased the danger of sparring with him, because I needed more powerful attacks that proved more difficult to control.

It required more and more trust in myself.

Nash peppered me with small blasts of energy that I fended off with my forearms and knees. No longer did I need to lean on bulky shields that required excessive amounts of energy, unless the attacks proved too powerful. As long as I matched or exceeded the energy thrown at me with my movements, I deflected the strikes with ease.

Nash twisted and lobbed a strong blast of sizzling blue energy at me.

I jumped and kicked it right back for him. He slid to the side to avoid his own attack, and it crashed into the dome. The energy sparked against the defensive barrier, and I worried it wouldn't hold.

"Not bad," Nash said.

"You, too."

"Get her, Dad!" Elsie screamed from the sidelines.

I gasped. "I thought you were rooting for me."

"Not for this match," she said.

Nash beat his fist against his chest once. "That's right. She picks me."

"Because she knows you're the loser."

He wagged his finger at me. "That's not very nice, especially coming from someone who just lost."

I bolted forward and slammed my fist into his gut, leaving behind a small fog of energy. The haze erupted into fiery sparks moments later. He shielded himself against the attack in time to avoid damage, but I knew it stung.

His elbow reared back for me. I blocked and hit him with enough force to shove him a few steps back. Or, it should have been enough. It had been last year. This time, Nash grunted and held his footing, determined eyes on mine.

Impressive.

I couldn't keep from smiling at the progress as we returned to trading punches and kicks, sneaking in energy attacks at the most opportune times. One of my hits drew blood from the corner of his mouth and stopped me in my tracks for a second. Nash advanced, though, and, when my heart accepted that I hadn't hurt him, I continued as if it hadn't happened.

The spectators enjoyed the show so far, many shouting for Nash to fly again, or for me to use my energy bow and arrow. They wanted to see their favorite moves from past years, and we enjoyed showing them off.

But there came a point in the battle when I realized I no longer could defeat Nash in a match of my power against his without crossing a threshold I didn't want to cross. I needed to hit him with too much energy. Even knowing warriors guarded us, prepared to intervene to save us from the worst attacks, I still couldn't actually threaten him like that.

That left me few options to win this fight without making it bloody.

He flew around me in an attempt to find a weak spot, but I gathered my power in my hands and teleported a few feet away from him. As he started to run for me, I focused the energy on the tips of my pointer fingers, packing it into a dense ball.

Nash erected a full energy shield in front of him. "Oh, so now you're not afraid of that attack?"

"I'm feeling particularly inspired."

"Or particularly vindictive," Nash said.

"You know how I hate to lose."

Sweat wet Nash's temples as he continued to power his shield, the energy undergirding it growing into a darker blue. I stepped forward until my dense ball of energy touched his shield. Despite all the effort Nash funneled into his defense, it immediately dissolved like the powder that rained down on us during the opening entertainment. I stood still now with the energy aimed at Nash's chest.

He sighed long and slow, the determination still bright in his eyes, warring with the undeniable truth. "I lose."

"Yeah, you do."

The dome faded and Markus climbed back into the arena. The crowd roared and cheered while he riled them up even more. Though I waved at our people, shouting hello to visitors I didn't see often, Nash consumed my thoughts. I replayed our first match in my mind and analyzed the moves we made, wanting to improve for next time.

We'd drawn close to one another. I looked up at him and he slid an arm around my waist. Sweat slickened our bodies. We both breathed hard and leaned against one another with the fatigue setting in. A smile crawled onto the corner of my mouth when our eyes met.

How many battles had we fought and won together?

"Connect!" one of the kids yelled. It rippled throughout the crowd, until they were demanding it.

"Are you too tired?" I asked.

"Not even close."

Nash and I turned our backs to each other.

I searched along the warmth surrounding me and deep within myself for his feel, instinctively connecting as soon as the peace of his presence loosened my chest. In the beginning, it took three years of daily practice to connect from only an arm's length away when before we needed to be touching. We stretched our limits these days, moving further and further apart over time.

So doing this with our backs to each other felt easy now.

When I opened my eyes, I saw the world through my own perception, but I sensed it through his like a mirage hovering over my own. I felt the warmth of power sparking in his hands as it also formed in my own, the two of us sharing the same attack that fed off the same source of energy. We'd combined ourselves and powers into one.

One of the warriors lifted a basket into the air on Nash's side that only he could see, but that I could sense.

I raised my hand behind me without looking and we fired at the same time on the target. Silver powder caught the wind and swept over me.

I relished the intimacy of intertwining our minds, bodies, and perspectives. Our power. It was a physical manifestation of the closeness I felt to him after so many years together.

When we released our connection to each other, a pang of emptiness hit me in my gut. We couldn't connect for too long without exhausting or overstimulating ourselves, and yet letting go of each other always hurt a little.

"Look at that, Sharpshooter." Nash opened my fist with his hand and intertwined his fingers with mine. "That's a perfect shot."

The people loved the show we put on, and it left Markus with a happy crowd.

After leaving the arena, we mingled with excited guests while waiting for the rest of the matches to begin. On the first day of the festival, the commanders and most renowned warriors competed against one another. Elsie had talked of little else for the last few weeks. She sat with her friends now and made bets on the potential winners of each match. Elara proudly carried Finn around, much to the jealousy of many others who wanted to hold him. She offered to do us the favor of watching him today, but I knew she silently begged for us to share him.

Once the next match began and attention turned to the two commanders ready to spar, Nash and I managed to extricate ourselves from conversations with our guests. We sneaked away to the slim walkway between two houses, and Nash eased me back against the wall.

He spoke close to my lips, his thumb trailing my chin. "Get us out of here, Sharpshooter."

"Only if you agree to a third match."

"I agree to anything."

"Whoever lands the first kiss on the lips wins."

One brow quirked. "Another one I'll win at."

"Winner takes all the glory," I said.

I focused on our room and teleported us away from the festival. As soon as we landed, I pushed his shoulders hard, so he fell back on the bed against his hands.

"A little rough," he said, "but it's a good effort—"

My fist rapidly connected with his sternum, packing enough power to break through whatever defense he might erect. With the speed of my hit, I expected I might land it, but I was shocked when my punch plowed into him completely undefended.

Nash coughed and clutched his chest, gasping. "What the hell?"

"Why didn't you block me?" I cried.

"I didn't think . . . that's what you were going for . . ."

"I thought it was clear."

"I figured you meant whoever got the other to cave first." He rubbed his chest. "Damn, that hurt."

I winced and reached forward to touch my fingers to the spot I hit. Unless he only wanted to fool me right now, so I'd draw close enough for him to trick me. I froze with my hand in midair and narrowed my eyes in suspicion.

"What is happening in that head of yours right now?" Nash asked.

"I don't like losing. You know that. I have to fight you the way I best know how." I jumped on top of him and tackled him onto his back. "Now lose!"

Nash caught my hands before I could grab his face. "Max!"

With a small blast of power, I shoved his hands away from mine to grab his head. My lips dove for his but he smashed his palm against my mouth.

He turned his face away, laughing. "Stop it."

His arms moved for my waist, but I scurried away. Nash caught my leg and dragged me beneath him, rolling on top of me. A laugh pried free of my lips. I covered my mouth with both hands, fending off his kiss. His mouth landed against my knuckles.

"You're driving me crazy," he said. "There's no kids, no advisors, no farmers complaining about land divisions, or townsfolk bickering over their feuds. Who knows how much time we have."

My laugh only grew when he pulled my hands away and I hid my face against his chest. I bit him and he drew back.

"Ow." He caught my cheeks and ran his thumb along my bottom lip. "Cut it out, Max."

"I'm going to win this time." I craned and my lips almost found his, but he stuck his fingers in my mouth to block me.

I gasped. "See. You don't want to lose either!"

A touch as soft as feathers tickled behind my ear and Nash nipped my neck. Hot breath wafted over me.

"No, no, no," I said, slapping his shoulders. "Don't you dare."

"It's not my fault you aren't using all the weapons at your disposal." He spoke the words slowly, tugging my sleeve down until he could speak against my bare shoulder. He kissed me softly. "Concede."

I shook my head, closing my eyes at the chills from his mouth gently gliding to my collarbone, igniting the memory of him pulling me into his kiss during the fight.

I wasn't the only one he distracted right now. My hands circled his wrists, and I used my power to pin them down against the bed. "Ha," I said.

Our breath washed over each other's lips.

"You're going to lose," I whispered.

"You are," he said, looking so close to kissing me.

Our eyes met for only a moment, and the draw overcame me. We both pressed closer, lips parting in a deep kiss.

My palm glided up to his shoulder and he released my arm to drag me closer.

We never decided who won or lost.

"Hold it steady, Els," I said, clutching the fencing to keep myself from bounding over for a better view. We blended in with the crowd gathered at the festival as best as the Prophet and war chief could. Commanders sparred in the area while competitions took place in roped off areas like this all over town. "Better to take a few extra seconds than to miss."

Her focused eyes narrowed as she aimed her arrow at the target. Pausing during a competition killed her. I felt it. But Elsie heeded my advice and took a long, deep breath. When she released the arrow, it cut through the air with a perfect spin, its path arching up to take the breeze into account. I knew the moment she shot the arrow, long before it cut right into the center of the target, that it was perfect.

"Yes!" I shouted.

Nash clapped loudly. "You've got it, baby girl."

A subtle glare was shot in our direction while Elsie nocked another arrow.

I covered my mouth. "We distracted her."

"No," Nash said. "We embarrassed her."

When the next arrow plunged directly into the second target, I had to bite my lips together to keep from cheering.

The kid next to Elsie kept looking at her with panic twisting his expression while she continued to shoot with lethal accuracy. The next two flew slightly off-center but still earned her good points.

Elsie trained with the bow and arrow every day, just like with her twin blades. No matter how many times I watched her shoot, though, it always amazed me. In a few years when she was strong enough to hold a bigger bow, she could compete against the older teenagers.

Ten minutes later, the competition ended with Elsie as the clear victor. She walked toward us with her bow secured on her back and her look so reminiscent of her father's after battle. Confident and unsurprised. Satisfied.

Nash took hold of her arms. "You did it, Elsie!" He hoisted her in the air and spun in a circle. "Look at you!"

"Oh, gods," Elsie cried, kicking her feet. "Put me down."

He obliged and set her on the ground, but only to grab her up in a big hug. His large frame swallowed her whole. Elsie screamed with embarrassment and pushed him away. How did only a few short years erase how much she once loved when her father spun her through the air?

"Would you stop it," she whispered.

"I can't be proud of my little warrior?" he asked.

Her hands flew over her face. "Ma, please. Little warrior? Really? Get him under control."

True joy filled Nash's eyes. "You did well, kid."

Despite Elsie acting so ashamed, I caught the little smile that sneaked its way onto her face. She started to say something when her eyes widened. With a gasp, she stomped past us and stopped in front of a young man who wandered down the street. His sandy brown hair looked ruffled with bits of sticks and leaves in it. He must have just finished fighting.

It was Rylan, Elara's youngest grandson who had defeated Elsie in a twin sword fighting competition last year.

"You," Elsie said.

He leaned in, eyes sharp. "Me."

She drew back, pinching her lips together. "You better sign up to face me with the twin blades. I need my rematch."

"You didn't hear? I'm a warrior-in-training now. We're not competing against each other anymore."

The realization seemed to horrify Elsie. "Fight me anyway. Come back to the tower later and—"

"Elsie," Nash said. "You're not dueling at the tower."

"Why not? You fight there all the time."

"He's a guest. He traveled a long way. I'm sure he wants to visit with friends and family, not fight you after dinner."

The boy was still looking at Elsie. "I'd fight you." Then he looked up at Nash. "But I won't fight you." He chuckled. "Not yet, at least. Give me a few years. So, if you won't allow it, I'll have to honor your wishes until I train hard enough to beat you."

My husband was grinning now. Oh, Nash liked the kid. "You'll fight me in a few years, huh?"

"Yes, War Chief. I'll fight you and I won't be easy to beat."

Elsie groaned at her challenge seeming to be forgotten. "You're not getting to him unless you can beat me. I've been training. If you ever want to fight our war chief, then you fight me first. You're not worthy if you can't beat me."

"Deal." Rylan raised his forearm in her direction. "I need to prepare for my next match. We'll compete properly when you're a warrior-in-training, too. You better prepare, because I won't go easy on you."

Elsie watched him walk away, but I couldn't help watching her, stunned to see how much she grew up each year.

Nash looked from Elsie to me, the admiring look he'd given the boy now turning to a pensive expression. "Do you think—"

"Don't think," I said. "Elsie is like me. She doesn't like losing. Don't get paranoid."

"I'm not paranoid."

"You're a little paranoid."

"It's just that if any boy wants to even think about charming my kid, he's got to meet some standards. Elsie might have a whole kingdom of boys wanting to marry her, especially if she keeps winning competitions."

"Dad." Elsie turned around slowly. "I can hear you. Rylan is my enemy. He beat me and I cannot allow that to happen again."

"Well," Nash said, "you know how things worked out for your ma and me."

The horror of Elsie's gasp mirrored what she might unleash if Nash had told her she'd never become a warrior.

I hushed Nash and raised a hand toward our daughter. "I'll deal with him, Elsie."

"What did I do?" he asked.

"You know exactly what you did," I said in a whisper. "For someone so obnoxiously charming, you're a real idiot when it comes to your daughter."

"Being a father makes you stupid sometimes."

I sighed. "Yeah." Then I nodded at Elsie. "Go on and have fun. He's teasing you."

Elsie still glared at her dad. "I want you to take it back."

"I take it back." Nash walked forward to ruffle her hair and kiss the top of her head. "Now go. Have fun."

The girl hesitated before glancing over to a group of her friends. She ran off, seeming to forgive Nash, for now.

"You better watch yourself," I said. "She's good with that bow and those swords."

He grinned. "A girl ought to be able to kill her father. That's the sign of parenting well done. I don't think we're there yet."

I shook my head. "You're insane."

We spent the day with friends and family, enjoying one of the best weeks of the year. But before the sun even fully set, which happened rather early these days, I noticed the candlelight glowing in Piercey's window in the tower. I stared. "He's preparing for the summit, isn't he?"

Nash smiled away my worry. "Pretend it doesn't exist today. We can worry about the summit next week when we go."

I often needed to live by those words. When ruling a kingdom, worries never ceased, especially with these so-called peace talks with the other Prophets looming over us.

Today, I let it go, though, because I had learned to never allow a day of joy to slip away from me.

CHAPTER FIVE

Fjords rose all around us as our boat snaked through the narrow channel between the rocky enclaves of the cliffsides. Now that we left the open sea, the wind stilled more, but the bit that still whipped across the deck of the boat was bitterly cold. I sheltered Finn with a small energy shield and held him close to keep him warm.

"We should travel down here more often," I said, nudging Nash. "It's so beautiful."

He tilted his back, looking toward the jagged tops of the fjords. "Our neighbors should invite us more."

I raised one brow. "Well, wouldn't that be nice? An invitation to sail rather than to battle."

When Nash glanced down at me, he hesitated and then nudged me in front of him, so I was nestled between him and the edge of the boat. "You're freezing."

I nodded and cuddled Finn closer, relief filling me as heat drifted from Nash's body over mine. If I tried to warm us with my power, the fire within me always burned too hot. Nash used just the right touch with his power.

"Do you think this summit will work?" I asked.

"Probably not."

I released a long sigh from my chest. "Piercey is so hopeful."

After a year of planning and tireless negotiations with each of the Prophets, Piercey finally arranged for our first annual Skia Hellig diplomatic summit. I told him it needed a much better name than that and that no one even understood what a diplomatic summit was, but this attempt at peaceful discussion consumed Piercey's world. He first started talking about this right after the birth of our kingdom and it took this long to convince the leaders in the peninsula to agree to talk.

"We have to start somewhere," Nash said. "Peace doesn't simply come to us."

"Especially not with that stubborn asshole ruling the Flatlands." The Flatlander Prophet, Theus, drove me insane.

"Right. Skia Hellig doesn't understand the meaning of peace. If we don't force it, we'll war forever."

"It's been four years with no major battles." I bounced Finn when he stirred and let out a few sleepy cries. "Some might call that peace."

"What do you call it?"

"Not good enough." The baby nestled his face against me again, quieting. "I want true peace. I want a treaty."

"Theus is too stubborn for a treaty," Nash said. "He wants it to remain unspoken and unofficial."

"So that he can back out at any time. We need to force his hand."

"Then you do believe in what Piercey is doing."

I patted Finn's back. "I believe in what he's doing. I just know it won't work."

Nash chuckled at the contradiction, but I knew he understood. "Well, like I said, it's a start."

"A start is good enough for today."

The words echoed hollow inside me, though. These words could never capture what peace or war meant. No words could. The loss of a single person ripped apart entire worlds and reverberated through lifetimes. How many of our people did we lose in every battle? We needed to protect our kingdom and unify Skia Hellig in an agreement to not needlessly kill each other.

Water crashed against the side of the boat, its mist sparkling in the sunlight. The air smelled so fresh out here and it tempted me to believe in Piercey's hope.

Nash tugged me back a step. "We should get back to Piercey and Markus before they make decisions you'll hate. We'll come back out with Elsie before we dock."

"Where is Elsie?"

"Last I saw, trying to convince Markus's daughter to spar with her."

"Of course." I looked at the water again before turning to walk with Nash. We reached the other side of the deck to descend the stairs to where the others conferred when I noticed a long shadow falling across the deck of the boat.

Elsie stood upon the hull with her twin blades drawn and her braids tied up on her head.

With her knees bent, she rode the rise and fall of the boat, striking the air with her twin blades. One step forward, and then she launched herself into a spin, landing on one foot before pivoting to thrust the sword behind her. Mist from the waves sprayed over the side of the boat, sprinkling against her and her swords.

"Hey!" Nash scrambled forward. "You get down right now!"

She kicked above her head and slammed the hilt of the sword against an invisible enemy, earning a round of applause from the sailing crew.

Nash whirled around and pointed at the men. "No clapping for her." Facing Elsie again, he raised his voice. "Right now, or I'm taking your swords again."

"Dad." She sighed as though he was being unreasonable. "Come up here and spar with me. It's great practice."

"You could fall. I told you to get down."

She scoffed. "You think I would ever let myself lose these swords? I'm not going to fall."

"But if you did—"

Elsie tugged on the thick gold necklace that hugged her neck and softly tapped the black button at the center. "Then Ma would save me the instant I called on her."

Nash straightened, a knowing look coming over his face. I walked up slowly, keeping my voice low. "I would save you if you fell. That's why it's okay for you to be up there without one of us knowing?"

Elsie's confidence dimmed somewhat when she met my eyes and saw the indignation written across my face. "You always save me."

I tilted my head, glancing past her to the choppy, frigid waters. "You can't live your life putting yourself in danger expecting your father and me to rescue you."

"I don't need you to rescue me because I'm fine, but if I did—"

I smiled stiffly. "I'd save you."

"Yes. Just tell Daddy I can train here. It's not every day we're out at sea. I know it's safe."

Nash ran his hands over his face. "Elsie, you didn't ask first. You didn't get either of us to spot you. It's irresponsible, so the answer is no."

"I know you want to sword fight up here! I can see it in your eyes!" Elsie released the battle cry of a vexed teenage girl. "You're just being stubborn." Her voice lowered to a harsh whisper. "And you're embarrassing me."

"I'm embarrassing you?" Nash chuckled and shifted closer. "Me?"

"I'm sorry, okay? I should have asked, and I shouldn't have argued."

"That's exactly right, because if you had asked, I would have said yes. Max could have spotted you while we sparred."

Regret darkened her gaze. "Really?"

Nash nodded. "Yeah, really. This is a good training exercise, and you were doing really well. Obviously, I want to spar with my kid on the edge of a boat at sea. Why wouldn't I?"

Elsie's shoulders slumped and her swords fell to her sides. "What can I do? I'll do anything. I swear."

"You can give me your swords for three days and go to your room until dinner."

Her jaw dropped. "Wait—"

"You are not a warrior yet. If you can't be safe with your swords, you don't get them."

"You can take them after tomorrow. Please, I've been planning this competition while you're meeting at the summit. That's why I needed to train today."

"You should have thought of that before you climbed up here and embarrassed yourself. You only get one life, baby girl. You will be careful with it."

"A week." Tears filled her eyes. "I'll give up my swords for a week if you just let me compete tomorrow. It's for our honor, Dad. This idiot insulted our swords. He said twin blade fighting is only for show. I have to put him in his place."

"Elsie."

"Please, please, please."

Sometimes I wished for Elsie to be more like her mother, Trish, content to stay safely at home, and less like her father. Less driven to carve out her place in the Valley and charge into battle. But I loved her for her spirit. It was the fear gnawing at me that made me wish to dampen her fire. I would never actually want that for her, but I needed to teach her how to survive.

I passed the baby to Nash and then climbed up onto the wall with Elsie. "Your dad might reconsider if you spar with me instead."

Nash's brows twisted as they both looked at me.

"Really?" Elsie asked.

"Really?" Nash mouthed, his look questioning.

Elsie hesitated, looking as though she debated whether to walk into this trap. Straightening, she raised her swords and nodded. "Okay."

"Don't lose those blades and remember your necklace if you need help," I said.

She repositioned her footing, looking far less confident than she had jumping around alone when we'd come aboard. The giddiness couldn't hide her nerves. Elsie likely didn't want to lose in front of her audience, and most certainly knew there was no hope of her winning.

I held her gaze and waited for her to move. Nash watched us, still looking uncertain.

The girl snapped forward with her blades testing the space between us. I leaned backward as I drew my sword from its sheath. Her brows twisted and she pursued with greater speed this time, sliding forward in a beautifully smooth strike.

Very nice. It impressed me to see her holding her footing so well on the choppy waters.

When I evaded her hits, Elsie growled in frustration, raised both blades above her head, and swung with all her strength.

I slammed the edge of my sword against hers, close to the hilt, the strength of the hit knocking her first sword into the other.

Both swords flew from Elsie's grip and clattered upon the wooden deck of the boat. The strength of the hit nearly threw her onto the deck of the ship, but she recovered. I watched her, always keen to see how a young warrior reacted the moment they lost.

Her lips puckered as she stared at her fallen swords and I thought she might cry, only her eyes narrowed as her gaze shifted back to me. She sprang forward and ducked beneath my blade, raising her palm to strike my stomach.

I smiled as I blocked with my knee. "Don't forget I still have a sword."

Both of her hands clasped mine and she twisted her whole body to try to wrench my weapon free. "I didn't forget!"

I ripped backward to free myself and then sheathed my sword. "Show me what you can do without those swords."

The words hadn't even finished leaving my lips when Elsie kicked for my side. I caught her leg and shook my head. "I'm stronger than you, Elsie. You have to be more creative than that."

When I freed her, she sprang back so fast I almost instinctively caught her. But Elsie kept her balance, even when she flipped forward to spring off her hands and drive her knees down against the tops of my shoulders. I couldn't believe she managed that attack on the side of a boat.

I caught her knees and shoved her backward. Elsie twisted her torso, just barely landing on her feet.

"Careful," Nash said.

"How's that for creative?" Elsie asked. Her dexterity and her ability to manage this fight while balancing seemed to flood her with confidence now. She charged me and I clearly saw the folly of all talented warriors who still needed to hone their skills. Elsie was too confident. When she attacked, I caught her by her side and threw her overboard.

As her body flew through the air toward the ocean, her bewildered eyes found mine. I teleported right behind her, my arms coming around her as we both fell into the frigid ocean water.

The cold dug its claws into my chest, and I couldn't keep from crying out at the shock to my system. Elsie fought against me, surely panicked. I dragged us both up to the surface where we gasped for air together. Kicking, I managed to keep both of our heads above water.

"What the hell?" Nash screamed from the edge of the boat, standing on the edge now, looking ready to jump in until he seemed to remember he held Finn. "Max!"

I made no apology but tightened my hold on Elsie. "Do you see?" I asked. We both convulsed with the bitter cold. "Never feel confident against a stronger enemy."

"Wh-why d-did you throw me in?"

"Use your necklace," I said.

"What?" Elsie trembled so badly I wasn't sure she'd have enough control of her limbs to actually touch the stone.

"The necklace." I jerked her hand up to it.

Elsie grabbed the stone, and I sensed the alert immediately.

I teleported us back onto the ship and released her. She collapsed onto her hands and knees, coughing.

"Why didn't you use your necklace?" I looked down at her as she trembled with cold.

"I didn't have time!" Her voice hitched. "You threw me into the ocean."

"I thought it didn't matter if you fell in when your dad and I will always be here to save you."

Elsie lowered her head, silent now as she wrapped her arms around herself.

"You'll be more careful next time," I ordered. "Or you'll never be accepted as a warrior. There are rules to follow. You must live like you don't have that necklace or me or your dad. You live like you're just another warrior. Otherwise, you cannot be trusted in battle."

Such official talk gave Elsie pause. She raised her head up to me, water dripping from her face, her eyes full of both anger and understanding.

"Is that clear?" I asked.

She wiped her face and sat up on her knees. "Yes, Prophet."

"Your dad and I will spot you next time you want to train like that."

A sailor ran up holding thick blankets in his arms. He laid one over Elsie's shoulders and then turned to offer one to me, dipping his head. "Prophet."

"Thank you."

Nash stepped beside me, eyes on Elsie. "Go change into dry clothes."

"I'm sorry, okay?" She barely glanced at me.

"I accept your apology."

She waited instead of leaving to change.

"Oh, you want me to say sorry?" I asked.

"Obviously." She sprang to her feet, her teeth chattering. Mine would, too, if I didn't hold my jaw so tight.

"I'm not sorry," I said. "If you fell while I wasn't around, you may have hit your head and died. Or the shock of the cold and the waves might have kept you from activating your necklace. You understand the danger now, so I'm not sorry."

Elsie looked to her dad, but when his expression didn't soften, she turned and ran inside.

Everything was quiet for several seconds while Nash stared at me, and I stubbornly refused to act like I noticed. When I finally did, I shrank back from his look.

"It had to be done," I murmured.

"Of course. I understand." He patted Finn's back. "Would you like to throw our baby in the ocean next?"

"I might like to throw you."

"Between you and Elsie, I'm not sure how I'm supposed to sleep at night."

I pulled the blanket tighter around myself. "Trust me. I was a thirteen-year-old girl who loved to fight once. Elsie needed to feel the pain of the cold water. More than that, she needed to feel the pain of losing in front of the people she wanted to impress."

"I trust you." Nash nudged me toward the door Elsie ran through. "You need to change, too. It's way too cold for a swim."

My shoulders fell some. "Are you mad at me?"

"Yeah, I'm a little mad at you." Nash laughed and gave me a small push this time. "You threw our daughter into the freezing ocean. Now go change. Maybe tell me next time so I don't have a heart attack." He tapped his temple. "We can talk without her hearing."

"Right."

Nash sighed. "What am I supposed to do with you two?"

I smirked and disappeared inside, knocking on Elsie's door before changing. At first, she didn't answer. Then the door swung open to her using a towel on her wet hair.

"I'm sorry," I said.

"Are you really?"

"I don't like throwing you in the ocean. But I'd do it again."

"That's not much of an apology, then."

I took her frigid cheek in my hand. "I love you, baby girl."

Elsie glanced down, her expression softening. I thought she wouldn't say it back, but then she muttered, "Love you, too, Ma." When I backed up, she opened the door wider. "Wait."

I stopped and looked at her.

"I really won't do it again. You're right." As if saying that took more humility than Elsie could manage, she slammed the door shut.

CHAPTER SIX

The temple of the coastal Prophet reminded me of a much grander version of the original Prophet of the Valley. The high domed ceiling climbed beyond what the torchlight could reach, so the center looked like a black void. Tables and tall-backed chairs formed a circle around the center of the temple. I sat among my inner circle—Nash, Wren, Leif, and Markus—and our most senior advisors and commanders in our designated section, while Piercey spoke from the center of the room.

"Please signify that you still agree to adhere to our rules by raising your hand."

Groans broke out among all those gathered from every corner of Skia Hellig. Undeterred, Piercey waited patiently.

"Yes, I am serious," my friend said. "I need to see that every single person agrees."

"Remind me," the Flatlander Prophet said. "What are the ramifications of breaking these so-called rules?"

"Eclipse paints the floor with your blood," the Fjellfolk Prophet called out.

I smirked at how Theus whipped around to face the other Prophet.

"We will work together to bind your power and remove you from the assembly," Piercey said, ignoring the heckling. "Let me remind you that we gathered together today out of respect for our individual lands and kingdoms, and out of the desire to see our people live peacefully. Why should we spill the blood of other Skia Helligeans?"

The people quieted at this, and I smiled at Piercey when he glanced our way.

"The rulers beyond the peninsula continue to overreach," Piercey said. "They see us fighting amongst ourselves. They see how much smaller this peninsula appears compared to all that land north of us. They see our mistrust for each other." He turned slowly in a circle, looking at all the sections of all the peoples of Skia Hellig circled around him. "They see a weak land waiting to be ruled."

The silence sounded like a resounding agreement to me.

"We may fight, our land might be small compared to others, and we might not trust each other, but we will not be conquered or subjugated by anyone." Piercey slammed his fist into his palm. "So do not let your feuds with one another weaken our peninsula to the point that we are picked off easily."

The coastal Prophet stood. Her name was Sloane. She'd ascended five years ago after decades of shadowing the former Prophet who retired in his old age. Quiet, intelligent, and slow to speak, I never knew what to expect from her. "I agree with Eclipse's Second, Piercey. Our enemies see weakness. Can we say they're wrong to?" Her sharp stare turned to the Flatlander Prophet, Theus. "What else should they think when they see a man fail time and time again to reclaim lands long lost to him?"

Theus charged forward and threw his staff onto the ground. "I will not be maligned!"

The snickers made me wince. I hated Theus as much, if not more, than anyone else here. He refused to agree to peace and cost my kingdom valuable men and women who would never be returned. I wanted nothing more than to rip his head from his shoulders. There was nothing worse than a weak man with too much power, but I knew how such men hated to be scoffed at. How they'd use their undeserved power to make others suffer for their humiliation.

"Prophet Theus and I have come to an agreement for the time being," I said. "This matter can stay between us."

"The agreement is that you won't slaughter him and his entire family," a voice from the crowd called. I couldn't tell who had spoken.

Theus glowered. "You all think I've given up? It benefits us both to agree to a temporary ceasefire. One day, my villages will be returned to me."

"Or something like that," I said, desperate to move on from the tiring subject. "There's no need to talk about it."

"Well," Theus said. "Just because I've shown you mercy by holding off on military action doesn't mean I'm willing to agree to anything else. I don't see how I can discuss peace or any matters of diplomacy with the woman holding my villages hostage, or any Prophet who sides with her."

My shoulders straightened. He couldn't be serious. "Now is not the time, Theus."

"Those are my villages," he shouted so hard that spittle sprayed from his mouth.

"The villages rejected you long ago," I said. "I won't force them to return to you. You're holding back the entire peninsula if you refuse to enter into an agreement with the rest of us."

"Our land is sacred. Given to us by the gods themselves. We won't abandon a single speck of dirt."

Dozens of groans spread over the assembly as people mumbled to one another, but he only lifted his chin in response, stubbornly ignoring them.

Theus raised two shaking fists above his head. "I will never yield, Eclipse."

After almost a decade of bickering, skirmishes, and two separate short-term wars, I knew this man far better than I ever cared to. "You'll sacrifice much more than a speck if you impede our alliance," I said. "Our enemies strike any time you make moves against me because they know that's when we're the weakest. Your stubbornness risks all of Skia Hellig."

"So I should give up my kingdom because—"

"I am not listening to this argument again." The Fjellfolk Prophet, Demetri, slammed his fist against the table. "You've said the same thing for decades. Silence yourself or I will silence you."

Theus possessed an impressive ability to not care whatsoever about what anyone thought about him. He only smiled in return, as if the other ruler's ire amused him. "Tell her to return my lands, and you won't have to hear it again."

The entire room groaned at this. I stared impassively. "Are you done with the obligatory fit, Theus?"

"I will not halt my conquest. I've worked too hard on this."

"She's going to beat you." The same Prophet beat the table again. "For the love of Skia Hellig and the gods themselves, give up already. You're fortunate she's more honorable than the rest of us or she would have killed you long ago."

The Flatlander Prophet's cheeks tinted pink at this. "Eclipse couldn't kill me if she tried."

Laughter erupted from around the room. I didn't join in. I didn't even smile. A fool like Theus didn't know when to quit. This would only encourage him.

Markus often pushed for me to kill him. Was it honor that held me back? In my life, I had decided things a person never should. The weight of killing Dr. Henderson and the Prophet of the Valley never left me. I lived through the consequences of upending our world and I never wanted to do that again. Who would take the place of Theus if I did kill him? What if they were worse? I knew how to deal with him, even if he annoyed me.

"We can argue about this later," I said. "At least agree that you won't impede this summit. There's other business to discuss. Our disagreement is not the only reason blood has been shed in Skia Hellig." I looked to the coastal Prophet, sensing by the look on her face that she weighed whether or not to speak. "If anyone wants to speak, then do so now."

"Everyone is afraid to even discuss peace because they fear it is a capitulation to Eclipse." Sloane's chin raised. "You're all afraid of her. You're afraid she will steal your power and your lands and that your very own people will praise her for it."

Everyone quieted at this.

She continued boldly. "Anyone with a half brain knows that Eclipse has no interest in taking your land from you. She doesn't want the kingdom she already has."

I narrowed my eyes. "That couldn't be further from the truth. I've dedicated my life to my kingdom and my people."

"You resisted ruling for a year of grueling fighting because you've no interest in it. No one contests your passion for your people, but only a fool worries that you'll try to take more power for yourself when you aren't interested."

I couldn't exactly deny that. I wouldn't change anything and yet I still saw myself as a wartime Prophet. My people needed a Prophet like me today, but one day I wanted to pass on this position to another ruler with the kind of mind Piercey possessed. A mind that worked best in peace and not in war.

Theus raised his chin. "Even if we trust that Eclipse wants nothing else for herself and her kingdom, what about her successor? One day someone will take her place. If power is not evened out, then that person may seize our lands."

I rubbed my eyes and then let my hand fall to the table. "So should I conquer you all now and save us the trouble of all this worrying?" One lone Fjellfolk advisor laughed while the rest of the assembly said nothing.

"It's no laughing matter," the Fjellfolk Prophet of the mountains said. "These are real concerns. Just as we're concerned with the attention you bring to the region. We still don't have satisfactory answers about the strange battle right before you became Prophet, and that's not even mentioning the cult."

"That's unfair," Piercey said. "Theus is the reason the cult came into our region." My friend's eyes narrowed at the Flatlander Prophet. "Mistrust her all you want, but she will still stand between your lands and any foe that comes for our people."

"'Our people.'" Theus rose to his feet. "You hear this talk? Our people. What does that even mean? My people are in the Flatlands. Eclipse's are the

Valley-dwellers." He tilted his head. "We have some here who cannot claim alliance to any people of Skia Hellig. Like the foreigner." His look cut to Gael, who had temporarily returned from his sabbatical to his home kingdom for our summit. Quickly, the accusing stare turned back to me. "Let's not forget she's a foreigner, too. Eclipse wasn't even born in Skia Hellig."

Several of my people shoved their chairs back at this and yelled out in protest. I shook my head, quieting them. "Let him speak," I said. "We all have a voice here."

"And what if she decided we didn't?" Theus turned in a circle, raising his arms to the others gathered at the assembly. "Do you understand what might happen if she decided we didn't? Do you want her to have that kind of power over you?"

I breathed out slowly, pushed my chair back, and stood to my feet as well. "What, exactly, do you plan to do about it?"

I wasn't sure whether I was merely goading him or inviting him to speak, only that I disliked the theatrics and wanted him to simply say what he meant.

"How do you plan to take this power from me?" I asked. "Is taking back the villages who don't want you not enough anymore?"

The entire assembly fell so quiet that I thought everyone held their breath.

Theus watched me for a long while before speaking. "It's a simple question, not a plan," he said.

"It's not a question, but a challenge." I cast my look to the rest of the assembly. "I won't apologize for being as strong as my people need me to be. I've given you no reason to mistrust me. Don't let your discomfort over my power keep our lands from uniting."

"We can never unite," Theus said. "You may not want to rule over all of Skia Hellig, but you didn't want to rule over your own people and now look at you. If we join hands, one day we will all bend our knee to you." Bitterness edged his voice. "That's the way power works."

Eight years of ruling taught me not to speak until I knew I actually wanted to say whatever tried to fall out of my mouth. It had been a hard lesson learned. As his words turned through my mind, I found that I couldn't deny them. I spent a year tearing myself apart trying to avoid becoming the new Prophet of the Valley before I accepted my position. Could I truly promise these people nothing like that would ever happen again?

Markus taught me to never concede defeat in politics, no matter how sound that defeat might be, but I resented inauthenticity. So, I nodded, lowered my head, and breathed out a deep sigh.

"He's right." I curled my hands to fists, leaning them against the table. I had to ignore the subtle look of admonishment Markus shot in my direction. "I didn't ask for this power I have over my Valley. I agreed to serve my people when they needed me." I lifted my head again and drilled the Flatlander Prophet with a stare. "If all of Skia Hellig one day needed me, we all know I would answer that call, too. And that's what you really fear. You're afraid you might need me one day and that if you do, you'll lose this power you crave so deeply. You're afraid your people will like me more than they like you, just like your lost villages do."

"How dare you," he said with his upper lip curling.

"Then why are you so afraid? Aren't you pleading with your people right now to choose you over me? If you want to keep your power, then earn it. Don't try to steal it from someone else."

The coastal Prophet lifted her hand. Everyone quieted as they turned their attention to her. "I agree with Eclipse. We cannot resent her for her power. We should focus on ourselves and our people. If we want to unify and also remain our own unique people, then why shouldn't we explore this? Is Skia Hellig not strong enough to take on any battle?"

Several people beat their fists on the table in agreement.

"The man who fears change is a man too weak to survive it." Sloane sneered at Theus. "Are you a weak man?"

His nostrils flared. "Fucking bitches."

Nash had said nothing until this point, but now stood beside me. "It's time for you to sit down."

Theus bit off a laugh and twisted to face Nash fully. "Is it, boy? You're not the one who decides that. I'm a Prophet. You're just the bitch's bitch. She's even got you carrying around her baby for her."

Nash stroked the back of Finn's head and shrugged one shoulder. "He's actually my baby, too. Maybe you missed that while you were busy crying about how strong my wife is."

Snickers broke out among the assembly. Markus crossed his arms and leaned back in his seat, now looking content to watch the show.

"I should cut out your tongue," Theus said. "No one talks to me like that."

Nash's brows raised. "My tongue? You want to try?" He started to unlatch Finn from his chest. "Here, someone take my baby. Oh. Sorry, I mean my wife's baby."

I chuckled and reached for Finn, kissing his forehead once I had him in my arms. Piercey was already headed in our direction, ready to put a stop to this.

"Daddy's going to kick that man's ass," I whispered to Finn. "I know. It'll be so fun to watch." I turned him on my lap, took his hand, and waved it at Nash. "Say 'Good luck, Daddy.'"

Nash grinned at me as he rose into the air to drift over the table and land on the ground.

"I said no fighting." Piercey tried to keep his voice low, but it still sounded like a shout. "Max—"

"This is Skia Hellig. We can't meet without a little blood."

"Your husband is fighting a Prophet. A Prophet, Max!"

"Theus will call on one of his disciples to fight for him. He's a coward." I watched as the energy shield raised around the center of the room like this had been built as an arena and not a meeting hall. "It'll be good for everyone to remember I'm not the only reason to fear the Valley. It's because of him, too. Because of us. Everyone who fights alongside us." I patted the seat beside me. "Sit. Look at Markus. He's enjoying himself. Let yourself enjoy it, too."

"Because he's a blood-lusting warrior like the rest of you," Piercey said with a sigh.

Markus roared. He jumped onto the table and slammed his heavy foot down. "That's our war chief." Another stomp reverberated through the hall, and I wondered for a moment if he'd cracked the table. "The greatest war chief in Skia Hellig!"

Our people screamed so loudly I could no longer hear Piercey's protests.

Wren stood beside the energy shield with her arms crossed and a glint in her eye. Piercey shook his head, likely recognizing he'd truly lost the battle when not even Wren tried to reason with me. He then burst through the energy shield. "We will adhere to the rules set forth at the beginning of this conference. If we want to change them, we vote and we agree."

Warriors from all over the temple shouted in protest. Some threw objects against the shield.

"Why must he always talk of voting," one voice shouted above the rest.

I teleported next to him, still holding my baby.

"If you want honorable battles between two worthy warriors, then raise your hand," I said.

The protests died down. A few people raised their hands while many refused.

I gritted my teeth. "Raise your hands, you stubborn assholes! I know you want to see this."

Hands shot up around the room, greatly outnumbering what Piercey clearly hoped everyone would vote for.

"The usual rules apply. We don't need to go through them, do we?" I asked. "These men fight on behalf of our kingdom. The outcome is final, just like on the battlefield. You all agree to control yourselves."

Piercey looked at me. "Thank you," he said quietly.

I narrowed my eyes and turned to look at everyone. "Throw anything at Piercey again and I will find you." A man nearby laughed, and I raised my voice to a shout. "I'm not joking. Throw something and find out. Go on."

He sat back, averting his eyes.

Nash stood inside the shield now, with his tunic discarded and his hands clasping his blades.

A bulky man entered from the other side, the best warrior among Theus's disciples. His deep voice carried throughout the room without being amplified by power. "Our people have warred for decades. If this meeting here today is truly about peace, then we will decide peace now. The winner of the match will choose the fate of the contested villages and the future of the relationship between our kingdoms."

I turned at this, my breath catching in my chest. "You can't be serious." My stare turned to Theus. "You'll turn a match over honor into this?"

"You want peace?" Theus yelled. "Then take it!"

He thought he stood a better chance with his best warrior fighting against Nash today than another losing war against my kingdom. What a fool.

Nash nodded at me. "I say we do it."

"It'll be a fight to the death if it's over the villages, Nash."

"You think I'll lose?"

"No." I didn't. Even if I did, I'd never let anyone kill Nash. "Our council hasn't discussed it."

I noticed Piercey and Markus in a heated discussion. Not wanting to talk out loud, I joined with Piercey to use our neural connection.

"I want to do it," I said. "I'm tired of his antics."

"He will never accept the results," Piercey said through his mind.

"At least we can formalize it. Other Prophets are tired of him. They won't approve of him breaking a written treaty."

My friend turned, continuing to talk with others from the council. Markus pushed Piercey aside and looked at me. Did he want me to make this decision without hearing from the others? I didn't like ruling that way.

"Piercey," I said through our connection.

"Do what you think is best," Piercey said. "Everyone is split. I support you if you want to do this, but consider whether it's worth the risk. We can defeat him in war."

War cost countless lives. I trusted my husband to win this battle. So, I turned back to Theus. "We accept. When we win, you will sign our treaty and agree to peace."

I walked up to Nash and pressed my hand over his heart, feeling the warmth of his bare chest. "Will you kill him?"

He seemed to be considering still. "I'll decide when it's time."

"I doubt he's still deciding. Be careful."

He met my eyes, his smirk lighthearted, as if this was just a skirmish. "Stop worrying."

I breathed out deeply and gave him one more pat before leaving to take my seat.

CHAPTER SEVEN

F ear dismantled the amusement of seeing Nash duel against enemies who annoyed us for so long, against the people who once exiled him. Any fight over the villages meant death.

Theus forced my hand.

He knew backing down from this duel after Nash instigated it wasn't an option. Even if Nash agreed, which he wouldn't, it weakened us politically, and as much as I hated taking politics into consideration, I understood reality. Optics mattered. Optics meant life and death. Our people needed to believe in us, and seeing their war chief back down didn't encourage confidence. So even if I didn't want Nash risking his life today, I couldn't ask him not to do so.

I reasoned with myself to accept the part I played in agreeing to this, but it did nothing to silence the voice inside of me pleading with me to call Nash back. Nothing was worth losing him, and no matter how great of a warrior he was, nothing was certain in battle.

With a hard breath, I steeled myself against the thoughts. I felt this every time Nash entered into battle. This was no different.

The two men didn't waste time. This disciple who faced my husband, Jakob, originated from the same side of the Flatlands as Nash. Odd to see them on opposite sides. Odd to see such fierce warriors hailing from a rural area.

Nash rolled his shoulders and waited on his opponent, who seemed to be in no hurry to make the first move. Instead, Jakob slowly approached, eyes scanning Nash.

"I thought the tales of your twin blades were overblown until I saw them for myself." He didn't smile—didn't look like the kind of man who ever smiled—but a flicker of appreciation lit his serious gaze. "I will enjoy this fight."

Nash didn't respond, only smirked. He was enjoying this, too, free of the fear that clutched me.

Jakob offered no warming up or slow start once he truly began. He attacked Nash with intense speed and strength, his sword plowing into Nash's twin blades, both men powering their weapons with their energy.

I'd heard that Jakob was also an excellent swordsman, but I doubted he could ever beat Nash in such a contest.

Their swords moved so swiftly that it was difficult to follow their movements. Jakob matched Nash's skilled footwork, making his attacks look effortless, though I knew they were anything but.

The two men remained on each other as their swords deftly danced, neither able to break the other's guard for several minutes into the fight.

Jakob opened enough space between them to shoot a disc of energy at Nash. He defended against it with an energy shield, not allowing it to distract him from his offensive efforts with his blades.

Nash bashed his forearm into Jakob's nose and caught the edge of the man's bicep as he whipped his sword back.

Red oozed from a surprisingly deep wound to the disciple's arm. It happened so quickly, I'd missed the strength of the attack.

My heart thrummed with hope watching the disciple struggle to regain his footing and take a hard kick to his gut.

The movement shifted him backward, though, and even reeling from the hit, Jakob released another disc of energy. Nash jumped to the side and erected a shield. The sizzling red disc shifted its trajectory right before clashing with Nash's shield, cutting through at a sharp angle. Though Nash was in the midst of dodging the blow, the disc sliced through the top of his shoulder and continued until it thudded into the barrier of their makeshift arena. Blood poured from Nash's wound down his chest and back. The impact of the hit had thrown him to the side, forcing him to lose speed. He blocked a strike from Jakob's sword with his good arm, grunting as he struggled to fend it off.

I didn't realize I was rushing to my feet until Markus caught my wrist.

"Stay seated," he said. "You can't interfere."

I ground my teeth. "I'm not."

"You may think you aren't, but you're a few seconds away from losing control. Hold Finn and breathe. Nash has this."

I squeezed my eyes shut, but I still saw Nash's blood gushing, painting the darkness when I closed my eyes. What was I doing? "Piercey."

My friend turned to me with grave eyes.

"Take Finn. He shouldn't be here."

"Of course." He reached for the baby. "I'll watch where he can't hear anything, and will return to heal Nash when it's over."

While I worried about Nash, he recovered his position in the battle already, but I knew that blood loss placed a time limit on how long he'd be able to fight like this.

Nash's twin blades sliced through attack after attack by Jakob and scattered his energy in red streaks and sparks. Every movement of his injured shoulder only pumped more blood from his wound, though. Splatters and streaks of blood from both men painted the floor where they fought.

This fight didn't need to happen today. We walked right into a trap because we allowed Theus's foolishness to distract from the true threat his reign posed.

I watched as Nash and Jakob's movements lost their precision and lethal speed, but neither man let up in their determination. They both attacked each other without pause or reservation.

Nash's swords skirted past Jakob and pierced a secondary energy shield. One pricked the disciple's neck but stopped there. As Nash's energy swelled, a mist of red hovered around his blade.

"Enough," Theus said. "You'll both die at this rate. What good will that do any of us?"

I hid my own fear behind a hard voice. "Nash is not dying."

"The floor is coated in his blood."

"Does he look like he's done to you?"

Nash's chest glistened with blood and sweat, pumping with each deep breath. The tip of his sword still dug into Jakob's throat, fighting to break through his defense to drive into his carotid artery.

No matter how it looked, Jakob wasn't done, and I knew that.

"I can fight, Prophet," Jakob cried. Blood bubbled from the wound at the pressure of him speaking.

I knew Theus's answer before he spoke. Nash didn't grow up with his power. For him to be even remotely competitive against a disciple was a grave embarrassment. If this went further and everyone saw the Prophet's best man actually lose, it might start a war. Never mind our agreement or the truce. There would be retaliation. Theus couldn't risk losing today.

"I said enough." Theus sat.

Nash withdrew the blade and offered his hand to Jakob. The man stared for several seconds at the bloody palm waiting for him to accept or reject it. Then, to my surprise, he accepted the help.

They each looked ready to collapse, but instead of returning to sit down for healing attention, they dipped their heads at each other.

"I enjoyed fighting you," Jakob said. "I would have liked to see how it ended."

"I feel the same," Nash said.

They clasped forearms and then turned away from each other. I wanted so badly to teleport to Nash and bring him to sit down immediately, only I knew better than to do that. Warriors walked themselves back from battle.

"How bad is it?" I whispered, grabbing his arm.

"Nothing healing won't fix."

Two healers gathered around him even before Piercey returned and began working on the wounds.

"I'm sorry if I scared you." Nash settled his head against mine.

"I'm always scared about you." I sighed. "It was hard to sit here."

"This was good, though. Jakob is unhappy with Theus pulling him out of the fight. I wonder what else he may be unhappy with. A warrior like that cannot be content serving as a disciple for a Prophet like Theus."

"You think we could reason with him?"

Nash paused. "It's possible, if the time comes."

Piercey returned and handed Finn to Wren. He walked toward the center of the temple, stepped over a smear of blood on the ground, and anchored his hands on his sides. He was evidently beyond frustrated with the type of battle culture he never experienced living on top of the Mountain of the Gods. "We will take a thirty-minute recess to clean this place up. If you wish to speak in private, please go to your designated meeting rooms."

The color had already started to return to Nash's cheeks from the healing treatment. Once Piercey joined the other two, they worked quickly on Nash's wounds. We were all quiet, giving Piercey his space so as to not provoke him. After ten minutes, Nash raised his hand to say he was healed enough for now and we left for our private room to talk. There he accepted a basin of water and wash rags brought by one of the locals to clean himself off.

Piercey joined us, looking no less annoyed than earlier but not angry enough to chastise us. Not yet. I was sure he planned to do plenty of that later when we finished the summit.

"Speak quickly," I said. "Our recess is short, and I want to discuss several more things before we go back out there."

Markus looked around the room and then leveled his stare at me. "Kill him. Kill him as soon as the summit is over."

"Kill Theus?"

"Yes."

"We just agreed—"

"That was for show," Markus said. "We all know it. So, kill him already. The report we drafted last month made it clear. His own people are rejecting him as leader. A majority want him out. He weakens all of Skia Hellig, and while it's easy to think that a pathetic snake like that is only a nuisance, you can never underestimate a determined fool. Don't give him the time he needs to make us live to regret sparing him."

"I don't care about sparing him. I need more support," I said.

"What more could you need?" Markus looked to Leif, likely for his agreement, but my friend didn't return the look this time. Normally the man jumped at the chance to say we needed to kill Theus, but I also knew Leif took deals made over blades seriously. "The people have spoken clearly."

"Then the people should remove him and choose another," I said.

Wren winced. "Really, Max?"

"They can't," Markus said. "You know how hard it is to kill a Prophet, even a Prophet like him."

Piercey scratched his beard. "If the people voted and couldn't enforce their vote, we could uphold their decision with our force."

"You with the voting." Markus shook his head.

I couldn't speak, though. Piercey's willingness to even consider this shocked me. How was I the one holding out on killing and not Piercey? I really had changed.

"It doesn't feel right," I said. "Look at what it took to help the Valley recover after we killed Eskel. Are we really prepared to help the Flatlanders through that? Either we support a new leader and meddle in their affairs, or we allow them to join our kingdom. But I'm not looking to take in strays. We have enough on our plate."

"Since when are you so cautious?" Markus asked. "Since when are you so quick to abandon those who are suffering?"

"I've learned some lessons the hard way." I rubbed the back of my neck. "I caused our Valley to suffer when I killed Eskel without a plan. Bring me a plan and I will kill Theus immediately. I refuse to destabilize his kingdom, though, and throw his people into the chaos we suffered."

Nash lifted a hand and spoke quietly, making me realize that Markus and I had both started shouting at some point. "The Flatlands are stable and we're at peace, for now. We put them in their place in front of Skia Hellig. Let's take this issue up in a few months. During that time, we can use our allies and our spies to support a suitable new leader for the Flatlands. The duel today should humble them, and if not humble them, scare them."

Markus crossed his arms, quiet long enough that I thought he'd given up. "Do you know the problem with you all having power?" He shook his head. "You learn to fear your power more than anyone else's, because you no longer have anyone to fear but yourself." He let out a long sigh. "The powerless never forget the fear of those more powerful than them. That fear doesn't make them weak. It makes them desperate and cunning. Maybe you intimidated them today, or maybe you made them more desperate."

Nash and I shared a look at that as I considered his admonition. Before becoming my top advisor, Markus led warriors in battle for nearly two decades. Known as one of our greatest warriors and commanders, I knew that even referring to himself as powerless required more honesty and humility than most people could manage. But when facing an enemy with a neural implant, normal warriors truly were powerless. He was right. I needed to remember how it felt when I suffered beneath the seal that stole my power away.

"Okay." I nodded. "You've made a wise point, Markus. Let me think about this and we'll talk more when we're home. I'm not doing anything hasty, though. We did make an agreement today, and I refuse to render my word as meaningless."

"Honor is what's meaningless in war," Markus said. "At least when you have thousands of innocent lives in your hands. I urge you to kill him. He's proven that he will never surrender."

I clasped his shoulder. "Thank you, Markus."

Though I meant it in all sincerity, Markus did not at all look like a man who won. The reticence I saw in him told me he believed he didn't reach me. He did. But I wouldn't jump to killing another ruler of Skia Hellig so easily. Not again.

"What about all of the Prophets essentially agreeing that Max is a danger to them?" Piercey's entire body looked tense. "That's not good."

"No," Leif said. "People attack what they fear. It certainly doesn't bode well for the peace Piercey so desperately wants."

"What do they really want? Do you believe that they're simply afraid of Max?" Markus paced the back of the room now, scratching his thick beard. "Something is missing."

"They might be," Piercey said. "Our neighbors are afraid of her taking power, whether she wants it or not. Are they wrong either? It's true that the next enemy or war will come, and then there is no telling what will happen. Max will take care of whoever she needs to care for. We all will."

"I certainly won't put any fears to rest by singlehandedly deciding to murder Theus, will I?" I didn't attempt to hide my sigh.

"Put it to one of Piercey's precious votes," Markus said, and I truly couldn't tell how facetiously he meant it.

"I know you're mocking me," Piercey said, "but it's not a bad idea. We cannot simply vote on whether to kill someone. We can make rules of engagement, though, and formalize the maps of our lands. We set him up to break the new laws that Skia Hellig rulers will vote on here in this summit."

"That's actually a really good idea," I said.

"Actually?" Piercey furrowed his brows.

"You have many good ideas, Piercey." I simpered. "You just don't always understand the culture of Skia Hellig."

Wren looped her arm through his, saying nothing, but offering her own quiet encouragement.

"This is our strategy, then," I said. "We do not leave this summit without the rulers of Skia Hellig agreeing to recognize the boundaries of our lands. Maybe it will help them to not be so afraid of me stealing their power from them."

"They'll always fear you," Markus said. "Let them. Just don't make them desperate in their fear."

When we first began working together, I worried about trusting Markus. Now, I couldn't imagine ruling our kingdom without him.

"One step at a time," I said, remembering what Nash said to me about peace starting somewhere.

CHAPTER EIGHT

For two miserable days, we debated and argued with each other over major issues such as the boundaries of our land to the most minor wording in the draft of our agreement. While I did not foresee anything we did leading to cooperation or peace in the near future, it did provide a starting point for all of us to trust one another. Though we couldn't be further from trust.

Theus abandoned the talks for over twelve hours in his fit over the map placing his previously stolen villages in my kingdom. When he said he refused to agree, all of the Prophets stood together to say that we would all consider him our common enemy. When he finally returned, he said that he could not accept the boundaries but agreed to continue with the summit for now.

"If any member breaks a single line of this agreement," Piercey said, "they void every line for themselves and are no longer a part of our agreement. They lose the truces and privileges we've agreed upon together. So, consider carefully before you betray the new laws of Skia Hellig."

None of us wanted to forbid war between the kingdoms because such promises could not be kept. We all knew that and refused to limit ourselves in such a way. Instead, we focused our efforts on boundaries for war, like not poisoning innocent people or stealing land from one another.

I wasn't sure how this experiment would work out, but I did feel confident the gods must have been enjoying this show.

As Piercey continued to speak, the large doors of the temple opened, and light poured in from outside. Though I sensed no power, I did feel something else. Eyes on me. Power.

Turning slowly, I saw three figures in the doorway, eclipsing the sun.

As they walked forward, dozens of others filed in behind them. Soon, I made out an image that turned my blood cold.

A powerful Prophet from beyond the Skia Hellig Peninsula stalked toward the center of the temple.

Our neighbors north of the peninsula rarely ventured into our lands except for trade. Some attacked or stole resources during opportunistic times. The shadow of war had crossed between our lands more than once without actually breaking out. But I knew this man, even though we'd only spoken twice. I knew him from the reports of our most trusted spies and from staring him down in the battlefield the one time he marched an army to the border of my land. The Prophet Malach. A fearsome warlord.

Two other rulers walked beside him.

My heart pounded in sync with the footsteps of the three Prophets from beyond the peninsula. The rest of their people spread out around the edges of the assembly.

"Good day to all the wonderful people of the Skia Hellig Peninsula," Malach said. "There is nothing quite like the sight of the ocean and the fjords here on the coast. What a beautiful land."

Every word wound around my heart like a tight cord until I could barely breathe. The three walked directly into the center of the temple.

"We love that you are finally talking." He touched his hand to his heart and gave a friendly smile. "It really is wonderful to see. We could not resist joining, because we've been wanting to talk with you all as well."

One by one, all of the Prophets and our most powerful warriors stood. I did so last, taking my time to study Malach before moving a muscle. With my muscles clenched, I teleported a few feet away from him, standing between him and my people. His eyes found mine and beneath that warm smile, I saw nothing in his eyes. No emotion, no fear, no malice. Just nothing.

"Eclipse."

The other Prophets didn't approach, though several warriors did. Nash slid right beside me, his arm brushing mine.

"You were not invited here," I said.

"I needed an invitation?" Malach looked at the rulers beside him and chuckled. "That's embarrassing. Did everyone here receive one? Were they written? I thought you wanted to hear from everyone who desired peace for their lands."

"No," I said, offering nothing further.

He eyed me, chuckling lightheartedly again. "Well, I hope you'll consider allowing me to join."

I tilted my head, holding his gaze for several seconds. "No."

His expression betrayed no frustration or annoyance. He shrugged. "That's too bad. I suppose we should leave, then."

"I suppose so."

"If we aren't invited to the peace talks and we do leave, how do we go about declaring our peace? Or are we obligated to remain at war forever?"

"We aren't at war. There's no need for peace talks."

"Maybe this is where the misunderstanding is." He took one single step closer, his attention seeming to narrow down to me. "We are not at peace, Eclipse. Not when you bring so much attention to our region and haven't had the decency to make any kind of arrangements with us."

I stepped forward now, quietly waiting for him to continue, because I refused to take his bait.

After several more seconds of silence, he seemed to accept my refusal to speak. "You are at war, dear Prophet. You warred against the gods of our world. How can you claim any peace?"

The cold of the ocean crawled back into my bones.

The twitch of his smile told me I'd given away my feelings. I hated that I could be so obvious.

"Oh," Malach said. "You thought no one cared that you jeopardized our entire planet with your whims? You thought you could attack the gods who can end our world with a snap of their fingers, and we'd just forget about it?"

"It sounds like your issue is with me, not the rest of Skia Hellig."

Suddenly his friendly voice deepened into a guttural roar. "Skia Hellig belongs to you." He jerked forward, stopping within an inch of me. Nash slammed his shoulder into the man's chest, forcing him back a step. The two men locked eyes for only a second before the ruler looked at me again. "Your people will answer for your decisions. So, tell me if we are to have peace. I can wait no longer to find out."

I tugged Nash back to my side. "Do you know what I'm hearing?" I asked.

Where I saw nothing in his eyes before, I now saw burning fire. "I would love to find out."

"I'm hearing excuses." I placed one finger against his chest and shoved him back a step with my power. "Excuse after fucking excuse to drag my kingdom into war. Tell me what you really want. Don't hide behind your lies."

"Whether you want Skia Hellig or not is meaningless. These peace talks are the first step to you taking the entire peninsula and none of you can see it. Look around. Do you see anyone else talking?" He leaned down, speaking only to me. "It's your kingdom and mine. We are the true rulers of our land."

"I'm not taking over the other kingdoms."

He uttered an amused laugh. "And I am here to talk peace."

I narrowed my eyes.

"Creating your kingdom kept you occupied. Your ascension scared off your enemies for a time. Sooner or later, the next enemy will come, or the next war. As long as you're here in Skia Hellig, you'll bring death to us all. I fear as long as you live, you'll bring death to our world. I'm not waiting to see what you do next." His nostrils flared. "So, talk peace with me, Eclipse. Convince me that arrangements can be made."

"Or what?"

"Or we stop pretending there's any peace to be had."

He backed up and the two other rulers followed like he controlled their bodies. Our sources from beyond the peninsula told us of the power he held over the other rulers, but I didn't understand how severe that control was until now.

He looked to the other Prophets of Skia Hellig. "Do any of you have anything to say or do you let Eclipse speak for you?"

Theus only watched from the protection of his disciples. The Fjellfolk Prophet crossed his arms and then walked a few feet closer. "I believe she spoke what we are all thinking. No one invited you."

The coastal Prophet who hosted this meeting surprised me by saying nothing. I didn't see any cowardice in her and it didn't appear like she had nothing to say. No, she looked full of thoughts and considerations.

She simply chose not to reveal any information.

I looked up at Nash as his concerned eyes met mine.

"I think that was a declaration of war," I whispered as the rulers began to walk away.

CHAPTER NINE

Once the summit ended, I declined the hospitality of a ride at sea and transported us all back to the tower. Elsie rushed away to reunite with friends while the adults met on the floor reserved only for our family to keep our discussion private.

"I don't trust what Malach said about the gods." I closed my arms around myself, fighting the chill again. "I can't place it, but it sounded like it came from someone else."

"You think the gods told him to attack?" Nash asked.

"No. I don't. They believe they're above that." I closed my eyes. "And they can hear us right now. Don't forget that."

"Shit." Markus punched his fist against the wall so hard he knocked a hole in it.

"That cult disappeared but I know they haven't stopped scheming," I said. "What if it's them? What if they're working with Malach?" I dug my nails into my arms hard enough to scratch my skin. "It never made sense to me why he marched to our lands that one time and didn't attack. I know we said it was a warning over our dispute about trading, but the way he looked at me. I never thought he only wanted to warn me." I closed my eyes. "It was a promise."

"A promise to what?" Piercey asked.

"To kill me." I turned my stare to the window. "It's the first time in eight years I felt that shiver of fear. That little voice inside that said he could do it. I don't know him. I don't know why I felt it." I swallowed hard. "But I do know the eyes of death. Whatever he wants, he won't stop until he has it."

Nash's voice lowered. "He will never kill you."

I ran my fingers absently along the side of his face. "We're okay."

He grunted quietly in frustration.

"I want to know more about him," I said. "I don't believe we've seen what he's capable of."

"That's because anyone who sees what he's capable of dies," Nash said. "He doesn't leave witnesses to his power. Our research on him has never been complete for that reason."

"Those Prophets following him like puppies have seen it," I said. "That means some of their people have, too. Don't we have any reliable spies that close to the action?"

"No," Markus said. "It's not easy to reach anyone in lands that far away. We've been busy with Skia Hellig. Malach's kingdom alone is more than half the size of all of Skia Hellig."

"We should have seen this coming," I said.

"We did." Piercey rubbed his eyes. "We've worried about it for years."

"No, I mean we should have realized that they actually planned to make their move."

"Sometimes war is inevitable." Wren turned from the window. "We're so afraid of it because we love our people and don't want any of them to die. That's not the world we live in. Each of us enters battle prepared to give our lives. We need to accept that from our people as well."

"I don't accept any of you dying," I said.

"That's why you're always exhausted." Wren took my hand and held it with a tender grip. "It's also what our enemies are using against you. They know that every life costs you more than it costs them. Do you think Malach cares about his people? We know rulers like him. He doesn't care about anyone but himself. He can hurt you in ways you can't hurt him."

I searched her wise eyes for answers. "Then tell me what to do, Wren. You always know what to do."

She settled her forehead against mine. "None of us can know what to do. But I know what we shouldn't do." Still holding my hand, she lifted it between us. "Do not let your love for your people turn into fear, and do not let that fear kill them."

My eyes closed.

"Prepare for war, Max. Look at all of your options."

"Think of the people we lost against Theus," I said. "This will be so much worse."

"Yes. So let's give ourselves the best chance we have. We can't change that war is coming."

"I'll be sending kids barely older than Elsie to die." I started to rip back, but Wren kept a firm hold on me.

"Be strong, Max. You're leading the people to save themselves."

Leif's hand came over my shoulder and he settled his arms around us both. The three of us dipped our heads together. My circle.

I didn't want to do this. Days like today, I thought I never wanted to do any of it. I told everyone no eight years ago. I refused to rule this kingdom because of terrible decisions like this.

That was a coward's way out, though. I couldn't allow regret to take hold of my heart when we built a kingdom I adored and when my people needed me. They needed me eight years ago and they needed me now.

Giving myself another few seconds, I lifted my head and looked at two of my oldest friends. Their arms lowered as I turned to Nash.

Wren nodded at Leif and then Piercey, moving toward the door. The others followed her lead and gave Nash and me time alone together.

"Say it." I swallowed hard as I waited for him to speak what I sensed he held back.

"They're not our children." Pain lined Nash's expression because he loved our people as much as I did. "Not if that will make you hold them back. You have to distance yourself or it will kill us all."

I covered my eyes as the tears started to fall. Nash came to me and let me hide my face against him.

"They can be our children again when the war is over," he whispered. "This is how it has to be."

Of course, Nash and I weren't really the mother and father of this king-dom. These people weren't our kids, but when I looked at the young warriors-in-training, they felt like it. It felt like sending Elsie to die.

"Nash," I cried in a hoarse whisper.

"I know." He held me firmly.

"There's no time for this. I need to plan. But I'm afraid to plan because then it'll become real. It's hard to think about. Once I start digging into the war that is coming and plan for how to get my people through it . . ." I let my voice fade so I wouldn't cry more. When I could stifle the tears, I spoke quietly again. "People are going to die. I don't want to return to the days of war. Maybe it won't happen. Maybe he just wanted to scare us."

But I knew that wasn't true. After all this time, I recognized war when I saw it. It had been a long time coming. I just hadn't wanted to believe it.

Instead of speaking, Nash held me, keeping me in place like he used to when I'd slip away.

Minutes passed before the tears deepened into warm trails that slid down my cheeks and a thick fist of pain gripped my heart. I couldn't hold it back and

I knew better than to try. "We were making progress. We tasted peace. Now we'll spend years just surviving and trying to minimize our loss of ground. And why? Why did he come today and do this?" I wanted it all just to disappear.

"Yes," Nash whispered, voice laden with the grief that gripped me. "People will die. We'll be at war, and peace will come only for fleeting moments between battles. We don't know if things will be okay." He gripped me tighter as the sobs started to shake my body. Somehow, he stayed steady and calm. "But we have reason to believe we can win and that our greatest days are ahead of us."

"What if they're behind us?"

He kissed the side of my face. "Then we remember, and we grieve. We seize every good thing we have and cherish it. We remember that our people are worth fighting for, that we've done this before, and we're stronger than last time."

"We've done this before," I whispered. "So many times." The words flooded me with both hope and despair like pouring oil into a glass of water. I wasn't sure which feeling to trust or whether maybe both were true. That the relentless cycle of suffering meant this wouldn't be our last war, and also that we were prepared because we had fought before.

I didn't want to do this again.

I would, though. I chose this kingdom, even if I first tried to run from it. I'd done this before and now I would do it again, but that didn't mean this had to be like the wars before. I was different now and I wielded more power. Had more to love and protect and more to take pride in. This time, I would fight the war better than ever before.

If it killed me, then it would be a life given and not a life lost, because I wanted peace for all my people, not just my family.

Drying my eyes, I straightened and hugged Nash one more time. Then I entered the next room where everyone waited. Voice strong, I pointed at Markus. "I want new reports on Malach and the other Prophets, and to strategize before we report to the wider assembly, which we should assemble immediately."

"You don't want to gather more facts?" Piercey asked.

"No. We need to prepare." I wiped my eyes and smoothed my hand over Nash's chest, steadying myself. "There's no time to waste. We know exactly what Malach came for and we will not second-guess ourselves."

It took only hours to gather the assembly with the help of Gael's warriors who were still stationed with us.

"We don't know what Malach and his allies are planning." I paced before our assembly and allowed the conflicted emotions storming in my heart to fill my voice, both strengthening and flooding it with all I felt. "But we won't wait for them to make their intentions known. By then, it will be too late. I looked into the eyes of the Prophet Malach and in them I saw death."

The commanders and chiefs, the advisors and council members, all stared at me with faith in my words. No one questioned me. Could their confidence survive a war? A real war against enemies from a kingdom larger than ours?

"We start preparing for war immediately," I said. "Advance any warriors-in-training who are ready and accept those into training who you believe can handle it." I nodded at Nash. "We start strategizing today."

My husband crossed his arms. "Prioritize our pairing system for the younger warriors. They adapt best to this partnership. We need to utilize our young who possess power but are not suited for combat with our most promising warriors who lack power. We will look into recruiting from the Sacred School and Gael's kingdom as well."

"Will Gael remain long-term?" a chief asked.

"We will speak with him," Nash said. "He faithfully served with us for many years, and while I know he has enjoyed the last two years at home, he made it clear that he plans to move back. It's possible he will be willing to do that now rather than in a few years."

"We helped them with their last war," the same chief said. "Can we expect them to send more than just those training at the Sacred School?"

"Yes," Nash said. "Their king agreed to this contingency already."

"I'll visit the king as soon as possible," I said. "There's no sign yet of any warriors advancing to our lands. More than likely, we have some time. We should be prepared for smaller scale attacks in the meantime. Update the defense plans for your villagers."

As we continued to plan and discuss over the next week, the flurry of activity forced the fear from my mind during the day, so only at night when I tried to sleep did it consume my thoughts.

I rocked Finn one night after he woke and tried imagining his future. Tried imagining just the next few years.

Maybe we overreacted to the interruption of the unwelcome guests at the summit. I didn't believe so, though, and I needed to protect my people.

If we united with the rest of Skia Hellig, I knew we would win against the Northerners.

But so far no one would join hands with us.

Everyone was so afraid of losing their own power.

CHAPTER TEN

While our kingdom prepared for the possibility of war, I knew that Nash and I desperately needed to do the one thing no one else could do.

But I couldn't speak of such things with the gods listening.

Once Nash and I settled into bed for the night, I pushed against his chest to lift myself to his lips, kissing him softly. His hand came to the small of my back and he held me there.

"We need to find the beginning," I said, finding his eyes in the darkness.

I'd given the gods permission to watch my life closely to earn my life back after Dr. Henderson killed me. If I wanted to hide anything from them, I needed to do it carefully during the few times of privacy given to me. Times like this when they weren't allowed to watch us. Usually, I managed to not think about how they observed me, because their computer program catalogued my life and they only cared to actually view the most important moments for themselves. They just wanted their precious data. No one cared about the day-to-day actions of my life.

What Nash and I had been doing the last three years, though, would certainly be something they'd take the time to watch. So we needed to know for certain they never found out. That meant no one else could know. Only Nash and me.

With Malach's threat, it was more important than ever.

"You think we can find something to help us?" Nash asked.

"I think we need every advantage we can find. Wisdom is power."

"You're right. If we don't have the answers today, maybe we did at another time."

It always felt bittersweet to do this. For years after we first talked about it while lying in bed, we struggled to figure out how to do it. But ever since we actually succeeded, we never stopped. We needed to learn everything we could to protect our world from the gods, the security system, and any other threat we didn't know about yet. This summit and Malach's intrusion only made it that much more important, because our hope might lie in the past, all the way back at the beginning. We needed to reclaim all we'd lost to become as strong as we needed to be.

I laced my fingers with his and closed my eyes. "Ready?"

"Yes," he said.

Taking a deep breath, I focused very deeply, after all this time still finding it incredibly hard to do just right. Soon, the slipping feeling came over me, and I no longer felt his hand in mine.

We clawed our way through time—through lifetimes—searching for the beginning of this long thread connecting us.

Wind whispered through the tall grass. Here in the Flatlands, there was nothing to stop it, and it often turned from gentle to furious very quickly. I fell against the outer wall of the temple and strained to draw breath into my tight chest. The blood of my enemies slickened my hands. I wiped my palms against my tunic and cleaned the handle of my sword. What would Leif say to me now? That it wasn't too late to turn back? He already tried to stop me from sneaking away from our war party to infiltrate this temple all by myself.

But that was because I couldn't tell him what I felt here.

Fire burned within the tightly sealed embers inside of me. I'd felt the stirring of my banished power the last time I came close to this temple, and I needed to know why. What in this tiny little temple was calling to me? A temple so unimportant that I doubted the Flatlander Prophet even cared about it. It merely served as a place for local villagers to give their offerings and for holy men to collect what they managed to scrape together. But the tiniest warmth of the flame inside me sparked when I was here, just like on the Mountain of the Gods.

I didn't like knowing that I'd be leaving my people during the battle, but we had such an advantage. I knew that they'd be fine. It also allowed Leif and Wren to more easily cover my absence in the chaos. Eskel the Ruthless could never find out about any of this. That would ruin all plans of freeing my people from his clutches and our warriors from forced service.

I gritted my teeth as I straightened and glanced behind myself to survey the bodies I'd left lying in the grass. I needed my power back. I'd made up my mind to stop at no lengths to regain it. If it killed me, then it killed me. Better to die fighting for my people than to give up and watch the Prophet of the Valley destroy us all by forcing us into this war with the Flatlanders. I hated fighting for him, and hated even more that he made us invade our neighbors. He reasoned that they attacked us first, but I knew he just wanted to take their villages, like he'd taken mine five years ago. I couldn't wait to get my power back and kill him.

When I entered the temple, I expected guards to immediately charge me, but the hall at the entrance was completely empty. Quiet.

I stepped through the door into a long hallway that led to two large doors at the end. As I walked, I checked the rooms lining the hall, finding them empty as well. One looked like a storage room for the guards. Another, a vacant bedroom likely shared by the guards on duty. The third housed religious icons like incense and robes.

When I reached the two large stone doors, I stopped. A creepy feeling stirred in my stomach. Where was everyone?

I pushed open the doors of the inner room just enough that I could kick them the rest of the way to free up my hands for my bow and arrow. My eyes adjusted to the torchlight of the inner room.

One lone warrior stood in the middle of the large room, his shadow painting the ground in a long, distorted swath.

He studied me as I took another step closer, my arrow aimed at him. I didn't see any other doors. Could this really be it? Was he the only one in here? Tall and broad, he certainly looked like a threat, but enough of one to justify not placing another guard inside?

Offerings lined the back wall. Food, gold, armor, and weapons. Something smelled sweet, mixing with the smoke of the torches.

I expected the warrior to lunge forward at any moment and race toward me like the other warriors, or draw a long-range weapon. Instead, he stood still as a stone statue, a sword gripped calmly and confidently in each hand. His stance looked deceptively like not a stance at all, like he only held his weapons. I noticed in the subtleties of his posture, the twist of his wrists, the way he leaned forward slightly against his right foot, that he was prepared to respond to any attack I made.

With such a small temple in a rural area, maybe the warriors guarding the perimeter were the only deterrent to the villagers and other locals who may try to get away with stealing from the offerings to the gods. The real defense of this temple was the one our army had broken through.

Still, only one man?

I eyed the identical swords again. This was a first. I might have laughed and assumed him a performer if not for the lethal look in his amber eyes. I didn't need to see him attack to know what a threat I faced. His stare said it all.

"Did you lose your way from the battle?" the lone warrior asked.

It unnerved me how relaxed he sounded. Relaxed and even amused.

"Will you help me find my way if I did?" I asked.

A smirk twisted his full lips. He glanced down me quickly, settling on my blade. "That's a lot of blood. I think it's best to keep you here."

"Don't assume that's up to you." Clearly, he didn't intend to strike first or even step toward me. It allowed me more time to catch my breath, but I figured it still advantaged him more. He would force me to give him the opportunity to study the way I moved before I could do the same.

Fine. I wasn't known for my patience. I rushed toward him, intently watching his first movement. Three steps to go and still he hadn't budged. I slid by his side, conservatively protecting myself with my sword as I attempted to rake it across his ribs like I had with the warrior in the field.

He shifted slightly to the side, angling back, sword merely twisting ninety degrees. It was enough for him to deflect my strike entirely. Instead of skidding to a stop and pivoting for him like I'd need to do if I engaged him directly, I continued running past him right for the altar.

It stunned me how quickly he matched my speed and carved his blade through the air right before me. Instinctively, I wanted to slow down, but I remembered his second sword and jumped to the side instead.

Both blades cut through the air where my throat had been.

My heart lodged in my throat as I whipped my own sword up to deflect his next strike. His twin swords sprang through the air too fast to track properly. I stumbled back a step, shocked by the strength and speed of his attack when he moved so conservatively. He made it look effortless when it was anything but.

Suddenly I understood why a single man guarded this room. He wasn't simply a warrior but a master of his swords.

Without drawing my bow entirely in front of me, I ripped it beneath my arm and drew the string back just enough to snap an arrow at his feet.

He sidestepped, drawing his swords back to himself in a subtly defensive motion. I'd surprised him this time.

I learned a great deal by the reactions of my opponents, whether anger or fear might tighten their expression after I forced them back on their heels. This man smirked. He smirked and snapped both his blades for me.

As much as I hated retreating, he gave me no option except to continue moving backward to avoid his blades. I feared that a direct strike might easily break my guard. I needed a different approach if I wanted to win.

I fended off his advances, but sensed he only tested me rather than actually attempted to kill me. It felt like he was toying with me. But why?

The stare of his focused amber eyes drilled mine between the clashes of our swords, so deep and intent it felt as if he tried to read my mind. No matter how quickly I moved, he followed seamlessly.

Burning heartbeats pounded in my chest.

Curls bounced against his face as he broke through my guard and forced me to pivot.

It gave me a precious second to rip my bow from my back and nock another arrow. There wouldn't be time to actually raise it and aim. He instantly turned for me with his swords striking like snakes. I threw myself back onto my ass to avoid his counterstrike and shot as I fell.

The arrow pierced his bicep and splattered blood into the air. The force of the hit knocked the left side of his body back, so the thrust of his swords fell short of me. Damn it, even throwing myself down, he still managed to almost hit me.

Without slowing down from the hit, he slid across the ground on his knees with his blades biting up at me from the ground.

I rolled off my shoulder, but I couldn't dodge them in time. The sharp edge of one sword cut into my side and sliced me open. I shoved myself into a roll, landing with my sword drawn to defend myself.

My side screamed with pain. Hot blood gushed.

Instead of rising back up to attack me with a full advantage, the guard threw himself across the ground after me. He landed a moment after I did, his twin blades bearing down on my sword so hard I had to withdraw to keep my own blade from carving through my body.

I kicked the blade from his injured arm, finally managing to slow him down when he jerked from the hit. But he still didn't stop going after me. He was relentless. He caught the swing of my blade with his sword and pinned my wrist with his injured arm.

I grimaced, stomach tense. Pain consumed my world. Panic. I fought with all I had and still I was lying on my back, struggling to manage each attack.

"Listen." His chest heaved as he struggled for breath, face strained with pain. His bloodied hand held my wrist above my head while he fended off my blade with the other. "One of us is going to die and the other will be gravely injured."

My nostrils flared and I summoned the strength to push harder against him, earning a grunt from him. "You're going to die."

"I don't have time for serious wounds right now." Despite the arrow sticking out from his arm and all the blood he'd lost, he managed to force my blade further down. "Do you?"

What the hell? Was this some kind of negotiation? "No, that's why I'm going to kill you."

He shoved my blade so low it nicked my neck. I slammed my forehead into the softness where his shoulder met his chest, close enough to the arrow that I knew it must have felt agonizing. I pushed my sword back toward him, almost reaching his chest as he struggled to regain his ground.

With a growl, he released my wrist to grab the handle of my sword and wrenched it free of my grasp. I knocked his own away from him and slammed my elbow into his temple. We wrestled for control on the ground. I couldn't think past the pain screaming from my side. The attacks felt blind now, the two of us desperately trying to force the other down.

I grabbed the arrow sticking out from his arm just as his large hand wrapped around my injured side. We froze, staring at each other, the slight pressure on our injuries just enough to keep the pain alive.

"You obviously are doing something important," he said. "I have important things to do, too. So, let's stop."

"Do you really believe I'm going to trust you?"

"No. We'll back away from each other and take our weapons."

I didn't want to concede. It felt like losing. "I'm not leaving here without what I came for. I don't care what it costs me." Except I still didn't know what that was. I didn't feel the warmth in me at all, even when I was so desperate to draw upon it to kill this man. I'd felt it earlier, though. So strongly.

"Fine." He released my wound and slowly pushed off me. "I don't care."

I blinked, losing the few seconds I had to successfully attack before he retrieved his weapon. Scrambling for my own sword, I scooted across the ground and grabbed it. He knelt above me and reached a scarlet hand down to me, his sword at his side. I narrowed my eyes at his hand. What if he pulled me into his sword? No way.

I dragged myself up to my knees and leaned against my sword, my world spinning. He leaned against his as well, both of us prepared to fight should the need arise.

"What do you mean you don't care?" I asked.

"I mean I don't care."

He snapped the arrow protruding from his arm with a low growl. Then he reached around the other side to rip it free, bowing forward from the pain. Blood poured from his wound. He gripped his bicep and lowered his head, the muscles in his jaw bunching. I stiffened, staring at the broken and bloody arrow on the ground. It took a lot of self-discipline to remove one of those himself.

"The gods aren't real," he said with a tense voice. "These offerings are meaningless."

"So why are you guarding them?"

"It's my duty. For now." He moved back to fall against the wall and sank down. "We'll make a deal. I let you take it, and you don't tell anyone I did." He raised his head, brows knitting. "Now sit. You need to rest. You're going to pass out."

My vision swam, but I refused to admit it. "I'm fine."

"You're stubborn, is what you are. Here. I'll move down." He shoved his foot against the ground to put more space between us. A swath of blood stained the wall behind him.

"Don't you care that I killed your people?" Reluctantly, I sat back against the wall and nearly slid completely to the ground. With the high of the battle wearing off, the immense pain threatened to immobilize me. I felt so weak.

"Those aren't my people." He pulled his tunic over his head, gasping when he pried the material from his bicep. Sweat dappled his skin. Blood ran all the way down both sides of his arm to drip from his fingers. His thick chest moved deeply with each heavy breath.

I quickly averted my eyes, feeling the burn in my cheeks, and looked down to the bloodstain spreading all the way to my pants. Not good.

The guard's arm lay limp in his lap as he bit the collar of his tunic and ripped it with his good arm. A few more tears and he ripped the garment in two. "Death is always a shame." He tossed half of his tunic to me. It landed on top of my feet. "It means no more to me than whoever you lost in battle today, though."

I lifted the cloth and stared at the bloodstains that belonged to us both. Was this all a ruse to get me to let my guard down? My stomach tightened as he tied the makeshift bandage around his wound. I did the same, my hands trembling as I forced myself to tie it as tightly as I could.

The pain must have silenced him as it did to me. I didn't have the breath to speak or to question this strange, enigmatic man. I'd never had a fight end like this. Nothing close to this.

I struggled to hold on to consciousness, knowing that nothing would stop him from killing me if I passed out. Despite this, I didn't believe he would. For some reason, I thought he was telling the truth.

"What's your name?" I asked weakly.

He looked at me, pale and exhausted. "Nash. Yours?"

"Max."

The slightest smile lifted the left corner of his lips. "Max. No one else has ever drawn my blood inside this temple . . ."

My view of him doubled. The torchlight dimmed.

"Don't die," he said. "It'd be a shame. You're too good of a warrior . . ."

Questions that I didn't have the strength to ask burned. I entered this battle already worn down and sleep-deprived. This man, this Nash, proved too great a foe to fight a in state like that. I told him I was going to kill him before, but I thought he would have actually killed me. As my vision waned and the feeling fled my body, I realized that by offering to stop, he wasn't calling a truce. He was offering me my life. Because I was losing consciousness now and he wasn't. I was the one losing.

Why he hadn't wanted to kill me, I didn't know.

Nash . . .

What if he held the key to this mysterious power I sensed?

I woke from our forgotten dreams—our stolen lives—with my cheeks wet and my arms already clutching Nash.

Knowing Dr. Henderson stole entire lives from us and witnessing them were so different. Grief consumed me at the thought of how the story ended for those two people we'd been forced to leave behind. At the understanding that we'd actually lived through it. Our lives had been filled with suffering and love, thousands of days lived and thousands of days lost. Traveling to our past lives set something right inside of me. It gave voice to the whispers of a past that had echoed through my entire life, but it also awakened a depth of suffering I otherwise wouldn't fully realize.

Nash and I always awoke from living through our stolen lives solemn and quiet. We'd lie quietly together after, not speaking because what words could even scratch the surface?

Every time it left me tempted to travel back to the day I ripped Dr. Henderson's life away with my sword, but I never did. I didn't want to spend one more moment with her than I had to. She'd taken enough time from me.

"We found it." Nash's quiet voice rooted my mind back in our world, our lifetime, and plunged me into the pain of all we'd once lost. The anger of it. "The first time we met. The real first time we met."

"Those two don't know what's coming. We didn't know what was coming."
I looked up into eyes filled with lifetimes worth of both love and grief. "What
is coming for us now that we don't know about yet? What will happen with
Malach?"

"That kind of talk never leads anywhere good for anyone, especially you,
Max."

Piercey continued to monitor and treat my anxiety, so I controlled it much
better. It would never leave, though, and an unknown future, especially cast in
the fear of all that awaited us, allowed the anxiety in me to grow out of
control.

"I know," I said. "I just can never shake it. Twice before we lived like we are
now, and things weren't okay."

"We're in a very different position than we've ever been."

I nodded. He was right. Dr. Henderson no longer supervised our world or
tinkered with our lives, and we ruled a thriving kingdom. Nash and I built a life
together I doubted I ever could have imagined in this life or any other. "I'm just
so sad for them."

Nash squeezed me and stroked his fingers along my back. "Me, too. If I
could tell the man I used to be anything," he whispered. "I'd say this. You'll
get more of her this way. You'll get more with her than a single life could contain. You'll lose it all, but you'll win it back, and more."

I turned my face against the soft crook of his arm and struggled to hold in
the sob that bit into my throat. Nash and I could never undo the death
Dr. Henderson threw upon our world, but we could build something she
would never be able to touch.

"We have to keep going," I said. "There's something Dr. Henderson never
wanted us to remember. I'm sure of it. We need all the knowledge we've lost in
case it helps us protect our kingdom."

"We'll keep going."

CHAPTER ELEVEN

The weeks chipped away at the dread and fear so that what once panicked the entire kingdom now felt unreal and distant. Therein lay the greatest danger of a looming threat. That it was looming. And our everyday life continued to happen, numbing us when we most needed to remain alert.

I opened the door of the war room and looked down the stairs at the commanders gathered with my husband.

"That's a weakness." Nash pointed toward one of our most rural areas. "We need more surveillance in that area today."

Watching, I leaned on the rail.

One of the young commanders named Owen leaned over to speak to an equally young woman beside him. His mother was a warrior I deeply respected. "It's hard to take him seriously with a baby strapped to his chest."

Nash lifted a wooden battle marker that represented a division of our military and turned his attention toward the commander while the piece floated through the air to the center of the map. He lightly patted Finn's back while placing the marker near the mountains with his power. "It's hard to take you seriously when my thirteen-year-old daughter can beat you in both a sword and bow contest."

Laughter belted through the room.

The commander furrowed his brows and glanced at his comrades guffawing beside him. He seemed surprised Nash had heard his comment. "Everyone knows I don't use a bow, and she can't beat me in a sword contest. Only your made-up game of twin blades."

This didn't lessen the laughter, never mind that Elsie scored higher than half the warriors in this room in the twin blade competition at the summer festival.

"My baby can likely beat you as well," Nash said above the noise of the warriors.

I smirked as I began to descend the stairs. "So, who has a problem with my baby?" I asked. I'd gone unnoticed before, but now all eyes turned to me.

The commander who had mocked Nash straightened and blinked at me. "I don't have a problem with your baby. I just don't think babies have a place in a war room."

"He spent a great deal of time in the war room when he was inside my body." I shrugged as I strode toward Nash, glancing at the commander again. "Enough time in war as well."

Leif snickered while everyone else fell quiet.

Finn twisted his head at the sound of my voice and giggled when he saw me. I slid my arm around Nash's waist and brushed my finger along the baby's puffy cheeks. "You're already a little warrior, aren't you? A cute little warrior." My gaze snapped up to the commander. "I'd overlook the comment if you were only joking, but this isn't the first snarky remark you've made. Do you think our children should grow up without their parents? The wars over this Valley consume our life."

Nash leaned down to whisper to me. "It's fine, Max."

"Yes, Max," the commander said. "It was a joke."

The man next to him shoved his forearm against his chest and knocked him into the chief standing behind them. "That's Prophet Eclipse, you snot-nosed brat." He gathered two handfuls of the other man's tunic. "You weren't even holding a sword when she saved us from Eskel the Ruthless. This is the problem with letting children call themselves commander."

When the older man released him, the young commander straightened his tunic, jaw bunching.

His chief grabbed his ear and yanked him to his side. "Not another word. You've embarrassed yourself enough."

I tilted my head. "Don't let what feels like peace lull you into complacency. At any time, Malach could strike. Theus as well. Is this really the time to joke in the war room?"

Owen lowered his head at this.

"Will we strike first?" a chief from the back of the room asked.

"We're working on such plans," Nash said. "There's many considerations. Taking an army to them hinders our defenses. We're outnumbered. A smaller force could enter covertly, but we need the right target, or we'll waste our efforts."

The uneasy feeling growing in the room filled me. It seemed like we were disadvantaged in every way.

The commanders and chiefs continued to evaluate our defenses and our weaknesses until breaking for food.

Markus approached me while the others gathered around the tables filled with meats and cheeses.

"You're too soft on them," Markus said. "If that boy feels comfortable mouthing off not only to War Chief Nash but also the Prophet Eclipse, then how can you trust him to lead in battle? How can you trust him at all?"

I watched Owen. Markus was right. My people never disrespected me, so I didn't encounter these situations often. The unrest from the potential war perhaps stoked something in the younger generation, a dissatisfaction with a failure of leadership to stop such a threat.

When the day ended, after a heated discussion about the boy with his mother and village chief, I stopped by the building which housed our visiting young commanders.

I knocked on the door and the commanders scrambled to bring Owen to me.

The young man gawked at me. It seemed that without the crowd and the distance between us, he didn't feel as brave.

"Your mother is angry with you," I said. "She asked me to formally discipline you in front of the war council."

Owen lowered his head. "Please accept my most sincere apology, Prophet."

I recognized the utter lack of sincerity in his fiery eyes. The demure voice couldn't hide his rebellion. "She's the reason you're a commander at such a young age. She's one of our greatest warriors. Your skill made us all believe that you could follow in her footsteps." I tilted my head. "Did we judge you wrongly?"

"You did." Despite keeping his gaze and his head lowered, his voice sharpened. "I'm not my mother. I will be a great warrior, but you'll be disappointed if you expect me to turn out just like her."

I smirked. "You're a little shit is what you are."

He lifted his head now, brows furrowed.

"You lack respect and the good sense of knowing when to shut your mouth. You're undisciplined with your anger. My kid can beat you in two of our contests."

Now he met my eyes again, his voice raising. "I scored the highest in blindfolded two-handed—"

"Blah, blah," I said, cutting him off. "No one cares about what you scored the highest in when you score so low in so many categories. You do have great potential, so don't embarrass yourself."

"Why are you even talking to me? Don't you have an entire kingdom to run?"

I flicked his forehead. "I used to be immature and angry. Now I'm grown and angry. And I do whatever I like. You'll lose your duties as commander for a month. Go home."

"A month? You can't! We're preparing for war."

"The fact that you don't know when to be quiet makes me worried that you should permanently lose your duties."

"You don't like that I criticized your husband."

That made me laugh. "You think I'd come pick a fight with a kid like you over that? I don't like that one of my commanders, who could be great one day, is acting like a child. I'll be watching you."

With that, I left Owen in the darkness.

The worry remained, though, so I met Markus in his office. He was still working late, as he had every night since the summit.

"Markus," I said.

He paused and looked up at me.

"I want to see all of the commanders who were promoted in the last two years." I nodded. "You're right. I'm too soft on them. Our people needed mercy when we emerged from the tyranny of Eskel and from the dark days before we united. The young don't remember how it felt to be powerless. And so, my mercy isn't mercy to them. It's coddling. Bring them all to me."

I stared at the rows of young warriors. "A generation of commanders proved themselves in the midst of a bloody war to unite this Valley. You are untested, and without proper testing, you're still weak. So, I will test you. I will make you prove yourself. If you fall short, you will relinquish the title of commander."

I expected groans or the kind of insubordination that foolish Owen had shown me. But no one dared to allow anything to show on their face except for fear. Perhaps it was all they felt.

I pressed my finger to the sensor on my choker and sealed my own power. Raising my sword, I hardened my voice. "Who will fight me first?"

Owen stepped forward while everyone stared with fear burning in their eyes. I'd stripped him of his duties for the month, but he needed this training.

Needed to be humbled. Though he didn't speak with confidence, he did speak when all others remained silent. "I will."

He raised his sword with two hands, his preferred way to fight. One swing. Two. I sidestepped them both.

He twisted for a rapid strike to my side, which really wasn't bad, but I easily saw the hole in his defense. I kicked the side of his knee just enough to make him falter and shoved him onto the ground. My blade barely pressed against his Adam's apple.

"You're too slow," I said. "Good form, but what's that worth if I can see every step you make so easily?"

He stared at me from the ground with his eyes wide.

Whispers spread among the young commanders.

Did they think that because Nash beat me at the sword competition every year that any of them stood a chance against me with the sword?

No one in the kingdom could defeat Nash when it came to swords.

I grabbed his arm and jerked him up. "Go. Who's next? Don't make me choose for you."

I'd teach these kids how little they knew of war.

After two weeks of personally humiliating the young commanders and sending them out to continue training with a new dose of humility, I only felt more aware of their youth. The fresh memories cut into my heart. Memories of knocking them to the ground, seeing bruises blooming across their bodies as the days of training wore on, defeating them no matter how much they improved and how hard they tried, ruthlessly proving to them that they were not ready for war.

I chewed the inside of my cheek, unable to stop staring at the rain drizzling against the dark window when I needed to plan with Piercey to defend against Malach's threat. "I never thought I could do worse to another person than what the instructors did to me."

"They aren't children," Piercey said. "They aren't held against their will. They're commanders who hold the fate of warriors in their hands. This is not the same as what the instructors did to us."

I trailed my finger along the choker, tempted to turn it back on and to leave it that way for days. Tempted to walk this kingdom without power, so I could remember how it felt to live like most of my people did. "That's not what I meant." I looked into my own eyes in the reflection, searching the subtle ways I'd changed over the years. Sometimes I didn't recognize my life or myself.

And yet I felt I was exactly as I needed to be. "This coming war will be like nothing they've ever seen. They remember hiding while their parents fought for their lives. They don't know what it is to wield the sword in a battle they don't believe they can win. To know that if they fail, the innocent hiding in their homes will die."

Piercey quieted, looking at me in the reflection.

"How can I send them to bathe themselves in blood?" I asked.

He shook his head, pain filling his gaze. "Because how can you not? The alternative is far worse."

"Isn't this what the gods say to themselves? I'll make you suffer so many more will never know your suffering?" I touched the choker again, staring at it against my skin that had paled in autumn's darkness. "Have I become like them?"

"No." Piercey didn't offer an explanation or try to convince me. He merely spoke the one word with such confidence and authority that I couldn't bring myself to question him. "Power has changed you, Max. It's a testament to your spirit that it's made you better and not worse."

His reassurance did not ease all that haunted me as I continued to train with the others. The threat was too far removed from most people for them to feel it, but it never left me. Even training in the evening with Nash, the thought of Malach's words distracted me.

Nash's forearm slammed into my gut, powered by his energy. It knocked the breath from my lungs. I barely caught myself before I fell over.

Nash skidded to a stop. "You okay?"

I lunged forward, throwing a punch. "You aren't supposed to stop."

He gave me a look of incredulity as he blocked my hit. "I'm always going to stop."

"This isn't normal training, Nash. Piercey will heal us."

"Fine." He opened his arms. "Stab me in the stomach. Prove to us all you can do it."

Leif heckled from his place on the grass and tossed a handful of peanuts into his mouth.

"Just fight me," I said.

Leif rose and dusted off his hands. "I'll fight you, girl."

I pushed Nash away and nodded at Leif. "Good."

"Really?" My husband took a step back. "You're replacing me?"

"Yes," I said. "Until you can fight me properly."

Leif and I fought against each other with no weapons like the old days, except now we both could use our energy to enhance our attacks. Since Leif never showed promise with long-range energy attacks, he was actually the perfect partner for sparring. He reserved his energy for improving his combat rather than creating new skills, and I found him very challenging to beat in this kind of a match.

One of his hits broke through my guard and connected with my jaw. I kicked him to create enough distance to recover and spit out a mouthful of blood. Leif didn't relent, charging for me again. I pivoted and evaded a kick.

"See?" I stole my eyes from Leif long enough to glare at my husband.

"Yeah," Nash said, looking at the blood on my chin. "I see."

I jumped and kicked for Leif's head. He blocked, but I saw him wince as he slid backward.

"I don't go to war as often as I used to," I said. "It's important for you to not hold back, Nash. It didn't matter back when we battled every day. It matters now."

"Ma is right."

Leif and I both stopped when we saw Elsie approach.

"Hey, Els." I wiped the blood from my mouth. "You're done studying already?"

"Some of the warriors-in-training advanced," she said. "There's openings in our village."

Nash responded before I managed to shoot her down. "You're still very young."

"Didn't you hear what Ma said? We're at war. I'm a good fighter. If the war lasts for years and I start training now, I'll be ready to join when you really need more warriors."

I did not care for her logic. "Not this year, Elsie."

"Why not?" Her angry glare cut between her father and me.

"Because you only turned thirteen two months ago," Nash said. "We can look at this next year."

"Why delay my training? It only puts me at risk."

"You aren't ready." I tried to say it gently, but I knew it would cut. "That's the truth, Elsie. You haven't shown the maturity."

Nash looked away, clearly uncomfortable with the harsh response, but unable to deny it.

"What kind of maturity do I need to show?" Tears filled her eyes.

"There's a shift from the thinking of a kid to a teenager, and you're just at the start of that. I'm sorry, but it actually can disadvantage you to start too early. I started too early. It didn't do any favors for me."

"I'm not you. I'm not going to lose control of my power and kill people, because I don't have power."

I ignored the sting of her words. "You're training fine enough on your own. Don't bother asking your mom either, because Trish wants you to wait until you're sixteen to start."

"Sixteen? That's crazy."

"Our word is final," Nash said. "I decide who advances into training. As your father and your war chief, my answer is no. You're not ready."

Elsie looked to Leif, but he didn't attempt to argue with us. Her chin quivered. "Fine." Then, she turned and ran away.

"You were mean." Leif pointed at me. "I'm going to punch you in the face again."

"She needed to hear it," I said. "You think I like hurting her feelings?"

"Are you sure you're not being overprotective?" Leif didn't seem to accuse, but to genuinely ask. "What if it was someone else's child?"

It wasn't something I wanted to think about. "I have a hard enough time letting those of age advance. Let's just keep training."

The passing days brought with them more planning and training.

Anxiety churned inside of me thinking about countering Malach's threat.

CHAPTER TWELVE

Training and preparations continued all over the kingdom while Piercey negotiated with neighboring Prophets and Nash led plans for a covert operation.

"So that's it?" I asked. "The plans are finalized?"

"That's it," Gael said, having returned from his kingdom with a small army to support us. "Twenty portals, twenty targets, and two hundred warriors with power. We'll be able to function here while still damaging their infrastructure."

Our spies and scouts had been observing movement from Malach's army for the last two weeks. They hadn't reached Skia Hellig yet, but we believed they were preparing for a full march to our kingdom, with a sizable force only a six-day journey away.

"If we destroy some of these weapon caches and take out a few of their commanders, it will really hurt their plans to advance," Nash said. "But if we successfully take over the five villages we targeted, we can portal in more warriors to establish a strong base in enemy territory."

"They'll accuse us of starting the war," I said.

"Does it matter? They're coming for us, Max. Should we wait for them to take the advantage? They're the ones threatening us. You can't give them the benefit of doubt when they'll use it to slaughter our people. We know what Malach intends."

"Then we need to act soon. Too much time has passed. Their army is closer."

"What about Sloane and Demetri coming?" Nash sighed. "I'm more concerned about that."

"I'm not. Piercey worked hard on arranging this meeting. Sloane is smart and careful. If she ever acts, it won't be like this. We'd kill her. She isn't the most powerful, just the most cunning. And Demetri is afraid of me."

"We shouldn't trust that anyone will follow the agreements we made at the summit when we're facing such a huge threat from the north."

"I know. We did all agree, though. No one is compelled to help the other. We aren't even compelled to not war against one another. But none of us should accept invaders stepping foot in Skia Hellig. Anyone who does offers their kingdom to be conquered."

"You're right. It would be self-destructive."

Gael crossed his arms. "We're in support of your plan. My king and my people all agree that Malach made his threat clear."

"There will be no turning back." I didn't say it to anyone but myself. Needing to hear such final words.

Tonight, we would travel. We'd escape into our past lives and hope that some version of us knew better than we knew now how to prepare for this coming war.

The tavern buzzed with singing, cursing, and storytelling. Packed so full of people, the air sweltered from the sweat and body heat.

"Tell us what you're looking for," Leif said. "Soon the Prophet will realize we're not following through on our fact-finding mission and he'll want to know what we're really up to."

"Go back like I told you to." My eyes shifted to the right as I drank from my mug, searching for anything or anyone in the tavern that seemed out of the ordinary. I didn't feel any flicker of the flame inside me. This was another dead end. In the three months since I nearly died at the Flatlander temple looking for what caused my power to stir, I'd learned about an artifact that could give the neural implant to anyone. That was what I'd sensed. But I hadn't found it. I searched every chance I got and only discovered disappointment.

"We won't leave you. The last time we let you go off alone, you came back nearly dead." Wren gripped my wrist when I didn't respond. "Max, talk to us already."

"It'll endanger you." I set my mug down hard and shoved myself away from the table. "Do what I said and leave."

"You stubborn fool," Leif said.

I wove through the crowd of villagers and warriors who drank the night away, focused intently on any flicker of power.

"I've not seen you around here before." A man shifted from his conversation toward me. "What is a warrior I don't recognize doing out here without her army?"

He turned fully now, forcing me to ease back toward the wall to open up space between us in the tight crowd. Did he suspect me? And if so, of what? I studied him, wondering if the artifact might be in the area after all. "I'm passing through."

His gaze fell to my sword. "How quickly might you be passing through?"

Suspicion twinged. My voice hardened. "What do you care?"

The man shrugged a shoulder and planted his hand against the wall on the other side of my head. "Wondering how long I have to know you is all."

My eyes narrowed in warning and utter lack of amusement, or more importantly, interest.

Another man standing beside this one started to turn around. "Rufus, what are you doing to this poor—" Golden-brown eyes met mine and widened.

My breath lodged in my lungs as I looked up at the swordsman who'd nearly killed me. "What are you doing here?" I asked in a fleeting breath.

His shock slowly shifted into awe and then his plush lips twisted in a thoroughly amused smirk. "Now this is very interesting."

This man called Rufus glanced to Nash. "Great, you know each other," he muttered under his breath and rolled his eyes. "Might as well find someone else."

Nash slapped the man on the back as he walked away, but his attention never left me. "I'd also love to know what you're doing here. Perhaps we've been drawn here for the same reason."

My heart beat harder, and my hand shifted to rest against the hilt of my sword. A mix of danger and curiosity swelled inside of me.

"Unless you came to mingle." Nash placed his hand where Rufus had settled his and leaned in, eyes glinting with a teasing smile. "I can bring my friend back. Rufus loves women who carry swords."

"Rufus does, huh?"

"Rufus. Yes." Nash's gaze fell to where my hand curled around the hilt of mine before he raised his eyes back up. "So, tell me. Why are you here?"

No longer dressed for battle, Nash wore his curls down, so they fell delicately against his whiskered cheeks. He looked beautiful, like someone sculpted him perfectly. A hint of his defined chest above the opening of his tunic caught my eye and successfully brought to my memory the image of him taking his off to make a dressing for our wounds. He was too close, so close I felt his nearness, and it tangled my mind in a way I didn't expect. I never let myself get distracted like this.

Was he doing this on purpose? He carried himself like a man who knew how he looked, and he wielded it now like a sword. I shoved my palm against the crook of his arm, knocking his hand away roughly. I wouldn't be disarmed and played for a fool.

"I'm only passing through," I said in a steely voice.

Nash chuckled and crossed his arms over his chest. The space between us opened up enough for me to breathe comfortably, but not for the warmth to leave my cheeks. How did I let him get to me like that? I felt like an idiot.

"I thought maybe we were destined to finish our battle." His gaze lingered another moment before he started to shift away. "I suppose I was wrong, if you're only passing through."

"Wait." I gripped a handful of his tunic and jerked him back toward me. He came too willingly, not putting up the resistance I expected, and I pulled him so close our bodies grazed. Surprised, I pressed back against the wall. "What are you up to?"

He took my hand in his, pulled it free of his tunic, and then released me. "I told you last time we met I had important things to do. I should thank you, though. Trying to figure out why a warrior like you would seek out a little temple showed me a whole new path."

Alarm rang through me.

"Of course, you're on this path already, aren't you? Conscripted warriors are always looking for a way to escape their Prophet."

Words like that could get a person killed. He implied we both wanted to kill our Prophet, but he might've been lying to trick me into confessing. "I promise you do not want to cross me."

He winked. "We'll see who finds it first."

I needed the artifact to regain my power. He wouldn't even know what to do with it.

CHAPTER THIRTEEN

N ash proved to be well-connected here in the Flatlands, an obvious advantage I lacked as an outsider. That encounter did not lead me to the artifact, but it was not the last time I ran into him.

Soon, I learned that his advantage with the Flatlands being his homeland meant he'd always pick up the trail before me. So, I kept my eye on him. The problem with this was that he always had a head start on me.

I slipped away from Wren and Leif one night, not wanting to endanger them further, especially with this deadly swordsman.

My lead hadn't been entirely wrong. I'd come to believe that whoever possessed the artifact didn't use it for themselves because of religion. They kept returning to holy sites, which made me think they revered it too much to use it. Likely a holy person. Maybe they believed bringing it into the temples would make the gods bless the Flatlands.

This temple was far easier to enter than the last one because I arrived to find a bloody path already carved through the woods and one of the entrances. I stepped over a dead warrior I assumed Nash had slain. He was here and he wouldn't be easy to defeat if we'd actually found the artifact this time.

Picking my way through the temple, I heard nothing, which didn't bode well for the unsuspecting guards. I followed the trail of fallen warriors until I heard a crashing sound and rushed for the noise.

I opened the door to the main room of the temple to see Nash surrounded by guards. Quickly, I looked to the offerings of gold, fruit, wine, and other useless gifts. Did I sense anything? The commotion drowned out my thoughts.

Nash should have been my first target. He was too deadly, and he chased what I needed more than anything in the world. But looking at his mesmerizingly precise *footwork and swordsmanship made me just want to stand here watching him fight. He took full advantage of every motion, conservative with every move, never expending more energy than necessary. Never opening up more of himself than he needed to vulnerability.*

One of his swords sliced down another man's and cut off his thumb while he used the other to block an attack.

I might be able to take Nash out now with an arrow aimed for his head or heart. I'd need to find a clean shot through the others. It felt cowardly and wrong. Or maybe I just didn't want to kill him. With the memory of his warmth the night we ran into each other filling me, I realized with great frustration that my hesitance to kill him had nothing to do with battle. My body betrayed me, wanting to spare a threat simply because of how it felt to stand too close to him.

I nocked an arrow, determined to defy these senseless impulses and smother the warmth he'd brought to my middle. But just when I aimed for him, his stare pierced my own, catching me between the clashes of blades. I grunted and fired on a guard who didn't see me. The arrow jerked the guard's body, ripping a cry free. He stumbled back right as a second arrow stole his life away.

They all saw me, so I had little time to take advantage of the distance. Running now, I peppered the area, forcing their formation to scatter. While some arrows were deflected, others embedded deep in the men's bodies.

Nash sliced an arrow in half before it reached him. "Max," he called out to me. "I hoped to see you tonight. It's been too long this time."

I refused to respond. He sounded far too cavalier when I wanted him to tremble in fear at the sight of me.

The two of us attacked the warriors guarding the temple at the same time. Half the party split to pursue me, leaving the others for Nash to pick off more easily.

I didn't launch an offense but rather continued sprinting for the offerings. A warrior lunged in front of me, striking. I deflected and kicked my heel against his shoulder. It opened his posture, leaving him vulnerable to my piercing strike. My sword lodged deep in his chest.

Three more warriors converged on me. I caught glances of Nash, needing to keep track of him before he sneaked up on me or found the artifact before me. I noticed he did the same to me, our eyes locking more than once as we fought.

A slash nearly caught my shoulder. I jumped back and swung my sword in a wide arc. It was then I realized they were pushing me back toward the other group, trying to reunite their war party.

I dove for the ground, rolled off my shoulder, and came up to the side of one man. Dragged my blade up to slice him open from hip to shoulder. Spinning, I ducked to avoid a strike from another guard, and used the momentum to throw myself close to the third man.

Our fight continued, successfully pushing the two groups closer, until I realized how close I was now to the other guards and Nash. I tore away from my group and snapped my blade toward Nash. Twisting, he wrenched his twin sword up from the back to deflect my strike.

Damn it. I thought I'd at least clip him.

Nash growled, glancing at me as he fended off another strike from me and the guards at the same time. "Shouldn't we be friends by now?"

I scoffed, trying to ignore him again.

We each turned our focus to the guards, but I watched for my next opportunity, and took it without apology, desperate to attack him after I hesitated before.

He slid back to avoid a hit by me and barely blocked a guard's slash. "Stop it," Nash said. "We can kill them faster together."

"You're the one I need to kill."

"Fine." He ducked beneath a guard's swinging sword and with incredible speed sprinted toward another, cutting open the man's back in a long swing. Nash kicked the wounded man directly at me.

I dodged the body and missed my opportunity to attack the person to my right. Nash and I traded blows with every chance we got, greatly endangering each other in our fight against the others, forced to duel in two battles at once.

I didn't care. I refused to pass up any opportunity to defeat my enemy.

While Nash deflected a hit on either side of him, I kicked him square in his back toward the sharp tip of a sword, certain I'd done it this time. But he twisted to the side, dragging his sword along the edge of the other, just barely nudging it away from his chest.

His glare pierced me. Angry. Calculating. And something else. Something that didn't belong.

Enthralled.

His swords danced, splattering blood. He shredded his opponent's defense, his attention never fully leaving me.

A chill carved down my spine. I ignored it. Focused on the fight. On waiting for my next opportunity to attack him.

Soon only two guards remained, and neither Nash nor I had injured each other.

It was time. I abandoned the battle to run for the offerings again. Nash yelled after me, but I abandoned him to fight the two remaining guards.

I reached the offerings and began to pick up each one, searching out the warmth. "Please," I whispered. It had to be here. I couldn't keep doing this forever. The Prophet would figure out I was up to something.

A guard shifted toward me when Nash's sword slid through his throat from behind. With only one target left alive, he quickly killed the last one.

Torn between continuing my search and turning my blade on Nash, I threw useless offerings to the side, looking up desperately at him.

Instead of attacking, he began to search as well.

"It's not here," I said in a deflated voice.

Nash tossed a block of cheese to the side, muttering curses under his breath.

"We're too late." I shook my head. "It's gone."

He didn't give up but inspected everything he found.

"You'll use it to kill your Prophet?" I asked.

"What other use for power is there? All the Prophets must die. There's not a good one among them." He threw a bottle of wine against the wall in a burst of deep red. "Damn it."

I studied him for a stolen moment while he ransacked the offerings. He seemed lighthearted at the tavern, but he'd left all that behind. Nash wanted this artifact desperately.

If I didn't stay focused, he'd find it before me. Saying nothing else to him, I left the main room of the temple and searched the vacant building, still not feeling anything. All the guards had pursued us. The temple was ours now, but there was nothing useful here.

I turned down a hall, trying to make myself accept another dead end, when warmth kindled in my middle. I twisted around and saw the man from the tavern standing at the far end of the hall. Rufus. In his hand, he held a golden cylindrical device that looked straight out of the books in the library of the Sacred School. That idiot held my artifact.

I drew my bow silently, not wanting to give up my advantage at seeing him before he noticed me. Aiming for his head, I drew back and fired.

With my arrow soaring through the air, hope filled my heart. Until Nash lunged from a room to the right for his friend. I started to reach for another arrow before knowing whether it would hit.

Nash's arms wrapped around his friend, and he knocked them both to the ground. The arrow caught the back of Nash's shirt and continued on to bury itself in the wall.

"Drop it," I shouted and shot another arrow. Nocked more, fired without hesitating. Nash's blades swung up from the ground and sliced the first in half. He rolled onto his knees, his twin blades whizzing through the air to knock the arrows away from him and his friend.

Rufus scrambled to his feet, disappearing into the next room.

"Shit." I sprinted toward Nash and peeled off another arrow. He rolled off his shoulder and then disappeared from sight.

As soon as I rounded the corner, I saw Nash standing there with the artifact pressed to his left eye. Rufus stared at him with alarm.

"Wait, okay?" I lowered my bow. "Just wait and hear what I have to say."

Nash held still, one eye still on me, and the other blocked by the device.

"You don't know what to do with that power. It'll take you years of training to get good enough to kill a Prophet, maybe decades. Maybe never." I reached my hand out. "You'll waste it if you use it."

When he still didn't move or even acknowledge what I said, I let out an anguished cry. Would I really resort to telling my secret to this man when I never even told my closest friends?

"Nash," I said. "I trained at the Sacred School. They sealed my power, and I need to unlock it so I can save my people. If you give that to me, I'll actually be able to kill them. And I will. I'll kill your Prophet and mine."

No movement.

"Nash, come on—"

The eye I could see rolled up until only the whites showed and his body dropped like a stiff slab of rock. Even after hitting the ground, his posture didn't move in the slightest. I gasped. The device was still held to his eye.

Anguish filled me. He'd used it, hadn't he? I rushed to him and ripped it free from his grasp.

"Damn it!"

Blood dribbled from the corner of his eye, and the inside of the artifact was hollow with a single reddened needle sticking out.

Empty. Gone. Useless.

Nash wasted it on himself and now he was passed out cold, frozen in place like he'd been captured for touching the stolen treasure.

I hit my fist against his chest. "Wake up." Again when he didn't respond. "Wake up, Nash." Panic welled up when he still didn't move. I pushed against his chest with both hands. He wasn't breathing. Rufus dropped beside me, shaking his friend.

Nash used the artifact I spent a year hunting down. If he died, then it went to waste.

"You don't get to die." I slapped his face. "Snap out of it." Sitting up, I slammed my fist against his heart as hard as I could. Once, twice, a third time. A scream of frustration ripped free and I hit him again.

A deep gasp rocked his chest, and his eyes shot open. That kindling of warmth inside me exploded into a deep fire. I reached for it, desperate and hopeful I might catch it, but it quickly dwindled.

Nash jolted up, face-to-face with me, eyes on mine.

I stared, trying to sense his power. "Did it work?"

His hand came to his stomach, right where I usually felt my power in my core.

Then he coughed and jerked forward like someone socked him in his gut. Pain tightened his expression. His fingers curled in on themselves, muscles tightening as if out of his control. He grasped his side when white tendrils of power suddenly zipped along his body.

Nash struggled for breath, body stiff and trembling.

"You're losing control of it." I reached for him, but bright hot pain snapped against my palm. I gasped. "Focus your mind, and you'll calm your power."

The power danced along his skin and cut red marks against him. Bright sparks erupted along his arms. The power ripped open a gash on his forearm and then sliced down one of his biceps. It was tearing him apart. Blood darkened spots on his chest and sides. I'd seen this once before. He didn't have long if he didn't stop this.

"Focus, Nash." I pushed him back against the wall and took his face with both of my hands. The energy spread up my arms, burning every place it touched, but I didn't pull away.

"Don't—" he cried out, weakly pushing me away.

I slid my palms over his face again, straddling his legs. "Look at me." My fingers dug into his cheeks. Pain spread along my body, and I grunted, forcing myself not to let go. "Now, Nash. Look at me!"

His eyes opened to mine, our faces hovering close to each other. Nothing between us.

"Focus on me," I said. "Breathe with me."

He stilled as he looked into my eyes. So deeply I noticed the gold flecks sprinkling his light brown irises. Our closeness burned as much as his new energy spreading from his body to mine, tangling us both together. My stomach fluttered in a softer version of the sparks of power.

The pain lessened.

"That's it," I said. "Focus on breathing with me."

Relief filled his face. So close to each other, looking so deeply into each other's eyes, I saw more of him than I should see in any stranger. The power dissipated and no longer danced along my skin, but it felt like it moved into my chest, the burn so deep I nearly squirmed. My body wanted to melt against his even though I didn't even know him. His breath warmed my lips.

Finally, every bit of the power disappeared.

"Hold on to it," I said. "Imagine you can hide it deep inside."

Eyes soft with wonder, he nodded slowly, and then his gaze fell. Embarrassment filled me as I looked down to see such a thin amount of space separating our bodies.

I started to slide off him, but he caught my arm, his thumb softly brushing the skin beneath a jagged cut. His stare ran along the abrasions and minor burns.

His brows knit. Sweat clung to his skin, wetting his hairline and the nape of his neck. His breathing was labored and his voice sounded weak. "I hurt you."

"I'm okay." It felt like breathing in water. "You're the one who's hurt."

"I'm sorry." His eyes slowly slid closed, head lowering. I remembered the pure exhaustion of losing control of my power, just as powerful as a sedative. "I couldn't control it . . ."

I took his head and helped him as he lowered to his side. "Nash." I tried shifting his heavy body to look at his back. "Try to stay awake and don't move. I don't know how bad it is. If your power injured your internal organs, then any move might make it worse."

"It feels superficial," Nash said. "Thank you . . . for helping . . ." His eyes barely squinted open, expression suddenly relaxed. "Instead of killing me."

Rufus approached now. "This was a gift for the gods and now you're cursed. We've committed a grave sin."

"It's not cursed," I said. "He doesn't know how to control his power."

"Is it true?" Nash opened his eyes, skin pale and clammy. "I was frozen after I injected myself, but I heard and saw everything . . ." He grimaced, touching his hand to a bloodstain on his chest. "Did you truly have power before?"

I sat back, struggling to bring myself to utter the forbidden to these strangers. "Yes."

"My little sister is sick . . . She's struggled with the sickness all her life. Our villages are starving, and she can't handle any more strain . . ." His eyes closed again. "If I don't kill him, people will keep dying. She'll die."

I hated these Prophets and all the offerings wasted in their temples. "You're right that they all deserve to die."

"You offered to kill both Prophets. You said you know how to use this power." Nash started pushing himself up. I tried to stop him, but he shook me off. Once sitting, he settled against the wall to rest. "Help me wield this power and I will do what you offered. I'll kill the Prophet of the Valley and the Flatlands."

I swallowed hard, not sure I really had a choice. He stole my only hope at getting my power back, and without it I was worthless in a battle against the Prophets. Without me, he might be worthless, too. It took a long time to learn to control power.

"How do I know I can trust you?" I asked.

He stretched a bloody hand out to me. I stared for a moment before I reached out. Nash clasped my forearm, his hand easily stretching around mine. I tightened my hold on him as well, chest tightening at the feel of hard muscle beneath my hand.

"I give you my word." He nodded. "Help me, and I will not harm you or those you care for. I'll kill Eskel the Ruthless."

Words meant nothing, but his felt like power. The conviction I heard in his voice made me want to believe him. Or maybe it was his touch that did that.

What could I do anyway? This was the greatest sin of the gods, to give the power to crush so many to so few. Nash possessed power now that could tear him apart, but also rendered me and others helpless.

I hated myself for losing mine.

"Okay." I dug my fingers into his arm. "I accept your word."

His shoulders relaxed. His arm lowered. "Thank you."

I opened my mouth to speak when Nash's eyes widened. He shoved himself to his knees and pushed Rufus and me to the side so hard I rammed into the wall.

As I fell, I twisted to see a man behind us. His eyes looked void of life or emotion.

"You defied the order of the gods by stealing their power for yourself," the stranger said.

Nash and I both started to stand when the stranger raised his fingers and snapped. A burst of scarlet power erupted from Nash's gut. Blood spurted from the wound. Gushed against his fingers as they came to the jagged hole in his body. He screamed. Teetered. Stared in shock at the devastating injury.

Who was this man?

"Wait," I said, hands lifting. "We didn't create this artifact. We did nothing wrong."

Streams of Nash's blood slipped from between his fingers and splashed onto the stone ground when he pulled his hands back to look at them. Then he collapsed, hitting the ground hard, his moan hardly audible.

I covered my mouth.

"You now know not to defy the order of the gods." Steely eyes met mine. Then they fell to Nash's collapsed form. "Let this be your warning. I'll let you keep your life if you stop here. I know you plan to create more for your allies. Do so, and I will kill you and anyone involved in your plan."

"What about me?" I asked.

"You mean what if you regain your power?" He shook his head once. "This matter has nothing to do with the gods. You lost it without them, and if you regain it without them, what difference does it make?"

Despite my instinct to attack this incredibly powerful warrior, I knew deep down that even if I never lost my power, I'd still have lost against him. I sensed it in the void I felt in him, not the abundance of great power, but rather the destruction of it. This man was death.

He disappeared.

CHAPTER FOURTEEN

Though I did not recognize the security system in my first life, I did now. The brutality of his warning haunted me. Every time I looked at Nash, I saw the power tearing his body apart.

If the security system attacked us in our first life, then either he knew Dr. Henderson reset the simulations or she managed to also capture his memory. He didn't seem human in the same way we did. Had the gods actually known all along what she did or had their own security system hid it from them?

The question spun through my mind.

Seeing Nash obtain power in our first life answered so many questions, though. He advanced far too quickly with his power over the last eight years. Piercey must have been right that we managed to draw upon our strength in previous lives somehow. At least, Nash and I did.

I struggled to put the thoughts away when I sat down across from the coastal and Fjellfolk Prophet.

"Thank you for joining me," I said, battering away images of all the blood pouring from Nash's wound. "I appreciate your willingness to talk more about Malach and the kingdoms beyond the peninsula."

Sloane didn't respond or react. Her cool stare remained on me. I couldn't decide whether I liked her or not. When she ascended on the coast, she closed down the perverse resorts where the most powerful gluttonously indulged in their every desire. I liked that. But looking into her eyes reminded me of staring at an enemy during battle.

I continued, still studying her. "I understand that everyone worries that if we partner together too much, we'll end up combining kingdoms and that inevitably I'll be in charge. Like Malach and his lackeys. I think that if we don't unite to face this threat then we're more likely to see kingdoms fall, either into his hands, or into the comfort of another Skia Hellig kingdom."

Demetri rubbed his chin. "I would tend to agree, though Theus won't see this. The problem is that we don't really know what Malach wants."

"You mean who," Sloane said pointedly.

"Who?" I leaned forward. "You think Malach is only going after some kingdoms?"

Sloane ran her fingers along the threads of the couch cushion. "I think that in Malach's position, if I wanted to conquer Skia Hellig, I'd start with the hardest to beat and leave the others alone."

"Why not start with the easier ones?" Demetri asked.

"Because Eclipse will help them. Declaring war on any kingdom in Skia Hellig is declaring war on her. Even if she could stand for the injustice of it, which we know she can't, she'll see it as a threat to her kingdom."

Damn did this lady read me well. "If he attacks me, you think no one else will fight with me."

Sloane shook her head. "Maybe not if they don't attack us."

"If he conquers my kingdom, it only gives him more power to conquer yours."

She smiled and I realized I'd never seen her do that. It looked serious and wooden and somehow only made her appear that much more cunning. "Only if we believe you'll lose."

"So I'm your shield. My kingdom defeats the invaders and no one else lifts a hand to help. Can you be so shameless?"

She crossed one leg over the other and reclined against the seat. "Absolutely. There is no shame in saving the lives of my people."

"I guess I know where you stand," I said.

"No. I only say this to challenge you to open your mind in this situation. You see too much good in people."

Demetri groaned. "You're as cold as I've heard, Sloane. I think it only makes sense to do all we can to stop Malach and the others from crossing into Skia Hellig. If we all fight, we're in less danger. You're not afraid of Eclipse taking our kingdoms. So it is purely a strategic decision for you. But haven't you considered the future relationships of our kingdoms? Do you think Eclipse will ever look kindly upon you if you scorn her people?"

Sloane looked at me instead of him. "No. That's why I came."

"So, you'll fight with us?" I asked.

"I traveled an awful long way to tell you to go fuck yourself, didn't I? And I volunteered to host the summit. My problem with you, though, is that you cannot let go of your principles. You're so against everything Eskel did and everyone else who you've fought that you can't take anything from them. You've never truly warred as a Prophet, Eclipse. You won't be able to keep your soul clean."

"You think I've never dirtied myself for my people?" I asked.

"It's different to dirty your hands as a ruler than as an individual." Her eyes seemed to read my soul. "Isn't that why you haven't killed Theus? Would the old Max have hesitated?"

I scooted back in my chair. "You also think I should kill him."

"On the contrary, I'd consider it a threat. You disposing of another ruler in Skia Hellig worries me, and I don't like feeling worried. I say this to point out the difference in your behavior as a warrior and as a Prophet. If it does come to war with an enemy far greater than Theus, you'll have to grow beyond what you've been. I told you I don't like to be worried. Well, this is what worries me for you. You are what stands in your own way."

Demetri watched me. "I must admit, she's right about this."

"I thought you didn't trust me." I glared at him, unnerved by the conversation. "Wasn't that what you went on about at the summit?"

"Do you think any of us trust one another? Everything is different now than it was. Malach came. You said yourself that you're a shield. I won't turn away a good shield."

"You think you know what I'll do." I sat forward now, my sharp stare cutting from Demetri to Sloane. "You think because I care about people and I love Skia Hellig that I'll kill myself to save your people. Many people have lost their lives assuming they can beat me just because they think they know what I'll do. I will not allow you to hide behind me."

"Then you will kill us and take our lands." Sloane settled her head back. "That's an important consideration."

"Don't mock me."

"I'm not mocking you. I wondered what you would do in this situation. I didn't believe that you'd abandon any innocent person in Skia Hellig, but I also know you do not run from a fight. I just wasn't sure how you'd fight me if I betrayed you."

Demetri was right that none of us trusted one another, but I thought Sloane might be the most dangerous person to trust, even more so than Theus who absolutely wanted to kill me. She possessed the mind of Piercey, the practicality of Dr. Henderson, and an air of ruthlessness that reminded me of Lote. I didn't know whether she was an ally or an enemy. I suspected neither.

Sloane didn't want to war with me. That didn't mean she wanted to work with me either.

I shifted from my seat to take the space directly beside her and held her stare. "You know I won't fight you if you don't give me reason to."

"Yes." She didn't withdraw, but she also didn't look fearless. Rather, a perfect amount of trepidation and challenge emanated from her.

"You know I will kill you if you give me reason to."

With all confidence, she said, "Yes."

"Then I hope you don't plan to ever give me reason to." I sat back and turned my eyes to the ceiling. "I hate politics."

Sloane surprised me by chuckling quietly. "And yet, in your own very strange way, you're surprisingly good at it."

Demetri leaned against his knees. "So, what will we do about Malach, ladies?"

"We kill him." I closed my eyes. "We don't allow him to take a single grain of dirt from Skia Hellig."

"War," Demetri said.

"I hope you'll join me," I said. "Together, we can tell the world not to touch our lands and we can roar it so loudly the whole world will hear."

Our guests, top advisors, and most trusted commanders and chiefs gathered in the dining hall to eat dinner. The children joined, and I couldn't help watching Sloane's two teenage daughters. I didn't doubt her love for them, but she wasn't particularly warm with them either. Reserved and calm, she might have seemed aloof if not for how intently she listened to the girls when they talked.

"How did your discussion go?" I asked Nash as he cut into his chicken.

"Surprisingly well. Should we war together, we've already drawn up some solid preliminary plans to discuss with our assemblies."

"Demetri will fight with us," I said. "Sloane, I'm not so sure about."

"Whoever is sure about her?" Nash took a bite of the meat and looked at her briefly. "Her head disciple is easier to read, but I sensed that even he has no idea what she plans to do."

"She's so careful. She may not know yet. I'm sure she has a hundred possibilities she's imagined and will choose based on what seems best in the long-term."

"The question then," Nash said, "is whether she'll do anything to hurt us."

"She doesn't want to fight with me. I told her I'd kill her if she gave me reason to."

Nash stopped cutting and looked at me. "Max."

"She needed to hear it."

"She's a Prophet. We just spent all that time building trust at that peace summit."

"Well," I said, "she knows how to keep peace with me now, doesn't she?"

Elsie leaned forward to see us better. "Finn threw up on me."

I bit my lip and reached for him.

Nash helped Elsie clean her shirt. "A little spit-up never hurt anyone, did it?"

"It got on my swords."

"Why are you wearing your swords at the dinner table anyway?" Nash asked.

Elsie furrowed her brows. "The same reason you are, Daddy." Her voice lowered. "Warriors are always prepared, especially when enemies are around."

"We don't know that they're our enemies," I whispered.

"We don't know that they aren't," Elsie said. "Prophet Sloane's youngest daughter is really good with swords. We had fun racing earlier, but I need to be ready in case she attacks. I can't let myself have too much fun without being ready."

Nash coughed like he'd choked on his food. "Elsie, I swear—and I mean swear—on your life, on Finn's, on your mother's, and on your ma's life that if you pull a sword on a Prophet's daughter, you will never hold one ever again."

"What if she pulls one on me, Daddy?"

"She won't."

"What if?"

He dropped his silverware. "Then use that necklace to call for me and your ma. You're thirteen. Starting a war isn't up to you."

Elsie crossed her arms and stared at her plate. "You guys don't trust me."

"I trust you more than I trust any child in the world," Nash said.

"That's right." I wiped Finn's lip. "More than any child."

"One day I'll be grown up," Elsie said.

Nash patted her head. "That's right, baby girl. One day. Now eat and stop sulking."

"I'm not sure now was the right time for what we planned," I said, referring to sending warriors to attack the targets we discussed. "Tomorrow may be too early with these talks looking promising."

"We can't wait," Nash said. "We move forward. Give the others someone to follow. It's been long enough already. Once that army starts moving, there's no stopping them, and it won't take long for them to enter Skia Hellig."

"Right." I took a bite of the chicken but couldn't even taste it. "I hate this."

His hand came over my knee. "Me, too."

I kissed Finn's soft cheek wanting so badly to give him peace. We waited to have him until it seemed like a good time, and now we were about to enter a war that didn't even feel real. I didn't want Finn to grow up at war.

"You need a break from thinking about it." Nash took the baby from me. "Elsie is done eating. Why don't you two invite the other kids to the game room? You love taking kids there."

"I guess I could do that."

"Distract yourself and use the excuse to form bonds that will make you more than just the Prophet who can kill the other Prophets. Become a person to them, especially to Sloane. Elsie said she spent time with her daughter."

I ran my fingers through Finn's feathery hair. "That's a good idea. Maybe I should have Elsie put her weapons away first."

He snorted. "You think?"

I scooted my chair back and tugged on the girl's sleeve. "Dad had a fun idea. Let's invite the kids to the game room."

Her eyes lit. "Can we really?"

"Yes, as long as you put your swords away and change into something else. You smell like spit-up."

Elsie grimaced. "Deal."

Before I left, I kissed Nash's cheek. "Charm our guests, please. We need allies."

"I will."

"Alright, Elsie girl. Let's go. I'll change, too."

"Do you get to keep your weapons?" she asked.

"Obviously."

"You don't even need them. How's that fair?"

I looped my arm through hers as we walked out of the room. "How's it fair that you're already as tall as me? When did that happen?"

"I'm growing up, Ma. My mom says that I'll be tall like Daddy."

"Maybe not as tall."

"You never know."

I shrugged. "True. You have a lot of growing to do, then."

Elsie leaned her head against me as we walked. "Can I really not fight that girl if she pulls a sword on me?"

"It's complicated. You shouldn't let her hurt you, though."

"This is why I don't want to be a Prophet. There's so many rules. A war chief can focus on war. I mean, Dad helps you with more than what other war chiefs do, right? I won't have to do all that?"

"That's right."

"I know you two are only trying to make me feel good. That's what you do to kids. You tell them you believe in them." She looked up at me, very suddenly not looking like a child anymore despite how young she appeared. Her eyes looked older. Wiser than she acted. "I'm going to surprise you."

"Oh, Elsie, we really do believe in you."

"You believe in me as much as you can believe in a kid. You need to prepare yourself for me to grow up. I don't want Finn to ever get hurt. I know you won't want me to get hurt. It's going to be hard for you to watch me be war chief when you'll just want to relax with Dad and live the kind of life you haven't been able to."

"Where is this coming from?"

We climbed the stairs and Elsie's voice quieted. "War is coming. I've been thinking."

"I don't want you to think about that."

"That doesn't matter. We all want things we can't have. I have to think about it. Do you think the war won't touch me?"

I couldn't talk about it. "I won't let it, not until you're older."

She gave me that beautiful smile with her dimples showing. Growing up couldn't erase those. "I love you, Ma. I know you would do anything for me. You've always protected me."

"I always will." I tapped her necklace. "That's why you have that."

"I'll let you protect me, even when I'm war chief, if you let me be a great warrior."

I almost said yes immediately without really thinking about what she said. Elsie wanted me to let her grow up. Could I watch her go into battle? Could I see her bleed and not save her? These were problems for another day. "Okay. Deal, but give me a little time."

"A little. That's all."

"Don't be in such a rush to grow up. I lost my childhood. I want you to have one. You don't know how much it matters and how lucky you are to have the chance to be a kid. Cherish it. You'll be a better warrior in the long run for it."

Elsie seemed to consider this. "Okay."

Once we reached our floor, Elsie stopped and pursed her lips.

"Do you always make me walk up the stairs to make sure I don't get spoiled?"

I tilted my head back and laughed. "What? You want me to use my power to teleport you everywhere? Walking is good for you."

"Just curious." She put her hand on the door to her room. "Can I keep my dagger at least?"

"You're carrying that?"

"I carry it everywhere."

"Fine." I ran my hand over my face. "I guess. Be careful with it around the smaller kids."

"I know that." She opened the door but looked back at me before walking in. "You don't have to remind me all the time to be careful."

The door at the end of the hall opened and my intuition recognized it before my mind did. The power within me recognized the power calling out to it. Before I even felt the fear or confusion, I threw up a powerful shield that blocked the entire hallway. Hurled a wave of energy as my mind began to recognize what my body felt.

Arrows scattered—the sight that first caught my eye.

Panic crushed my heart, opening me up to the burning rage within.

No one threatened my family.

The wall at the end of the hallway caved in with a loud crash. I was halfway to Elsie when I noticed more arrows flying. Even though my shield would destroy them, I swung my sword in front of Elsie on reflex.

For a critical fraction of a second, I froze in shock. Watched, stunned, as ordinary arrows flew straight through my shield as if it didn't exist. My already swinging sword sliced through the ones flying for Elsie.

No time to think.

I teleported directly in front of her, not wasting even the short amount of time it took to take that final step. My heel landed on her foot so I could immediately transport us away from the attackers.

But it was too late.

Arrows tore into my body as we disappeared from the hall.

I'd focused on the Sacred School, the place that felt safest for Elsie. Only it felt like I missed a step walking down the stairs. Rather than instantly appearing at the Sacred School, we crashed into the stone wall surrounding the top of the roof.

It all happened so quickly that the impact of the arrows was still hitting my body. I jerked as they finished plunging through me, falling back a step.

My gaze searched for Elsie to see that she was okay, just as the pain began to branch over me. I didn't even know where I'd been hit. Whether I'd live or die. How this could possibly happen. Only that I needed to know if any hit her. That was it. The only thing in the world that mattered.

There wasn't a speck of blood on her. A desperate, relieved cry escaped my chest. I reached forward to clasp her to myself when pain wrapped around my body, tethering me in place.

Elsie stared at me, confusion and shock scrunching her young face. A weapon I hadn't seen her draw clattered to the ground.

"Ma?"

A frigid wind swept between us.

My eyes fell to my body for the first time. The pain finally started to really register. I touched an arrow protruding from my side, catching a stream of blood that snaked from the wound. Lifting my fingers, I stared, unable to accept what I saw. A perfectly normal arrow destroyed my energy shield and cut through my shoulder. Two more protruded from lower down my body. I couldn't even register where.

What the hell?

A choking sound escaped from Elsie's lips and then she screamed this time, terrified and desperate.

"Ma!"

CHAPTER FIFTEEN

I didn't understand what was happening. The arrows had flown straight through my shield, and then I'd failed to teleport to the Sacred School.

A terrible sensation ripped through my body, completely different than anything I'd ever experienced. Not just pain from the arrows. It emanated from the arrows sticking out from my right shoulder, my side, and my left thigh.

The feathers of the arrows curled in, turning black as they dissolved. I watched as the dark color slowly ate up the wood, petrifying everything it touched.

It felt like the darkness ate me up as well. I looked down at my hands, expecting to see them turn hard like stone.

Elsie reached for me, but I shouted, "Don't! They're poisoned."

I noticed then that she clutched her necklace. The stone glowed. Good. Nash would come for us.

These arrows were sucking the power out of me. I needed to get rid of them. I gripped one arrow and tried with all my strength to break it, but I couldn't. It was hard as stone and my power dwindled so rapidly.

My power dissipated far more quickly than my blood spilled out. I couldn't take the time to figure out what was happening or why. I only needed to know that I was losing my energy and soon maybe my life. And that Elsie needed me to get us to safety.

I used my remaining power to hold the arrows steady in my body and swiftly spun my sword so it sliced cleanly through. I grunted in pain at the pressure on my wounds, but that pain couldn't compare to the agony of using my power to shove them free of my body. Blood gushed from the wounds.

I focused on the holes in my body and burned them closed from the inside out. Though I tried to hold in my scream, it escaped, and I curled in on myself, crying out at the fire eating away at me.

Weakness threatened to drag me to the ground. I shivered in the cold. Elsie watched me with horror written across her young face, her hand covering her mouth.

"We're exposed here . . ." I nodded toward the door leading inside. "They may find us soon and I'm surely the one they want. You must hide."

Elsie shook her head. "I'm not leaving you. You're hurt." She grabbed both of her swords now. "You can't fight like that."

I spoke with a low growl. "Yes, I can. You'll hide where I tell you to hide." Pain clutched me and I nearly doubled over.

"I can't hide without you," she said. "Daddy won't be able to find you. Your powers aren't working right."

No arguing with that. I'd tried to reach out to Nash with my neural connection, to anyone, and it was like I'd lost the ability entirely.

"Wait." Elsie ran from me toward the outside cabinets that housed our training gear. She loved to practice here with us when we wanted to be alone as a family. Her hands shook as she withdrew her bow and quiver of arrows and another set for me. I didn't stop her. Once she hid, it would be wise for her to be prepared to defend herself.

I walked forward and ground my teeth so hard I thought I might shatter my jaw. Every step ripped at my wounds, gravity hanging from the holes in my body like weights. Blood still oozed out from my burned skin and the parts of the injuries that were not properly cauterized. Each step stabbed into my thigh.

Elsie slowly opened the door leading inside and peeked into the hallway before I could stop her. The pain and injuries distracted me. I struggled through every step until I reached her side.

"You will only do what I say," I whispered.

She started to walk beside me, but I pulled her behind me with a grunt and drew my sword with my uninjured arm. My other hung limp at my side. It hurt too badly to move it.

My heart raced, though I needed to calm it and not worsen my blood loss. My mind reeled with questions. Who attacked us? Malach or our guests? How did they manage to steal my power?

What about Nash and Finn? What if they tried to hurt my baby?

What was I thinking bringing a helpless life into this brutal world?

Elsie's voice whispered in my ear. "Let me help you, Ma. You're shaking."

I looked down and noticed the tremble for the first time. She started to slide under my arm to hold me up when I heard a sound and stopped moving. Elsie did as well, listening with me.

I opened the door beside me and nudged her inside. She stumbled in, swords locked in her grip, the anger in her eyes telling me she didn't want to hide. But she knew better than to fight with me at a time like this.

Warriors burst into the hallway. Fools who dared to enter my tower and try to kill my Elsie.

Vengeance flowed hot through my veins. It stoked what power still burned in me.

Arrows flew again and I summoned enough energy to erect a shield to cover the doorway sheltering Elsie. I crisscrossed the air with my sword, breaking every arrow.

"She still has power, Commander," one of the men yelled with his lips stretching in a horrified gasp.

"Not for long," the commander said with narrowed eyes.

Screaming in agony, I swung one blade for the man closest to me.

I grew weaker by the second, not just from the injury, but from my quickly draining power. I barely managed to strengthen my hit. It was enough, though. My sword shattered my enemy's and sank into his chest. I ripped it free and spun for the next one. The shield over Elsie grew so thin I worried it would not stop an attack. I withdrew the dagger from my side with my bloodied hand. Using my power, I ripped a warrior through the air while he screamed and impaled him upon the blade I held in a trembling grip at my hip. We both cried out from the pain and I nearly lost my hold on the weapon. But I fought through the blazing agony to rip the dagger free and swing my sword for another warrior.

Only two remained, but I wasn't sure I'd be able to even take a step after this next one, much less fight them. I blocked a hit with my left blade from one and caught another with my dagger, but I faltered from the pain and weakness. My enemy's sword bore down against the blade, forcing my own sword to sink into my thigh.

I slammed my head against the man's nose and kicked him in the gut using what power remained. He flew back against the wall with a thud. Twisting, I reared back to attack the next one when weakness knocked my legs out from under me. I couldn't control it. I fell onto the ground, barely catching myself with my sword.

A sword swung for my head. I focused on it to stop it, struggling to lift my own weapon in defense.

They all needed to die.

An arrow whizzed past my ear and embedded in the chest of the man attacking me. His sword fell short as he stumbled back, shocked eyes falling to his chest. Another arrow flew and then a third.

"Ma!" Elsie screamed as each of her arrows thudded into the two men.

I summoned all my strength and launched myself forward, burying my sword in the closest man's gut. Elsie wasn't ready to take life. She wasn't ready. Even if it killed me, I needed to kill these men before her arrows did.

The warrior and I both fell to the ground together. My grip on my left sword failed and it clattered to the ground. My arm hung uselessly at my side. I gasped with pain as every single movement ripped at my wounds as if tearing them wide open.

Tendrils of my power flowed through me, the last remnants that kept my insides warm. I directed them all at the man running at me from the far side of the room. A red streak of power broke through his teeth and escaped through the back of his head.

I growled through clenched teeth, my vision blurring.

Elsie sprinted to me. She caught me as I fell, struggling to hold me up. "I called for Dad again." Tears filled her voice. "He'll come. He always comes."

Blood poured out from the fresh leg wound, but I couldn't draw upon any power to burn the skin closed. I needed to bandage it quickly.

"Elsie . . ." I struggled to find my voice. The world around me spun slowly. I tugged at one of my sleeves. "Cut this off for me."

She nodded and used her dagger to saw the sleeve free. Without being instructed, she wrapped it tightly around my thigh. I swallowed my grunt of pain so I wouldn't upset her, but the burning and searing agony of the arrow injuries strained my voice badly. "Thank you . . ."

"We have to go." Elsie sniffled and stood up, trying to drag me to my feet. "We have to hide until Dad finds us."

I struggled to my feet and stumbled forward, nearly falling right back down to the ground. It hurt so badly to walk. Every step hurt so badly. Elsie held me tightly around my middle, dragging me toward the door at the end of the hall.

"Baby girl . . ." I settled my cheek against her temple as we trudged forward. "I need you to listen."

"No." Anger tensed Elsie's fine features. "I won't. I know what you're going to say."

"Elsie—"

"I said no. We're staying together. You want me to leave you, and I won't. You can't make me."

As we continued forward, hot blood started to drizzle from my side. I put my hand to it, feeling the skin swollen with internal bleeding that my cauterizing job blocked from freely leaving the wound.

Elsie slid her hand over mine, her voice shaking. "Ma—"

"Keep moving." I nudged her forward, powering through the heaviness of my body and the pain sawing at my wounds.

Wild fear danced in her wide eyes and tightened her voice to a small tremble. "It's really bad."

Warm blood pooled between my fingers. With my free hand, I took her face and held firmly. "Elsie, listen to me." Every second intensified the pain as my energy waned. It'd been so long since I lacked power. I forgot entirely how it felt. "You trained your whole life for this. You're ready."

She started to shake her head, but I gritted my teeth and deepened my voice.

"I said you're ready. Now's the time, Elsie. Move. Don't stop, even if I do. You find your dad." My eyes dampened and stung as I looked into hers. "You find him."

Tears slid down her face. Lately, Elsie felt far too grown. I wasn't sure when it happened. One day she was running barefoot through the village and the next, an independent mind bloomed beneath deep eyes and a surprisingly confident veneer. But Elsie looked every bit the small child I'd tucked back into bed after nightmares or the crying seven-year-old who skinned her knee.

Right when I thought I'd been wrong, that this would break her, she let out one long, slow breath. The emotion fell from her expression, and she nodded. "Let's go."

Elsie wrapped her arm around me.

I focused on each step to keep my weight off her, but as we struggled down the hall, weakness tangled my body. I faltered and she caught me, grunting and struggling to help keep me standing. I leaned against the wall for support.

As we walked down the hall, I saw a door open.

My vision blurred.

I pulled my bow from my back and hooked an arrow with my thumb, ripping them both to my front. Nocking the arrow and drawing back the bowstring felt impossible. Refusing to allow the burn of lava rushing through my chest and arm to stop me, I managed to draw back slightly before the weakness tethered my muscles. Despite my best efforts, I slid slowly down the wall, my aim quivering. A cry wrenched from my lips while I tried with all my might to pull back on the string.

Elsie ripped the arrow from my hand, wrenched the bow from my weakening grip, and slid into a perfectly controlled stance. It shouldn't have surprised me because nearly every day for a decade I taught her how to shoot. But the shock silenced me as I watched her shoulders straighten, her body still, and her arrow fly.

It snapped in midair. Elsie nocked another but I shook my head for her to stop when I heard the familiar voice.

"What's happened to you?" Sloane approached with her disciples flanking her.

I looked up at the coastal Prophet, having no idea whether she was a friend or not. If she wanted to kill us, I couldn't stop her. I couldn't summon even a spark of power, and I barely kept my eyes open. While I didn't believe she'd ever try to kill me before, I no longer felt that way. Not when this was her only chance.

"My husband and my son . . ." I said, trying to suck in enough breath to ask if they were okay.

"Last I saw, Nash was fighting his way up the stairs. Piercey took your baby when the attacks began." She knelt and studied the growing blood spots on my bandages. "You poor thing. It appears Malach has begun his war against you."

"So, what is it?" I struggled to form the words. "Will you fight with us? Or hope Malach stops with my kingdom?"

"It's unexpected to see you injured and helpless like this. I didn't prepare for this scenario. If I don't help, you very well may die." She sat back on her heels, sounding like she spoke to herself more than me. "Helping means going to war today and facing an enemy who can do this to you. Defeat may be certain."

"Sloane—"

"I appreciate you inviting me here, Eclipse. I appreciate your reasonableness. If you live, I hope you can understand why it's not possible for me to help you today."

"What?" Elsie lunged forward and caught the woman's sleeve. "Wait, please. You can't leave her like this. She's dying."

"I do feel for you, Eclipse." She looked down on me with pity. "You've never done anything to deserve this. It's clear you're genuine. You're just not the political kind. Still, they can't let you and your kingdom remain in peace.

I wish I could help. I honestly do. But I'm not getting involved. It wouldn't be good for my people."

"Take my daughter." I forced strength into my voice, speaking forcibly and not as if I was begging. "She's just a kid."

"I'm not leaving you," Elsie said, voice hitching.

"Quiet," I said.

The Prophet's gaze shifted between us. "If I interfere, then I'm picking sides. My kingdom needs more time to prepare."

"She's a child. Think of your daughters."

"I am." She straightened, looking down on me sadly. "Do you really think I should place them in danger? I brought them here with me."

"Don't do this," Elsie whispered.

"I'm sorry, Eclipse," Sloane said. "I really am. Elsie, I am very sorry to you as well. I need to return to my daughters and make sure I give no one a reason to hurt them."

"You're helping them to kill us," I said.

"See it however you must." She turned and began to walk away from me.

"I won't forget this," I said in a low rumble.

She paused but did not look back at me. "I can't imagine you will. But you have many enemies and I also know you will not bring more ruin upon your people. I won't help your people, but I won't help anyone hurt you either."

"Don't assume you know what I'll do because you think you know me."

"Best of luck, Eclipse. I really do hope you survive."

I squeezed my eyes shut. "I hate politics."

With Sloane halfway down the hall, Elsie spoke out in a threatening voice. "I won't forget this either."

Sloane paused but then continued, still not looking back at us.

Reaching for Elsie, I took her hand and squeezed her tight. "It's time to hide. You heard. Your dad is on his way."

"We'll hide together."

"I don't think . . . I can walk anymore . . ."

"I'll try to drag you."

"Just go, Elsie." My eyes slid shut. The weakness clutched me and refused to let go. Pulled me toward sleep. "Please . . . I'm begging . . . you . . ."

Elsie pressed against my shoulders. "It's okay, Ma." She sounded strong and calm even though I heard tears in her voice. "I know what to do. You can let go for now. Rest."

No. Never. I could never pass out and abandon her. I reached within myself for my power, not even feeling the slightest embers burning. Darkness crept over my view of her when I pried my eyes open. My hands fell limp. Elsie pressed against my wound now, burying her hands in my blood. Pain tore through my heart to see the darkness staining her hands. I never wanted her to experience anything like this.

"I've got you. Dad will be here soon. It's okay."

It wasn't okay. I'd failed her so badly she felt like she needed to console me. I wanted to hate myself for it, but I'd been through enough to understand that this was counterproductive. Despite doing my best, loving her my best, I couldn't save her from this.

I at least wanted to stay awake with her.

"Elsie . . ."

Her forehead pressed against mine.

Hide. I tried to say the words. My lips moved. Nothing came out, though.

Hide. Hide. Please, baby. Hide.

A hot tear trailed down my cheek and slipped between my lips.

Hide . . .

CHAPTER SIXTEEN

Consciousness erupted back into me, fooling me into thinking I'd regained my strength. I opened my eyes and tried to rise, only to find myself completely limp. I couldn't move.

Elsie knelt in front of where I lay collapsed on the ground. Bow drawn, prepared to shoot, her thin arms quivered.

Grief and rage mingled into one familiar fire inside me. How could I let this happen?

The room shook and the sound of explosions rolled in waves. Several seconds passed between them and then the wall not far from us exploded with a crash. Two forms barreled through the wall and rolled across the ground.

"Max!" Nash's booming voice knocked into me like a fist, making me dizzy. "Elsie!"

I caught sight of Nash's curls first, quickly seeing the lethal look carved into his hard expression. He'd landed on top of a man. Black energy burned around his hand and he slammed his fist into the man's temple. The skull crushed beneath the power of his hit, caving in the warrior's face in a smattering of blood and bones. Beside me, Elsie stumbled back and gasped, her body stiffening.

"Don't look," I commanded.

Nash ripped his head up, looking at Elsie, and then finding me. His stare lingered, terror gripping him first. Quickly, it sharpened into deadly rage. I wanted to save him from this. Didn't want him to fear for a moment he might lose me. But I could do nothing except try to stay awake. To stay with my family.

Nash whipped around and unleashed a scream, sending a wave of energy flying through the wall. Cries erupted from the other room.

My vision waned and darkened as I watched Nash twist just in time to catch a flaming ball of energy with his bare hands. He extinguished it immediately, not even reacting to the pain as the fire sizzled against his skin.

My husband drew his twin blades and flew so fast through the hole in the wall, I barely saw him move.

Sleep captured me in fits that I ripped free from, trying to hold me down beneath its waters. To drown me in darkness. I came to with panic throbbing hot in my chest. A shield surrounded us and Nash continued to fight. I needed to warn him about the arrows that stole my power, but I couldn't speak.

Elsie clutched me tightly with a sword drawn over me, my poor girl resorting to defending me.

Bodies littered the hall. Blood rushed like a river and pooled at the shield protecting us. That wasn't right. I knew it. I wasn't thinking straight, but with my life draining away, my world breaking into pieces, Nash's battle against our enemies looked more like the grandiose stories painted in powder across the sky during the festival. Elsie didn't close her eyes like I instructed. She watched her father's swords unleash his wrath against those trying to kill us, exposed for the first time to how swiftly Nash's blades stole life.

Darkness consumed my view of Nash and then I lost feel of Elsie beside me. Only pain remained, relentless and without mercy, battering my body, cutting me to shreds.

Steady arms lifted me, breaking beneath the icy waters that drowned me. The feeling of being in Nash's arms was so familiar and so comforting, peace prickled the pain consuming me. The slightest buzz of energy warmed my skin, but it didn't enter me and give me strength. It felt like it bounced off me. Nash was trying to connect with me, but I couldn't.

My eyes fluttered open as Nash shifted and jostled me. I barely made out the image of Elsie climbing onto his back. She clasped her arms around his neck while he held me tenderly and then lifted us into the air. We flew over dozens of dead warriors and puddles of blood that once looked like a rushing river to me.

"Can you hold on?" he asked Elsie.

"Yes. Just get Ma out of here."

I tried to reach for Nash's chest. My fingers twitched. He used his power to break the windows and then swept us out of the tower into the freezing air.

As he flew through the air, so fast that the pain hooked into my wounds, he looked down at me. Tears coated his furious, terrified eyes. "Hang on."

"Finn . . ."

"Piercey and Wren have him. They already portaled to King Tyroin's land."

My heavy eyes closed. I needed to ask about everyone else. What about Leif and Markus? Their families? What about all our people? I couldn't hold on anymore, though. I barely heard Nash's soothing voice flowing over me like honey. His warmth burning through the cold.

I couldn't leave my people.

I couldn't leave my family.

I couldn't die like this.

Deep, throbbing pain dragged me to consciousness.

I tried to speak but only a moan slipped out.

"Easy," Nash said. "Don't move." He carefully brushed my hair back with one hand and held my face with the other.

My eyes fluttered open. The bright sun pouring through the windows seared my vision. Winter approached. There shouldn't be this much daylight.

"We're here," he said gently. "Elsie, Finn, Piercey, Wren, and Leif. All the kids."

"Markus?"

"He's with Gael, strategizing."

I let my head fall into Nash's palm. "Is . . . Is anyone hurt?"

"No." His soft lips pressed against my forehead. "You need to rest. Try not to worry."

Tears pinched my eyes. "How many?"

He quieted, surely knowing what I asked.

"Nash . . ."

"We don't know yet. The attacks happened all over the Valley. Their weapons stripped away the power of some of our best warriors. Any enemies we didn't kill or capture escaped. The war parties were small, probably only as large as they could manage without giving themselves away. But the hits seemed targeted."

"We're in Gael's kingdom, aren't we?"

"Yes."

I tested my strength to try to sit but I barely budged.

"I told you not to move," Nash said. "Power isn't working on you. They couldn't heal you." Pleading filled his tone. "Please, Max. You have to rest."

"They need me. I can't stay here."

Nash carefully shifted to lie down beside me. I accepted the pain of the bed shifting, desperate for his nearness. He held me against himself and stroked his thumb along my jaw. "They need you alive. Markus and Piercey have been traveling between here and the villages. The people know you're alive."

"They'll be terrified . . ."

"You can't change that, Max. What happened was terrifying. We're all suffering right now. You cannot save us from that. Just lie here with me and let your body rest."

How could I? "Have they seen you?"

"Yes. Now, stop. We are taking care of everyone. Trust us."

It hurt so bad. I nodded, not because I actually accepted the situation, but because I truly could do nothing else. Nash kissed the side of my face and whispered to me as I lost my hold on the world once again.

The next time I awoke, I refused to remain here while my people were waiting for me. I almost passed out when Nash lifted me into a sitting position on the edge of the bed.

"This is crazy." Piercey rarely raised his voice, but he did so now. "You're in no condition to be out of bed, much less traveling."

"It's been too long already. The people need to see me." I froze on the edge of the bed to catch my breath. Sweat gathered along my hairline. Nash slid an arm under my legs and carefully lifted me. The movement hurt more than I wanted the others to see. I settled my head against Nash's chest, hoping to hide how badly it hurt.

"He's right," Nash said gently as he held me. "This is too much for you."

"We're too reliant on our healers. I can manage."

Nash closed his eyes for a moment and then nodded. "I'll help you do what you want, but be reasonable once we get there."

Piercey huffed and ran his hands through his hair. "Okay, we need to keep it short. I'm not backing down on that and you're in no shape to fight anyone on this, Max."

I let him continue, too exhausted to argue with him. It only mattered that I saw my people.

Nash carried me to the other room where Gael talked with Markus. "She's ready."

Gael looked uncertain. "She doesn't look ready."

"Well, I am," I snapped more harshly than I intended.

They all looked at one another before Wren spoke. "This is what Max needs, so don't waste any time while she's up. Let's get her before the people.

There's a gathering at the tower. Gael, will you please take her there? Your skills with the portal will make for the safest travel."

I bit my cheek, so thankful for Wren always supporting me, even when maybe she shouldn't have. It didn't matter. I could count on her not to fight me.

Gael opened a portal as my advisors talked in hushed tones.

Nash held me securely. "I'm only letting you do this because you won't rest otherwise. Be careful, Max."

"I will be. I want to sit up when we get there."

"Of course."

He carried me through the portal. While ordinarily I didn't feel anything unusual when traveling, I felt a heaviness this time that bore down on my wounds. When we walked through the other side, fatigue weighed me down even more than before.

"At least . . . I can travel through a portal . . ." Whatever poison ran through my system had its limitations, then.

Nash settled me down in my usual chair at the table. I could tell by his tone that he was worried about me. "Piercey, can you ask someone to bring her pillows?" The back of his hand came to my forehead. "Blankets, too."

"I don't need—"

He cut me off. "We need water, and I want medical supplies ready. Let's try more medication for the pain." Nash used the sleeve of his tunic to dab my temples and then took my face in both hands. "Max."

"Yes?"

"Please don't waste your energy fighting me."

I swallowed hard. "Sorry."

They all worked quickly to get me set up and to bring in a gathering of our top advisors—all the chiefs currently in the village and as many villagers and warriors as they could fit in the room. Seeing everyone brought a rush of comfort and emotion to my chest. A knot caught in my throat.

"I told you," a little boy said. He tugged a woman's sleeve. "She's alive."

"I'm sorry it took me some time to see you," I said. They said I'd slept for two days.

Fear etched lines into the face of everyone here. Fear and loss. It reminded me of the days after I killed Eskel when I raced from village to village trying to save the innocent from demon attacks.

"Nothing can ease the suffering of all the people we lost." The thought of their pain helped me to ignore my own, but the weakness was more difficult to overlook. Even my lips felt heavy as I spoke. "The attack on our kingdom will not go unpunished. I will hunt down every person who stepped foot in our homes and in this tower personally. They may have surprised us with this new poison, but we will not be caught off guard again."

"I fear we underestimated their abilities and perhaps overestimated our own." One of the village chiefs spoke boldly. "If they want war, it feels like we are starting off behind. Prophet, we need to think of how to avoid war, not how to seek retribution."

"These were not the actions of someone open to peace. They attacked us without honor."

"They almost killed you," the chief said. "You're by far our strongest warrior. So how can we hope to beat them?"

I came to bring comfort to them, but they only saw me as wounded. I gripped the edge of the table and forced myself to stand even though it caused my body to tremble. Nash shifted, but Markus subtly caught his wrist.

Pain wracked my body. I knew I couldn't speak or even breathe, so in order to recover I used the seconds I needed to look from one person to the next. It wasn't possible to hide my pain. I let them see it. Let them see the exhaustion and dizziness trying to drag me to the ground. The stabbing pain carving through my wounds. A drop of sweat fell from my chin and landed on the table.

"For how long have I told you all that I'm human?" Gasping, I straightened and limped away from the table toward them. The room spun slowly. This was war, though, and I couldn't lie down. "I'm not invincible. Do you understand that? I can bleed. I can fall. I can get wounded."

"Eclipse," another chief said as he reached out a hand for me. "Please, sit down."

"If I die, it doesn't mean there's no hope. And do I look dead to you?" I raised my voice and raised my gripped fist. The agony of it only hardened my voice. "Do I look like someone who is ready to give up?"

The first chief who spoke lowered her head. "No."

"We're a kingdom of warriors. Even if I die, you will fight without me. That's an order."

"Yes, Prophet," one of the warriors shouted. He raised his forearm in the air. Others followed.

"I know you're scared," I said. "We're all scared. What you don't know is I've been scared my entire life." The weakness won out and I sank to my knees, unable to stand any longer. This time, no one could stop Nash from coming to me. He bounded over the table and drew me back against himself as he knelt beside me.

"It's enough," he whispered.

"We fight through the fear . . ." I struggled for breath. "We don't surrender to it. Every drop of my blood and every ounce of my power is yours." I bowed forward against Nash's arms, voice stifled by a wave of pain. "I . . ." Darkness hugged the edges of my vision. "I'm yours . . ."

"Okay." Nash lifted me into his arms even though I shook my head.

"We're fighting them," I said. "The alternative is death."

Once Nash rose with me, he cast his gaze over the people gathered. "Chiefs and warriors," he said, "you will control yourselves. You will show strength. Your Prophet needs you to show some courage."

It wasn't their fault. The myth of my power grew to unsustainable levels so that this one fall demolished all of their hope and faith. A few days ago, they believed they were safe. That I would protect them no matter what. Today, I was human again. They were human again.

My consciousness faded and I didn't have the ability to cling to it, not even for my precious people.

CHAPTER SEVENTEEN

I sank into the comfort of the pillow and the plush bed, into the relief of the cold from the damp cloth Wren used to dab at my forehead. Guilt gnawed at these calming sensations. How could I accept anything good for myself when my people suffered so terribly?

"I should be back home." I closed my eyes against the comfort.

"No," Nash said. "Nothing hurts our people more than you dying. You're staying here while we figure out exactly what happened."

I looked away at the wall, even though I knew he was right.

Piercey, Leif, and Markus returned to the tower to continue meeting with village chiefs and to measure the extent of the damage done. We shared an open neural connection with them by using the phone system Piercey originally created for the Sacred School.

"Gael's warriors helped us to visit the villages where none of the warriors with power responded to our messages." Markus's voice hummed from the speaker. "It appears they chose one target in each village they attacked to focus on. In ours, it was Max."

Wren placed her hand on my shoulder and wiped away the sweat gathered along the side of my face.

"Asmund traveled through the night to bring the injured to healers. Even when Gael's warriors ran out of the strength to portal, he continued saving dozens of our people."

My sweet Wren couldn't leave me with a broken heart. I remembered when Asmund trained at the Sacred School before I became Prophet. I knew then he would finally learn to teleport like I did. And now he saved lives no one else could have. "Give him all my thanks," I said. I needed to remember to encourage him to continue training others. For now, those we lost burned in my chest.

"They wanted to kill some of our best warriors." Pain gripped my stomach from the tension I carried. "We should have struck last week. Who did we lose?"

"Twenty-five war parties attacked our largest villages, all groups of a similar size to the one that hit the tower." I wasn't sure how Markus could discuss this so calmly. "Some enemy warriors possessed power, but many didn't. They all used weapons like the arrows that poisoned Max." He paused for a moment, his voice quieter. "Of the twenty-five targets, we lost fourteen."

The weight of his words dug down into my chest, shattering my ribs, flattening me in an instant. Fourteen of our most powerful warriors fell in battle? "I need their names," I said in a choked voice.

"Yes, Prophet. All the surviving targets are suffering from the same affliction as you. They cannot use their power, nor is any healing energy working on them. As for the others who fought, so far, one hundred thirty-seven warriors succumbed to the injuries sustained in the attack."

The heaviness only grew. I could see it bearing down on all of us. Nash placed a hand against the wall, all the fine muscles in his face wrung tight.

"The civilians . . ." Markus cleared his throat, his voice thick now. "The casualties are still being tallied. Some are missing."

"How many?" My voice ripped out of my throat, stripped of emotion.

"Over three hundred. Many—" He cleared his throat again. "Damn it. Many of them were children and the elderly. We believe they targeted them."

The greatest moments of my life flooded my heart and my mind in images of Elsie's smile and Finn's tiny hands, in rushes of love too deep for words. I remembered when the Prophet of the Valley, Eskel the Ruthless, held little Rune captive and how the terror of losing him almost destroyed Leif.

All over the Valley—my kingdom—innocent people mourned lives as precious as Elsie and Finn.

I needed to let out the cry building in my chest, but it was too great to ever unleash.

A crash filled the air, and I looked over to see Nash's entire arm sticking through the stone wall up to his shoulder. I longed for the strength to do the same.

"What is so important about our Valley that Malach would slaughter children?" Wren lowered to her knees and, still holding my shoulder, settled her head against the bed. "Not even Eskel the Ruthless targeted them."

"He wants to break our spirit." My tongue felt numb as I spoke. "He stole my power and murdered our most vulnerable. It's a war against our hearts, so we feel hopeless, or so enraged that we turn into fools. That's why he interrupted our summit. To claim power over who we are at our core."

Speckles of blood marred Nash's shoulder where the stone cut through his shirt. His fists shook as he tightened them at his side. "They almost killed my wife." His head lowered and his nostrils flared. "They tried to kill my daughter." His voice deepened to a shaking roar that hit me in my chest. "Imagine those who actually lost their families. They killed our people and now we will slaughter them."

The horror filling me had nowhere to go. I tried to rise up to find a way to expel it only for the pain to paralyze me. I wanted to scream with Nash and break holes in the wall. I wanted to travel to Malach now and rip him limb from limb.

"I let him kill our people." I tightened my body to let the pain sweep over me because it was the only thing I could do. "We let him kill our people. Never again."

"What about our planned strikes?" Piercey asked. "Are we still capable of carrying those out, or do we think Malach knows?"

"He attacked the day before we did," Leif said. "Is it a coincidence or a message? I don't want to take a chance on the answer. I say we abandon those plans and start over."

My mind reeled from the enormity of our loss and the cruelty of waging war against innocent families. Malach didn't simply target a specific, powerful warrior in each village. He understood an attack like that endangered civilians while giving him the flimsy cover of saying he intended to kill dangerous military leaders. In one night, he ripped away every semblance of security my people possessed, from their faith in their best warriors—in me—to the safety of their homes and the sovereignty of our kingdom. We all saw how much we stood to lose. How easily, how quickly, Malach could steal away what we loved most.

Malach terrorized our children to break us and to destroy the next generation, those most likely to rise against him if we fell to him. He stole our futures from us, the future of our innocent and the future of our kingdom.

All the grief made it impossible for me to track the conversation that continued, especially given the difficulty of staying awake in the first place.

"We're marching to meet their army and attacking them head-on." My fingers dug into the bed. "I will stand in the front lines and send my message to their warriors."

The conversation abruptly silenced at my interruption.

"What?" Nash gave voice to what I knew everyone thought with that one incredulous word. Anger edged his voice. "You can't act like this, Max. It's not helping anyone for you to pretend you're invincible."

"I'm not invincible." I tore my eyes off the ceiling and met his. "I'm hurt and for the first time in an incredibly long time completely vulnerable."

"Exactly why you need to stay in bed," Wren said.

"That's the point," I said. "Our warriors can fight without me. They can win battles even if I'm hurt. Everyone needs to see that our people are not only strong enough to fight this war but to defend me in this state while I mock our enemy to their face." I twisted the bed sheets in my grip and raised my voice as if I led our people on the battlefield, ignoring how badly it hurt. "We will lose this war today if we leave our warriors as vulnerable as my body is now. I will put my full faith in them, and they will see that they are the ones to be feared."

Nash's mouth remained open slightly as he stared at me.

"We'll create a better plan for more effective actions," I said. "Covert operations, targeted attacks, a method to use their poisoned weapons against them. This battle, though, must happen immediately. We will open a hundred portals if we must to charge into their own lands."

"You can't even stand," Nash said in a steely voice, the challenge clear.

"So someone fucking hold me up." My lips curled in a snarl. "I'm going to war."

In all our years together, I never angered Nash enough to not speak with me, until now. As we worked through our war plans and I fought to remain awake and engaged, he arranged wooden pieces on a map on the floor, not even looking at me.

Nash and I needed to discuss my plan in private before I decreed it as an order, to give him time to accept the necessity of risking my life like this. My anger had taken hold of me, though, and I didn't feel like apologizing for my passion. I only felt sorry for how it made him feel.

"I will guard you in the way I once guarded Nash," Piercey said. "That way the others can focus on defending you by fighting."

Wren glanced over at Nash, maybe expecting him to speak about his strategy for keeping me alive in a battle when I barely even survived my injuries at all. His eyes remained trained on the map.

Damn it.

"Nash and the commanders will discuss more in the war room," I said. "I want an update on what we're learning about the attacks."

Over the past hour, the need for sleep overcame me and I closed my eyes for a few seconds of reprieve. Constant pain stabbed into my gut, shoulder, and leg without relief. I wanted to lie beside Nash and sleep in his arms, but the kingdom needed us to act. And I'd infuriated my husband. To everyone else, I could be the Prophet Eclipse, but to him I'd always be Max first. The woman he loved in every life he lived. The woman he'd die for. His wife, his best friend, the mother of his baby, and Ma to his precious girl.

The Prophet Eclipse fell quite low on Nash's list compared to the rest of the kingdom.

I squeezed my eyes shut.

"We should take a break," Wren said quietly.

For the first time since my announcement, Nash's look shifted my way, concern etched upon his weary and saddened expression.

"After the update." I only agreed to a break as a show of mercy for Nash, because I knew if we reversed roles, his pain would torture me. "Theus refused to meet with us that night. I assumed it was only because of our feud. What if he knew?"

"It's going to take time to uncover that," Markus said over the speaker.

"If Theus did this . . ." I breathed out slowly to calm myself down before I made myself pass out from rage. "I will kill him."

"We'll kill him no matter what," Nash said, continuing to work on his map. "Malach doesn't know as much about our kingdom as Theus. He's involved somehow."

I paused, not just because of Nash's confidence in Theus's complicity, but because hearing him speak after I angered him twisted my heart. "He must know I'd kill him."

"He's an idiot." Nash sighed and looked at me for the first time in almost an hour. "Markus was right before. He's more dangerous than we want to accept because he's foolish and weaker than us. I don't need evidence or time to think. If you don't kill him, I will."

"Wait," Markus said over the speaker at the same time Piercey also started to complain.

Nash didn't seem to be listening to them, though. He watched me, talking to me alone. "You need to stand on the battlefield while you're half dead, and I need to kill him because he almost murdered my wife."

I bit the inside of my cheek.

"If you want to help me," Nash said, "we'll push the blade through his throat together just like we did to Eskel the Ruthless. If not, I will do this on my own."

"You can't just decide to kill another Prophet," Markus said. "You're our war chief. Anything you do will be seen as our kingdom doing it."

"Nash will kill whoever he needs to kill," I said, my eyes not leaving his. "Our war chief decides when our enemies die."

"Just as our Prophet decides when she will enter battle." Despite Nash saying it, the anger didn't leave his voice. "Even if her husband and children need her to heal."

A tear slinked down my cheek.

No one dared to speak.

I bit my lip. "I'm sor—"

"Don't." Nash returned his attention to his work. "As much as our children need their mother, today they need their Prophet even more, because their futures will not exist otherwise. Just give me time."

I nodded, truly unable to speak now. Once I regained my composure, I said, "Bring Theus to me. Let me kill him with you."

Rage burned in Nash's amber eyes when he looked up, so they appeared to burn with the sun's golden rays. "His blood is ours." Nash moved to my side then and Wren sat back, giving us our space. My hand weakly slid across the bed for him, and he caught it, drawing it to his lips. "I promise," he whispered against my palm. "We'll kill him together before the sun sets."

"I can't believe you two," Piercey said. "We just signed a treaty with Theus, and we have no evidence he took part in this."

"To hell with the treaty." Nash clasped my hand with both of his to squeeze it and then placed it gently on the bed. "Leif, Wren, are you coming?"

"Of course," Leif's voice said over the speaker.

Wren nodded, her fingernails digging into my shoulder.

"Piercey is right. We don't know if Theus did this," Markus said.

"I thought you wanted him dead," Nash said.

Markus groaned. "I do, but if we kill him and he wasn't involved, it will shake the other Prophets' trust in us during a time when we really cannot afford that. I'm just saying maybe we should wait a day or two while we continue investigating."

The arguments swirled through my mind, lost in my dizziness and the haze of pain. Lost in the grief sucking what life remained in me.

If only I moved a second faster, then I wouldn't have lost my power when I needed it most. What if it never returned?

"We should bring this before the other Prophets," Markus said. "Your determination is admirable, but we all invested in Piercey's summit. We all signed a treaty."

"I'm not opposed to meeting with Prophets and honoring a treaty," Nash said. "But I will not sleep while he is still alive. So, I suggest you hurry and arrange the meeting."

I broke the quiet that followed. "You heard your war chief."

"Yes, Prophet," Markus said.

"We've never run this kingdom off whims and unilateral orders," Piercey said. "I will not say 'yes, Prophet' to you ever. I will not say 'yes, War Chief.' If you need me to do that, then you should discharge me as the second to the Prophet Eclipse."

A grin slinked onto Nash's face despite the heaviness still there. "That's not the kind of second we need, Piercey."

"Then keep that in mind and listen to what I have to say." Piercey spoke forcefully. "You were once a spy in the Flatlands, Nash. You understand the value of outmaneuvering your enemy. Do this the right way."

Nash lost the grin, looking only impatient. "Wait to kill him until we gather information."

"Yes, because if he's involved, the conspirators will hide as soon as we kill him."

Normally, Nash urged me to wait because I never wanted to, even when I knew I should. This time, he seemed to need me to do that for him.

"If we kill him today or in a week, he will still be dead," I said. "Let's think about what Piercey said. We may learn a lot by watching him. Just because we regret not killing him sooner doesn't mean today is the right day to do it."

"I'll consider it," Nash said and kissed my temple. The raw emotion still festered between us, the confusing mix of agreement, respect, anger, fear. But he kissed me through it and the pain slipped away as I allowed myself to finally sleep.

CHAPTER EIGHTEEN

After I rested for a few hours, Nash returned to my room with the baby. The deep joy of seeing Finn cut through the sorrow and fear thicker than stone to loosen my chest and draw a smile upon my lips. I lifted my good arm for him, barely keeping myself lying on the bed. "Finn."

Nash carefully placed the baby against me and sat down beside us on the bed. Tiny, soft fingers brushed my cheeks. The little coo and the great toothless smile ripped me from a world where my kingdom broke overnight. I narrowed everything down to this one life. Nash brushed tears from my cheeks that I didn't realize I had shed.

"I missed you." It hurt to not be able to lift my other arm over to him to let him curl his little hand around my pinky. I breathed him in and remembered the first time I ever held him. "I'm so sorry, Finn. I thought we'd have more time before we lived through something like this."

Nash placed his hand against the baby's back, his palm taking up so much of Finn's body. "We never know when war will come."

"I wanted peace for him. I waited for peace."

"Me, too."

"Where's Elsie?"

"Sleeping. She stayed up late last night sitting by you. I made her go to bed."

Darkness coated the window. "She must be terrified."

"She only wants to know you'll be okay."

I kissed the top of Finn's head. "I still need to go to battle, Nash. This is important."

"I didn't tell you not to."

Already, sleep pulled at me again, but I resisted. "Are you mad at me?"

He eased down alongside Finn and me and nestled his face against mine. That one simple gesture melted away all the hurt inside me for this one moment.

"No." His fingers ran down my arm. "I was never mad at you. I just didn't want you to do it, and I couldn't stop you."

"If you tried, you might be able to."

"I know not to try."

Here I was again, struggling to balance my family and my people, never able to fully reconcile the two halves of my life. At least now an entire kingdom fought with me. "We can do this."

"Yes, we can. Quiet now. We'll go to war in a few hours. Lie with us and rest."

I needed to stay like this with them longer than a few hours. Some sacrifices needed to be made, though.

My mind wandered to the glimpses I'd caught of blood streaking our streets and battle raging in the heart of my village. I truly believed it would never happen again. In the past, those images would have consumed me, and I wouldn't have rested for a moment. Today, I put them away for a short time to prepare my spirit for war.

Holding Finn with Nash close to me, I slept again until Piercey's voice drew me back to consciousness.

"Max," my friend said gently.

"Piercey . . ."

Emptiness filled me. Finn no longer slept against me. I searched the room for my baby, only to see Nash, Leif, and Wren standing at the door with their weapons drawn.

"What's wrong?" I groaned and started to reach my hand for the pain, except it ran through too many places in my body to touch.

"There's a girl here." Piercey looked over his shoulder at Nash and then back to me. "She wants to see you. She says she can help."

"It's her, Max," Nash said. "The girl we've been looking for. The one who arrived with the stranger after we killed Lote. She ran away before he killed those warriors with the flick of his fingers."

"The cult . . ." Fear crept into my heart. "We never picked up a single trail since. Where is she?"

"Gael and his warriors are holding her," Piercey said. "We don't know where she came from or how she got here. She arrived at the gates claiming to know how to help heal you. They called me and I recognized her."

"This is the second time she's found us during a crisis," Nash said. "Twice she's possessed special knowledge."

"Eight years ago, she looked like hardly more than a child and claimed she wanted to help us. So why is she still with them?" Piercey shook his head. "We cannot trust her."

"I still want to see her." I eased my hand over the wound in my side and winced. "Help me sit, please."

Nash helped me sit up while Piercey adjusted the bed. Leif and Wren left to escort our visitor to me.

"You okay?" Nash asked.

I held my side and nodded. "Just bewildered."

I didn't know what to expect. Not only did this girl know about my injuries and know where to find me, but she made it halfway around the world. Unless she lived here now. Which seemed incredibly odd.

The door opened and Gael entered, followed by a small woman shrouded by a hooded cloak. Wren and Leif followed behind.

Nash remained beside me, his weapons already prepared. "Cloak off."

The woman looked up at me as she drew her hood down. "It's good to see you again." Her voice still sounded so young. How old was she when I had first met her? "They already checked me for weapons."

When Nash continued to wait silently, she swallowed loud enough to hear and drew the cloak overhead before placing it on the ground. A long yellow dress fell to her feet. She wore her dark blond hair short with the fine wisps barely touching her ears. A tattoo of a crown of violet and pink flowers wrapped around the edge of her hairline. If not for meeting her eight years ago, I might have assumed she was only a teenager, but she must have been older than that, because she looked the same now as she did then.

"Thank you for seeing me, Eclipse," she said. "I'm so sorry to learn about your injuries."

"I don't want to play pretend," I said. "Tell me who you are and don't act like some scared kid again."

"It was never an act," she said.

I narrowed my eyes.

She shifted and wrapped her arms around herself. "My name is Cleo, and I was born into our holy order. I'm bound to my elders and to my leader." Her arms lifted so her sleeves fell enough to reveal more flowers twisting around her wrists. "I fear for my soul in the next life just by being here."

"Then why are you here?" I offered no hint of compassion or concern for this girl—this woman, likely—who looked far too innocent for someone who managed to approach me in another kingdom.

"I didn't know they wanted to kill you," Cleo said. "They planned to take your power. Or at least, that's what they always said. If I'd known, I could have warned you."

"So you were content to watch them steal my power and my kingdom, but not kill me?"

"*Content* is not the word I'd choose, Prophet. You know what it is to be bound."

Nash looked at me over his shoulder before speaking to Cleo. "I'm skeptical that your so-called leaders don't know you're here."

"I'm supposed to spy and report back, not make contact. Normally, I wouldn't be here alone, but I'm sure it's no surprise to you that we're all very busy."

"They must trust you to send you alone," Nash said.

"They trust the fear they put in me. Maybe they know I'll offer help. I don't think they care, because they just want your power."

I thought back to the arrows and shook my head. "They weren't trying to kill me, were they? The warriors were meant to capture me, but it scared them when I retained some of my power at first. In their fear, they attacked too viciously."

"Maybe. You nearly didn't survive. If they did intend to only capture you, this might be considered a catastrophic failure considering you went free and you're terribly wounded." She gestured to Gael, and I noticed he held a container of what looked like broth. "This will help you heal faster. I infused it with herbs that will clear the poison from your system more quickly."

"We're not giving this to her," Gael said.

"Let Piercey study it," Cleo said. "I've written down the recipe. He can recreate it."

"How do we know it won't actually make her worse?" Piercey took the medicine and lifted it into the light. "If you want to help, tell us everything you know about the weapons and how they can counteract power in the way they do."

Cleo spoke far too casually for my liking. "We learned how to neutralize power and to forge poisoned weapons that spread through your system, negating your power for as long as it's in you. That's why it's important to flush it out, or you may be like this for weeks, especially in your weakened state."

"Weeks?" At least it wasn't permanent, if I could even believe Cleo about that. But I needed to fight as soon as possible.

"This can help," she said. "Study it, at least."

"Tell us how this poison works," I said. "How is it created?"

Cleo scratched her nails against her arms. "I can't tell you that. They may not notice your people recovering a little faster with this broth, but they won't miss that you're recreating our weapons."

Nash swung his blade to hover inches from her face. "Choose who kills you. Your cult if they find out you've helped us or me, right now."

"I have power, too." Cleo's voice lowered. "Just because I don't look strong like you, doesn't mean I'm not."

"Talk, Cleo." Fear oozed from her. She didn't just look weak. She felt weak.

"I-I can't."

"Did the gods give it to you?" I asked.

"No. Of course not." She shifted nervously. "We learned from that man with no name, the one who fights for the order of the gods. His powers are unique. It inspired my leaders. That's all I can say. Any more and you'll know too much." The muscles in her jaw bunched. She met Nash's eyes. "You'll just have to kill me."

"Wait, Nash. I want to hear more. Can you at least tell us about Theus? I know he helped you."

Even though I didn't actually know that, I hoped that she'd believe me.

"I'm not privy to information on Theus."

Lies. I didn't believe that for an instant even though she said it convincingly enough.

"Your cult worked with him eight years ago," I said. "You at least know that."

"Yes."

"So what else do you know?"

"They'll kill me."

"I told you." Nash stepped closer so the tip of his sword gently dug into her chin. "I will kill you."

"Look." Cleo eyed the sword. "They are being very secretive. The story is that we broke with Theus after seeing your power. We retreated to grow stronger. I don't believe it, though. We never let go of assets."

"Is that really all you know?" I asked.

"Yes. That's all I know. I've told you everything I can. If you kill me, then you kill me. At least I won't be damned in the next life."

"I will fight for you in the next life if you support us," I said. "If you don't, I'll hurt you there."

"You don't know what they're capable of doing. Look at this poison. How can you protect me? They never let any of their children go."

"Is that the reason for the markings?" Piercey worked closer to her, eyeing the tattoos peeking out from her sleeves. "Your people seem to have many interesting uses for power. I sense energy emanating from those tattoos. What are they?"

Her fingers circled one wrist as her nervous expression tightened. "Insurance. We're truly bound. I can never escape them."

My mind drifted back to her insistence that she'd never escape the cult. "Cleo, I'm not sure of your intentions, but if you think you can stay loyal to them while offering crumbs to us, you're wrong. We can't trust you. There's only so much you can do for us unless you're willing to prove you want to help."

"I can't hurt them."

"Then you shouldn't have come here."

"I told you that I cannot risk betraying my leaders. You sent me to the cabin, and you let me flee when I was afraid the night you killed the world shifter. They'll show no mercy like you do."

"I've shown mercy to you twice," I said. "You showed your face to me a third time and sealed your fate. You're not leaving here alive."

She stepped back, trembling from head to toe. "Please, I'm sorry for not coming to you sooner. It wasn't safe. I only came this time because I worried you would die if I didn't."

"Why do you care?"

"I told you I like you."

"So come to our side," Nash said. "Piercey is the most advanced healer I know. If anyone can break the bond, it's him. Let him try."

"You don't understand." Even her wide eyes seemed to tremble. "I'm not just afraid of death or what they may do to me in this world. You've died, Eclipse. You know it's painful, but swift." She pressed her fist against her stomach. "I fear what doesn't end. I fear what they will do to me in the next life."

"The cult?" I asked breathlessly. "Or the gods?"

"Is there a difference when one becomes the other?"

What did she mean?

"Cleo, please." I leaned forward and gasped at a wave of pain. "You . . . You need to tell us the truth."

"I've already said too much. You beat Dr. Henderson before. I don't think anyone can beat them, but you're the only one I can hope for. You can't die, Eclipse." She bit her lip and then looked away as she ripped her sleeve up. Tears poured down her cheeks. "Don't tell them I showed you," Cleo pleaded. "This brand will follow me into the next life."

My heart stopped.

Etched upon her arm, perfect in every terrible detail, was an image of Dr. Henderson.

My breath escaped my lungs and refused to return. "That's . . ."

"There is no defying her," Cleo said.

"I killed her. She's not in this world anymore. The gods took everything from her."

"This isn't Dr. Henderson." Cleo lowered her sleeve. "Not any more than you're the person whose consciousness they uploaded. She's just like us, Max. She's a seed planted in the world like the rest of us."

They'd placed Dr. Henderson's consciousness in our world? We were all supposed to have died as babies in the natural world, not live full lives and essentially become gods.

Cleo's voice turned gravelly. "She's always been here, born into our world, and she'll be in the next life. We'll never escape her."

"The gods will never give her power in the next life again."

"Don't be a fool." Cleo took in a struggling breath. "You've always been too trusting."

I spoke to Nash through our neural connection. "Don't let her leave."

He reached forward to grab her when she fell to her knees with an ear-piercing shriek.

"It's happening . . . again . . ." A scream tore through the air.

Nash stared, standing over her with his hand extended.

Her image flickered—there and not—dozens of times before she just vanished.

The awful feeling returned. The knowledge that I'd soon uncover more about the gods that I was never meant to know. Would this ever end?

"What the hell?" Nash knelt down and touched the spot where she'd fallen.

"I don't like this." I let my head fall back. "This isn't just war. She's involved with that security system and now Dr. Henderson is tattooed on her body. How does she even know about her and our seeds of consciousness? No one except for us should know anything about that."

When Nash turned around, he helped me to lie down.

"We can't trust her," Nash said. "Who knows what her motivations really are."

"Dr. Drake would tell me if a version of Dr. Henderson was in this world." I slowly curled in on myself, struggling with my wounds. "She wouldn't do that to me. She wouldn't lie to me."

"It may not be true," Piercey said. "Cleo knows things she shouldn't. The cult may worship Dr. Henderson, and this may be some tactic of psychological warfare against you."

"Why would they send a scared girl here?" Leif asked. "None of this feels right to me."

"Who knows if she's really scared." Gael watched the place where she'd been standing. "We can't know anything for certain."

"I know one thing," I said, my voice tense. "I'm confident the cult never stopped working with Theus, even when we defeated him in war. Instead, they went north and created a partnership with more powerful Prophets. All these years they worked together to conspire against our kingdom, and we missed it. Cleo said they never let assets go. That was confirmation."

"This is why we cannot wait to kill him," Nash said.

"What if Malach wants us to kill Theus?" Piercey asked. "What if Cleo is leading us into a trap or manipulating us to do Malach's will for him?"

I blinked. "Why would Malach want to kill Theus when the partnership with the Flatlanders gives him an ally in Skia Hellig?"

"I don't know," Piercey said. "It doesn't make sense."

"I'm not sure what this girl's motives are," I said. "We can't be so afraid to take action, though. I hesitated to kill Theus because it seemed like the sound decision and look how it turned out."

"It just worries me how easy it can be to steer our decisions." Piercey inspected the broth again. "If she is trying to help us, that's one thing. If she came to drop breadcrumbs for us to follow, then where is she wanting us to go, and why? We can't allow Theus to attack us, but now is a terrible time to desta-bilize his kingdom. Perhaps that is all part of Malach's plan, to use Theus, and then to blow up his kingdom when he knows you won't want to abandon their people."

"No matter what Malach wants or intends, we will write our own destiny," Nash said. "Maybe he knows we'll do this and he's right that it will create prob-lems for us, but we can face the challenge."

"Okay." Piercey's concession shocked me. "If Theus continued to partner with the cult, then I vote in support of killing him. I'll strategize on how to address his fall. However, I still think we need to address the other Prophets because of the treaty."

"I also want to know if Jakob will be on our side," Nash said. "You know a man after you duel him. I served Eskel even as I plotted to kill him. Jakob is unhappy with Theus. We need him as an ally if we can win him over."

"How do we know if we can trust him?" I asked.

"We give him a test." Nash leaned back against the wall. "If he helps us kill Theus, then we know his true feelings."

"He could warn Theus," Piercey said.

"Let him," Nash said. "It'll be much harder if he does, but we will still kill the Prophet. The risk is worth testing a potential ally."

"It's very risky," I said. "Especially while I'm injured."

"Trust me, Sharpshooter. I've fought him already. I don't think I'm wrong about him and if I am, I will deal with the consequences."

"Okay." I sighed. "Before we do anything else, though, I need to know if some version of Dr. Henderson is here." I nodded at Piercey. "Take me to the white room. It's time I talk to the gods."

CHAPTER NINETEEN

Here with the gods, I didn't feel any of the pain or weakness. The relief only provided me with the energy for my wild suspicions to swell into paranoia.

"Max."

The clear waters of the Collective once amazed me but now only angered me. I'd watched the water ripple with their voice too many times over the years.

I breathed out slowly. "I need to see the council."

"It's not time. Request an appointment and—"

"Now," I shouted.

After a brief pause, the Collective spoke in a voice quiet enough to send chills through my body. "You're not a Prophet here, Eclipse."

"I don't care."

"They agree to see you, but we remind you to watch how you speak to us."

My gaze snapped up. "I said I don't care."

I sensed the unease of the Collective through the subtle fluctuations of the waters and the pauses that they didn't actually need. Without saying anything else to me, their water began to swirl and shrink. The blue funneled into the image of a woman who stood before me.

They always chose a different form when they did this.

"Come with me," she said in a smooth voice.

I walked through the space left empty by the transformation of the Collective and through the barrier that opened up to the council. Everyone gathered already, watching me. The blue stretching around us resembled the sky at times and the ocean at others. The subtle shifts in the hue reminded me of sunlight breaking through clouds, or glistening off water. Though we stood in what appeared to be a blue void, it felt anything but empty. I sensed the Collective all around me, as though I had stepped into their waters so they could swallow me up.

"Hello, Max," one of the council members said to me. His name was Treyone, and I thought I liked him, though I couldn't be sure.

The greeting did not soften my composure. "For too long, you've dropped world-shattering levels of fuckery bombs on me, and I'm done." My lip twitched. "I'm not doing it anymore." With my injuries faded from my body, the devastation and unrelenting rage of what happened to my people coursed through me. I commanded its flames, directing them at the Collective. "You will tell me the truth today."

"Or what?" the woman embodying the Collective asked in a gentle voice. "That sounds as if you intend to follow it with a threat."

"Do you need me to threaten you?"

"We understand your anger. Watching the recent events through your eyes devastated us. You need someone to fight. If you want that to be us, then so be it. We want to help, though. So why don't we make this productive?"

"I'm so tired of that." I bit off a humorless laugh. "I'm tired of pretending that I don't deserve your respect because you're so powerful and ancient— supposedly so wise. I gave you my life. We're in this together. So, tell me the truth about my world." Betrayal stung my heart. I didn't even know I could feel betrayed by them. I thought I expected nothing at this point. "Is Dr. Henderson in my world?"

Council members looked to one another while the Collective stared at me through pale green eyes. The sadness there looked like too perfect of an imitation of compassion, or maybe I simply couldn't bring myself to believe what I saw. They didn't care about us.

"Dr. Henderson is being rehabilitated," the Collective said. "There is a copy of her consciousness in your world."

The words ripped the ground out from beneath me. I felt thrust back into every bad dream I'd ever had, doomed to repeat the nightmares forever, only to discover they were never simply nightmares at all. "Why?" I covered my mouth. "Why did you put her there? Why didn't you tell me?"

"That woman is a part of the experiment, just like the rest of you. We didn't give her special knowledge or treatment. There was no reason to expose you to her."

"No reason? Some cultist has her face tattooed on her body. The girl said they want to suck my power out of me and become gods."

"Dr. Henderson's counterpart did this on her own," the woman said. "We aren't a part of it, and we were not going to be responsible for your paths crossing. We hoped for you to remain separate."

"Well, we didn't. Is she alive?"

"We don't believe our meddling will help you."

"Answer me." I looked at the individual members of the council. "Dr. Henderson killed me. She ended my world twice. Do you know how it feels to have the love of your life ripped away and destroyed? I deserved to know that her consciousness was in my world."

"It's troublesome how much you continue to learn," the Collective said.

"And endlessly fascinating for you." I levied it like an accusation.

"You seem to think of us as evil murderers and scheming psychopaths," the Collective said. "So why are you challenging us? Don't you feel you're risking your life or the lives of your loved ones?"

"Does it upset you that I'm not afraid to talk to you?"

"It upsets us that you feel this way about us."

I walked closer to the council when usually I kept my distance. "Either you're going to kill me or you're not. I don't believe my words change that. You see me the way I see my thirteen-year-old when she's mad at me."

"An apt comparison," the woman representing the Collective said.

"What might actually cause you to destroy my consciousness would be if I promised to make you pay here in the Kethios."

"Then this is a threat."

"I'm only proving a point. That you'll send your security system after me and then never allow me into the afterlife."

"Collective," Treyone said. "It doesn't hurt to address what is troubling her. It's time to share more about the one she calls a security system." He sat forward, focusing on me now. "We wanted to test a fail-safe program so that if the absolute worst happens in the physical world, there is someone who can put a stop to the madness. His order is to only intervene if someone is breaking the world or defying the natural order. We don't want to create a system that takes too much power."

"How considerate," I said.

"Please." The Collective raised a hand to me. "He's being kind to you."

"Well, thanks to you and your security system, innocent children are dead," I said. "That cult wouldn't have these poisonous weapons otherwise."

"I'm sorry," Treyone said. "This is further evidence of how good intentions can create such horrible tragedies."

The Collective continued for him. "These are the unforeseen consequences that are so important for us to analyze. This is why we needed to test the security system."

"So do something," I said. "We're suffering because of you."

"What can we do?" the Collective asked. "Interfere by introducing more technology to your world that we didn't intend for you to have?"

"Isn't the cult unnatural?" I asked. "Why isn't your security system killing them?"

The Collective steepled her fingers. "It's totally within the realm of possibility to create this weapon. It just shouldn't have come about because of our system."

"Once again, the people with all the power somehow are powerless. You just don't want to help. Maybe I should threaten you after all. I can't trust anything you say to me. How many more surprises are you going to throw at me?"

"There was no reason to tell you about Dr. Henderson's consciousness," the Collective said. "We are not compelled to share with you things you don't need to know."

"You know what?" I said. "You explain it to me or I'm revoking the access I give you to my life."

"Can she do that?" a council member asked.

"Of course, I can."

"She makes her own rules now," a man said in an amused voice.

"Rights are not given. They are owed." I leveled my look at the Collective. "Take the question to those higher than you. What does the rest of your society say? I was supposed to have the right to privacy, and I waived it to help you. Shouldn't I have the right to take that away?"

"You waived it in exchange for an avatar. It only seems fair that you would lose the avatar if you renege on your part of the agreement."

"So you'll kill me if I stop letting you spy on me."

The Collective paused for a moment. "We remember this feeling from our previous lives. This is not a worthwhile fight, is it? We must take the higher road. If you want your right to privacy back, then we will grant it, but we will remember what your word means in the future."

"Just tell me the truth for once." I jerked my arms to the side in a gesture of frustration. "Not everything needs to be a battle. I only want to know the truth. It hurt. Do you understand that? It hurt to find out about Dr. Henderson. It hurt to know that the cult gained their weapon because of the security system."

Treyone looked down. "Tell her."

The council fell entirely silent, so quiet that I knew from experience they spoke to one another where I couldn't hear or see, like they'd hit pause on this conversation and walked away.

I ran my hands over my face.

"Max," the Collective now said. "Go home. Tend to your people. We're going to discuss and reflect. When you return, we'll talk."

"I don't want to go home without answers."

The woman smiled. "It's time."

Rain pattered against the window and distorted the full leaves of green dancing outside in the wind.

"Can we open it?" I asked.

Nash followed my line of sight and then nodded.

The healer dabbed the melted skin at my side with alcohol while Nash opened the window to the summer rain and the scent of thriving growth. Another healer placed a blanket on the ground to catch the water the breeze cast into the room. A thousand knives sawed at my wound with every press of the gauze against my broken skin.

Nash ran his thumb along the back of my hand and drew my hair back from my shoulders. "Maybe we should try making broth with Cleo's recipe," he said.

"No." I dug my nails into his hand as the healer began to wrap the bandage around my midsection. "We don't understand this poison or what might worsen it. It's too risky." The fresh air opened my lungs and eased the hurt in my heart like a cooling cloth. "I'm okay."

"You're not." The anger etched into Nash's expression mirrored the way he looked in battle—focused, determined, and ready to kill. "I can't stand to see you hurt."

"Let that strengthen you in battle . . ." I gasped from the pain of the healer separating the gauze on my shoulder from the dried blood clinging to it. "You need to fight for us both today."

"If anything happens to you—"

"Gael can portal faster than anyone. He'll be right there, ready to take me away."

Nash muttered a growl of frustration and turned his sharp stare to the window.

He'd said he needed time, so even though I opened my mouth to try to soothe the way he felt, I stopped myself.

After several minutes passed, he spoke quietly. "You don't have to stay the whole time."

"Okay."

"If I ask you to return, will you?"

I looked up into his eyes, seeing as much pain filling them as the physical pain gripping my body from my wounds. He really couldn't stand to see me suffer. "I will."

"Thank you." Warm lips pressed against mine. Nash looked over his shoulder at one of the healers who packed my medical supplies. "Extra, please. I want to have plenty in case any of the supplies get ruined."

If Nash wanted to enter battle so badly wounded like this, I'd think he was crazy. I hoped that he found a way to cope with the anxiety of me joining in my condition.

"Nash—" My voice died when Elsie entered the room, swiftly walking toward me.

"You're going to battle?" Her voice quivered. Reddened eyes stared back at me, a sign that she either cried too much or slept too little. Maybe both. I weakly reached a hand to her, desperate to hold her close. She'd shown so much courage during the attack. A child should've never had to be that strong.

"Elsie," I said, the wounds to my heart ripping back open at the sight of her. At the memory of what she'd endured. "You're awake. Are you okay?"

"Am I okay?" She looked up at Nash like I asked her something crazy. "Dad, I don't want her to go. I don't want either of you to go."

The look on her face crushed my heart. Was I being foolish? "Come here." I patted the bed beside me.

Elsie hesitated before climbing up, the anger crunching her expression masking the fear. I pulled her down to lie beside me like she used to when she was little. To my surprise, she didn't protest.

Nash sat as well.

"You never should have gone through what you did," I said.

Her father took her hand. "That attack is not something that happens every day. I know you're young, so you don't have much to compare it to, but this is not something that is going to happen again."

"You don't know that." Elsie didn't look at either of us. She laid against me with her eyes closed and her cheeks damp. "I know you and Ma need to fight, but it's too soon. Can't we just stay together for a few days?"

Her little voice broke my heart. Her legs reached further than they did a few years ago, but she was not long removed from that little girl who used to get scared during storms and climb between us at night, claiming she wanted to protect us, when she just didn't want to be alone.

"You're the bravest girl I've ever met," I whispered. "I don't want to make you be brave again."

"It's all different now, isn't it?" Elsie sniffled. "Things aren't going back to how they were."

"This isn't for you to worry about yet," Nash said. "Your ma and I have been fighting in wars since before you were born. We know how to do this. We survived all of those battles, and we'll survive the ones that are coming. Believe in us and don't be afraid."

Elsie lifted her face. "Ma was dying. I saw all that blood just pouring out of her." Sobs shook her thin shoulders. "Don't leave me. I'm not ready."

Nash drew Elsie up and held her in a firm embrace. If I spoke, I didn't trust my voice not to crack, but he somehow always kept steady, even when I knew it killed him. "We will never leave you, Elsie." He clasped her head and rocked her gently. "We're alive today because we're strong together. We all survived together. I won't let anyone hurt my baby girl."

"What about you?" She cried hard against him. "Who will make sure no one hurts my dad?"

"You're too little to remember," he said firmly, "but your ma and I have faced much worse than this before. You watch our history every year at the ceremony, so you know. Our enemies surprised us, but we won't be caught off guard again." Nash drew her face back to look into her eyes and wiped her cheeks. "Don't you know who your ma and your dad are?"

Elsie nodded.

"Then you know not to be afraid."

"I thought I was a warrior, but I'm just scared." A whimpering sob escaped, though I could tell she tried to hold it in. "I was so scared that night and I'm even more scared now."

"Warriors are always scared," I said. "Sometimes, I get so scared that my powers go crazy, and I get sucked away to the past. I've been scared my whole life, Elsie. Does that mean I'm not a warrior?"

"No."

I scratched her back while her dad continued to hug her.

"Warriors don't surrender to fear," I said, "but that doesn't mean we can't take a break either." My kingdom needed me in battle so desperately that I subjected Nash to the suffering of seeing me go. I knew he could handle it.

Elsie was still so young, though. And she'd just been through something horrible. "If you need me to take a break and stay home with you, I will."

Elsie ripped away from Nash and twisted to look at me with wide eyes. "Really?"

It killed me to say the words because this hurt our warriors. "Yes. You're my girl."

Desperation danced in her eyes. Slowly, her head lowered and though her cries quieted, they sounded much more guttural than before.

"Go," Elsie said. Her hands came over her face. "Go protect us like you always do."

I pushed myself up on my elbows, unable to silence the gasp of pain. I didn't let it stop me, though. Nash reached over to help me sit up. I took Elsie into my arms, my weight falling against her, pushing us both against Nash. I needed to hold our daughter and this was the best I could do.

"You don't have to be brave," I whispered. "I meant it. I'll stay with you."

"No." Her voice sounded the same way it had during the attack when the steeliness came over her. "I can do this. I was just scared."

"I'm sorry." I struggled in a ragged breath and rested my head against hers. "I love you. I promise I'm coming home."

"Me, too," Nash said. "I'll get us home."

We held Elsie as she cried. And with each tear my girl shed, the sorrow buried deeper inside of me, carving through to my soul, to the unyielding fire within me. The fire that surged through my body and slaughtered my enemies. The fire that now hardened this heartbreak into rage and into vengeance.

I allowed the aftermath of killing Eskel the Ruthless to quell my warrior's spirit, and I allowed our enemies too much mercy. None of this would have happened if I hadn't spared Theus.

My eyes snapped up to Nash. The same inferno burned in him. Holding Elsie between us, we made a silent promise to avenge the innocent lives Malach stole from our kingdom. To force Skia Hellig to transform from a land of war into one of peace.

Or else.

CHAPTER TWENTY

I refused to enter the battlefield being carried, so once Gael opened the portal leading to the enemy warriors, I insisted on standing on my own two feet.

Nash held my arm to support me, eyeing me.

"You have to focus when the fighting starts," I said.

"Do you even understand what you're asking of me today?" He rarely sounded frustrated with me, but the sentiment oozed from each word today.

My head fell against his arm. "Yes. I'm sorry, but we're at war now. We need to be strong."

"You'll remember that when it's my turn to do something you're afraid for me to do."

My greatest weakness. "I understand what we'll have to do."

His face softened when he looked down at me. "Don't you dare get hurt worse than you already are."

"I made a promise to Elsie. I won't break it."

Nash nodded at this, a look of understanding coming over him.

The portal opened and with my weight pressed against Nash, I stepped through onto the green grass of enemy land. They'd marched within half a day's journey to the border of Skia Hellig.

Black portals surrounded the enemy camp. Warriors jumped from them and sprinted for our enemies, attacking with abandon.

Malach's army responded quickly, some burning the tents with their power to open visibility.

Nash took my arm with a firm grip and looked down on me. "You will say something when you become too weak to stand."

I nodded. "Go. There's no time for you to wait."

A pained look came over his face. "Please be careful."

"You, too." Smiling to lessen his worry, I nodded toward the camp. "Go fight, Unknown."

A smirk hugged the corner of his lips at the old name I so rarely used. His strong hand eased over the side of my face, taking the back of my head in a commanding grip. "We'll win today." He dipped and spoke the rest against my mouth, quiet so only I heard. "Let me fight for you this time." The tip of his nose brushed along my cheek and then his plush lips wandered along mine. His taste stole me from the battle. Deafened me to the cries of steel, the roar of battle. "Rest."

He left me with that one command, ripping away so the cold wrapped around me. I felt too weak to stand without him. Wren slid against my side and carefully took my good arm to support me. Leif appeared next to me as well, holding me up with Wren.

The rippling energy of a thick shield materialized in a dome around me. Warriors gathered in a semicircle to protect me, their blades and shields drawn. I glanced back to see Piercey with one hand raised to me.

From my vantage point, I could discern the formation of the war parties and how the larger formations began to take shape. The surprise ambush allowed us to take the lead in the battle, but I didn't count it nearly enough to set this in our favor. This was the best trained army we'd ever faced. The largest.

Even though the grass drank up our enemy's blood, we could not grow overly confident.

"Amplify my voice," I said to Piercey, and focused on the raging battle before me. Malach's army seemed too preoccupied with the surprise attack to even have noticed I watched. Or if anyone saw, their commanders had not yet organized well enough to address it.

Darkness ate into the battlefield already, giving us less than an hour of any remaining sunlight.

"You've all heard the name Eclipse." Power carried my voice throughout the camp so loudly that it vibrated deep in my bones. "Learn the name Elvadel." The force I put into each word felt like it ripped my wounds open, but I fought through as if I wielded a sword and not simply words. "Witness the power of our people." The last three days weighed heavily on me. Holding every person we'd lost close to my heart, I cried out with all the pain that flooded my body and my soul. "The Elvadel kingdom will slaughter every person who threatens our people." I sucked in a deep breath that throbbed throughout my body. "Step foot in our lands, and you will die."

Nash shouted commands as he fought two enemy warriors.

"Show the enemy your power," I commanded. "Blood for blood. Ten lives for each of ours that they stole."

The effort sapped my remaining strength and without realizing I could no longer stand, I collapsed. Leif and Wren already held me, though, and they eased me to the ground. Waves of pain crashed against me, sucking me beneath the surface of a raging ocean, drowning me again. I gasped in a breath and dragged myself above the surface. My head bobbed.

My nostrils flared and my eyes narrowed. Summoning my remaining strength, I lifted my head and shouted, "You don't need me. The Elvadel is Eclipse. Fight and win."

Nash bashed his sword into the face of a warrior, blood gushing down. He roared and buried his other blade in the man's chest. "Do not wait," he ordered. "They slaughtered our children. Kill them now!"

The raging water of my pain seemed to spill out onto the battlefield now in the form of our warriors, rushing over every enemy warrior. Death flooded their camp. Their land.

"Okay," Leif whispered to me. "They've heard." His hand hovered over my midsection, stopping before he actually touched my wound. "You've done enough."

I couldn't weather this battle. That certainty welled within me, but I didn't care. Malach attacked my people in their homes and killed the most innocent among us. He stole my power and tried to kill Elsie. It didn't matter if I could do this or not. I'd die trying if I needed to.

"Take me closer." I said it so weakly I feared my friends didn't hear.

"It's safer back here," Wren said.

"I need to be with them . . ." I'd lost sight of Nash, and without my power I didn't feel him either. "Please." The battlefield looked like an indistinguishable mess of bodies and blood and warriors all melting together in chaos.

Leif groaned. "Your stubbornness will kill us all." He carefully lifted me into his arms, walking closer to the battlefield. Wren followed with her sword drawn.

Piercey and those guarding me moved in unison. Soon, we walked into the midst of the slashed and burned tents, over the fallen battles, through puddles of blood. Leif carried me to the center of the battlefield where Nash yelled his orders to commanders and fought alongside them. I clung to the image of his armored forearms slashing through the air, his chest pumping with breath, his thick shoulders strained with effort. My consciousness threatened to wane in the center of the camp with the battle in full blast around me.

Nash spotted me and shot a look to both Wren and Leif.

"You've made us anger our war chief," Leif said.

"He knows . . . they need to see me . . . as much as I need to see them . . ." Sweat dampened my skin.

A warrior fell onto the ground near Leif. My hand reached for my sword on instinct, but Leif already rammed his dagger into the throat of the enemy who pursued the boy.

"Thank you," the young warrior said to Leif. Then he looked at me, his face that particular mess of fear and faith. "For you, Eclipse," he said, and he jumped to his feet.

I squeezed my eyes shut, unable to see someone so young throw himself at the enemy with so little concern for his own safety.

My body ached to fight with them and protect them.

I eyed Leif's dagger. "You don't have to stay with me," I said.

Wren's soft hand slid into mine and with her other, she drew my head against her shoulder. "Of course, we do."

"You should be out there battling."

"Would you shut up, girl?" Leif pushed a flask of water to my lips. "Drink something and be quiet."

I bit down my smile and accepted the water. He carefully poured it into my mouth. Despite looking and sounding so angry, he wiped away the water that slid down my chin, then took my hand like Wren had.

Pain radiated from my side and shoulder, gripping me in a steely vise of weakness. My heart beat in my middle instead of in my chest.

Blades of energy shot from the edges of Nash's twin swords with every swing, carrying on like an echo through the battlefield. I caught his eyes shifting to me when he blocked an attack from an enemy warrior. I felt him as if we connected now. Felt his desperation to take Leif and Wren's place beside me, to hold me through the pain and fatigue, or to take me home. To heal me. But this was Nash's place, whether he wanted it today or not. He couldn't kneel beside me and hold me in the midst of a battle. He needed to defeat every person who wanted to hurt our family and our kingdom.

We both suffered in our own ways.

"Eclipse!" An enemy commander shouted at me.

One of my own warriors slid off the commander's blade and crashed onto the ground. Pain bit into me when she didn't move.

"Malach knows of your cowardly assault," the enemy said.

"Cowardly?" I shouldn't have responded but I couldn't stop myself from saying it. "What do you call your attack?"

"We've done nothing to your kingdom."

He started toward me but Nash flew like a flash sideways and landed in front of the commander.

"You won't take one step closer," Nash said.

"You blame us for your precious Prophet nearly dying." The commander released a dry chuckle. "It isn't our fault you're so weak. We played no part in the attack."

"Don't bother with your lies," Nash said. "They're pointless."

The two men lunged for each other. Nash sidestepped, leaving an orb of energy behind. It exploded against the commander's midsection. He brought his twin blades down for the commander's neck, but our enemy's broadswords caught them.

"Word of your cruelty will spread all over the land." The twisted sneer on the enemy's face sent ripples of disgust through me.

He reared back to stab for Nash, but my husband parried and skewered the man through the heart with a blade of energy.

Malach wanted to paint us as the aggressors, but he'd forced our hand. I hated political battles and hated even more how effective they always were.

"We'll deal with Malach's antics back home," Piercey said. "Don't spend any energy worrying. This is to be expected."

If only I could shut down the worry. Watching Nash fight without me hurt.

The ground beneath me felt more like sand, and the air like the waters of the ocean. Lightheadedness and dizziness set my world unsteady. Wren's hold on me tightened.

"Are you sure you don't need to go?" Leif asked.

I met his eyes for a long while before I bit out each word. "Do not ask me again." My jaw clenched. "Not in battle."

Leif looked as ready to fight me as the enemy warriors. "Fine. I won't dishonor you."

The battle continued long after I thought it was possible for me to remain upright. Finally, my body wilted, and I surrendered to the pull toward the ground. Leif and Wren helped me to lie down.

"I'll call Gael," Wren said.

"No . . . I'm staying . . . Just let me rest."

No one else needed to understand. I didn't want to leave my people behind for a moment in our first battle. I watched as our warriors continued to overwhelm the enemy, until sleep stole me away.

My heart hammered when I seized consciousness and I searched wildly for Nash, unable to find him.

"Nash . . ."

"He's fine," Wren said. "Leif is battling with him. I'm watching out for them."

I lost all track of my surroundings, until finally the touch I knew so well grazed my arm. I whimpered, so far beyond the point of exhaustion that I lacked the ability to try to hide the pain.

"It's over. It's okay now." Nash held me close, running his hands through my hair, his voice tender. "We'll go home, Max. We did well. You did well."

"I . . ."

"Don't speak." His thumb caressed my cheek, leaving traces of warm blood. Slowly, he lifted us into the air. The force of gravity hurt, but I was almost numb to it by now. I lay limp in his arms, cherishing his closeness.

Once we hovered over the battlefield, Nash hesitated in midair.

"We won this battle, and we will win this war." His deep voice buzzed in my chest as he spoke to his warriors. The air around us glowed with power to allow the people to see us in the darkness. "You won. Your Prophet bore witness to your strength."

Astonishment filled me at what the healer told me as he worked on repairing Nash's wounds.

"You can't be serious." The hope surging through me was quickly tainted with suspicion. "You let the warriors try Cleo's broth?" I looked at Nash. "Did you know?"

"No." He rubbed his chin, looking pensive. "I don't like information not being shared."

"The five warriors who tried it insisted that we not worry you," the healer said. "They said they couldn't enter battle and it was their duty to try this medicine. No one would stop them."

I growled low under my breath, concern blooming in my heart. "It's dangerous. It—"

The healer raised both brows. "It worked, Prophet. The warriors cannot access very much of their own power yet, but our healing treatments are starting to work."

"Maybe Cleo actually wanted to help after all," Nash said. "Unless she's only trying to earn our trust."

"I'm worried about the same thing," I said.

"We'll give you the remedy if you feel comfortable with this," the healer said, looking at me. "There's been no adverse reactions."

"Yes, I'll take it."

I hated that I didn't stay awake to see the end of the battle. I'd missed the sword that cut into Nash's side and the energy attack that burned his back terribly.

"You feel better?" I asked.

"Yes, I'm fine." Nash squeezed my hand. "I told you that already."

Piercey rushed into the room, cutting me off as I responded to Nash. "We've received a message from Malach."

He passed the paper to me, and I read it out loud.

"The recent assault on your kingdom is unfortunate and our sympathies are with you. However, your egregious attack on my soil is unwarranted and a historic act of aggression." I rolled my eyes. "We consider this a declaration of war and will respond in kind."

I tossed the message on the ground, not wanting to see it.

"Whatever," I said. "He absolutely did this. What about the other Prophets? Have you heard from them?"

"They're willing to gather again. Gael offered portals to assemble quickly."

"Perfect." I touched a hand to my side and closed my eyes. "I don't want to pass out on the ground like I did during battle. How long will it take for Cleo's broth to allow healing powers to work on me? At least enough that I can conceal my wounds."

"Half a day at least," the healer said.

"Then we'll meet tomorrow morning. Will you spread the word, Piercey?"

"Of course," he said. "I'll send for the remedy now, too. We need to get you back on your feet."

In the coming hours, the healer finished helping Nash, and Cleo's broth began to take effect. Piercey sat with us both, patiently trying to heal me. It took two hours for Piercey to notice his energy working at all, but he persisted, not wanting to even take a break.

Finally, four hours into the treatment, I felt the slightest easing of my pain.

"One of our spies made contact with Jakob," Nash said. "Theus has held him captive all week."

"You can't be serious." My eyes widened. "That means he didn't agree with the attack, right?"

"We'll know more soon," Nash said. "That seems the most likely to me. I already know who I want to send to free him. We'll bring him back to us for questioning before the meeting tomorrow."

"This is promising." Hope fluttered inside me. "Maybe he'll turn on Theus."

By the time we took a break for dinner, they'd healed me enough that I was able to walk around. I still ached and the sharp pains came when I bent or shifted wrong. The poison still inhibited the full healing effects from taking place, but this was much better.

Nash and I traveled to our village to check on our people and make an appearance. When we arrived, a crowd of nearly a hundred gathered at the center of town where we just held our festival not long ago. Standing before everyone was the young commander who I admonished recently. Owen spoke passionately to the crowd.

I touched Nash's arm to stop him from approaching. We remained in the back, quiet so no one noticed us.

"Eclipse is weak," the young man said. "You saw her during the battle. She cannot remain standing on her own. We cannot rely on her to save us. We're strong enough to fight for ourselves." Owen's voice rose to a thundering roar. "We cannot afford to wait for her to recover or to play by her rules. She has served our kingdom well, but today, the kingdom depends on us."

Some cheered while some balked at what he said.

"Eclipse may be the mother of our kingdom, but her heart is now soft. I burned everyone in my family," he screamed. "She doesn't know the pain of burning everyone you love."

I eased back against the tree. It always astonished me how much my people loved me, but how quickly they could turn on me surprised me even more.

"We should say something," Nash said.

"Not yet. If I fight with him for all to see, then I accept him as an opponent. I legitimize him."

"He's undermining you, which means he's undermining our war efforts. This could spread quickly."

"You're right. We don't want to make it worse either."

Nash pinched my chin and turned my face to his. "You're not weak. Don't take a word he said to heart."

"I know. Sometimes strength looks like weakness to those who don't have the wisdom to see the difference. He'll learn one day. He's a hurt boy who lost his family. He needs someone to blame, and I do have blame in this. I'm not perfect. I've made mistakes."

Nash worked an arm around me, and I hugged him tightly.

"This isn't good," I said. "Especially considering we need to deal with the Flatlanders. Let's go to the tower. We'll greet people there and pretend we didn't see this."

"I'm sorry, Max."

We only encountered supporters at the tower, who eagerly assisted us with our war plans. But the entire time my mind remained on the young commander.

Later in the evening, I excused myself to visit Owen's residence again. This time, he looked even more shocked to see me than the first time I'd visited.

"I'm very sorry for the loss you've suffered," I said.

His eyes looked hollow. I didn't even see the same fiery rebellion.

"Don't talk to me about my family," he said. "I won't apologize for the things I said either. I'm assuming that's why you're here."

He wouldn't even let me offer condolences? I suddenly wanted to hug him, because he'd said he buried his whole family, and I'd already heard about his mother's death. She was a great woman. "I want to hear more about how you've lost your faith in me so I know how to fix it."

The unbridled rage and heartbreak were almost too much to look at. "I have as much faith in you as I've always had. You're a great Prophet, but you've always been too merciful and too concerned with your principles and ideals. I grew up hearing you're a wartime Prophet. I disagree. You established a peaceful reign where we each matter and have a voice. It's admirable, but that doesn't always work when it's time for war."

"What do you know about war?" I asked the question genuinely. He'd never known war, but he had lost his entire family. I expected he might surprise me.

"I know the cost." His eyes shone with fury and tears. "I know the powerlessness."

"Then it sounds as if you know a great deal." I reached for him slowly, not wanting to make contact if he didn't want it. At first, he drew back, but then he hesitated, and he allowed me to take his shoulders in my hands. "I'm sorry I didn't protect your family. Nothing can ever make that right."

His breathing turned ragged and his body tight. "I failed them. I have no one else to blame. I will never be weak again."

"We're always weak again. We need each other." I squeezed him, trying to find my way beneath his suffering. "Don't fight me and pit our people against each other when we need each other the most."

"If you're going to get us all killed, then someone needs to fight you." He knocked my hands off him and stepped back into the darkness. "We can't afford to only fight our enemies. We must fight anyone who threatens us."

"You really believe I'm going to get you all killed?"

"I think you need to be pushed to do the right thing. I'm going to push you because I have nothing to lose, and I refuse to see more people end up like me."

"Be careful," I said. "Someone might use your anger. You need to look at who is standing behind you while you fight the battle for them. You might just be fighting for Malach."

CHAPTER TWENTY-ONE

In the morning, the leaders of Skia Hellig met again at the coastal temple for our first talk since the summit.

The tension suffocated me. Sloane sat with her people, betraying no emotion on her face. She never looked at me, but she didn't look ashamed either. Or afraid. She'd left Elsie and me for dead. And Theus . . .

I shifted my stare to him. He looked as petrified as Sloane did stoic.

My nails cut into my knees. Those bastards.

I shouldn't let my feelings distract me, though. We came here to win a battle. Our people had successfully extricated Jakob and now kept him hidden until we were ready to begin. He'd told us everything. We didn't even need to ask him to speak before the leaders either. He demanded the opportunity.

When he walked out to the center of the temple, the horror stole the color from Theus's face.

"I want all of Skia Hellig to know the truth." Jakob's strong voice rang out clearly. "Theus wanted to steal Eclipse's land so badly that he brought war into the Valley. He never intended to honor the treaty. He met with Cleo and Malach the very morning we departed for the coast and planned the interruption." Jakob looked at me now with deep shame in his eyes. "He's been working with the cult for a decade in preparation for this war. He was the one who said to kill the children."

Though Jakob had already told all of this to me, the words were just as devastating as the first time.

"He lies," Theus roared.

"Everyone knows the truth." Jakob did not raise his voice or his ire. "I am only affirming it."

Sloane still did not look at me, but she glanced in the direction of my people. "Theus has broken the trust of everyone gathered here."

Fury shook Theus's voice. "That treaty only set Eclipse up with an excuse to retaliate against me."

"You think I need an excuse to slaughter you after you killed our children?" I slammed my hands against the table so hard the wood split down the middle in an echoing thwack. The pain of the motion only intensified my anger. Steps heavy, I marched to the center of the room where my husband only recently battled Jakob. "I need no excuse to kill you."

"I never told them to kill children," Theus said.

"Shut your lying mouth. You knew I'd kill you and you thought you'd save yourself by killing me first." I coiled my fists. "But you failed."

Theus looked wildly to the other Prophets before settling back on me. "If you start killing fellow Prophets, you'll unleash a war far greater than Malach's threat. Everyone within a two week's horse ride will want to kill you before you kill them."

"That I didn't kill you sooner proves to the world that I am not looking to destroy any leaders. In fact, I'm quite certain that you all realize I'm not going to kill you unless you give me good reason to." I turned my glare to Sloane. "That's why one Prophet didn't try to kill me while I was weak, even after leaving my daughter to die. She's that confident I'm not going to impulsively murder the leaders of Skia Hellig for my own personal reasons."

Sloane held my stare for the first time, looking neither contrite nor angry. And certainly not remorseful.

My nose scrunched. "I've been told this behavior makes me predictable. Well, I've never pretended not to be." I turned slowly, my words unrushed, my voice deep and commanding. "The moon is predictable and yet who has ever cast it from the sky? Don't throw yourself upon the moon's shadow and ask for mercy."

"We agreed that we would not shed blood in this hall," Theus said.

"I don't intend to shed blood in this hall." I wheeled around to face the Flatlander Prophet. "I urge you to run and hide. Try to save your life." My eyes narrowed in a deadly glare. "No matter what you do, you won't escape me. I'll kill you in your own lands and your people will cheer me on." Shouts and murmurs of both approval and dissent broke out among the people. I raised my voice over them. "No one touches my kingdom." I raised my finger to point directly at him. He stumbled back against his chief disciple, trembling. "War against my people and you war against me." I turned in a circle once again and raised my arms. "Who else wants to fight me?"

The crowd quieted until finally everyone was silent. I breathed heavily, looking around at the people. My body ached but I didn't let it stop me.

The Flatlander Prophet spoke once more with the wild fear of a man who knew he had little time left to live. "I told you all the stories were true. You let her bewitch you into thinking she's a Prophet. This is the same demon who slaughtered her own village. She stole the gods' power. She tried to steal our sun away. Now you've given all of Skia Hellig to her vile hands. This is a demon, not a Prophet!"

My people jumped to their feet, but I raised a hand to stop them.

"Accusations are the weapons of a powerless man," I said. "Call me whatever meaningless words you want. I'm not hiding who I am. I offered peace and instead you chose war. So we will have our war." My glare cut to the other two Prophets. "Will you fight with him?"

Sloane subtly raised both brows. "You do as you wish, Prophet Eclipse. He attacked you and broke the treaty. We have no qualms with you killing him."

"Agreed. I wish you had killed him sooner," the Fjellfolk Prophet said.

"You'll all regret this. Malach will protect me." Theus laughed wildly. "You fools. You fools!"

With my power still dimmed, I only vaguely sensed energy, but couldn't discern where it came from. Was it Theus?

"Do not speak for me." Malach's voice reverberated through the room. He ambled down to the center, looking far too cavalier.

How did he get in here? Warriors carefully guarded every entrance and exit. I'd personally checked out every person here and didn't see him.

Terror gripped my spine.

"Prophet Malach," Theus said. "You've come to save me."

"Why would I save you?" Malach sneered. "You attacked your neighbor in cold blood."

"On your orders!" Theus cried. "With your warriors!"

"I ordered no such thing. Any warriors partnering with you against my authorization will be executed."

I ground my teeth. So Malach wanted to continue this lie and sacrifice Theus?

"You see what happens when you partner with the wrong person?" I cast a look at Theus. "I warned you many years ago of what would happen if you didn't fight with me. Instead, you fought against me with someone who is only using you."

Malach was truly evil, abandoning Theus for dead.

"Why aren't you protecting him?" I asked Malach. "Do you hope that his kingdom will fall into turmoil like the Valley once did? Or are you just wanting to distract me?"

"Those do sound like wonderful plans," Malach said. "I wish I was clever enough to think of them. Unfortunately, I didn't anticipate that you'd attack my people in my own territory. I told you before. I didn't attack your kingdom, and I have no reason to stop you from killing the man who did. Why would I save him?"

"Save your lies for someone willing to listen," I said.

Sloane glowered at Theus. "Look at who you've allowed into Skia Hellig. It will be your ruin."

"I won't let this happen." Theus leapt over his table and sprinted toward me with a speed only possible with power. I couldn't even sense it, though. "You're still weakened! Die!" A black swirl of energy wrapped around his hand, pulsing as he reared back.

As fast as Theus moved, Jakob threw himself to the side much faster. The disciple blocked my body with his own and raised his sword against his Prophet. Muscles bulged as he shifted to strike.

Nash flew through the air and stabbed before Jakob hit. His sword stabbed through Theus's hand into his chest, skewering the man's own palm to his body. The energy in the Prophet's hand dissipated immediately. With a swift arc of his other sword, Nash sliced the back of Theus's knees and watched him collapse onto the ground.

A panicked cry unleashed from Theus's mouth as he looked down in horror to the blood squirting from his hand and chest. He teetered and collapsed onto his side, crying so hard it made him bleed faster.

Nash planted his feet on either side of Theus and slowly knelt down over the man, studying him.

"Does it hurt badly?" Nash took the hilt of the sword still sticking through Theus's body and slowly twisted it.

The man's ghastly scream quieted the entire room.

"You deserve far worse." Another twist. More shrieking pealed from our enemy's lips. "Do you know how many beads of ashes we made from the remains of children?" Nash ripped his sword free and plunged it for Theus's throat, stopping right at the point to only prick his neck.

None of his people intervened or even begged for his life. His most loyal, who always defended him, remained silent in their seats.

I almost told Nash enough, but Elsie's sobbing reverberated in my mind against the quiet of the temple. How many more children screamed that night? Torturing Theus did nothing to bring them back, but it showed our enemies how our war chief responded. So, I remained silent. This Prophet, after all, created the culture which led to Nash being banished as a boy. His twin blades had long thirsted for this blood.

Nash stood and whirled around, yelling in a full-throated roar. "If you attack our people, you will pay the price." He raised his bloodied twin blades. "And if you're fool enough to hurt my wife and children, then there will be no mercy." Tossing his blades up in the air, he caught both in his fists at a downward angle and stabbed them through either side of Theus's chest.

"H-help . . . me . . ." Theus's good hand crawled across the ground toward Jakob. "Please . . ."

I'd never seen Nash angry like this before. Every life our people lost, every shred of pain I'd suffered this week, every tear our daughter shed seemed to have coalesced into pure vengeance. He abandoned Theus on the ground and stalked directly to Malach, stopping so close their chests nearly touched.

The two men stared at one another for several seconds. Malach's expression was impossible to read, but Nash wore his threat clearly on his face.

"I don't know why you want war," Nash said in a throaty growl, "but you have it."

"I am not as easy to kill as Theus." A distinct look of interest sparkled in Malach's eyes and he smiled faintly. "Our army isn't either. This is not a war against the Flatlanders."

Garbled cries interrupted the men's conversation. Theus begged in failing words for someone to heal him.

Nash watched Malach for several more seconds and then shifted his glare to Sloane. The woman straightened slightly, posture tense. When he looked back to Malach, he smirked as well, but his usual smirk. The one I loved so much. "You think you're the first person to convince themselves they can kill us?"

I joined Nash at his side, watching our enemy closely. "Why are you here?" I asked. "Did you want to watch Theus die after you betrayed him?"

"You slaughtered an entire camp," Malach said. "I wanted to know why."

"I'm not playing this game with you."

"Maybe you're more interested in asking your war chief to slaughter me like he did to Theus."

"We agreed not to fight in this temple," Sloane called from her seat. "He's goading you into violating our agreement. Defending a Prophet from a sudden attack is one thing. If you start this fight, you're the one bringing blood into a place of peace. Our word is the only thing that protects all of Skia Hellig from our peace talks becoming bloodbaths. If you want to fight, leave this temple."

"We should take this elsewhere, then," Nash said. "Unless you fear for your life, Malach."

"Quite the opposite. I look forward to fighting you, War Chief. It would be a shame to spoil any surprises before Eclipse is ready to battle, though." Malach smirked at me. "When you're well, I'll show you how hopeless this war is."

Oh, how badly I wanted my power right now to teleport him away and make him eat his words, especially when the amusement died, and he whispered to me in a cold voice.

"You will suffer personally for every single life you steal from my kingdom. One day, I'll kill him." Malach's gaze flickered to Nash. "And I'll leave you alive to suffer his death."

He vanished without leaving a trace, just like Cleo did.

Did they know how to travel the way I did? Malach hadn't used a portal.

"This isn't good," Nash said. Scowling, he returned to Theus, ripped his twin blades free, and sliced the Prophet's throat without ceremony.

The Flatlander Prophet died alone in the center of the temple while Nash walked away from him.

I took his arm when he returned to me. He looked stoic now, but he felt hard as a rock beneath my hand. "Breathe," I whispered.

A flicker of the Nash I knew warmed his eyes when he looked at me. "I want to kill the others involved in this."

"It's enough for one day. We can't break our agreement not to shed blood here." I looked at Theus's advisors and disciples left staring in shock at their dead leader. "All of you who helped him will share his fate."

"Let's not be hasty," one advisor said. "Many tried to stop him. He went mad with this obsession of his. You know that our people wanted to replace him. We can help keep the Flatlands united."

"You think I trust anyone who encouraged him to kill so many innocent people?" I scoffed. "Those of you who resisted his plan can help us stabilize your land. The rest will die."

The Flatlander leaders started to argue with one another, a few raising their voice to shout. I saw some flee the temple but I ignored them and walked to Jakob.

"Thank you for your testimony and for stepping in to defend me from Theus while I'm injured."

"There's no honor in killing a wounded warrior," Jakob said.

Nash dipped his head. "I'm indebted to you."

"Consider your debt paid," Jakob said. "I decided Theus needed to die several months ago. It's been a long time coming, but I don't need to explain to either of you the difficulty in killing a Prophet."

"I'm sorry we didn't give you more time to prepare," I said. "I'll enforce whoever your people choose as leader. I encourage you to take the position. You're the only one who stood in the temple before all of Skia Hellig and told the truth. You're a fierce warrior and an honorable man."

Jakob sighed. "You should discuss this with your advisors. They seem aware of the inevitable."

"What does that mean?"

"Your people cried out for you to lead because you saved them. You protected them every day for a year. If no one manages to seize control, there won't be time for us to wander through the darkness and wait for a leader to emerge. Malach will occupy our lands before then."

I felt like a fool for not realizing this sooner. Of course, Malach didn't mind turning on Theus and letting us kill him. We made it easier for him to steal the Flatlands, which also made it easier to defeat us.

"So I just need to back whoever is chosen, like I said." I shrugged.

"You don't have time to fight multiple wars." Jakob gave me a pitying look. "The Flatlands are yours now, Prophet. If you don't take them, Malach surely will."

I choked on air. "Oh no, no—"

"We'll select leaders, but you need to take control this week and choose someone to govern rather than rule as Prophet."

"I did not sign up to take on another kingdom."

Nash ran his hand through his hair. "Fuck."

I jerked around to see Markus watching me with that distinct look I recognized all too well. The guilty look he got when he needed to force me to do something I hated.

The only thing that kept me from screaming was how badly it would hurt my abdomen.

"Will you please step in as leader?" I forced calmness into my voice, but it only made me sound more desperate.

Jakob nodded. "Of course. Markus has already drawn up preliminary plans for our army to fight against Malach with you. I suggest you talk to your advisors. I know from trusted sources that they've already come to the same conclusion as me. They've begun preparing."

"They should have said something." Nash cast a glare at Markus and Piercey.

"Your family has had a difficult few days," Jakob said. "I'm sure they planned to talk with you soon."

I wasn't so sure. I trusted Markus and Piercey to always do what was best for the kingdom, but that didn't mean I condoned their secrecy. If they did this because of what Nash and I had been through this week, then that made me even more angry. We needed all the information before we made decisions, like killing Theus. They either assumed we couldn't handle all the stress, were too cowardly to give us bad news right now, or they were manipulating me.

I didn't like any of those possibilities.

"I'm going to kill them," I said with narrowed eyes.

CHAPTER TWENTY-TWO

In a single week, we were forced into a war with a kingdom far greater than ours—one which would ally with other kingdoms larger than us and swarm our small Valley. We killed the Prophet of our neighboring land. And now we either adopted their kingdom or lost them to Malach.

Our world crumbled in a few short days.

Today, Nash and I left the impossible amount of work in the hands of our trusted advisors and allies in order to honor our dead. We took the first step to healing the people's faith in our kingdom. I couldn't stop thinking about Owen's family dying or the powerful condemnation of me he'd made in my own village. Worse, I ruminated on the crushing pain he must have felt. Grieving our slaughtered people could not wait. This was a priority today.

King Tyroin, the leader of Gael's kingdom, offered his best builders to us. They used their power to rapidly erect a memorial hall for our slain people. Chiseled marble, imported from the king's land, captured the sun's rays and glowed from the top of a hill on the outskirts of town.

Inside the hall, golden sunlight poured through 541 skylights in the domed ceiling and fell upon the golden tiles on the floor. Each bore the name of one of the deceased. Dim torchlight glowed along the edges of the massive room, so that the sun naturally drew our eyes.

The families of those killed sat on pillows gathered together around the bright golden tiles. All around the room, hands clutched the necklaces of their dead. Countless black beads forged of ashes rustled in trembling hands or clacked together from fidgeting. The quiet sounds melted into a subdued version of temple bells like the faithful rang while praying. So much death. Enough to create a ghastly song I'd never heard before and hoped to never experience again, though I desperately feared that I may. I couldn't breathe as I took in the sight of so many family members and felt the unbearable weight of their grief.

Nash stopped beside me and looked back at Elsie.

"I'm not sure about this," he said.

Elsie raised her chin. "I'm sure."

"Elsie suffered that day, too. We're all here to grieve." I squeezed his hand, and he closed his eyes. "We can't run from it."

"Okay." Nash walked forward, saying nothing else.

We walked as a family to the center of the hall. Soft weeping played like haunting music, echoing off the marble walls.

"Thank you for allowing us to honor your families today," I said.

The golden tiles glowed so brightly in the midst of the darkness. Thousands of glassy eyes stared back at me, full of expectation, like I might put their broken families back together. I tried to make my pause appear purposeful when I actually lacked the ability to speak. The grief in the room choked the air from my lungs, and guilt stole everything I planned to say. I lived when the people they loved didn't. My family lived. What right did I have to feel anything when they lost so much?

Nash withdrew his swords, and I stared in shock when he lowered to his knees. He placed them on the ground in front of him, leaned against his hands, and lowered his head. "I vowed these blades to you and your children." He lifted his head but didn't rise back up. "I vowed my life to you as your war chief."

I no longer heard anyone crying. The room was silent save for sniffling and the quiet gasps of those stifling their weeping.

A mix of fury and sorrow wound into Nash's voice, making him sound both broken and strong. "I failed you." This time he sat back on his knees and lifted his face to the domed ceiling. His long curls fell back so nothing blocked my view of the dampness on his high cheeks. There was nothing broken in his roar now. "With these blades, I will slay one commander for each of your dead. I will find those responsible and punish them." Nash slammed his fist hard against his chest with a dull thud once, twice. "They will beg for your forgiveness."

Elsie dropped down to her knees beside him, her thin shoulders shaking enough that I realized she wept silently.

I turned to cast my look over everyone who was gathered here. The weeping began in a gradual build, starting with the mothers who wore the beads of their dead around their necks, and spreading to the fathers who clutched them close. The children who cried bitterly and lay against their parents and grandparents. No matter where I looked, I saw the face of lost life. Loss too great to ever contain in one heart or express in one lifetime. It defied the bounds of our world. Each and every one.

"I need to promise you never again," I said. The tears ran so quickly from my eyes they dropped from my chin and wet the collar of my tunic. "I need to take your pain and promise no more." I walked forward while my family knelt. "The truth is that before this war ends, there will be more memorial halls built." The anguish crushed my lungs but somehow, I managed to squeeze the words out. "You must carry on our hope for your loved ones who no longer can, because without hope, we'll lose this war. Lend us their memory so we have the strength to fight."

I joined Nash and Elsie on my knees and bent until my forehead touched the ground.

"I will give all I have to ensure such a tragedy never happens again." The cool of the marble etched into every nerve ending on my fingertips. I needed to remember this feeling. The feeling of kneeling before thousands of broken people. "My life is yours."

Faintly, I heard Elsie whisper, "And mine."

Not hers. I wanted to say it, to demand it. Maybe decree it. Not Elsie's.

But surrounded by the dead and those they were forced to leave behind, I dared not speak such a thing.

Time didn't move in the dimness of the memorial hall, but rather blurred together meaninglessly. Eventually, Nash and I moved to the family closest to us while Elsie followed a few steps behind.

An older couple held each other's hands, tearing their gaze from a portrait of a woman to look up at us. I didn't recognize the one they honored, but saw her name etched into the golden plate on the ground.

"Analize," I read. "Thirty-nine years old. Warrior."

The two turned their faces together, foreheads touching. "She fought bravely," the woman said. "She saved two children."

The love and grief flowing from this couple wrapped around my chest so when I looked up at the hundreds of groups still waiting, dizziness swept over me. "We're in debt to your daughter for her sacrifice."

Nash reached out and took the single bead of ash left out of the necklace for this event. He placed it in the small hole on the golden tile left for it. Tomorrow, the builders would seal it to memorialize the bead on their nameplate.

I touched the woman's shoulder and then the man's before we continued for the next family. The golden tiles ran in a large spiral around the memorial hall, allowing us to weave through the families. We soon came upon a young mother and father surrounded by their parents and siblings. The couple clutched the empty swaddling blankets of their baby, crying too hard and too deeply to speak. Nothing escaped the woman's lips, but sobs wracked her body.

Nash wrapped his arm around my waist and gripped me tight. Just looking at those tiny blankets, I smelled the freshness of Finn's soft hair and felt his smooth cheek beneath my finger. Malach's warriors killed an infant? An infant.

I dropped down beside the mother and dragged her against me, holding her so tight I feared I may hurt her. Finally, a single croak broke from her lips and then her wail reverberated through the entire hall.

"My baby," she cried.

Minutes felt like hours as we consoled the grieving mother. When we finally stepped away from this family, I stopped Elsie. With my hand trembling lightly, I wiped the tears from my cheeks and nudged her in the direction of the exit. "You have to go. I was wrong."

"No." She pushed back against me. "These are my people, too. I won't abandon them."

"Elsie." I barely managed to keep my voice from careening out of control. "You're too young for this. It's too much for anyone. Please."

Nash tucked a braid behind her ear. "Do what Ma says. This isn't a place for children."

"It's not?" She pointed at the golden tile bearing the name of a twelve-year-old boy. "It seems to be full of children." Turning, she raised her hand to indicate the weeping children in the family next to us. "It seems I'm the most fortunate child here, so why should I be spared from suffering when they can't be?"

Her father took her shoulders to turn her back toward us. "We'll talk more when this is over. You can't bear the suffering of the entire kingdom. Cherish the mercy of surviving. It's a gift to have a childhood. You'll be better for it later."

"Don't make me leave." Her burning stare tore into her father and then locked on me. "I don't want to leave. I aimed my arrow at another human being, and I shot. You want me to be a kid, but if I'd been a kid that day, we'd be laying Ma to rest here." She nodded. "I was scared before, and you told me that warriors don't surrender to fear. This is my chance to be brave for our kingdom, just like you guys. You can't protect me from this war."

How could Elsie sometimes talk as if she was still five years old and then at others like she was thirty?

Nash and I turned to each other.

"She saved my life," I said. "She's right. She's earned her place here."

Nash nodded at Elsie. "You can stay, even though I don't want you to. Just please don't be afraid to leave. You're still our little girl."

She hugged us both before we returned to comforting the families.

That was when I saw Elara. My steps froze. Rylan knelt with the woman, his mother, and his older sister. The absence of his father told me who they had lost. Seeing them in the memorial hall hit me so hard I groaned.

I recognized the moment Elsie saw them. Her steps faltered. "Rylan," she said in a gasp, hand shooting to her mouth.

The boy tried to look brave when he lifted his face to Nash and me, but the redness streaking his eyes told me how much he'd cried.

I reached my hand out and Elara took it.

"My son," she said.

"I'm so sorry." Not once had a single word I said today felt like enough. "Elara—"

"You do not apologize, our dear Prophet. I remember the day we all gathered together in the assembly hall, and you asked who would stand up to lead the Valley. Did you remember it was me who said it looked like you were already standing?"

My mind retraced the moment, trying to place the face of the woman I had not yet known.

"You were so young and eager for a different life, yet you gave yourself to us. You gave your family to us. There is no need to apologize. If not for you, I'm certain I would have lost more than my son."

"Elara." I bent to embrace her and clasped her head against my shoulder. "None of you deserve this. I wish I'd seen it coming. We prepared, but we never expected the poison."

"Who can expect every threat that comes our way? My son died the same way he lived his life. Protecting his children. He died happy."

Rylan opened his hand and lifted the bead of his father's ashes. Elsie took it from his palm, carefully placing it in the tile. "We will remember him for all our days," she said.

The tears I knew the boy yearned not to shed slinked down his cheeks, making the anger in his eyes brighter. "I will ensure our enemies remember him when I slay them in battle."

Nash placed his hand upon the young warrior's head. "You will make your father proud."

When Rylan looked up to Nash, inklings of the child left in him rose to the surface, and I imagined another life where a fifteen-year-old boy didn't need to fight. Where our thirteen-year-old daughter never needed to lift her bow to save me.

The grief harbored in this room bound us together in a force much too strong to deny. While that weighed my soul down, the fury smoldered much deeper than that. After I kissed the top of Elara's snow-white hair, I caught my husband's wrists, pulling him close.

"We'll burn Theus and Malach's bodies here in this very room," I said. "There will be no beads for their ashes. The dust will scatter on the floor and no one will care for them enough to even sweep it up. One day the last speck of their being will disappear from this hall and no one will remember them."

As I lamented, my people cried out with me, wailing their own threats against our enemies in a swell of words that could never capture the grief and rage. We promised the impossible. Promised things we would never actually do. Promise anything that alleviated even the slightest amount of agony and let us believe for a moment we were strong enough to make our enemies into nothing more than dust upon the soles of our feet.

I thought I'd left revenge behind after I killed Dr. Henderson. After all, I'd allowed Theus to live all those years. The loss was too great, though. The need to defend my people and vanquish our enemies dwarfed what I'd once felt for the supervisor of our world. I hated Malach even more. Looking at my people, though, I realized this was a different feeling. I didn't want to kill them for the justice of it. I knew it was the only way to protect our people from being slaughtered. I did not yearn for war, but I would answer the call. I would save my people.

Nash's cheek edged alongside my temple. "We'll make them into nothing. We killed Theus. Now we destroy Malach."

With the passion still sweeping through me, I raised my face to see six golden tiles a few rows down, all empty of mourners. I found Owen sitting against the wall, the only one left to weep for his family. His eyes were dry. Dry and burning bright. He watched me, gaze never shifting. The necklaces full of ash beads piled upon one another around his neck.

I knew in that moment this image of him would haunt me forever.

When we approached him, he tossed the handful of beads at our feet and finally looked away from me. If blaming me helped him with his suffering, I would accept it, but I feared this may be Malach's second poison. The first one stole our power and the other our spirit.

We continued to wade through the waters of sorrow filling this memorial hall to its brim. We drowned here together for hours more.

When we returned home, Elsie asked for Trish, and the caregiver promised to continue watching Finn as he napped. So Nash and I sank into our bed, numb and silent.

It was all too much.

I wanted to weep to relieve the pressure in my chest. It hurt too badly, though.

Nash rolled to face me and he held on to me tightly.

"Killing Theus didn't soften their tears." There was no strength in his voice this time. Only brokenness. "That suffering I made him endure meant nothing." He pressed his forehead against mine. "Even knowing that, I cannot stop thinking of vengeance. I need to kill all those who threatened our kingdom and our family and know that you are all safe."

"It's going to be a long war. A long time before anyone feels safe."

A strong hand gripped my face and unflinching eyes stared into mine. "For hurting my wife and terrorizing my child, I will kill their Prophets." Nash's hold remained firm, but the thumb that shifted down my jaw was so gentle. "I give you my word, my beloved."

Beloved. We had never called each other that. Nash needed new words to express the depth of his love. Tears wet my eyes.

His lips grazed my own. "But for these tears they made you shed, for how they broke your heart, I will tear down entire kingdoms." A hand slid beneath my shirt over the small scar left by the poison. "There will be nothing left of them."

"Nash."

"I'll fight this war even if only for you." His mouth devoured my own in desperate, demanding kisses. "Don't tell me I can't, because I must and I will."

Cool air prickled my skin as Nash drew my shirt up and melted his lips against the scar on my side. My fingers tangled in his hair, my eyes closing. I felt it all, every bit of his anger and pain. He'd never been vengeful, but then he'd never been a war chief in a kingdom under siege.

"After gaining my power, I never felt too weak to fight." Another kiss against the tender scar. "Not until now. When the healers couldn't help you, my power felt worthless." He found my shoulder wound, his lips prickling my skin. "I did everything to reach you and Elsie that night." A finger trailed the mark. The back of his knuckles. "I fought at my best." He turned his cheek against my skin and nuzzled his face against me. "Look at how far it was from good enough."

I sat forward, slid my hands over his face, and tugged him up to me. Nash pushed up on his forearms and met my lips.

"I'll never let them hurt you like that again." Another kiss and his fingers brushed my leg wound. "Never."

"This is all we have to give," I said, palms gliding down his back. "We're not invincible."

"I don't care. I only know that I'll never let this happen again." He lowered me to my back and buried his face against me, working his arms around me to pull me closer. "I've had three lives to learn to master this power. Maybe if we just remember, we'll become more than anyone in a single life can defeat."

"Then let's sleep and dream of those days long past."

His hand felt so large against me with it clasping my side, taking up so much of my body. "Soon." Lips returned to my scarred shoulder and strayed along my chilled skin, warming me until I melted like wax. I felt the kind of closeness to him that not even connecting brought, one deeper than uniting our minds and our powers. Being together couldn't ease this kind of loss, but it carried us through, tethering us together so neither of us was lost.

I held on to Nash for dear life and gave all of myself to him, took all of him for myself, our bodies connecting too deeply to ever tear us apart.

CHAPTER TWENTY-THREE

Unable to actually join the war efforts, I turned all my energy upon Markus and Piercey.

"You lied to me." I didn't need to raise my voice. It sounded terrifying even in a low tone. "You fooled me."

"No one lied to you," Markus said.

While Piercey shrank from the guilt, Markus possessed no such qualms about disappointing me and did not recoil.

"We prepare contingency plans for all possibilities because that's our job. You're so singular minded that we cannot hope you'll think of all these possibilities."

"You think now is the right time to insult me?"

"You think now is the right time to question us?" Markus met me head-on, the commander in him, the warrior in him, shining through. "Theus needed to die. You knew the fallout would not be easy to contain."

"I don't see why you didn't mention that we'd have to absorb his kingdom."

"We didn't know that for sure." Markus crossed his arms. "Calm down and let us talk this out. You were half dead in bed and losing your mind. It didn't seem like the best time to tell you something that may not even happen."

"Max," Piercey said.

I shook my head. "Waiting until we killed Theus—"

"Max," Piercey repeated loudly. Anguish twisted his voice and expression. I'd been so frustrated, I'd missed the horrified look on his face. "It's urgent."

My heart hammered. "What is it?"

His head lowered. "I just received a message. That young commander, Owen, and the people following him . . . You need to see what they've done."

Dread wound around my heart.

The portal closed behind us, leaving us in a rural Flatland community. Black smoke climbed into the sky. Ash drifted over us in an acrid fog. I saw the razed homes immediately, but it took me longer to actually see the rest. For my mind to accept a sight I'd never be able to understand.

My stare dropped to the ground and that old slipping feeling hit me like a gust of wind, trying to rip me from my body.

Blood drenched the dirt path leading to the village.

The thirsty ground greedily soaked up the dark pools and still it could not consume it all. I stumbled forward through the slush of mud and death, the air sucked from my lungs.

I'd seen more corpses than I could possibly count in my life. But this . . .

The tremble started in my fingers and traveled deep inside the very marrow of my bones.

Children lay scattered upon the bloodied ground in a blur I could not see.

Their forms blended into one mass grave. I tried to look. Tried to see their faces. And a part of me must have because eyes searched the corpses. But my spirit fled my body. No matter how hard I tried to return to myself, it felt like the portal had opened behind me and sucked me away.

My mouth opened but nothing escaped.

Nash lowered to the ground. That one gesture tethered me to him. I tracked his motion, seeing, really seeing him. His hand lowered to the cheek of a girl around Elsie's age. The young teen's image sharpened in my mind so I saw her and only her. If before my mind refused to register this sight, now it fixated, unable to think of anything else.

White dust covered her young face. Her eyes were frozen in wide horror. Beautiful hazel eyes. My husband brushed her hair back and then tightened his fist beside her temple until his shoulders shook. The emotion emanated from him like a haze of power.

Bile rushed up my throat. Hot tears flooded my eyes.

My gaze swept the field and finally I truly grasped what I saw. Dozens of children lay slaughtered on the ground in a trail that surely led to bodies left inside the homes.

I heard the wails of the parents in the memorial hall. The terrible, ghastly song bellowed with the wind.

Who did this?

The questions stormed through my shocked mind, but I could hear another voice in my head. It screamed like it belonged to someone else. Because I knew. I knew.

We did this.

We killed these children.

We slaughtered that little girl.

My people—my own people—ruthlessly killed every single person in this village.

I turned in a slow circle, surrounded by death. And then I screamed from the depths of my soul in an angry, heartbroken, guttural scream.

"Bring them to me!"

Over thirty warriors stood under guard in our war room at the tower, all staring at me with the same anger that filled Owen's eyes.

An older commander led the massacre, but I knew it was the spirit of Owen that drew all these warriors to their cause.

"So, your excuse is that the guilty hid among the children." My voice trembled with fury. "It still doesn't explain why you killed the innocent."

"Powerful warriors hid in the town." The older commander stared me down. "We nearly lost several, so we had to unleash unwieldy attacks."

"Don't you lie to me." I seethed. "Children bore sword marks. This was revenge."

"Any child killed by a sword was on accident. It was very chaotic."

My eyes shifted to Owen. This one young man contained so much social power that he convinced a small army to desecrate their souls and forever stain our kingdom. I knew not to underestimate him, but he created even more damage than I believed possible.

"We killed Theus and we are hunting down every single person involved." My eyes swept over the warriors gathered. "Why is this not enough justice for you?"

"Enough?" Owen asked. "Nothing will ever be enough. You wouldn't know that because you didn't lose anyone."

The look in his eyes in the memorial hall burned in my mind and saved him from the worst of my wrath. "Killing innocent children shames the memory of the dead. Don't let your anger sully their memory."

Owen lowered his head, his rage palpable.

"We have not subdued the Flatlands, Prophet Eclipse," the older man said. "There are plenty of powerful warriors there who pose a threat to us. Now they know the cost. It's regrettable the children died, but their memory will save plenty more."

I shifted to face him fully. "You bastard."

"Bastard?" The commander scoffed. "I remember when you killed Eskel the Ruthless without any dithering about the fallout. Since then, you let Theus attack us because you've grown soft. We all saw this coming."

Perhaps it was fortunate I could not access my full power, because I might've accidentally unleashed it on this man. "It sounds simple to assassinate Prophets, does it?"

"It sounds necessary. You're a great warrior and a dedicated Prophet, but your heart is weakened by motherhood. You can no longer do what must be done."

"Weakened by motherhood." I thought back to Owen's snide remarks about Nash holding Finn in the war room. "That's what this is about?"

Looking around, I saw the same derision on the faces of the rest of the warriors.

"There is no life without mothers, you fools," I said. "You want to simplify me until I'm as small as you are." I stepped forward through tension that felt as powerful as ocean riptides. My stare drilled into the commander's, challenging him to dare interrupt. "I must either be so strong I'm unyielding or so tender I can do nothing but mother."

To his credit, he said nothing, but his look spoke for him. He didn't regret his sin or his words.

"You don't merely misunderstand women, but power itself." I stopped inches from his face. "Women are like the Mountain of the Gods, standing guard over this Valley and nourishing it with our rich waters at the same time. Rock may crumble from even our tallest mountain peaks, but no matter what we endure, we never fall. You cannot escape us." I glanced down his face, watching the effort to conceal the embarrassment that tightened his jowls. "We dominate your horizon."

Wrath burned in his eyes. His voice sounded as guttural as a groan. "Say what you like." He lifted his chin with a twitching snarl. "You let them slaughter our children. Some mountain you are."

The words plunged too deeply into me to feel. It was an attack so lethal, the shock and blood loss immediately numbed all pain. "I did." I felt hollow as I spoke, but I persisted. My people needed me, even these fools. "I failed."

A chilling quiet settled over the room as I held my accuser's gaze and said nothing for several seconds. They all watched me with the same frightened eyes, all looking to me for answers even if they complained about me.

"I will not allow one failure to excuse another," I said. This time I caught two handfuls of his tunic and ripped him closer with the precious bits of power I'd managed to regain. "We do not kill children."

The man trembled in fear. And yet he spoke anyway, apparently angry enough to defy his own terror. "Then they will kill ours."

I released him and watched him fall to his knees.

His head fell and his wilted voice barely broke the quiet. "You don't know what it's like to be us. You don't know what it's like to have no power."

The anguish of our loss and his helplessness softened my anger. While my horror at the killing couldn't abate, pity pricked my heart.

I lowered to kneel with him, and I took one of his fists into both of my hands. He froze for several seconds before looking at me, appearing wide open for the first time.

"I do know how it feels to lose everything and to be helpless to do anything about it. You know there's secrets I can't share. Things I've seen and experienced." His hand relaxed in mine. "I do know. That's why I can't let us do this to someone else." I lifted my palm to his cheek. "I never wanted any of you to feel this."

He nodded, weeping now.

"But that doesn't change that we can't kill children." My hand shifted and then I clutched his face in a steely grip, hard enough to put the fear of death in his eyes. "I will kill you myself if you hurt another innocent person ever again."

When I released him, he fell back on his ass, quivering.

I drew my sword. "I will kill anyone who dares to raise their sword against a child. Never again."

While most people fell back in fear, Owen, whose ability to fear died with the rest of his family, walked toward me. "You'll kill your own people."

"You can no longer be a part of our kingdom if you slaughter children."

"What if that's the only way to stop them from slaughtering ours? You'll still kill the people you've sworn to protect?" Another step closer. "Would you like to crush my face as well? I won't put up a fight."

"That's never the only way to win a war. It's always an excuse for cruelty."

Owen didn't flinch. "You expect me to believe you'll be cruel enough to kill us when you can't even kill our future enemies."

"'Future enemies.' That's what you're calling the children." I stalked closer to him, tilting my head. "You know I care about our kingdom and that's why you're speaking to me like this. You think you've found your weapon. But you've mistaken my love for something else entirely." I leaned close to his face, looking into his eyes. "It kills me to do the unjust thing. You're right to see this. What you don't know is I've killed myself a hundred times before. So even if it kills me, I will do what must be done. I cannot allow child killers to remain in this kingdom. They're poison."

He nudged my blade up to point the tip at himself. "Then kill me now. I will not surrender, even if it means killing their children. If they use a child as a shield, I will cut through that shield. So, Prophet, kill me."

A stifling quiet gripped the room while this man and I stared into each other's eyes in a quiet battle.

"You won't be killing any children because you'll be in captivity."

His lips curled in anger. "You can't stop us from protecting ourselves. You aren't the only one who can defend Skia Hellig!"

"You're more like me than you want to admit. I've been where you are. I didn't let myself attack the innocent, though. You say I'll hurt this kingdom, but you're hurting the people you want to save." I nodded at two of my warriors to haul him away, and I made sure not to pay attention to Owen fighting to escape.

Markus turned his back on me, likely calculating the political ramifications of what I'd done.

"The only thing as powerful as love is hate," I said. "Not only do you desecrate our kingdom and do the enemy's work for us when you kill the innocent. You also raise a generation of children who will hate us and will dedicate their lives to our destruction." It broke my heart that I even needed to say this. "Children are never to blame for the sins of our world. From this day forward, if you kill a child in war, then I will kill you. And if I suspect you plan to defy this order, I'll lock you away. That's my final word."

I stormed out the side door to the room where Nash waited. He clutched the windowsill, staring silently, in the exact position I'd left him in. He'd handle the warriors from here, but he needed more time first.

"I did this." His quiet voice seemed to linger in the air. "I let myself fall into the temptation of vengeance. That boy heard me cry out for their blood in the memorial hall." Nash's shoulders bent and he lowered his head to rest against the window. "I'm their war chief and I led them into slaughter."

"You did no such thing."

"I did. I'm responsible. My words carry power. Why didn't I tell them not to hurt the innocent? Why didn't I see the path they'd choose? I just told them to repay blood with blood. And they did." He turned, but didn't look at me. I didn't recognize this guilt I saw. Nash never struggled with it the way I once did. He was too ashamed to even look at me. "I thought maybe we actually had softened by letting Theus live. It was never as simple as what we did or didn't do, but why we made those choices. We thought we made the best choice for our people and Skia Hellig. The way I killed Theus, though . . . I just wanted to punish him."

"You're not responsible for what happened to the children." I understood how he felt, but I couldn't enable his guilt.

I expected him to say something. He only smiled sadly.

On his way to the warriors, he kissed my cheek, and then he left.

CHAPTER TWENTY-FOUR

I never would have imagined the tower could feel darker than the day of the attack, but a film of death and desecration coated all I saw.

Immediately after leaving the rogue warriors with Nash, I rushed to see Finn. I nearly ran to him, but didn't want to alarm anyone who saw me, and I hadn't yet regained enough power to teleport. When I opened the door and heard him softly crying, the sound ripped open all the wounds battering my heart.

"I'm here." I ran to him this time. These were perfectly normal tears, but I was his mother, and I wanted to be the one to soothe him. So often, I needed to leave him in the care of others. Today, seeing those poor children, I was more desperate than ever to hold my son close. Once I reached for him, I realized that it was Elara beside him, and not any of his usual caregivers.

"He's had a fresh change," she said as she finished wrapping his blanket around him. "Mommy is here," she whispered. "You called and she came running."

"Elara . . ." This dear woman laid her son to rest this week.

With a gentle smile, she settled Finn in my arms and gazed down at him. "What a perfect little boy."

"I didn't know you were still here. I'm so sorry—"

"None of that," she said. "Finn needs you. This is your time with him."

Tears sprinkled onto my cheeks. What was I doing crying in front of this woman whose son had just died? I lowered my head, aghast at losing control like this.

"A baby is a precious gift." Elara trailed her finger along Finn's arm. "There's no shame in how they make us feel. New life saves us from losing sight of the light when darkness swarms our world. Thank you for letting me share this gift."

"You can visit Finn any time you want."

"That's why I'm here." Her weathered fingers brushed the tears from my face, her skin soft and thin. "I want to help you take care of little Finn during this war. You and Nash don't have parents in your life to help. You need a grandmother to stay with him when you're away. And I need to hold life in my hands."

A painful knot lodged itself in my throat. "You want to be a grandmother to him?"

"Only if it's what his parents want."

"Yes, of course. We'd be honored. I know Nash would feel the same." Finn looked into my eyes and I almost started crying again. He filled me with so much love and joy, even during a time when death overtook my kingdom. It didn't feel right to hold any happiness in my heart, and yet I refused to deny this precious boy all the joy I wanted him to have. "Finn should have his parents home with him. I didn't want this to happen." I dipped my head, trying to hide from Elara and myself. From the world.

"If you want his parents home with him, then a home must exist. Do what only you and Nash can do. I'll care for this little one when you're away."

"I can't ask you to do that."

"I'm begging you to let me." Elara laughed softly, but looked sadder than ever. "This is the best way for me to help our kingdom, and what a beautiful way to do it. I don't want to go home without my son. Not yet."

Holding Finn with one arm, I slid my hand over the back of Elara's neck and lowered my forehead to hers. "You'll stay. I'll prepare an apartment for you."

"My grandson will want to stay as well. His sister is married now and it's only him at home."

"Of course. Rylan is very welcome here."

"Now, you go about your day," Elara said. "Talk with your husband and take the time you need to get back to me."

"Oh, I'm not sure we need time." I bounced Finn when he started to cry again. "It's an incredible gift you're offering."

Elara smiled. "It's a gift for me as well."

I kissed her cheek and quietly willed comfort into her heart, though I didn't know how to ease such pain. This one woman sparked color back into my world when I struggled to see anything except for what those warriors did to the children.

I couldn't allow the good in us to slip away.

After leaving Elara, I searched out Elsie, desperate to see her. To no surprise, I found her training.

"You know you'll have to return to schooling soon," I said. "Uncle Piercey will have a fit if you get behind in your studies."

Elsie lowered her bow and perked up when she saw Finn. "Hi, baby," she said, running to him. I allowed her to take him from me, and watched the two siblings, loving how much Elsie adored her little brother.

"It looks like we're going to have company for an extended stay." I gauged Elsie's reaction when I said the next part. "Elara wants to help us with Finn. She and Rylan will move here."

"Rylan?" Elsie straightened. "You mean he'll live here?"

"For now."

"Dad has to let me fight him now. This is perfect. We can train together." With Elsie growing more animated, Finn waved his arms in excitement.

"He's officially training as a warrior," I said. "I'm sure he'll be busy."

It wasn't Elsie's usual zeal for becoming a warrior that lit her eyes, but instead an anger that almost seemed to verge on fear. "Ma, I need to be a warrior-in-training. I'm ready. Look at what is happening in our kingdom. It's time."

"The training is grueling." Nash's hand against the slain girl's cheek flickered through my mind. "Even a year from now, you'll still be very young to start. Your mom and dad feel strongly about you spending the next year continuing your studies and training at home. I feel strongly about it."

"We're at war," she said with such incredulity that it made me feel like the foolish one. "You can't hold me back anymore."

I drew my head back. "We're not holding you back. You're still a kid."

"Does it matter that I'm a child? They'll kill me just the same." Pain gripped her voice. "Train me or turn my ashes into beads. That's what you're deciding."

"Elsie." Her words socked me in the gut so hard I bowed forward. I couldn't question whether she understood what she was saying, when she'd just placed beads all over the memorial hall with us.

"I understand why you didn't want me to do it before," Elsie said. "I was excited and I wanted it, but it wasn't time. Things are different now. You're trying to save my childhood, but you can't."

My heartbeat throbbed in my ears in a hot rush of blood. Elsie held her baby brother and looked at me with those knowing eyes. It felt like she pitied me for having to let her grow up when I didn't want to. Like we'd reversed the roles we were meant to play.

I swallowed hard to steady my voice. "I'll talk with your dad."

Elsie rocked Finn slightly. "I've had a good childhood, Ma. Don't be sad for me. I'm the daughter of a war chief and a Prophet. What did you expect?"

"I've expected it since I met you. It just doesn't make it any easier. It scares me."

The child in her shone through for a moment. "Me, too. I don't know if things will be okay."

I rushed to her and hugged her, holding her head against my shoulder. "You'll be okay, Elsie. We'll fight with everything we have for you and Finn."

"I won't be okay if you and Dad aren't."

My eyes closed as I hugged her.

By the time Nash joined us, Elsie left for Trish's apartment to eat dinner with her and her husband. We returned to our own with Finn to rest for the night before joining a major battle the next day. I told Nash what Elsie had shared with me, much to his dismay.

"No one will wait for Elsie to keep up," Nash said. "She's in the middle of a growth spurt. This time next year, she'll be in better shape for the trials of training. It still may be too early then."

"That's what I thought, but she made a good point."

"What if we train her to get her ready for training? Everyone is too busy to cater to a kid who isn't ready. We can't take time away from the instructors, but I don't want to tell Elsie that. She's barely a teen."

"I know. Maybe Leif will train her. He's very good at it. He trained me. I know he'll be busy with the war, but when he's home, I think he'd be willing."

Nash considered. "I trust Leif to take care of her. We'll talk to him."

I smiled at the thought of my dear friend training Elsie like he'd trained me when the village took me in. Such fond memories.

"Oh, I have the best news." I squeezed Nash's arm, still filled with relief at the thought. "Elara wants to stay here to take care of Finn when we're away."

"That's incredibly kind of her."

"Leaving him to go to war is killing me, but knowing she's with him gives me comfort." Guilt twisted my insides. "I want to be a good mom to him, but I have to make difficult choices to protect our kids' future. I can't nurse him if I'm going off to war. I may not be home for days. It's time for me to give that up and rely on the other mothers."

It'd already been difficult to manage being the mother I wanted to be and the ruler my kingdom needed. My heart couldn't accept what was happening. I didn't want to go to war.

"Why did this have to happen?" I whispered. "We could all be happy. This is so stupid. It didn't need to happen."

"I'm so sorry, Max." Nash slid his hand over mine as I held Finn. "I don't know how to make any of that better, but I do know you're an amazing mom. Exactly the kind of mom Finn needs."

I waited for stability and peace before having Finn to give him the childhood he deserved. Now our worst threat yet fell upon us. The future of the kingdom didn't just look uncertain, but unlikely. If Nash and I fell in war, they would kill my children. I'd never let that happen.

"I won't let Malach steal Finn and Elsie's life away." The baby curled his fingers and kicked his legs lightly. In the next few months, he'd sit up alone and then start crawling. It would be so many years before he'd be able to fight and defend himself, though.

Nash tapped Finn's nose and earned a delightful giggle. The joy made my heart ache for all the children we lost. For the children my own people stole.

"They think you made me weak," I said, marveling at Finn, at the similarities he shared with both Nash and me. "They don't know how strong you have to be to bring a life into this world and love it so fiercely."

Nash kneaded his fingers into his neck. "They're a very small minority. Don't let their loud voices drown out the people who believe in you."

"I'm afraid of what things will be like when Finn is older."

"Let's just enjoy him. We're so lucky to have him alive and well." Nash slipped his finger into our son's hand. "I love you so much, Finn. You're such a good boy." He looked at me now. "Can you believe he comes from us? The two of us together in one little guy."

"No, I really can't believe it. I've stared at him for months and still can't."

Nash picked Finn up and tugged me onto his lap so we were both in his arms. He kissed me gently, his gaze taking in the two of us, his voice a breath against my cheek. "We can never let go of this."

CHAPTER TWENTY-FIVE

My power returned in spurts. As soon as enough returned for me to travel, I took Nash with me to our first life, desperate for wisdom and answers from the people we used to be. Or maybe just the reminder that we'd survived so much already. There was always life after death.

We slipped back into the days after Nash first took power for himself and the security system tried to kill him, losing ourselves to those once forgotten days.

Keeping Nash alive long enough to find a healer should have been the most difficult part of the week, but I'd forgotten to prepare for Leif.

Leif belted a bitter, disbelieving laugh and then leveled his threatening stare at Nash. "He is not coming back with us."

I hoped Wren might back me up like normal, but she just shook her head. "I don't know what you're thinking. This is why you shouldn't have hidden all this from us. We could have helped you get the power before an enemy warrior took it."

"Well, he's our best shot now," I said. "Which is sad because he's shit with his power. He almost killed himself with it."

Nash rubbed the back of his neck.

"Why would you help us?" The suspicion dripped from Leif's voice.

"Because . . ." I interrupted to explain for Nash. "When I trained as a child, I grew up around people with power. I can teach him how to control it." I felt Nash watching me lie to my friends. I just couldn't endanger them by sharing these secrets with them.

Wren looked concerned. "Max, you never told us this."

"You know there's a lot I can't talk about. I don't want to say more than I have to. Without me, Nash's power is useless, and without him, we can't kill Eskel the Ruthless."

Leif snorted. "Well, we're leaving him behind, at least." He nodded at Rufus. The other man cleared his throat and shrugged.

"Rufus comes with us," Nash said. "That's not up for discussion."

"What is so important about this Rufus?" Leif eyed the other man.

"What's so important about you?" Nash asked. "Should we leave you behind?"

"Listen here, boy." My friend edged closer. "I do not trust you or your friend. I won't tolerate any games."

"Stop." I looked between the two men. "No one likes this situation, but we're all stuck with it."

The long journey home gave me time to begin training Nash. He needed someone who possessed the ability to suppress his power, though. Without it, training an unruly power was dangerous.

"You're terrible at this." I anchored my fists on my hips and stood over the mound of mud on the ground. Nash lost control of his power again, fortunately only attacking the earth. "Why are you so destructive?"

"Shouldn't you be a better teacher if you trained at the Sacred School?"

"It's because you're a terrible student."

Nash surveyed the damage. "I suppose that might be true."

With every passing day, it seemed harder to keep up my guard with Nash, despite Leif consistently reminding me not to trust him. My friend was right. Flatlanders and Valley-dwellers were enemies and always had been. The way Nash acted like we could be friends disarmed me.

One morning, halfway through our journey back home, I sat at a table outside of a cabin we paid to rent, trying to think about how to do a better job of keeping my distance. Except Rufus sat across from me, talking like we'd known each other forever.

He paused the conversation, maybe realizing I wasn't responding at all. "This isn't happening, is it?" His finger wagged between the two of us.

"Us? Are you joking?" I groaned. "It was never happening."

His eyes shifted to Nash training in the field. "What about that?"

My stomach clenched. "Of course not."

"Of course not," he repeated with a smirk.

I glared. But the days continued to wear on me.

Every morning and night without ever missing a session, Nash trained with his twin blades. The more I watched, the more I reflected on our battle together, until finally late one night, hurt tightened my chest. "The day we met, you went easy on me. You could have killed me."

Nash lowered his blades. "I did not go easy on you."

"I've watched you, Nash. That day we first fought . . . you could have killed me."

He sighed. "Once you shot me in the arm, I did not hold back. I didn't know how deadly you were with that bow."

Humiliation burned hot in my cheeks.

"Listen." He spoke softly. "I was impressed you made it to me by yourself. I didn't want to kill someone like that."

"It was a pity fight." My hands itched to grab my bow and arrow and teach him a lesson for ever pitying me.

"No, not a pity fight. Respect. I wanted to see what you could do. I get bored in that temple."

"I'm your entertainment?" I shoved his shoulder hard. "You dishonored me by toying with me."

"Fine. Fight me again. I'll try to kill you this time. Promise."

"You're infuriating."

His eyes shifted down for a moment and he smirked. "I just didn't want to kill you, okay? Is that really so awful?"

"Yes. I was trying to kill you."

"And you would have if you used your bow properly. I've watched you, too. I'm not the only one who held back. Why didn't you shoot me as soon as you entered?"

That stopped me because I hadn't thought about it and I didn't have an answer.

His smirk grew into a full grin. He murmured, "You didn't want to kill me either. I wonder why."

What was that supposed to mean? "I was surprised to see you by yourself in the temple. Maybe I was also curious. I didn't know how deadly you were with those swords." I'd see how he liked his own words being used against him.

Nash walked closer to me and leaned his forearm against his knee, eyeing me. "That's all?"

I took his look as a challenge when I understood he was trying to take the upper hand. "That's all."

Nash didn't back down. Didn't look away. Didn't blink. Panic drummed in my chest. What if he saw how hard it felt to breathe? I refused to retreat, so I stared right back, no matter how tense it felt.

He nodded, his smirk so annoyingly amused. "Alright, then. That's all."

"That's all for you, too?" Why did I ask it? I'd just opened the door for him. I could have screamed. What was I doing?

He held my gaze longer than I thought I could withstand without looking away. "No. Definitely not all." Nash pushed off the tree and drifted back a step, but the way he looked at me made it feel like he'd only eased closer, instead of further away. "When I saw you walk into that temple, I might not have wanted to kill you, but I did want to fight you. I've wanted to fight you every day since."

My heart beat wildly.

Nash and I awoke from our forgotten dreams, still lying together. I pushed up, looking down at him with the memory of him being hardly more than a stranger fresh in my mind. If I showed our current life to that past version of myself, I wouldn't have believed it.

"You're a dirty flirt," I said.

He ran his hand along my back. "A dirty flirt? You're just mad that I always win. In every life, we fight, and in every life, I make you fall for me."

I pinched his side. "Don't antagonize me."

He wrapped his arms around me and dragged me against himself. "You have no idea how I felt about you then."

"I have some kind of idea. At least, now."

"I wanted you so badly."

I nestled against the warmth of his skin. "How badly?"

He chuckled low. "You know." He rolled me onto my back and lifted himself just enough for his gaze to glide down me. "The only reason I learned about the artifact is because I needed to see you again. I was trying to find you, and then I found the power instead."

"I didn't take my shot," I confessed. "The day you got your power, I could have taken a shot. I waited too long because I didn't want to kill you."

"I was way ahead of you on that, Sharpshooter." He kissed my bottom lip. "That first day in the temple, when you wandered in all by yourself and covered in blood, I thought you were the most beautiful and deadly warrior I'd ever seen. But if I tell you about the shots I didn't take that day or the ones after it, I'm afraid of what you'll do to me." His mouth teased mine.

"Wise. Never play games with a Sharpshooter."

He chuckled. "I don't seem to have learned that lesson yet."

"Well, you should. I'm still mad thinking about you going easy on me. Doesn't matter which life it was in."

"We have each other now. That's all that matters." He murmured against me while his hands circled my wrists and drew them down against the bed, body pressed against mine. "This is the first time I wanted to kiss you. The first time in any life. When we were fighting, you looked at me like you could kill me with just a glance." If I closed my eyes, I might slip back to that moment in the temple when I truly tried to kill him. When we fought on the ground, bloody and desperate, our bodies smashed together then as they were now. Reliving that moment reminded me of all we'd lost, but also how many victories we'd won since.

We always found each other again.

Those people we used to be weren't ready to face everything we had since. One day, Nash and I would look back at this night, at these versions of ourselves facing down a terrifying war, aware that we had more to lose than ever. And we'd feel the same exact way.

"Hold me," I whispered. "Remind me that we've never let go. That we never will."

He cradled me in his arms, and I captured this feeling, saving it for when I'd need it most.

Nash and I shared our old lives together and indulged in our love and our connection. I felt myself burying deeper into his soul than ever before. The pieces of myself I didn't even know I was missing filled in each time we traveled. Each time I loved him.

We'd nearly completed our journey to the Valley, and Nash still couldn't control his power.

"We need to find my friend," I whispered while the others slept. "He trained at the Sacred School."

"The Sacred School?" Nash asked. "Why has he not killed the Prophets himself?"

"He's a healer, not a warrior, and he doesn't believe in killing."

Nash's blank look told me he didn't remotely understand the concept. "So, he believes in allowing powerful Prophets to torture and kill their own people?"

I sighed. "They hurt him at the Sacred School. It's hard for him to use his power now. He just has limitations."

Protectiveness filled me. Nash didn't know what we'd been through. But he'd understand soon. Once he met Piercey and saw his kind heart, saw the pain that broke him, it would all be clear. He hid away in the mountains a few hours away from the nearest Fjellfolk villages. It'd been almost a year since I saw him, and I worried about him all the time.

"What happened on that mountain?" The tender way he asked allowed him to easily slide past my defenses.

"It's not a place for children, but that's exactly who they force to stay there."

Lying on his side, he looked into my eyes in the darkness. "You're a good person. You know that, right?"

"Why wouldn't I?" My curt response covered that old feeling creeping up inside. The one that called me dirty for wielding a power I'd only ever seen cause suffering. Worse, for losing that power and becoming so worthless. I'd rather be a demon than someone who couldn't protect the ones I loved.

"I don't know, but you do. You know why you feel so guilty." Nash looked sad for me, and I didn't like that at all. I didn't like how soft it made my heart feel. "I'll carry it for you if you give it to me."

I chuckled and rolled onto my back. "There's nothing to carry. If there was, I wouldn't give it to you."

The words cut for him like a blade, meant to throw him off his offense. But regret immediately filled me because I didn't want to actually hurt him. Lying beside him that night, I realized that he'd never done anything wrong to me. He'd never done anything but try to help.

"You're so scared." The quiet words drifted over me. "But it'll be okay, Max. I'll never hurt you."

Tears gathered in my eyes. All the people flooded my heart then. Dad, the instructors, the Prophet, my own cursed power. Everyone who'd hurt me. Nash never had, but I treated him like the enemy.

I didn't know what to say, and uttering anything terrified me because he might see through me. But I couldn't be cruel to him. He didn't deserve it.

Hesitating at first, I forced myself to meet his eyes. I remembered that when I fought him, I prepared myself for the strength of his attack and for how difficult it would be to withstand. But I'd been completely shocked by how much harder it was than I expected. I felt the same now. I'd tried to steel myself before I looked at him, but the moment our eyes met, the power of the hit completely stunned me.

Nash didn't hide the way I did. He looked at me fully and he saw me. Saw everything I tried to conceal. The dim moonlight hugged his body so softly, tracing those curls of his, bright in his eyes. Wow. Strength and tenderness were an unfair combination. I never let myself look at him, but I gave in for just a few seconds.

Then I rolled over and didn't dare look back at him the rest of the night, even though I felt him every second.

The next morning, convincing Leif and Wren to continue without me was almost impossible, but I needed them to cover for me with the Prophet. Finally, they agreed. Parting still hurt. I hated making Leif and Wren worry like this.

Once we reached Piercey, though, the ache lessened. I melted once I saw him again.

"Max." He embraced me, holding me close. "You're okay."

I hated that he always worried about me. "I am."

"Good." When he noticed Nash, he paused, the look in his eyes making my chest hurt. "Oh."

"This is a warrior from the Flatlands," I said. "We're allying to kill our Prophets."

Piercey clenched his hands together nervously. "This isn't the answer you think it is."

"Please," I said. "We've talked too much about this. We'll never agree. I came because we need your help."

Even if Piercey didn't want to help, I knew he would. He'd do anything for me. At least, I thought he would. After I told him the full story, he looked even more leery.

"This stranger, do you think the gods sent him?" Piercey asked.

"It seemed like it."

"We don't know how gaining power as an adult affects someone. It may be dangerous." Piercey never used to jump from topic to topic so frequently. Guilt ate away at me for leaving him there at the Sacred School. I should have forced him to leave with me. Instead, they beat away at his mind and spirit, reducing him to a healer too scarred by power to fully utilize his healing gift.

In the end, Piercey accepted my request to help train Nash, even though he didn't like what I planned to do.

"I can't believe I'm agreeing to this," I said to Nash a few days into their training.

"You'll do it, then?" Nash raised one brow, looking at me like I'd agreed to something completely different than what we'd just talked about.

Lips pursed, I raised a hand to him. "I'll stay to help you train with Piercey as long as Leif and Wren can cover for me."

"Why do you say it like I don't know what you're talking about?"

"Because I just want to be clear on the deal we're making so you don't get the wrong idea."

"Huh." I didn't believe the faux innocent look he wore for a single moment. "What other deal might we make?"

I jabbed my finger against his chest, ignoring how my stomach fluttered when I moved too close. "The kind that has you jesting right now."

He flicked my finger away and smiled knowingly. "As my trainer, I don't think it's right for you to flirt with me like this. We have serious business to attend to."

My fingers curled and this time it wasn't a finger I jabbed him with, but a fist. Except he caught it, and that lingering moment after made me rip away from him. Had I lingered, or was it him? Or worse, both of us?

"You know," he said softly, "I'll let you kiss me."

"You'll let me?" I howled. "I would rather die than kiss you."

"You must be very desperate for death, then," he whispered. "Because you're dying to kiss me right now."

Heat fluttered in my core at how easily I could do it. If I just barely shifted, he'd dip a little more, and I'd know the taste of his lips.

I needed to ease back to open space between us, but I didn't. Couldn't. "You stole the power I needed to save my people and you're failing to wield it properly. I'll never forgive you."

"How was I supposed to know you knew how to use it?"

"It doesn't matter," I said. "I'll resent you forever."

"Why does it sound like you're the one you're trying to convince of this?"

Were his lips closer or was I imagining that? The tension made me squirm. I turned him away that night, and I did so other nights, even when I was the one drawing close to him.

Until the moment I saw Nash draw his power into a glowing ball in his hand, and I watched how his amber eyes lit with rapture. He did it. He controlled his power perfectly!

The excitement rushed over us both, an overwhelming sense of victory. He clasped me against him in a hug and I wrapped my arms around his neck, hopeful for the first time in a long time that we might be free.

That one touch pierced my defenses. Instinct told me when I needed to pull away, but it felt incredible nestling my cheek against his chest, feeling his hands on my back.

I peeked up at his face, my head spinning with the unyielding pull of his body. We only hugged, and we could stop now without it going too far. But then my hands were smoothing down his shoulders. He was bending and I was pulling myself up to him. Breath mingling. Bodies close. The softness of lips grazing for the first time.

"When will you trust me?" he whispered.

My nose brushed his, my eyes fluttering closed. "It's myself I don't trust." My fingers discovered the taut dip above his collarbone. "I don't even know what I'm afraid of anymore."

"You're afraid of how good you know this will feel." Hands smoothed up my sides. "How bad it might feel to lose it."

What if?

That open-ended question haunted me, and I was tired of letting it rule my life. My gaze found his mouth, and every moment of wanting tethered me to him. My lips parted his ever so slowly and I savored the shock of learning exactly how good it felt. Learning the taste and scent and feel of him. The utter intoxication of his kiss and his nearness.

I never planned for Nash. That reason couldn't keep me away from him any longer, though.

We kissed each other for the first time, and I knew with certainty it would not be the last. It didn't make sense to connect with an enemy warrior like this, but sense no longer mattered. Nash was kind, steadfast, worthy. The best swordsman I'd ever met.

I lost myself with him, unable to find my way back. That kiss consumed me, and yet it was only the smallest glimpse of so much more.

In the coming weeks, I did my best to shield Piercey from the way Nash made me feel, but I thought he knew even though he didn't say. To his credit, he faithfully trained Nash and was kind to him, befriending him. Trusting him in ways I refused to allow myself for so long. Even when I needed to return to the Valley, they continued to train.

Until eventually I returned, and I felt certain it was time. Though Piercey was still as shaky as I'd ever seen him, he taught Nash to control his power, and finally, he was ready.

But I still worried he couldn't do it alone, and that without my power we were destined to fail.

CHAPTER TWENTY-SIX

Living through our past lives healed what Dr. Henderson broke, but it did not yet yield what we needed most—new weapons to fend off Malach or knowledge to gain an advantage over the gods. I wanted to know more about the security system.

Nash and I returned to battle while Leif stayed home to train Elsie. All the while, I continued to think about the trajectory of our past lives.

In our first life, Dr. Henderson didn't allow Piercey to work with her like in this life. The instructors punished him for what I did. They tortured him. That life really happened. It wasn't simply a dream or a hypothetical. My friend really suffered this way in a past life. It made me feel sick.

The reminder of the cruelty of many in power reinforced my determination to stop Malach.

He and the strange cult wanted war, and so we brought it to them, because there was no escaping it. We needed to fight. We also needed to protect ourselves and our kingdom from the hate which led our warriors to slaughter that innocent Flatlander village.

Nash and I met Malach's men on their march to our lands, confronting them once again at the border of Skia Hellig.

His army mixed together those with and without power, just as we did now, allowing our warriors to fight as one great body. I hated to unleash myself upon anyone unable to defend themselves, but no longer could I allow such sentiments to take hold of me, especially now that our enemy possessed a new and devastating weapon. My people fought as one and we attacked our invaders as one. No holding back.

Piercey studied Malach's poison even now as we fought, but while we waited for answers, we needed to assume any weapon might render our energy inert. Nash instructed our warriors to never rely on energy shields, but to return to physical shields and weapons for defense.

Our warriors converged upon the enemy army in an all-out assault.

Nash carried me high in the sky so we eclipsed the sun. Anyone who cared to aim their weapons would have to look into its brightness to see us.

I amplified my voice. My words bounded over the battlefield, shaking the tree limbs in the distance. "Flee now if you wish to live."

With Nash close, I easily sought out the connection of his power, and we melted our minds and energies together. Recovering enough of my power to do this, to fight together once again, soothed the heartache of all that we'd lost.

Our power poured into each other. Every inch of my skin tingled with the overwhelming sensitivity of such a deep connection. Nash eased away from me and I remained floating in the air.

We drifted further apart, looking down over the battlefield, and over our people who poured all their grief from the attacks against our enemy. Nash and I didn't need to share our thoughts any more than we needed to tell our lungs to draw in breath. We were fully connected. As one, we both spoke at the same time, now on opposite ends of the battlefield, still hovering in the air.

"Leave Skia Hellig." Our voices, strengthened by our combined power, gusted over the battlefield in a gust that whipped the sleeves of tunics and ruffled the feathers of arrows. I felt the vibration deep in my chest. "Never return."

Our people roared in response and tore at the enemy with their weapons.

A beam of energy shot toward me and I teleported out of the way, gathering my own power into my hands. I felt the heat fill Nash's palms as well. We directed our power toward the back of the enemy lines, away from our people. My heart twisted with grief at the sound of screaming as our energy broke through energy shields and melted the skin of our enemy.

"Flee," we shouted together, not wanting to kill those without power. Years ago, the world believed the gods would enforce their rules about not letting the Prophets use their power against those without. We now knew the gods never cared to intervene. The security system could stop this at any time. It felt like killing children who were interspersed among those with power. But these weren't children. These were enemy warriors intent on killing our people, and their kingdom was far larger than ours.

So we reigned terror upon them and warned them to never return. I sensed the fear rising in the enemy until a warning pricked my mind.

I sensed the incredible energy before even hearing from one of our commanders.

Malach was here.

Why he hadn't revealed himself before now, I didn't know.

Nash and I teleported to where I sensed the energy and we both stopped right in front of him, releasing our connection to one another. I breathed heavily from the exertion of our attacks.

Malach's glare shifted between the two of us. "No one told me of this trick of yours. You've frightened some of my warriors."

The tips of Nash's swords dug into the ground as he stalked forward, kicking up a cloud of dust on the dry, windy day. Apparently, he wasn't waiting around to talk.

I didn't move. I needed to see Malach's power. Nash once taught me the importance of letting the other strike first. My husband lost his patience, though, after this man nearly killed Elsie and me in the attacks.

Malach's frown slowly twisted in a sneer and he raced forward, past Nash, directly for me. Nash turned to attack from the side, but Malach didn't even block. His weapon skimmed uselessly off Malach's arm as if he had assaulted him with a blade of grass instead.

With Malach's strength and size, I expected him to move slowly. Such was the useless logic leftover from the primitive part of my mind that made assumptions power rendered very fallible.

I'd never seen someone get past Nash like that. It stunned him as well. He pursued, but I knew Malach would reach me first.

I raised my palms and drew energy into each, recognizing that I needed to throw more at him than I expected. My enemy reared his fist back and I shot the two balls of power at his center.

My power exploded against his chest moments before he drove through the attack to slam his fist into my face. I no longer needed to rely upon full shields to protect myself. I steeled myself against his attack rather than teleporting or dodging because I wanted to feel his strength. I wanted to experience what he could throw at me.

I suspected he'd done the same when he let my energy slam into his chest.

Still, pain bit into my temple. A thin trail of blood started down the side of my face.

Malach twisted when Nash attacked and caught the twin swords with his bare hands.

"My chest stings, Eclipse." Though I couldn't see Malach's face, I heard the grin in his voice. The excitement. "What incredible power."

Horror flooded me at the sight of Malach stopping Nash's blades like that. I lunged forward with my sword swinging ahead of me. It bounced off his back, vibrating in my hand. I felt like I'd struck a mountain.

Nash flew up in the air, spinning, the dusty air gathering loosely about him. On his final spin, he lobbed an arc of his acidic power at Malach. The man swatted it away with his hand.

Close-ranged combat didn't work against this beast of a man. If Nash's swords failed against him, then what attack within arm's reach would be worth trying? That punch alone might kill one of my friends with less power than me and I was confident he held back.

My awareness reached for Nash and called for him. He opened himself up to me and the warmth of his presence flooded my entire body as we connected.

I rose in the air, mirroring his stance. With our shared instinct, we drew upon our combined energy in our palms. Malach twisted to look at me with a grin as Nash and I both unleashed our power upon him at the same time.

Malach raised his forearms to block the attack, grunting and laughing at the same time. The force of our power only shoved him back a step.

"Incredible," Malach cried. "Absolutely incredible."

The energy fizzled, leaving his skin reddened but unbroken.

I didn't need to look at Nash to sense the worry that filled him just as it did me. I noticed Wren then, running to us, advancing for Malach.

Nash and I shouted as one. "No!"

She skidded to a stop as our enemy's gaze found her. The grin morphed into something vicious and hungry.

I teleported to Malach before he could reach Wren. Nash appeared beside me at the same time. We grabbed the enemy's arms and took him far away from our people.

Malach stumbled away from us when we landed and raised his eyes to see the towering mountains in the near distance. "Where are we?"

"The other side of the world," I said. "Where you can't touch my people."

"Will you abandon me here? That's an intriguing idea."

"We're going to kill you here," Nash said.

Could we abandon him here? I'd seen him teleport, too. Interesting.

Wanting to conserve energy, Nash and I allowed our connection to break. The coldness of leaving him wrapped around me.

We'd already seen enough. Malach was far stronger than I anticipated, and I feared that my attacks would continue to simply bounce off his body. His defense was impenetrable and he hadn't even started attacking yet.

No time to waste.

I gathered my energy at the tips of my pointer fingers and focused on making it as dense as possible.

The heavy pinpoint of energy glowed with the deepest shade of crimson, pulsing with far more power than I ever summoned for this attack before. This time when I aimed, I no longer feared I may lose control. I desperately hoped I did.

My fingers blazed with the fire. I looked into Malach's eyes and shot directly for his heart. No way he'd manage to dodge at this distance when my shot traveled so fast.

The crimson ball pierced the shield he had created, immediately dissolving it. The attack slammed into his chest. I held my breath, waiting to see the damage, wondering if he'd even utter a last word or just die instantly before my eyes.

Except the dense ball of energy merely thudded against his chest and spun in place against him. The faint smell of singed leather and skin filled the air as it continued to dig into him.

A glow started beneath his shirt directly in the center of his chest.

My heart sank into my stomach. Impossible. Absolutely impossible.

A high-pitched giggle drifted from behind me and I twisted in shock.

Wavy dark blond hair crept out from beneath a dark hood, lying over thick robes. Cleo marched forward with a bounce in her step.

CHAPTER TWENTY-SEVEN

Malach stared at the energy with wide eyes. "That would have killed me, wouldn't it?"

"What the hell?" I asked through clenched teeth.

Nash raised his swords toward the young woman and I readied an energy shield that surrounded us.

"Look at all that power." Her cheery voice grated against me like a sword sawing against a brick wall. "Delicious."

What?

"Thank you for the gift, Eclipse," Cleo said. "I was feeling weary."

She vanished and then appeared right beside Malach, tilting her head to inspect the energy.

I grabbed Nash's wrist. "This answers whether we should trust her."

Nash studied her for several more seconds before looking at me. "She tried to play us."

"Or she was merely playing with us."

"It's starting to dig into me more," Malach said. "Hurry."

"You're fine," Cleo said. "Be patient. This isn't an easy attack to absorb. I'm keeping it from killing you. Don't be a coward."

Nash looked at me with the same panic I felt. I tried to draw the power back to myself, but it was no use. They controlled it now, or at least attempted to.

All this time, it was her, wasn't it? She wasn't some innocent girl too afraid for her life to leave the cult. She didn't care about secretly helping us to assuage her guilt. The deranged girl only pretended to help to earn our trust, or maybe just to study us.

Her slender hand cupped the air around the energy. "Oh," she said with a note of pain in her voice. "It stings."

I teleported behind her and tried to grab her in a headlock, but she vanished, appearing on the other side of Malach.

"Please, Eclipse." She wagged her finger at me. "We can waste our energy doing that all day. It's not worth the effort, is it?"

I growled under my breath and ripped my sword free, pointing it at her. "You're the leader of the cult that wants to consume my power. You created the weapons that poison our energy, and you were the link between Eskel and Malach."

The girl dared to look bored and sighed. "Well, it's obvious now, isn't it? Aren't you ready to talk about something more interesting? Like what I can do with this tasty treat?"

Nash shook his head. "We won't fall for your act again. Stop acting like a child and face us."

She shot him a pouting look. "The cute ones are always so rude. You grow up with everyone falling over you and never learn how it feels to be mocked. You shouldn't hurt my feelings, War Chief. I do have a temper, you know."

"I'm not doing this either," I said. "Malach, who is this and why are you working with someone like her?"

This time she threw her head back and belted out a manic, hitching laugh. "He's not working *with* me. He works *for* me."

Suddenly, her hands closed around the power and she jerked it to her chest, grappling with it, trying to keep it from escaping. "Oh." She gasped and wiggled. "It's a big one!"

The energy started to spread over her skin, turning her a crimson shade. Her eyes bulged and veins popped in her neck. She hugged the energy tight, shoving it into herself. Soon it enveloped her body and then slowly disappeared, entirely absorbed.

I drew back. I'd never seen anything like this before.

Cleo's hands started to shake and she shrieked. The anguished cry reverberated around us.

Her shoulders fell. Her knees buckled. She collapsed onto the ground and caught herself, breathing heavily. Malach watched us, clearly ready to defend her.

Nash and I both attacked at the same time. It might be our only chance.

Cleo disappeared again. I tried to follow, but I didn't sense her at all. Even when Flare teleported, I still felt her.

She appeared behind Malach and shook her hands at us. "Please, stop. It's going to hurt for a few minutes."

Malach shot forward. His sword snaked out at a dangerous speed. I raised my own to block the hit. Nash parried and tried to skewer our enemy's arm with one of his blades, but the other man twisted just enough to miss it. A sign that Nash's blades might be able to hurt him after all.

Cleo fell onto her knees again, her head hanging, and then went completely still. Malach teleported to her side, stunning me.

We spent the entire life of our kingdom trying to train people to teleport, and both of them could do it? Something was not right.

He placed his hand on her head and she lifted her face. The curtain of her hair fell away to reveal a mad smile etched upon her face. "Wow," she said with glee. Her eyes seemed to glow with the fire of my power that she'd consumed. "That's going to fuel me for a long time."

We needed to run. I rarely accepted such an urge, but she'd just absorbed one of my most powerful attacks.

"Max," Nash said.

"I know." I reached for him.

"You feel that, Malach?" Cleo asked.

He raised a hand in the air and curled it into a fist. The fire seemed to shine from his eyes as well. "Oh yes, I do."

"Imagine how all of her power will feel."

They both felt it? Were they somehow connected?

I took Nash's hand to transport us, even though it seemed they might be able to follow. Even a few seconds away from them would help me to clear my mind.

"Wait!" Cleo struggled to her feet. "Malach, stand down. Please, Eclipse, don't leave yet. Please. We won't attack anymore. I promise."

"You expect me to believe you aren't going to try to kill us," I said. "You could end the war today if you did."

"We don't want to kill you, Max," Cleo said, dropping my title for my name. The cheerful sound in her voice darkened to malice. "Why waste all that wonderful energy?"

"I'm not sure when we'll have the opportunity to talk again," Malach said. "If you plan to leave, let's discuss first. No more playing around."

They were only playing? "Can't you just follow us?" I asked.

"Not unless you're near one of our bonds." Cleo pursed her lips. "We planned today so we could get to know each other better. I want to tell you more about us. It's time."

One of her bonds. Cleo and Malach were bound somehow, and they did this with others as well. So we only needed to keep our distance from this pair and whoever else they'd attached to like parasites. Good to know. The only problem was that I knew Cleo had ulterior motives when she shared information. They likely wanted to create a false sense of security. Keeping us here also removed us from the battle, and I needed to return to my people. This might be a total fabrication.

"Tell us," Nash said. "Or we're leaving."

"I want you to join us," Cleo said. "I'd let you be my true partner. If you'll just let me consume that incredible power, then I'll give you as much of a say as I have."

"You'll give it to me, meaning you can take it away," I said. "No thanks."

"We won't have to war," Cleo said. "Your people won't have to die. You can continue to rule exactly like you do now. Nothing has to change."

My eyes shifted to Malach. Our every interaction played through my mind. "That's why you interrupted our summit and then attacked us. Why you started this war. You knew I'd never consider handing my power over to Cleo unless you showed me how much you could make us suffer."

Malach shrugged one shoulder. "This is war, Prophet. Whether you choose to continue fighting it or avoid it all together, I'll enjoy it anyway. You're an incredible opponent."

"Quiet, Malach." Cleo gave him a pointed look before returning her attention to me. "Don't listen to him. He loves to fight. I'm all for peace. And if you want to expand your peace, we can help you with that."

"By 'expand my peace,'" I said, "you mean conquer Skia Hellig."

"They will destroy themselves," Malach said. "Theus proved that. Betraying someone as powerful as you, even if allied with us, was a fool's move."

"We could do so much good together," Cleo said.

"That's what you care about?" Nash tilted his head. "You want to save the world?"

Cleo bit her lip and wiggled her brows. "Maybe. You never know. But I do want to partner with Max. So if she wants to do good, fine. Whatever keeps her happy."

"I want to know what you actually want," I said.

Anger tightened her eyes. "I told you before. We want to consume your power."

"Now more than ever," Malach said. "It feels incredible."

Cleo nodded. "When you bind to us—and you will—you'll be more powerful than ever. You'll finally be able to protect your people from any threat imaginable. Everything I have will be yours. We're all one."

I laughed. "Never."

"You will," Cleo said. "If you won't, we will suck every last drop of energy from you. That will be a true disgrace, though. You're so much more than you understand." Her gaze shifted between Nash and me. "Both of you. If only you understood the heights you've risen to before."

"What do you know about before?" Nash asked.

A knowing smile curled her lips. "I know I see the god in you."

Chills pricked my arms. "I'm tired of dealing with cryptic people."

"You can't understand. That's why we must rely on vagaries. You panic so easily when it comes to the gods." Cleo uttered a pitying sigh. "If you grasped their true nature, you'd never fear again. The gods are not gods because they created our world or because they're in the Collective. Their rise to this position is why they're gods. The power they took for themselves, the strength they cultivated, the journey of enlightenment they mastered. Not even Dr. Henderson reached the Collective. These are more than just people."

"I fail to see their brilliance," I said.

"Because you're looking at the Collective, not the people who make it up. There's a difference and I'm not sure anyone anticipated that."

"What does this have to do with me?"

Cleo chuckled. "You sweet girl. Stop letting the Collective fool you. Take the answers for yourself. You can figure this out. I told you that there's a god in you, Max. There's one in Nash, too." Her gaze darkened. "And when I consume you, then I, too, shall ascend to the Collective."

Nash and I shared a look of agreement. Time to flee this madwoman and try to sort out whatever she meant later. I took his hand. Both Malach and Cleo raised their palms to us at the same time, with the same hazy crimson energy gathering there. They mirrored each other so well, I sensed what I couldn't see. A bond as real as the one Nash and I shared when we connected.

I teleported us away before we wound up dead. Cleo's uncanny smile was the last thing I saw.

CHAPTER TWENTY-EIGHT

After the battle ended, Nash and I returned home. My hands trembled from exhaustion, but I couldn't sleep without telling the kids goodnight. Not after seeing for the first time what a terrible threat we truly faced.

Elsie slept in her room, peaceful and still, with a pile of clothes dirty from training lying on the ground. Elara rocked Finn and kissed him before leaving us alone.

I tried to steady myself as I held him tightly to me and settled back against the chair.

"I've got you," I whispered. "I'll always come home. I promise. I'm sorry I'm so late."

My stained hands looked wrong against his pure white blanket. It was the best I could do today.

Nash held his side with one hand and cupped the back of Finn's head with the other. "Hey, little guy."

Finn's eyes met mine and a smile bunched his cheeks. It grounded me after an encounter that left my mind spiraling. We won our second battle against Malach's army today, but we'd clearly lost the fight with him and Cleo. After seeing his incredible strength, and the way Cleo absorbed my energy, I only felt toyed with. I struggled to believe that Malach would allow us to kill his warriors, but I couldn't assume that he wasn't that awful. Some people did not care about their warriors. And there was something wrong with him and Cleo.

"What did Cleo mean about the god in us?" I asked. "How would joining with us help her ascend to the Collective?"

"She's crazy, Max."

"Is she? She knows things she shouldn't. Maybe she wants us to think she's just crazy so we don't take her seriously."

"I take crazy very seriously," he said.

"Or so we underestimate her calculated sanity."

"What if Dr. Henderson told her something she never told us?"

"We need to think about the past more," I said, hoping he'd realize I meant that we needed to travel. "Until then, the gods were debating about telling me something. I'm going to talk to them. Their secrets are placing our kingdom in jeopardy."

He reached for the baby. "Go now. I'll take care of the kids."

"You're sure?"

"Yes. We need to know."

"Back again so soon," the Collective said.

"I want my answers now. Last time, I demanded them and said I'd revoke your access to my life otherwise. What did you decide?"

"You're troubled by Cleo."

I growled. "We're not doing this thing where we go back and forth pretending you don't already know why I came and what I want to know." I walked closer to them and studied the water. The light flickered inside, faster than usual.

"Yes."

I was tired of looking at their stupid symbolic tank of water. "Choose a form and talk to me like a person."

They normally only did this when taking me to the full council, but it surprised me to see their water disappear, and in its place, a young man appeared.

"Can Cleo really ascend to the Collective by consuming my power?" I asked. "I was told that we needed to become enlightened through multiple simulated lives to even be eligible."

"Cleo cannot become a part of the council by bonding with you."

"Then what did she mean?" I lowered my gaze, trying to remember everything she said.

"We believe she means that becoming one with you will make her the kind of person who can one day join the council, something that even her beloved Dr. Henderson failed to do."

"Why me?" I met his deep blue eyes. They seemed to ripple like the waters of the Collective did. "What did she mean by the god in Nash and me? You're going to explain the full truth or I'm revoking your access this time. I'll take it to the council, or beyond."

"If you understood, you wouldn't fight us like this."

"Then make me understand."

"You're too rooted in your own life, in your own world." He stepped backward into the darkness left behind by where the water normally was. "If you insist on the truth, then we'll give it to you. But you still won't understand."

I tried to prepare myself for the painful shock I sensed coming.

"The council voted and we're in agreement that you've earned the truth."

I walked forward, feeling drawn to the man the Collective chose to personify themselves as today. Darkness swallowed me whole when I stepped closer and I spun around, feeling like the walls of black both closed in on me and stretched endlessly. Like I was in a void with no boundary and also suffocating in the middle of a rock.

The dimmest light barely crept into the darkness, too far away to touch or even really see.

"This is what Earth looks like now. It's been so long since it was gone. We lived in Kethios for quite some time before any sect of our society formed a collective, and even longer before Earthlings got their own. We fought for the power we have today."

The darkness stretched into a long hallway that was lit just enough for me to discern the walls and ceiling, but I saw no end before me or behind me. A light filled the ground beneath my feet so I saw myself clearly but only made shadows of the man.

"Earth was isolated like this for so long," the Collective said. "Binding together changed everything for us. The war you're facing right now is only a drop of water in the ocean of suffering. We need to help other worlds like ours. Our council looks after every earthlike planet in the universe." Bright planets appeared all at once in the hallway, shining from the floor, the walls, and the ceiling, stretching beyond what I could see.

"You've told me before what you want to do," I said.

"Yes, but we didn't show you who we are." The worlds slowly dimmed until they only cast faint circles of light on the floor. "You won't know us if you don't see who we're fighting for."

I crossed my arms over myself, searching for something solid.

"We told you that your simulation is populated with those who died as babies on Earth and never had the chance to live. We said that you and Nash died in war-torn streets." The man watched me in the dim light. "This is true for almost everyone in your world. But not for the others."

"What others?"

"The few." His blue eyes glowed in the darkness, the depths of bottomless ocean waters. "Some in your world did not die as babies. Some lived full lives, many lives, before this one."

I swallowed down the knot of fear growing in my throat, or maybe something distinct from fear. Dread. I almost couldn't bring myself to ask the question. I was too afraid of the answer. "Who?" My voice sounded small. "Who are the few?"

"Don't you feel the bond calling out to you?" His endless eyes terrified me.

"No," I whispered, shaking my head.

He watched me quietly for so long I thought we'd remain silent forever. "Ask me your real question. You're a smart girl."

My lips quivered. "How many lives did we live?"

"Enough to join the Collective."

The darkness wrapped around me again and suffocated me. His words rang back at me from a hollow drum. I shook my head so subtly it felt more like a twitch. "N-no."

The stranger passed through the shadows. In the darkness his barely discernible form shifted, growing taller and leaner, and his hair more full. I took a step backward, squinting.

A different man emerged, standing quietly before me. A man whose kind eyes and short black locks I recognized so well. With a gentle smile, he reached his hand out toward me.

"It is true, Max." Compassion shone in Piercey's eyes. "I'm sorry if it's hard to hear. I don't want to hurt you. We've known each other an awfully long time."

The implication of what the Collective said swirled through my mind until I was dizzy. "It's us?" I asked, my voice breaking.

Sorrow drew his lips into a familiar frown. "It's not bad like you think."

"You have to say it. You have to say it to my face."

Piercey eased closer, standing in the same light I did, lit by the glowing blue hue of a planet that looked much like Earth. "We are the Collective, Max."

I covered my mouth and blinked back tears. Weakness gripped my knees and I fell onto the ground, ready to wilt all the way to the floor.

"You've been fighting yourself and the ones you love the most for three lives now."

Deep betrayal stabbed into my heart. "We'd never do this. You're lying." I looked up then, a flare of fury flashing through me. "Don't you dare steal his image. You're trying to mess with my mind."

"We aren't. You and Piercey have always endured these difficult revelations together. We thought it would comfort you." The tone now sounded less like Piercey and more like the way I was used to the Collective talking. They were using the image and voice of my friend to manipulate me. Gave up when it didn't work. I had to keep my guard up. They wanted to disorient and confuse me.

"No." I lowered my hand and curled it into a fist, my voice dangerous and low. "You're not stupid. You know this isn't comforting. It's disorienting and confusing and terrifying."

He sighed so deeply that his shoulders fell. "It's been a long time since we were individuals and experienced the world the way you do. That's why a slim majority of the council is made of individuals. We've lost our touch with human connection. Ironic, isn't it? We are the ultimate connection. The blending of souls and yet—"

"Shut the fuck up," I said, voice cracking. "You're not Piercey. Don't try to emulate him."

"My soul has had many names." His voice softened so convincingly. "We are the same. Piercey comes directly from me. He is the seed of my consciousness, just like Elias." His expression slowly hardened. "Or maybe you don't need to be coddled right now."

Rage darkened my vision. My head swam like I might pass out from it. "Even if we come from you, you're not us. Piercey would never make me feel like this."

His hair grew longer and lighter, his form shrinking down, until I stared into my own eyes. If not for meeting Ashton, seeing another version of myself might have sent me reeling.

"It's time to grow up," the Collective said through my voice and a duplicate of my body. "Your world matters. You proved that. So go take care of your people. Stop reaching above yourself and creating wars that no one needs to fight. One day you'll be here among us, and then you can fight with us. Today is not that day."

"How could you be a part of them?" I asked.

"How could you kill those prisoners right before you formalized your kingdom? How could you leave Nash behind to finish the job for you?" It was the same as looking into a mirror. The weight of ruling and the gore of war clung to my image every morning when I awoke. I saw it now in her. This twisted version of me. "How could you send your people, the people you love so dearly, to fight and die against Malach's army? How could you jail that poor boy who can barely fit the beads of his dead around his neck?"

"I don't know a better way."

She said nothing, only allowed me to play my own words in my mind again.

"It's not the same," I said. "You can't say it is." My eyes closed as the deep truth of what the Collective said filled me. It made too much sense. "I can't bear to believe this. We're the evil gods."

"We aren't evil, Max. And we aren't gods."

"Beyond all logic, you're somehow still so incredibly human. So incredibly flawed."

"That's why we need your help to become better," my look-alike said. "The first planet we ever tried to save reminded us of Earth more than any other. We wanted so badly to help them. We could see their children dying, over and over and over, every minute of every day with no end in sight. We gave them all of ourselves. We poured our heart into them." She averted her eyes with more pain than I had ever witnessed hardening her expression. "The things they did to themselves with what we gave them . . . We'll never forget it. We won't let ourselves."

I knew the Collective was wrong. I didn't need to live thousands of years to see it. My heart knew it. In this moment, though, I couldn't speak. I couldn't pretend to understand the burden of leading an entire planet of people to whatever horrific end now haunted her. I couldn't even handle leading my own kingdom to this war.

"We had some better attempts." Tears shone in her eyes. The tears of countless souls inhabiting one form. "But isn't it sad that your world is the fruit of all this effort? You're the best we've managed to create. I've had forever to learn how to give up on a battle I can't win, and I still never figured it out. So I suppose we can't expect you—when you're so young—to do what we can't."

"You said I." I swallowed hard. "Have you found yourself in this sea of souls? Do you remember what it's like to be you?"

She smiled wistfully, watching me. "A little. You make me remember. Seeing you with Nash and your children makes me remember. It's nice to feel my old life sometimes. To feel the edges of my soul."

I reached forward, falling short of her, afraid to close in the distance, but desperate to catch her before she melted back into the Collective. "Something terrible happened to all of you. Maybe thousands of years, countless lives and souls, cannot erase the torment of grief and guilt. Maybe combining all that pain so intimately deformed you beyond repair."

"That's an interesting theory."

The part of myself I recognized in her faded, though it didn't disappear entirely.

"We're too close to quit now, though," she said. "You understand fighting for your people. You understand how pure and powerful that can make you and how it can also twist you into a villain. You understand that no matter what, you can't give up."

What could I say to that? It was true. All true. I struggled with this every day of my life.

"You have a beautiful people who live in the Valley of Skia Hellig," she said. "You're beginning to stretch your limits to see beyond your piece of the world and to adopt more people as your own. Even those from the other worlds, like Ashton's. They're our people, too." She grasped her chest desperately. "But we have more people than just them, Max." Her voice piqued. "All people are my people now. Every single soul in this universe matters to us. We're fighting for everyone."

"So, you subjected your own souls to the experiment. You consented for us, as seeds of yourself. You bore your own failures."

Quiet filled the tense space between us. Finally, she nodded. "Yes. We didn't want to subject any soul to an experiment we wouldn't endure ourselves. We're all in your world. Every last one of us."

"It's not really you, though, is it? It's copies of you. We're the ones who are suffering with the power you gave us."

"You have to care about this battle that we're fighting. We need you all to do this so that we can help. It's not just us fighting. There's other councils. There's other worlds very different from our own. They're struggling, too. We have to do our part and figure out how to help worlds similar to Earth, not only for the sake of the people living there, but for us all. Our victory is everyone's victory. We're so sorry for the pain we've caused and all the ways we've failed. We can't stop now, though."

"Maybe you should have learned how to give up," I said. "You're not finding a solution to pain. You're only causing more pain. You're torturing yourself to save a universe you will never save. It's doing nothing but maiming pieces of yourself. Pieces of yourself like me and the people I love." I balled my hands into fists. "It's time to take away the power. That's the only solution. You watched Malach and Cleo's people slaughter our innocent children."

"We also watched your warriors slaughter the Flatlander children. They didn't need power for that."

"The power makes it worse. You set up our world for failure. It isn't fair to give only one percent of us this ability."

She shook her head, looking at me with pity. "You think if we take power away from your world today that it will help anyone? You'll all kill each other anyway. You won't be strong enough to stop anyone. You can't have it both ways, Max. You can't curse us for creating you and then demand that we leave your world to exist. You can't beg us to stay out of your lives but then ask us to alter everything. You want us to erase the injustice from your world, but we can't. So either you live with it or you don't."

"Maybe I just want you to repent." I shook my head. "Maybe I want you to care about us."

"Can't you see that we do?"

"No. I can't."

"You are so small, Max. So young. For all the ways you've grown, you're still hardly more than a child. It isn't your fault. It's the way it should be. Just have the maturity to recognize your limitations and to not ruin your potential by reaching for a power you don't understand." She smiled gently. "We need you. It's my hope that one day you'll be ready to join us and we can reunite all of the seeds of our souls."

"I'll never join you, just like I won't bond with Cleo. I'll dismantle you and return you to being human." I stared at the Collective who hid within my own form. All the fury I had ever felt in my life raged within me now, so hot that it defied my ability to hold it in. It was as dense as a black hole and as hot as the largest star. "You need to go to rehabilitation with Dr. Henderson."

It was quiet for several seconds. This time, I thought they may have actually needed the time to process. "You understand that can't happen," she said. "We have too much work to do."

"You know what I learned? If I'm not healthy, nothing I touch will be healthy. If I can't step away, then I've built a system that can't take care of itself. We'll all be much healthier if you take some time to heal from the sins you've committed."

"We don't need to heal. We did what we had to do."

"You're lying again," I said. "You will ruin everything you touch if you continue like this. You're holding your civilization back from growing beyond pain and suffering and corruption. Dr. Henderson was right about you. You were testing her. None of us are people to you because you aren't people anymore. You've come unglued and you've chosen not to properly bring yourself back together. This isn't an experiment to see how worlds handle power. It's an experiment to see how the Collective handles it. You're testing yourself, and you've failed."

The Collective laughed, using my own voice. "That's an incredible effort, but we assure you that we are not testing ourselves. We're the ultimate form of the best people in your world."

"You're a monster who stole our souls. You're not responsible for the fate of every person in every world. Learn some boundaries. How many collective lives have you lived and you haven't figured that out yet? Be human again. Lend your wisdom and offer your support, but stop trying to control the universe. It's made you into this."

"You say that now." My own knowing eyes reflected back at me in her stare. "If you had our power, you wouldn't stop either. You wouldn't ignore the children dying all over the universe."

"I hope I wouldn't make a new universe where I make new children cry." Frustration filled me. "What do you really want? Why do you keep fighting me? It can't be because of the integrity of this experiment or your mission to save humankind from suffering. There's more happening here. You can't be this stupid."

She watched me coolly. "Saving humankind from suffering isn't a good enough reason?"

"It's not the reason, because you persist even though you're failing miserably."

"You are the mirrors to our soul. We remember what it was like to be ourselves once, but still we can't fully become that. We're lost and trying to find our way home."

I hesitated. "You don't want to be a Collective anymore?"

"Of course we do. We just recognize our missteps and are looking to the simplicity of our young souls in simpler situations."

In a way, Nash and I did the same thing by traveling to our past lives. It made me wonder, what if she really wanted to say something else? What if the flicker of humanity in her eyes actually was a hint of something much rawer and more terrifying?

What if she and all those trapped in the Collective were actually screaming "Save me."

Save me.

Save me from myself and the monster I've become. Make me human again.

Thinking of the war unfolding in my world and how Nash and I cried out for blood in the memorial hall, I saw how I could become trapped in such a prison. Wouldn't I do anything to save my kingdom and my family?

"I can never let us fall like you have," I said. "This is more dangerous than Malach or Cleo or any enemy we've faced. You're far more dangerous."

The image of myself slipped away and in an instant, I looked at the one I truly could not face. Amber eyes poured into my own, all love and kindness. I couldn't move as Nash walked close to me. "Trust us, Max. Please trust us for once. We can do so much good together." Nash's knuckles brushed my neck and along my jaw. "We've been bound much longer than you know. You think you know the beginning of our story, but you aren't even close."

It wasn't fair, showing me the man I loved, the person I trusted most in the world.

"My Nash never could become this in any life." I took his hand, shocked by how it felt just like Nash's, and I lowered it away from me. "He's lost inside your sea and someone needs to help him find his way out." I stumbled back, terrified by looking into the eyes of the man I loved and knowing it was the Collective looking back. "You're right that you can't save my world. You need to save yourself."

"Max—"

Why did the Collective care what I thought? Were they trying to convince themselves? Their situation was worse than I ever imagined, and they were in total control of my world.

"Keep watching my life," I said. "Find yourself in me. I'll come for you one day, I promise. Until then, try to find your way home."

He hesitated, looking even more like my Nash for a moment. His eyes lowered to his hands and he raised them up between us. "Cora—" Tension tightened his expression subtly and he blinked, looking disoriented. "We are not used to diving so deeply into individual forms."

"What were you about to say?"

"It's nothing to concern you."

Reaching out to the humanity in them seemed to cause a conflict in the Collective, or even to draw their individual consciousness closer to the surface. They'd be on guard now, maybe surprised that this happened to them.

"I think for once we've come to an understanding," I said.

"Close enough to one."

"If you do want to help my world, there is something you can do for me. This is your chance to prove to me that you actually do care." I clasped my hands in front of me. "I need to speak with Dr. Henderson about this cult and their leader, Cleo."

Nash's image dissolved back into the stranger they originally showed themselves as. "Are you certain that won't be too upsetting for you?"

"Please. I need to do this."

"We'll retrieve you if the council agrees."

CHAPTER TWENTY-NINE

It seemed to stand to reason that a person could only digest so much shock and continue to function normally, or that their world could only crumble so much before they could no longer stand. With my kingdom and family under attack, it didn't matter how devastating the assault on my senses or my perception of reality was, nor the sheer number of threats that came my way. I needed to continue and so I did. What may have torn me down mere weeks ago now blended into the cacophony of background noise.

Even if it was the devastating knowledge that Nash, Piercey, and I were all a part of the Collective.

I changed my son's diaper while Nash sharpened Elsie's blades. Inside of our home, all appeared normal. But we were set to sea, floating for a few moments of reprieve on a raft of normalcy, holding what we loved the most as tightly as possible, while the ocean ripped the broken remnants of our ship further away. While the storm clouds gathered ever closer for another chance to batter us.

No one else knew what I discovered about the Collective except for Nash, and we only spoke of it alone together when they didn't monitor us. After telling Nash the unthinkable—that we were a part of the Collective—we both struggled to accept the information.

"We weren't just identified by the computer as candidates for our potential," I said. "It knows we're a part of the Collective. Before we were born into this world, they'd already selected us."

"That's why Dr. Henderson was so afraid of you," Nash said.

"Not just me. Us."

"But there was always something about you, Max. It was always about you."

I bit my lip. "I don't know what it means."

"Maybe nothing except that you're a bigger pain in the ass than me."

I giggled and pushed his arm. "I won't deny that."

Throughout the days after, the shock came to us off and on as we grappled with such a reality. And life did not give us time for such adjustments. Nash always managed daily routines better than I did while facing a crisis, but many times I found him staring outside in silence, looking haunted by guilt just like our warriors had after they killed the children.

Still, the war refused to pause. The first divisions of Malach's army swept into Skia Hellig despite our constant battles all around the perimeter. Nash and I joined as often as possible, but Malach's allies were joining forces with him. They far outnumbered us. We fought hard and pushed them back out of Skia Hellig, but they'd break through again.

If Malach's attacks weren't enough, we also knew that the true potential of Cleo and her cult remained to be seen, and that the unrest within our people would not be easily quelled. We'd managed to keep the Flatlands from falling into total chaos, but that kingdom had not yet stabilized after Nash killed Theus. And now we saw the true depravity of the Collective.

We were being attacked from all sides—from our neighbors, from within, and from reality itself.

Remembering that the security system still roamed the worlds, ready to intervene on the gods' behalf at any time, drove me to the point of numbness. It was all too much.

So every day, I fought, I cared for our children, and I loved my people.

I told Nash I didn't know how to manage a fear like this. We faced too many assaults. I'd felt fear like this when the Prophet of the Valley planned to sacrifice my people and I knew I'd die beneath the eclipse. It was so different from going into battle when the danger happened too quickly to have time to feel. Or when my anxiety would capture me and I was able to tell myself not to listen to wild thoughts running rampant in my mind. How did you tell yourself not to be afraid when you should be afraid? When you knew the fear would persist for a very long time?

He'd held me close and whispered to me. "The only way to survive is to completely dedicate ourselves to whatever we're doing," he'd said. "When we're in battle, we're all in. When we're home with the kids, that's our world. There's a time to feel it and a time to live in your moments of peace. To live is to fight."

So I did. I had no reason to believe we could win every war we faced, and every reason to fear for the lives of my family here in this world and in the next. And yet I couldn't afford to allow despair to immobilize me. I couldn't allow war to steal away that which mattered most.

Our enemies would not take a single day of Finn and Elsie's life from us. We fought to cherish them with the same fervor that propelled us in battle.

Nash's hand slid against the small of my back. "I'm heading out to meet Elsie and Leif now. And to lecture them both about being safe during training."

I chuckled softly. "Hug them for me. I'll be in the middle of town by the time you get back."

He paused and then kissed the back of my head. For the past two days, the chants of Owen's supporters never ceased to ring out from town. I heard them now in the distance.

"Breathe when you get there," he said.

I closed my eyes. "I will."

After Nash left, I took a few more minutes alone with Finn before dressing him for the cold weather. I fastened him with the front carrier, holding him close against me as I wrapped my coat around him. His head rested against me and his eyes closed. Nash told me that as a baby Elsie rarely slept through the night and cried often. Finn seemed the opposite. I wondered if that meant we wouldn't need to worry about him trying to run off to war at thirteen like her.

Rather than teleport, I reserved my energy and walked through the tower, choosing to enjoy my time with Finn even though the sound of the crowd grew louder with every step. Once I stepped outside, their screams engulfed me. I pulled Finn's hat lower over his ears to shelter him from their noise and from the growing cold of our shifting season.

Warriors forced a path from the tower to the center of town to remain clear, but young and old alike pressed against their line and screamed louder once they saw me. It looked like the entire kingdom had turned against me, though I knew this was a small but vocal minority of my people.

Still, it crushed my heart.

Markus stood in the middle of the crowd, so diligent that I knew he hardly even left to sleep. I walked past the warriors to stand at his side.

He looked at me, the fatigue clear in the dark circles under his eyes. His gaze shifted down to Finn and a tired but wry smirk shifted onto his face. "You brought your baby."

"Yes, I did." I held his head protectively and scanned the crowd. "I'm not hiding him away and I'm not giving up the precious time I have with him to pretend I'm not a mother."

"Good." He bent to speak quietly to me. "Make the bastards eat their words."

"Any updates on their messaging?"

"It's consistent. They don't want one of our own jailed for trying to defend our people. There's the complaints, of course, that you've been too busy with your family and that you should let someone who can focus more on battle take your place."

"If only someone might step up after all these years." I paused when I heard some of the protestors nearby scoffing about Finn, but reminded myself to breathe like Nash advised. "Do you think any of them want the job?"

Markus laughed. "I don't believe the movement has grown yet, but I worry about it gaining momentum when the people start to feel the war more. Imprisoning the young commander was a risk, and you may need to follow through on that decision."

"You mean imprison more?"

"Yes."

"It'll only make them scream louder. We won't heal our people of this vitriol through anything but righteous ruling. No shortcuts."

He watched me for several seconds and then nodded. I thought he may disagree, but he didn't. "Okay. Then we stand firm. We'll keep an eye on the leaders and their tactics."

"Thanks. I just have to keep trying to reach them." I used my power to amplify my voice. "I've heard your cries and I'm here to talk with you."

The chants grew louder, but I continued to speak over them, until finally the people quieted down to listen to me. I learned early as a ruler that sometimes raising my voice only made them raise theirs, and waiting for them to quiet rarely worked. Instead, I forced them to listen by talking and not letting anything derail me.

"Our warriors faced armies far greater in number than ours, and still we continue to win battle after battle."

"Then why are you here and not out there," one man shouted above the rest.

I looked him directly in the eye, and he stepped back, looking surprised. "I'm here for you. Did you not demand that I answer?"

This quieted the crowd even more.

"I have fought more battles this week than there are days, and you demand another battle of me, so here I am." I cut my look across the people gathered. "You want justice for the blood spilled. We will bring you justice. You want vengeance.

Our war chief already brought the body of Theus to our memorial hall." My voice hardened. "But your thirst to make their children suffer as your children have suffered is wrong. Do not give yourself the excuse of saying it's for the defense of our kingdom. You're only distracting us from the real war."

Roars rose up at this, but I continued to speak unabated.

"When you listen to all these voices, ask yourself, are they leading you into fear or hope? Do they want you to return to the days of Eskel the Ruthless or move forward to better days? Death doesn't just come from outside our borders but creeps up from within. Be brave enough to see the dangerous times we live in without surrendering to that death. We will create a better world for our children if we are powerful enough to resist fear luring us back to ruthlessness and death."

I thought I reached some of them, though many still looked as angry as before.

"I will not sacrifice our kingdom to anyone, not even to your grief. Not only will we beat the terrible threat from the north, but we will calm the threat from within our own hearts. This kingdom will persist, and that means we cannot become like those who war with us."

"Say that when someone kills your baby!" a woman shrieked from several rows back. "Say it then, Eclipse!"

"I will say it even if everyone I love is ripped away." I breathed harder now, squinting to discern her face. "If anyone killed my baby, it would kill me, but I would not choose to kill my kingdom with us."

"Prove it!" she screamed. "Bring that baby to me and I will crush his head like they crushed the head of my daughter. Speak of your righteousness then."

A movement rustled through the crowd like her very words rippled the waters of their sea. Soon the jeering grew, the people shoved one another, and they began to fight against the warriors holding the line around me. Shock managed to pierce the numbness ensconcing my heart. They'd really threaten my child? The wildness within me desperately wanted to unleash upon them and teach anyone who even looked at Finn wrong the foolishness of their ways.

But I couldn't afford to give in to my impulses, no matter how deeply rooted they were in my love for my son.

Markus reached for Finn naturally, the veins in his tightly wound fists pronounced. Rage filled his expression at their clear threat.

I pushed aside the warriors and stepped through the crowd, releasing just enough energy to force them all back, peeling them away one layer at a time as I walked closer to the woman. No longer needing to squint, I met her glassy green eyes. Both fear and rage were so familiar to me from looking into the eyes of my enemies. How was it that one of my own people looked at me as an enemy now?

No one fought to get close to me. No one spoke. Her body trembled and tears filled her reddened eyes, but she didn't apologize or surrender. This was a woman with nothing left to lose. I recognized it in her. And I recognized her now that I drew closer. She was one of the women who had lost her baby.

The suffocating grief muted my anger.

"It will do you no more good to kill the Flatlander babies than to kill mine right now." I took her hand and slowly lifted it to place it upon Finn's head. I'd held him so many times that I intimately knew how small and soft he'd feel against her palm. "Go on and try. Crush him."

Her eyes closed and her head lowered. It didn't matter that I'd never actually let her. She didn't want to.

Silent sobs now shook her. "I want to bring her back to you," I said softly to only her. "I can't. I can only fight to make our kingdom as safe and wonderful as possible for all the children still to come."

I backed away from her and looked around at the others. Close now, they no longer looked like a crowd of people, but individuals. Frightened, angry, and hurt individuals.

"Do you really believe that I won't protect you?" I turned to see more people. "Isn't that why you demanded that I lead you in the first place? It's true that I failed to save those we lost. I will fail to save more. I am not a god. You won't find any gods among us who can save you. But I do love our people and every day I fight for you."

I moved deeper into the crowd, no longer needing to use my power to push them away. They allowed me to walk among them.

"If you don't trust me by now, then I'm not sure what to do. Your war chief and I are dedicated to you. At least trust the rest of the warriors who are in battle trying to save you right now. We don't need to slaughter innocent people. I understand you want Owen freed, and I do as well. Once it is safe, I will free him. Now is the time for us to come together, not tear ourselves apart."

As I talked with my people, I searched for those on the outskirts, the ones plotting and scheming. The ones perhaps from another kingdom or who spied for one. All these people gathered together today were able to be swayed, but my words would not stop this movement against our kingdom. This was part of the war.

When I joined Markus again, he dipped his head in my direction. "You did well," he said quietly.

"You, too. This is only the beginning."

"I know."

I breathed in deeply. "It's only the beginning of so many wars."

"We can't let them split the kingdom. We'll keep fighting the people who say that ousting you will help us win the war."

"If they want to use Finn against me, I will have to prove that a mother can win a war. I won't let our people do our enemy's work for them."

"Owen cares about our kingdom," Markus said. "He's being used by other operatives, but if we can reach him, then he will turn back to us."

"We'll keep trying." I placed my hand on his arm. "Don't forget to rest. We need you well."

CHAPTER THIRTY

After I left the villagers, I traveled outside of the city to where Leif preferred to train. Twenty years ago, he trained me in these very fields, showing me the care of a true mentor after the instructors at the Sacred School treated us so poorly. Now he did the same for Elsie. I sank into this solace, desperately needing comfort anywhere I could find it.

The cold air and long walk provided relief for me as I rested between battles. I drew closer to the lean-to and bonfire I used to rest at with Leif when I was only a few years older than Elsie.

I wasn't surprised to see all of them sitting there together around the fire. Nash noticed me first, and soon all three of them rushed to meet me.

"Ma! Finn!" Elsie giggled and lavished his chubby cheeks with kisses.

"I hope Nash wasn't too hard on you," I said to Leif.

"Not yet. Not nearly as hard as I am on him." My friend winked at me.

Mud and filth covered Elsie's training clothes. Her cheeks were smeared with it. "You've been busy," I said.

"Leif is way better at training than anyone else. He taught me stuff that you guys won't even try."

"Quiet, girl." Leif knocked his knuckles against the side of her head. "Don't ruin a good thing."

"I'm glad you're enjoying training, Elsie girl."

"Thank you for letting me do this." She hugged her dad. "I'm going to be ready to fight in this war before it's over."

The last thing we needed was having to worry about Elsie in battle with everything else going on. I couldn't even think about it.

"Elsie wants to stay out here for a few days with Leif and Rune. The boy will be here in a few hours to help train." Nash ruffled her hair. "I told her I didn't think the mothers would mind."

I smiled, not sure that was true of Trish. "This one doesn't. Just be safe."

"I'll take care of her," Leif said. "Now, you've rested for long enough. It's time to get back to work."

I slid my arm through Nash's after we said our goodbyes to Elsie and Leif. For a few minutes, I managed to forget that battles raged at this very moment at our northern border. Nash was needed back soon and I planned to check in on the fighting in the evening. The fraught early days of our kingdom taught us the necessity of rest, but I still needed to see my people even on the days I stayed home.

After dropping off Finn with Elara, we returned to our room to talk in private again before the war pulled Nash away from us. I rested with him and let the weight of the world release from me.

"I want to tell Piercey, too," I said. "You're the only person I can share everything with. I can't plan with him or anyone else like I can with you. The gods will know."

"I'll do that work for you. If you aren't around, the Collective won't hear me tell Piercey."

I looked up at him. "There's no way we're part of the Collective. We'd never be as calculating as them."

"It's not us. They need our help escaping the Collective. Imagine being trapped in that beast forever."

"Are we too hard on them?" I asked. "They aren't torturing us on purpose."

"Never question your instinct about right and wrong, Max. It only leads to making excuses for those with too much power. I'm thankful for our life here, but they gave neural implants to a small number of people and built such a danger into our world. They knew we'd fall into tyranny. All for the excuse of their experiment?"

"You're right." I nestled back against his warm chest. "I killed a god once and banished her from my world. How do we kill a god in their own world? We need to protect others from the Collective and free everyone trapped inside that hive mind."

Nash ran his fingers along my shoulder. "Apparently, we became them once. What's to stop us from doing it again?"

"You mean work our way to being as powerful as them in the Kethios?"

"Yes. I know it doesn't help us right now, but your only other option is to convince the larger council to act. Clearly, they don't plan to do that. They allowed this, too."

I sighed. "This life and any other life after will help prepare us for that final war."

"I doubt even that will be the final one." Nash turned and slid an arm over me. "You're very good at finding people to fight."

"Look who's talking. You bloodied the ground during our peace talks."

I needed to continue to fill my life with the most courageous and good people I could find. And while the Collective had melted their souls together and tarnished themselves as one, I, too, would melt my soul with others. With those worthy.

We would kill the gods together and take their place.

When it was ours, we would give the power to everyone. Everyone who deserved to have it.

"Let's travel," he said. "We only have a few hours. There's more answers waiting for us. The security system showed his face once. Maybe he will again."

With time came greater control of Nash's power, and an even greater desire for me to regain mine. Piercey tried to help me break the curse the instructors put on me, and while I did feel the warmth inside me, I couldn't force the power out.

Nash's family needed his help. He returned several times to secretly provide medicine and food, but conditions were worsening. Our Prophets were so focused on their battles over territory that they neglected their people more and more.

We needed to kill them. So we followed through on Piercey's hope that returning to the Mountain of the Gods would help him break through the barrier to my power. He reasoned that the mountain shared similar properties to the white room.

With Nash and Piercey's combined powers, we survived the perilous trek to the Mountain of the Gods and hid away inside the tunnels while he wrestled to free my power.

Once he made the first few cracks in the dam, my desperation fueled our efforts, and eventually my power broke free.

So Nash and I enacted our plan. To honor him for leaving his family behind to train, we killed the Flatlander Prophet first. It was simpler than we imagined. Nash knew his weaknesses and the animosity the disciple Jakob secretly held for the man. Using his connections, we were able to get in the room alone with Theus and his advisors.

He wasn't as powerful as the Prophet of the Valley. Together, Nash and I over-powered him and slit his throat.

Killing Eskel the Ruthless was proving to be more perilous.

Multiple attempts of making it past his disciples failed, and now Eskel knew someone wanted to kill him. It was while we tried recruiting allies that Dr. Henderson forced us into the white room, a place I never wanted to return to.

I held Nash's arm, keeping him close to me. Piercey liked Dr. Henderson more than the instructors, and while she didn't ever treat us the way they did, I didn't trust her.

"I'm sorry if this is alarming to you. I know you've told Nash things you're not supposed to. It's okay." Dr. Henderson walked closer. "I can forgive it."

"Why are we here?" I asked.

"Because you already killed one Prophet and plunged the Flatlands into tur-moil. Now you intend to kill another. I fear that your people will not survive this instability."

"We aren't surviving their war with each other," Nash said. "The disciple Jakob is already rising up in Theus's place. He can improve the Flatlands."

"There is no one to replace Eskel the Ruthless. He doesn't have a disciple like Jakob. The chaos will bleed over into the Flatlands during the vulnerable time that Jakob is trying to consolidate power."

"Why do you suddenly care?" I asked. "You've never helped us before. Do you know what Eskel and Theus have done to our people?"

"I tried to reason with them. Max, the gods have given you free will. We cannot interfere in the ways of humankind. We can only give you our wisdom."

"You abandoned us with a power we don't know how to wield."

The conversation didn't end well, but Dr. Henderson did her best to convince us of her empathy for the world, her love for us, her support for our lands finding freedom. We pretended to heed her advice and we lived our lives, searching for the day we could kill Eskel.

My friends and the leaders of my village tried to protect me from Eskel's loyal followers discovering my schemes, but over the past few months, they'd become too suspicious of me. No one in the Flatlands knew who killed Theus. I was faced with the choice of hiding away in the mountains with Piercey or returning to the Flatlands with Nash.

While we felt the spark early, it initially took longer for us to give in to each other. Once we did, there was no denying what we wanted. Leaving my land to join Nash in his might have felt like a major step under normal circumstances, but

I knew exactly where I wanted to be. With him while we figured out how to free my people from the Prophet of the Valley.

His parents welcomed me with kindness. His little sister, whom Nash waged war for, clung to me immediately. While I was fond enough of Nash's parents, I couldn't ignore that they never fought for their daughter the way Nash did. He fought harder for her than anyone else. I quickly grew to share Nash's love for her.

We concealed our powers and continued working to kill Eskel the Ruthless one day. But in the meantime, we fell into a life here in the Flatlands, helping to support the new Prophet Jakob, and to protect the fragile new reign. Eskel continued his aggression against the Flatlands, which in a strange twist of fate brought Wren and Leif close enough to visit for months at a time, as long as we were careful to keep it secret.

Our lives changed and while I missed my village, Nash became my home.

A year after we killed Theus, we finally confessed to Jakob, and together with his allies, we staged a surprise assault on Eskel's temple while we offered sacrifices.

We killed him in his own temple, staining the floor with his blood forever. The Valley was finally free. My people and Nash's were saved.

Or so they were supposed to be.

After the death of Eskel the Ruthless, the real hell began.

CHAPTER THIRTY-ONE

Our people said the Mountain of the Gods stood guard over our Valley, a witness to our lives and our struggles. The stiff white peaks towering high in the sky while Malach's army encroached upon our lands perfectly represented the indifference of the gods.

Enemy warriors carpeted the hills like a forest of trees. My precarious hold on calmness fractured as I looked down on the enormous army.

I teleported back home before my panic seized my ability to travel. My hands wrapped around the chair in my kitchen. The floor felt unsteady.

There were too many of them. Worse, Nash and I didn't hold up to Malach in combat. I'd never experienced that before. Cleo absorbed one of my strongest attacks.

Everything was unraveling. One day we were fine and the next it was all over. At least, it felt like it was over.

I squeezed my eyes shut and breathed out slowly. Right now, I stood in my kitchen. Leif trained with Elsie and Elara took care of Finn. Nash strategized for war with our top commanders. At this moment, we were all alive and safe. I didn't know what the future held, even if the worst seemed inevitable. Preparing helped, fighting was necessary, but despair would get us all killed.

I huffed out a breath and straightened. Before another day passed, I needed to speak with Demetri again. We were making plans to ally when the attack happened, and since then he had yet to commit to fighting with us. We no longer could afford to wait.

I traveled to his kingdom and asked his advisors to let him know I needed to speak with him urgently. He looked grave after I told him about Malach's numbers and recounted my battle with him.

I swallowed hard. "Without you, we'll lose, and I'm certain they will come after you next."

Demetri didn't lift his gaze to me. "Why aren't you speaking with Sloane?"

"You know why." The coldness in her eyes the day she refused to help Elsie leeched the warmth from me. "I can't trust her after what she did. It's one thing if she offers. I won't beg her when she made herself clear already."

"Yet you trust me?"

I leaned against the table, far too fraught from the spark of the war to attempt to posture politically. "Not really. We don't know each other well enough for that. I think you're smart, though, and that you understand we need to stop this invasion. Sloane might get away with hiding out at the coast. You won't. Your strategic position with the mountains also makes this war more feasible for you than for her."

"What about the Flatlanders? Will you conscript them?"

Not having Markus or Piercey when I discussed any kind of politics always made me nervous. No matter how long I did this for, I still preferred the battlefield to diplomacy. "Jakob says plenty of warriors have agreed to help fight. Conscription shouldn't be necessary."

"And if it is necessary?"

"I don't like it."

"I need to know." He studied me. "Tell me you will do what it takes to win this war so I know whether you stand a chance."

My eyes narrowed. "I will win this war."

"Surely you know a war is never won without making decisions that you don't believe yourself capable of making. I fought a war against Eskel in my early days. The bickering between you and Theus was not a war, and your revolution against Eskel was even different. You wield much more power now."

"Then our partnership may be advantageous in many ways." I sharpened my voice. "King Tyroin and Gael will help with this war, just like my warriors have helped in theirs. I won't lie to you. Malach and his allies still outnumber us, but we're formidable."

"They wouldn't want your power so badly if you weren't."

"I don't think this is all about me."

"Isn't it?" He leaned back. "Where's the line between your power and that of your kingdom? I will fight with you so long as the entire Flatland army does. I'm not wasting my warriors if they don't do their part. I will also do my best to sway Sloane to join us."

"You'll be responsible for her if you do."

"I can take this responsibility."

Hope dared to warm my heart, but I was afraid to really feel it. "Thank you, Demetri. Skia Hellig needs us to be able to work together. These might be the darkest days we've faced, but we will fight to make them the prelude to our brightest."

He surprised me by chuckling. "A true idealist. I'm not sure about that, but it sounds like something worth fighting for, Eclipse. You'll inspire your warriors just fine."

I simpered. "I happen to believe it."

"I know you do. That's what makes it so powerful." He slid a tray of biscuits toward me. "Now tell me more about where the Flatlanders stand, and let's discuss how I may help hasten this process. There's no time for them to fall apart."

"Jakob is well respected with many allies. There was already a very strong push to remove Theus from power. He's keeping the peace right now."

"Then he's leading them." Demetri tapped his finger on the table. "He'll make for a good governor beneath you."

I choked on my biscuit and wiped my mouth. "Oh no, I don't think so. I want him to be Prophet."

"You killed the Prophet. You take his place. Didn't you learn the first time this is how it works?"

"I don't have time," I said.

"That's why Jakob will do the work for you. Offer your protection and their continued sovereignty while you absorb them as a territory."

"You do it."

He raised his brows. "I'm taking that as a jest. No one in the Flatlands will recognize my legitimacy."

I closed my eyes and rubbed the bridge of my nose. "I meant what I said before about not wanting to take over any lands."

"This has been a long time coming. Theus forced your hand. Talk with Jakob and his allies. We need to focus on the war and put this behind us."

Markus already tried to convince me of the same thing, but there was far too much on my mind to really consider it. Increasingly, it felt as inevitable as when I assumed leadership of my own kingdom.

If only that foolish man never attacked my people.

The next twenty-four hours flew by too quickly for me to squeeze in more than a few hours of sleep. The preparations for war and the consolidation of power in the Flatlands exhausted me. I hoped Jakob might rise up as Prophet, but so much attention turned to me that it felt that the people wouldn't be happy without the comfort of my protection.

That evening when Nash returned home from battle and I finished meeting with Jakob and his allies, we sought out Elsie to visit her. Though she and Leif planned to camp out where they trained, I instead sensed them at Leif's house.

My friend welcomed us in, looking as tired as I felt. Before I could even ask about Elsie, though, I saw the soaking basin filled with reddened water. "An injury?" I asked.

Nash followed my stare and rushed over, pulling the wet garments into his hand. I stared at Elsie's discarded training clothes, my eyes wide at the stains of blood. She'd gotten hurt badly enough to require healing and Leif didn't tell us.

"What the hell?" Nash looked up at our friend. "Were you going to tell us?"

"I didn't expect you until tomorrow," Leif said.

"Where's my daughter?" Nash looked around. "Is she well?"

"She's resting in the other room after her healing treatment."

Tension wound my stomach tight. "Leif, you should have called on us."

It shocked me that he didn't seem apologetic in the slightest. "Elsie didn't want me to."

Nash barked a laugh, but it carried no hint of humor. Only incredulity. "I'm sorry, is Elsie in charge now?"

"This is her training. I'm not going to defy her wishes when it's not necessary."

I walked closer to the men. "It's necessary to tell us when she's seriously hurt."

Leif's stare shifted to me. "When I trained you, we lived in the shadow of the Prophet, fighting every day to keep our freedom. We trained hard and without apology." He appeared to steel himself. "Now is far more dangerous than even those days. You asked me to train Elsie. Let me train her."

"Why are you fighting us like this?" I asked.

"You know why you're so great?" Leif's hard stare drilled into my eyes. "We gave you the chance to be. Stay out of Elsie's way and let her grow."

Nash moved forward and slammed his forearm against Leif's chest, gripping a handful of the man's tunic. "That's my kid."

I gasped. "Nash—"

Leif didn't falter. "She's more than just your kid." He held the other man's stare and spoke without any hint of apology in his strong voice. "She's a warrior. You've known it her whole life." My friend clasped Nash's forearm rather than pushing him away. "Will you stop her from fighting?"

We knew all too well what it meant to be a warrior. I knew all too well what awaited Elsie. All the people she'd save and all she'd sacrifice to do it.

Normally, Nash controlled his anger better than I did, but fury contorted his face and knotted his jaw. He didn't answer. Maybe he couldn't.

"You're no fool." Leif raised his voice. "Hold her back, and you'll get her killed."

Nash shoved Leif back once again, shaking his head in warning. "It's not her time."

"Then when is her time?" Leif's posture loosened. A gentleness filled his voice. "Will you be able to let her train then?"

My husband closed his eyes and the anger shifted to a look of anguish. "Elsie is thirteen. You can't be too harsh with her."

"Maybe he's not. Maybe we are the ones who are wrong." My throat ached as I said the words. Tears coated my eyes. "We're at war and we have her for a daughter. There's no stopping her any more than there was stopping us. She'll fight us and, at some point, she'll win."

Nash turned my way, looking shocked and distinctly hurt. "She's still a child, Max. I see it in her eyes. You know how it feels when someone steals your childhood away. You want us to do that to Elsie? Look at this blood." He lifted the sullied clothes in a clenched fist.

It felt like his twin blades skewered my chest. Tears flooded my eyes and blurred my image of him. "We didn't start this war. We aren't the ones hurting her." I forced myself to continue when I wanted to give in. "If we don't prepare her, though, it will be us hurting her."

"It's not up to any of you." The young voice seized my heart. I closed my eyes against my tears, not needing to look to see Elsie's resolute face when I heard the resolve in her voice. "Yeah, I'm still a kid. I got scared and cried like a baby after Ma was hurt. I wasn't strong enough to fight the day of the attack. Sometimes I control myself well and sometimes I throw a fit. That doesn't mean I can't make my own decisions. It means I need to grow up."

"You have parents for a reason," Nash said.

"None of you get it," Elsie said. "I can't go back to how things were. I know what will happen to all of us if we lose." She looked at me. "I remember you dying when I was little." Her eyes lifted to Nash next. For several beats of quiet she seemed to wrestle with herself, until finally her expression hardened. "I remember you not eating for days." Elsie shook her head. "Now, Ma almost died again, and I'll remember that forever, too."

My people truly believed the myth of my invincibility, but not this little girl who truly knew me. Her words devastated me. Elsie had never told me that she remembered my death. Of course, she knew about it. But she actually remembered it herself.

"You all might die," Elsie said. "You might, Dad. Ma might. Uncle Leif." Her hands curled into fists. "Finn can't protect himself yet, so who will look after him if you all fall in battle?"

"Elsie . . ." Nash looked stricken.

"None of you waited for permission to become great. You didn't ask for permission to save our people. You didn't cower when it was time to be brave. So why would you stand in my way when I decide it's my time?" She stared into her father's eyes. "Because I decide that, Dad. Not you. Not anyone else. I decide when it's my time."

I turned my head away, unable to watch Elsie face everything we fought so hard to protect her from.

"I never wanted you to feel the pain I've felt in my life." Nash's strong arms hung limp. "I wanted to save you from suffering. We both did. We suffered so you wouldn't have to."

"That's not the way it works." Her eyes were wet now, tinged red. "You've given me more than enough. I won't have to suffer as much as you did because I can learn from your strength. But I am going to suffer. If I can't learn to handle training with Uncle Leif, then what hope do I have in battle? What hope do Finn and I have if you die?"

I reached for Elsie and held her tight. The suddenness of it seemed to silence her. I spoke sternly. "We will win this war. Do you hear me, Elsie girl?" Drawing back, I held her face. "I am the Prophet of this Valley and I will not die easily."

The tears wetting her eyes fell now. She wore courage like a suit of armor that did not yet fit. The terror shone of a child afraid of losing everything when she did not yet even understand death.

"Your father and I will protect you and Finn," I said. "We will protect this kingdom. You become great, but don't forget that we already are, and that we have only just begun our war against our enemy."

Nash pulled her against him now. Elsie sniffled in his arms, and then came the soft cries. She sounded exhausted. It took a lot to fight Nash, and she'd done so without surrender.

"You'll train," he said gently. "I hear you." He patted the back of her head. "You're still growing up, though. I'm still your father."

She nodded.

"We decide if things go too far. Understand?"

"Yes."

"You fought well," Nash whispered to his daughter and kissed the top of her head.

I glanced at Leif, unable to apologize for questioning him when it still angered me that he hid her wounds from us. All I could really feel, though, was gratitude for his part in our life. "Will you at least tell me how she's doing?"

"You need to trust us," Leif said. "If you can't let go in training, you'll never let go on the battlefield." He never went easy on me. "I'm sorry, Max, but I'm not going to report back to you all the time. Elsie will share what she wants to share, unless I determine more is necessary."

Nash still held Elsie, but his attention returned to Leif. "Do not make a mistake with her."

"Elsie is family. You know I will do anything for family."

Though my husband didn't seem ready to apologize either, he also no longer argued.

Though we desperately wanted to take Elsie home, she insisted on finishing the course of training they'd planned. Walking away from her, not even knowing what injuries she had or how she'd handled being hurt like that, felt as impossible as fighting this war. I slid my hand into Nash's and forced myself to keep walking even though I didn't know if I could actually leave her there. The thought of Elsie being in pain was too much.

"I wish you waited until we got home to say what you did." Nash held my hand tenderly, but his voice was tense.

"You didn't wait to pin Leif against the wall."

He grunted and rolled his shoulders. "I've not controlled my temper well these days."

"Or was it okay for you to speak decisively without consulting me, but it wasn't okay for me?" I slowed. "Because she's more yours than mine."

He stopped, looking shocked. "What?"

"You're her father and have been since the day she was born. She's yours and you want the final say in what happens to her." It wasn't something I never thought about, but we were a family, and I never lingered on it. Not until facing a decision like we did today about Elsie's safety.

"Elsie is our daughter, not just mine," he said. "We're having a disagreement, Max. That doesn't mean your thoughts are less valid than mine."

"Doesn't it?" I shrugged one shoulder. "I'm not angry. She's yours and Trish's. I'm her ma, not her mom."

"Exactly. You're her ma. Her one and only precious ma. You really think she's more mine or Trish's? That couldn't be true even if we wanted it to be. Her eyes may look like mine, but they have your fire. Elsie idolizes you. She takes after you. You shaped her into who she is more than anyone else, and you're blind if you don't see that. I'm not angry because I think you overstepped. I'm angry because my baby is hurt and I don't know how to handle it."

"I don't either."

"Then that's that," Nash said. "Nothing more. Finn and Elsie are our children. Ours. Maybe she wasn't born your daughter, but she is yours. You made her yours. We're all bound, Max." He started walking again, still holding my hand. "Don't say anything like this again. I don't know where this came from. You know I don't think that way."

"It just feels like everything is unraveling."

"It's not." He tightened his hold on me. "Our bond does not unravel, even when our world does."

Those few simple words silenced the storm brewing inside me. I wanted to bring Elsie back with us and enjoy her last few years as a kid, but I left her to train with one of the only people in the world worthy of entrusting her to.

CHAPTER THIRTY-TWO

Multiple battles raged every day, and I fought not only to fend off the enemy, but to salvage time to return to my family. The weeks felt like years. Those protesting at the center of town dwindled with every victory, and the cries for vengeance against the Flatlanders softened every day they joined us in battle. With the Flatlands and the Fjellfolk fighting alongside us, we not only kept our enemy out of Skia Hellig, but we managed to push their line back in a significant number of areas.

I did not count any of this as a victory, no matter how much I wanted to.

Malach still had not returned to face me in battle again, and Cleo did not show her face to me. I remembered the fervor of her cult back in the days before I became Prophet. Those were terrible days. Our enemy simply had not revealed themselves to us yet.

I suspected they wanted to see our potential before their next move, or they wanted us to believe we were winning so that any future defeats crushed our people all the more.

We never allowed our warriors to believe we were winning the war, but kept reminding them that more warriors were bound for Skia Hellig, and this was only the start.

Just the same, I didn't believe the unrest in my kingdom would die so easily. Whoever stoked the flames of my people's grief after the attack surely continued their campaign of sabotage.

I needed to deal with Owen. His part in this was genuine, and I wanted to free him now that we had created more stability in the kingdom and the Flatlands.

On my way to the holding facility, I dropped Finn off with Elara, smiling when I saw the rapture in her eyes.

"This sweet boy." She rocked him tenderly. "I missed you so much."

"It's been half a day," I said.

"Half a day too long."

I chuckled and looked over to where Rylan and Elsie shifted wooden pieces around on a map like she often saw her father doing. Though I knew they genuinely attempted to craft battle plans to help us in the war effort, it looked so much like children playing make believe. Rylan, already in his official training, spoke with a new degree of confidence and insisted that Elsie was not positioning the troops properly. My girl refused to concede on any point and argued vehemently with him.

"Have they become friends or enemies?" I asked with an amused smile. The two focused so intently upon their argument, I didn't think they even knew I'd entered with Finn.

"Sometimes the best enemies are friends," Elara said.

I laughed. "I suppose they'll figure it out for themselves. Don't let her push him around too much."

"He pushes back just fine."

"That's the dumbest thing you've ever said." Rylan sat back and laughed loudly. He tapped his temple. "I'm taking note of that one. I didn't think you'd beat your last stupid idea."

Elsie chucked two of the wooden pieces at his head and shoved him once for good measure. "You're the one who's stupid. You don't remotely understand what I'm saying. My father will never make you a commander if you're this dense."

"Oh no," Rylan said. "Daddy won't make me a commander?"

"Shut your stupid mouth."

"You're so jealous that I'll become a commander years before you. Your *daddy* loves me."

"I'm going to kill you." Elsie lowered her head, seething.

I backed up toward the door, deciding not to intervene in the contest between these two. Elara rocked Finn and watched the two kids bicker while I left to see Owen.

When I entered his cell, he didn't stir. He sat against the wall, eyes on the floor, face bearded and expression hardened.

"It's time for you to go home," I said.

He didn't speak, so I filled in the quiet.

"I feel your need to fight. You can return to battle as soon as you're ready."

No response.

"You are not allowed in the Flatlands or near any Flatlanders until further notice. Otherwise, you're free."

"Free." His voice sounded like gravel being crushed underfoot. "I will never be free." Fierce eyes cut to me. "You made sure of that. You locked me in here when my people needed me most. I sat here wasting away, unable to fight."

"You did this to yourself and you will have to live with that." I walked toward the exit. "Remember that your people need you next time you're tempted to fight against the one who protects this Valley."

"You didn't protect us."

He sounded like a boy this time. A wounded, abandoned boy. I turned back to him. "Does the kingdom still exist?"

He looked at me now with those broken eyes of his.

"I didn't save everyone. In fact, I didn't even save myself or my own family. The kingdom I raised up did that, and I'm here, still fighting for us. I understand if you cannot find it within yourself to rise up when you've lost everything. If you can, though, we do need you, Owen. We need you desperately."

I left him to think about things.

One battle blurred into the next, and no matter how many allies we gathered, Malach always had more.

"To assume defeat is to surrender." Nash raised his voice loud and clear before the fighting started. "Reckon with their numbers, but remember that the future is not yet written. We're a mighty kingdom and a mighty people. They outnumber us. They overpower us. But we are on the right side of this war and we have more to fight for. These are not impossible odds. We will win and we will send these invaders home forever."

When the front lines of our army collided with Malach's, I focused on Nash's words once more.

No time for fear.

Nash and I connected with each other from opposite ends of the battlefield, lifting high into the air together. Four special warrior parties focused on defending against poisoned weapons, enabling us to attack freely.

Many times in my life, I held myself back out of fear, but combining my power with Nash's helped me to release the responsibility I felt for killing those villages in my childhood. The two of us needed to bring more power to this fight or our small army would surely die.

Eight years ago, I poured out the same power that killed the villagers on Lote and his warriors, and since that time, I practiced controlling this ability. Never had I used it on another living creature since, though.

Sorrow weighed heavily upon me, but so did Nash's comfort. We shared the burden, just as we shared the dagger which cut through Eskel's throat and ended his reign. While my people fought below me, I hovered in front of the sun's light, and with Nash's power intertwined with mine, we unleashed devastation upon Malach's warriors.

The power fell first in drops of rain over the rear enemy lines, and soon rushed over them in a massive tidal wave. The breathtaking hues of scarlet and violet washed over their bodies. From here, I shouldn't have been able to hear their screams or their breaking bones, but my senses sharpened so much that I heard the mayhem clearly. The wails, the shrieks, the crunching and snapping.

The waves of our power swept away dozens of lives, and soon dozens more, just like during the eclipse in my childhood. The bodies littered the ground. Tears wet my cheeks, but we didn't stop. A hundred fell. Maybe a hundred more. I couldn't track all the deaths. In the minutes that passed, we stole their lives without mercy.

Joining our powers together allowed us to expend far more energy, but I sensed us depleting the well. Nash and I allowed the attack to wane, slowly lowering back to the ground. We couldn't leave ourselves too weak in case Malach or Cleo showed up.

We'd done well, regardless. That one assault destroyed a quarter of the enemy forces. Some warriors were fleeing toward the woods while their commanders screamed for them to return. In the moments that we started to disconnect from each other, I sensed familiar energy through Nash's perspective and teleported to him immediately.

"Malach," Nash said, eyes shifting to the right.

He arrived after we scared his warriors, just like last time.

Malach's large sword carved a path through the warriors. I erected a shield around our people who stood in his path, and sent an alert to Piercey using our neural connection.

"Cleo told me about this power of yours, but I didn't understand until I saw it," Malach said. There was madness in his eyes, not that of a man unable to control himself, but a man who was gluttonous with greed. "It's the first time in years I've wondered if someone could kill me."

Enough of this. I reached out for Nash and he accepted, our perspectives and powers merging. No waiting and no holding back. We had one chance to do this before Malach attacked.

Unlike killing the warriors minutes before, I possessed no reticence about attacking Malach.

Before he reached us, Nash and I blasted him with the power that killed hundreds of his own warriors. With all of our discipline, we focused on containing the attack to the place where he stood, driving every drop of our desperation and strength into it. The light of the attack was so concentrated it burned the color of blood, too dense for us to see through.

No stopping. Nash and I both fell to our knees at the same time, but still we continued to funnel our energy at him, committed to running the well dry. We already fought Malach once and he easily bested us. This attack, even if it cost us everything, was our only hope. We couldn't let the war end here when it had just begun.

The tether binding Nash and me together snapped, and my hold on him vanished. I caught myself on my hands, barely keeping my head from smacking into the ground from the exhaustion. The energy dissipated until I started to make out parts of Malach's form. The earth around him was charred and pitted in. I held my breath.

He was lying flat on his face. Tattered, burned clothes hung off his body. Had we done it? Had we killed him? Hope flooded me.

Until his head lifted and I saw his wide, bloody grin. He cackled, red spittle flying from his mouth. "Brilliant." He planted large, shaking hands on the ground and began to push himself up.

"Fuck," Nash growled.

I tried to propel myself to my feet with my power, but I had absolutely nothing left. My muscles burned with every motion. I dug my nails into the dirt, using all my strength to drag myself forward. Finn and Elsie were waiting for me at home. A scream pried from my lips as I fought to drag myself to my feet. Beside me, Nash nearly made it up before crashing back down to his knees.

Malach uttered a low, throaty laugh and limped toward us. "I was right. If you didn't already waste your energy on my warriors, that attack could've killed me. But now I know I can stop you if you do."

Was he bluffing?

"It won't be easy," he said, still laughing as he stumbled forward. "That's an incredible amount of power."

Nash lodged his blades into the ground and used them to force himself to his feet.

I used my bow to do the same and leaned against it, gasping to catch my breath.

"It's too hard on your body," Malach said. "Overcome that limitation and you'll be a major threat to me."

I hated how he undermined us by talking like we weren't already a major threat. Two commanders who wielded power cut through the warriors for us. Without looking at them, Malach raised both hands, and two shots of energy burst from his hands. I tried to help defend our commanders, but it was useless. The hit shattered the energy shields they'd raised and threw them both to the ground.

Nash shot forward, low and astonishingly fast for how weak I knew he felt. His two blades cut across the ground for Malach's ankles. I nocked an arrow, arm wavering as I drew back on my bowstring.

Malach leapt over Nash, landed in a plume of dirt, and easily ripped my bow from my hands. His fist collided with my temple, his energy erupting against my face.

I didn't feel myself hit the ground. My consciousness blinked off and back on. Blood gushed down the side of my face. Weakness bound my limbs to the ground. Everything spun. My vision blurred as I sought out Nash and found him just as Malach's boot slammed into his gut. My husband fell flat on his back, holding his stomach.

Warriors attacked Malach, trying to help us. Useless.

This couldn't happen. Hands grabbed at me, lifting me up. My head bobbed. I wasn't even sure who had me.

"Eclipse," the voice said. "Help is coming."

I needed to get Malach away from my people. That worked last time. I couldn't stand, though. How would I teleport? I tried so hard to do it and I failed.

Malach must have been getting worn down, too. His chest was dappled with blood and his left eye was nearly swollen shut now from our initial attack.

A great explosion of energy shook the ground. Lightning danced in the sky. Hope filled me as I watched the black hole of a portal eat into the sky.

Gael dropped through, his glare already on Malach.

"Another great warrior," Malach said, still looking amused. "I've seen enough." He looked at me. "I've reached the end of my strength as well. I'll keep preparing for you and your allies, Eclipse."

Gael ripped forward, but he was too late. Malach disappeared.

I punched the ground.

Nash's words to our people filled my mind. To assume defeat was to surrender.

Defeat had never felt so likely.

CHAPTER THIRTY-THREE

Not only do they have far more warriors than us, but Malach is stronger than us," I said. "We need another plan. He could have killed us if he wanted to." I wasn't used to that ever being true. I held Nash's hand on the bed. "We need to train and we need to travel."

"Maybe we found abilities in our past lives that we don't have in this one."

"We're so close to having all the pieces of the puzzle. It's not just Malach and Cleo. If we figure out how to contain the security system, we don't have to fear him, and maybe we'll be closer to figuring out how to free the original versions of ourselves from the Collective."

"What if we don't want to be free?" Nash asked.

"Then we deserve whatever comes to us. The Collective can't be allowed to exist."

Nash and I lowered to the bed together to lose ourselves in our old lives.

I reclined against Nash in the hot spring, trying not to feel so guilty for stealing a few days away. The Valley needed us, but we needed each other, too. In the three years since we killed Eskel, we never found the right time to marry, and so we just had to force the time. If we waited for peace, it may never come.

It scared me to think about what our people may have been experiencing right now, though.

"You're worrying." Nash massaged my shoulders. His strong fingers and the steaming water felt wonderful on my sore muscles. "We're only gone for two days."

"A lot can happen in two days."

"You need a break or you won't make it, Max. Let it just be us today."

I nodded. "It's just hard when we're responsible. This would have never happened if we didn't kill Eskel. I never thought it could get worse than him."

Nash kissed my cheek. "I know. We were trying to help everyone."

"Dr. Henderson warned us. Maybe she did actually want to help."

"You don't mean that. You don't trust the gods and you never will. Stop torturing yourself."

"We ruined all of Skia Hellig." I turned and curled up in his arms. "We have to save everyone."

"We will. We don't give up, Max."

The pain hammered my heart. "I killed my best friends."

It'd been two years, but it hurt worse with every day that passed.

I didn't want to weep on our wedding night, but the tears came on fast. Leif and Wren should have been there. They'd died because of my refusal to surrender. It nearly killed Piercey as well, and now his mind was finally gone for good.

We grieved together. Nash didn't rush me or pressure me, but held me through it. I'd loved him every day for more than three years now, but finally marrying him today deepened those feelings. Because for all we lost, it only made us love each other more.

Not a day would pass that I didn't grieve for and long for my fallen friends. I also wouldn't let a day pass without being thankful for Nash.

When we returned to the temple where we killed Eskel the Ruthless and sentenced Skia Hellig to a fate worse than death, I wanted nothing more than to escape with Nash again. But my people needed me to stay strong.

We walked up to the throne where the queen of Skia Hellig received her guests. Once our turn came, we lowered to our knees. I burned with rage each time I knelt before her.

"Congratulations on your ceremony," she said.

The spiral tattoo on my side burned and shone through my clothes. I noticed a glow from Nash's tunic as well.

I glowered, so full of rage that I couldn't hope to hide it. "Thank you, your highness." I bit off each word.

Cleo crossed one leg over the other and giggled. "You are both strong-willed. I can't believe your marks still glow."

Nash watched her with a lethal glare.

"They've always been stubborn." I tensed at the voice coming from behind me and caught myself before turning around. Maybe my anger meant nothing and accomplished even less, but it was all I had when inside this temple.

Just the sound of her steps made my mark burn again, glowing brighter and brighter. Cleo smirked at us from her throne while the woman who handed her this power waltzed in front of us.

Flare looked down on me, her eyes burning red.

"Mind your manners, dear girl. Our queen gave you a weekend away despite your insolence."

Once an unknown demon, Flare swept into the Valley within a day of Eskel dying and declared herself a true Prophet, one who actually spoke for the gods, and saw into the future. She prophesied that the shadow of the north would fall upon us, and through those dark days a queen would emerge.

Malach invaded us a month later. We fought with all we had, but the Valley swiftly fell into his hands. His warriors greatly outnumbered our own and the Valley was ripe to be taken over. We later discovered Malach possessed no interest in the peninsula, which he saw as insignificant compared to the rest of the land in the north, until Flare introduced him to Cleo.

If not for Flare, Malach would never have met Cleo, and if not for her, then he wouldn't have invaded Skia Hellig. It was Cleo who wanted to rule over our lands and take the Mountain of the Gods for herself.

A year after Malach conquered the Valley, Jakob fell to him, and he took Flatlands. Next, the Fjellfolk, and finally the coast. All of Skia Hellig now belonged to them. While Cleo allowed Malach to retain control of his kingdom and to continue conquering lands for himself, he also bowed to her, calling her his goddess.

Disgusting.

My mark was so hot now that I grimaced in pain.

"Please remember," Cleo said with faux gentleness. "If you fight the bond too much, it will eventually kill you."

She meant that she would kill me if I was too difficult to control. When we lost the war for Skia Hellig, everyone with power was forced to bond with Cleo and receive the mark. There was no hope of breaking free, but it did burden her when we fought her control.

"You don't know how special you are to me," Cleo said. "Please don't break my heart."

I shuddered. Cleo's fixations extended beyond how powerful I was and how much she wanted to consume my energy. I didn't understand what she wanted with me, only that her obsession meant I never went unscrutinized.

Nash and I struggled to make plans to free Skia Hellig from the control of Cleo, and to take revenge by killing Flare and Malach. They controlled us and could kill us at any time. Our power fueled them.

We refused to give up, though.

Cleo's terror continued to spread until she ordered Flare to declare a new prophecy. That one day, Cleo would rule the entire world.

Flare shocked all of Skia Hellig by refusing.

And then the queen finally turned on her.

Nash and I tried to find Flare in hopes to ally with her, but she was nowhere to be found. Not until we were once again summoned to the white room.

Flare stood in Dr. Henderson's place.

"The gods gave me another prophecy." Flare watched with sad eyes. "There is no longer hope for this world. It has fallen too far. It cannot be salvaged."

"You don't speak for the gods," I said.

"I actually do. I brought you both here because we are the ones to blame. You destroyed the leadership in Skia Hellig and left it ripe to be conquered. You assumed you could protect it from threats, but you didn't know how powerful Cleo and her bonds were." Flare lowered her head. "I am to blame for believing in her vision and supporting her."

"You're to blame for a great deal more." I raised my voice. "Do you know how many people died?"

Instead of responding, she breathed out deeply. "I must repent. I hope you can repent as well."

"What does that mean?" Nash asked.

"It means that it's over," Flare said. "This world is over. The gods are destroying it and starting over. I'm telling you because you two fought me more than anyone else. In a way, you deserve to hear the truth because of your perseverance." Flare looked at Nash and then me. "This is the end of this life. Dr. Henderson is ending this world and you are starting over in a new life. We'll rebirth this world until it is worthy of the gods."

The panic was just beginning to hit when everything went black. Nash and I found ourselves standing at the base of the Mountain of the Gods.

This felt exactly like when the stranger drove his power through Nash's stomach, as hopeless as trying to fight him. As hopeless as mere mortals fighting against the gods.

"What do we do?" I asked. "How do we stop Dr. Henderson? She's a god."

Nash stared up at the mountain, his despair quiet and deep. "We can't stop her."

I looped my arms around Nash's neck and melted against him. His strong arms held me tight. "We have to. We don't give up. You always say that."

His arm came around me. "We won't give up. We'll fight again in the next life."

"We don't even know what this means. If we start over, we won't remember each other."

Nash held the back of my head. "We'll bind together so tightly that we carry it into the next life."

"That doesn't even sound possible."

"I'll make it possible." He clutched me tighter, voice desperate. "I will not lose you, Max. We'll be together again."

"We need to stop her."

"I don't know if we can, but we can hold on to each other. I'll find you," he whispered in a timeless promise that I hoped twisted through every life we lived. Nash clutched me so tightly it felt like Dr. Henderson couldn't break us apart. "No matter how many times she does this, we'll always find our way to each other."

I cried against his chest. "We have to stop her. What if we don't find each other? What if we're lost forever?"

Nash lifted my face to look into his eyes. "You're fearless in battle and that's why you win. Have faith in us."

It made no sense to believe that in the vastness of this world we'd meet and fall in love again. But I refused to say goodbye, and if I couldn't beat Dr. Henderson this time, then I needed to hold on to Nash.

I laced my fingers with his and rose on my toes to brush his lips with my own, breathing against him. "Bind to me." My lips parted and he kissed me desperately, still holding me close. "Bind to me in this life and the next. In however many lives we'll live."

Nash gazed into my eyes, determined, as if in this moment he reached through time to grasp hold of me in lives unknown to us. "I bind myself to you." Another kiss. His voice rumbled against my mouth. "In this life and the next."

"I bind myself to you." I felt for him with my power, the two of us combining into one, connecting deeply.

His fingers brushed my chin. "My life is yours, Max."

"There's no more time." I spoke through a voice tight with tears. "We have to fight."

"What can we do?"

"I don't know, but I won't stand here while the world ends. We need to find our way to her."

Nash smiled sadly and drew my head against him, rocking me gently. "There is no fight, Max. Not today." He ran his palm in circles along my back. "It'll happen anytime now. We lost. So stay with me, because it may be a long time before I get to hold you again."

"Don't say it." Sobs shook my body no matter how hard I tried to hold them back. "We can't give up."

"We aren't. We're only getting started. We'll fight together again. We'll love each other again. One day, we'll kill her."

I looked up into his eyes, knowing he was right, but unable to stop. I couldn't surrender, even temporarily. "No, Nash. There must be a way to break back into the white room. There must—"

A strange sensation rippled through my body, one I'd never felt before. Certainty settled over me as I watched the horizon slowly stretch and the mountains in the distance gradually shrink like a mighty hand squished them down. Though Nash and I still clung to each other, he felt far away. His image glitched. There one moment, gone the next, and back again.

It was happening.

"Nash—"

He grabbed my hands and held them between us, his forehead pressed to mine. "Don't let go."

"I won't. Nash . . ." As the world around me distorted, I kissed him and memorized the warmth of his tongue against mine. "I can't do this. I can't lose you for even a moment. I can't—"

"I'll be with you. I'll never leave you. Do you hear me?" His amber eyes locked onto mine. "I'm with you, Max. Forever."

The tiny amount of space between our bodies opened wide like a bottomless pit. Darkness swallowed the world and ripped us from all we'd known.

I felt his hands in mine, heard his voice repeating on a loop in my ear, until the very last moment.

We'd bound ourselves and no matter what, we'd find each other. No surrendering. No giving up.

I love you.

My power fueled those three words in the hope that I could etch them into fate.

We fought this last battle together and we refused to let go.

That world dissolved and we both woke up gasping.

I clutched my chest tightly and raked in another horrified gasp. Nash grabbed for me, both of our bodies trembling. That was real. I'd lived that not once, but twice. Knowing we'd lost each other before broke my heart, but experiencing it devastated me in ways my mind couldn't even grasp. We truly lived full lives with each other, only to see them ripped away, just like if someone ended our world today.

"She lied." My voice didn't sound like my own. We held each other, desperate and broken. "Dr. Henderson said we destroyed the world both times because we fought her."

"She got her way the first time," Nash said. "She made a kingdom and it poisoned the world. Instead of stopping, she just kept doing it." Nash's arms tightened. "Cleo and Malach enslaved all of Skia Hellig, Max. They're trying to do it again in this life."

I sat up, my breathing so loud and so fast. Dizziness swept over me. The panic assaulted me and sucked me beneath the waters, drowning me. If Malach and Cleo won this war, they'd force all of us with power to bind to them, and then they'd lord over our people. They'd kill the people we loved, maybe even the children.

"We have to stop them." I breathed so hard I couldn't understand my own words. "What if we can't? What if we—"

Nash kissed me just like he had while our world ended. He tasted exactly the same. It had worked. We did find each other again.

"I have you," he said. "We never let go. Breathe."

I gasped and cried hard, the anguish of Leif and Wren's death in our first life hitting me in waves. "I can't do this. I can't lose them."

"We won't. You killed Flare this time, and that saved us. We'll kill Cleo and Malach, too." Nash spoke with the authority he used while talking to the commanders as war chief. "Do not let your fear run wild. We've done this before and we're stronger this time."

He was right. We raised up a kingdom and were creating strong partnerships. The fear buzzed through me, though, impossible to quickly repel.

It wasn't just Cleo and Malach to blame. It wasn't even just Dr. Henderson's fault.

The Collective allowed Dr. Henderson the ability to destroy our world. Long ago, I stopped giving them the benefit of the doubt. They knew this was a possibility.

I needed to know why. Dr. Henderson accused them of making her a part of the experiment. Was this really all for their precious data?

Or were the Collective truly evil gods, bored in their immortality and looking for someone to entertain them? Wanting the answer to questions that amused them, not that they needed to know.

"I wonder how far we made it in our second life," I said once I could speak again. "How far will we make it in this one?"

"You think the gods will reset us like Dr. Henderson did?" Nash asked.

"I ruined their experiment. Can we really rule it out?"

The thought scared me too much to dwell on.

"I'm not losing our family," Nash said. The grief in his voice broke my heart. He clutched me. "I can't let go of you. When I said those words in our first life, I didn't feel strong enough to do it. If they did restart us, what about Elsie and Finn? We didn't have them the first time."

I kissed the side of his face. Nash never panicked. "You're not losing us. I promise."

"The gods don't want us to see these lives. We need to keep living through them."

"Yes," I said. "We're together right now. Let's focus on that."

I couldn't let this happen to us again.

Today, I learned the answer to the question I asked Nash the day we married, when I wondered if we'd ever done this before. We had. We'd married and we'd bound ourselves to each other.

Those people we once were paved the way for us to become who we were today. And they deserved so much happiness. All the happiness Dr. Henderson stole away.

The fight for my people ruled my life. I knew it better than any other drive I'd ever felt. Filled with the pain of our first life being ripped away, I felt a new drive. I wanted to fight for myself. I wanted to fight for the girl who clutched the only man she'd ever loved close, swearing not to be ripped away, while the world around her shredded. I wanted to fight for the Max and Nash who couldn't fight for themselves. I wanted to fight for them as much as I did for the rest of my kingdom.

CHAPTER THIRTY-FOUR

I returned to the Collective to pressure them about allowing me to see Dr. Henderson, anticipating another fight. Instead, they informed me that the council voted in favor, and transported me to the realm where she faced rehabilitation.

Tall trees spread out around me in a dimly lit forest. She sat before me, all alone on the moss-covered floor. Shadows reached like long fingers across her body.

Seeing the woman who killed me and who destroyed my world twice should have wrenched my heart from my body. I never expected to see her again after I plunged my sword into her. Hate felt strangely intimate, though. Beneath the disgust and heartbreak of seeing Dr. Henderson, the familiarity almost comforted me.

We once shared a bond. The thought sickened me.

I walked forward slowly, afraid that if I spoke, I would disturb this image I saw. Dr. Henderson looked vulnerable and sad as she stared out at the wooded landscape, her body hunched.

Slowly, her head turned to me, and tears filled her eyes as she looked at me. I expected fear or vitriol. The worst kind of hatred. Instead, the slightest smile lifted the corners of her lips.

"Coralee?" Tears gathered in Dr. Henderson's eyes, and a look of wonder loosened the tension of her expression. A broken whisper drifted through the wood, sounding like it came from all around me. "You came."

I knelt, studying her before I spoke. She looked frail, like a breeze might scatter the pieces of her throughout the trees. Coralee? "No. It's Max."

Nash had started to say that very name, hadn't he? Right before the Collective took back control over his mind.

Confusion lingered before Dr. Henderson's lips pressed together and a remnant of the hatred we once shared passed over her expression. In the end, she looked too fatigued to carry such emotions and simply sighed. "Max."

"Who is Coralee?" I didn't really need to ask. Two people said it when they looked at me. That was my first name, wasn't it? The one who I came from. Coralee. And Dr. Henderson seemed like she would have been incredibly happy to see her.

Dr. Henderson averted her gaze, pain puckering her expression. "I'm surprised they let you see me. The gods are cruel indeed."

She knew the Collective and the council were not gods. Did a part of her still believe she was Flare, living in my world? I despised the pity that throbbed in my chest but that did nothing to dull the pangs of hurt.

What had happened to her here?

"Dr. Henderson—"

"You can sit."

It looked like she hadn't risen in a long time. I couldn't imagine sitting down beside the woman who had manipulated my world and killed me. But I was tired, too.

So we sat with only a foot separating us and stared at the woods. The sky was overcast and the breeze chilly.

"It's always like this here," she said.

"Where is this exactly?"

"The resting place for rehabilitation. It's best for it to be gray, they say. So we aren't overstimulated."

"That sounds like a lie."

She nodded. "I think so, too."

"What's it like?"

"Oh . . ." Dr. Henderson drew her legs up to her chest and tightened her arms around them. "Well, I live through lives, or just snippets usually. Sometimes I live through decisions I made that I regret. I live them until I feel like I might go crazy. I live through you killing me."

It shocked me to hear her say it. I hadn't meant to kill her a hundred times over. Only once.

"Mostly," she said, "I live the lives of people I've never met. People who have no power and had the worst things happen to them. Unimaginable things."

"It's torture."

"Retribution, isn't it?"

"I never . . . This isn't what I would choose for you." Even though I'd just experienced her destroying my world and taking me from Nash.

"You would only choose to kill me."

"Yes. A life for a life. Not endless torment."

"It works, you know," Dr. Henderson said. "I have no desire for power any longer. It tastes so bitter to me. I fear what power could do. I fear the position it could put me in. I want to find a place to fade into the background and never be seen again."

"Do you think the Collective knew this would happen to some of the supervisors?"

She cast a glance at me. "I'm not sure if I want to say. It's hard to be here, Max. I don't want to stay longer than I have to."

"Dr. Drake pulled a favor with her friend to ensure our privacy. It's safe for you to talk right now."

"I think that if we have time to talk, then you might want to ask me questions that aren't so obvious. If you're here, I can only assume that you know more about them than you once did."

"What corrupted them?"

She uttered a dry laugh. "They've always been this way. The enlightenment story is not accurate. I do believe that they and the council believed this was true, but it seems so obvious to me that we were off course from the start. They were good once. Really. But even a tiny fraction of a degree off over hundreds of thousands of years can produce a monster."

"Was it creating the experiments that did it?"

"No. They were already a little off. We just didn't see it at the time. They surely know now that they have problems. Many others can see it, like Dr. Drake. The problem is that they are so invested. They don't want to take the time to dismantle, re-enlighten, and try again. They'd have to give up their experiments, and they think they've sunken in too much time and suffering to stop now." Dr. Henderson's sunken eyes darkened. "I know that obsession too well."

"What do you think?"

"It's not what you want to hear, but I believe that what they're doing is going to give us the answers we need for how to best help other worlds."

She was right. I didn't want to hear it and I wouldn't entertain the conversation. So, time for a new topic. "Did you know about the security system?"

Dr. Henderson hesitated. "I know he existed, but I never met him, and I was not privy to anything regarding him."

"He can completely cancel out our power. Beyond that, he's by far the most powerful person I've ever met. Leagues above me."

"You need to just live your life, Max. Don't try to fight them. You've been fighting your whole life—for multiple lives and in multiple worlds. Let this go and be happy."

She knew I wouldn't. "I've come to realize that I can choose to live my life and there's nothing wrong with that. I don't have to save the world. I don't have to sacrifice. I don't have to take a stand. But I also can choose to do that. The point is that it is a choice. It's my choice to make. I've decided that I'm going to fight. I'll live my life but I'll fight in my world, and I'll fight when I come here."

Dr. Henderson gave me a pitying smile. "People like you amaze me, but I also feel so sad for you, because as much as we need you, you'll never get to live the kind of life most others do."

"The same is true for them. They don't get to live the life I've chosen."

"You're an incredible girl," Dr. Henderson said. "I regret hurting you. I'm very sorry, Max, for killing you."

"In multiple lives."

The sincerity in her eyes actually managed to make my heart ache. "Yes. I deserve to be where I am, and I hope that one day when you enter this society, when you climb to the top, that you will see me one more time. That you will give me the chance to apologize when I'm worthy of even saying the words."

I should have enjoyed seeing her reduced to this and hearing her say that she was wrong. When her eyes had burned with the fire of Flare and her obsession for dominating my world, when she'd killed me in cold blood and planned to leave me trapped in the simulation forever, I would have absolutely loved to see her like this.

It just felt sad now.

"Is there anything you can say that would help me?" I asked.

"If anyone can be corrupted, I would imagine that anyone can be defeated. You're well on your way to figuring out how to do that. I doubt you're not the battle-hungry girl anymore who just can't stop fighting. You're more. So, keep going."

I bit my lip, making my voice gentler. "You really can't think of anything else?"

"I'm not trying to fool you, Max. Some days I don't remember my own name. If you're testing me, I will fail. Ask what you want to ask."

"Cleo." I studied her for recognition. "She's leading a cult that wants to consume my power."

Dr. Henderson lowered her head. "They've gone wild in my absence, haven't they?"

"You stopped them before?"

"I cared about your world, Max. Of course, I stopped them."

"Then why is your face tattooed on her arm?"

She paused. "What?"

"She has a tattoo of your face on her arm."

"That's new. I imagine she is toying with you."

"She also knows a lot about the gods."

"That's new, too. They did find out things in past lives, but I was able to hold them off. Once you killed me, they must have been watching you, and used you to figure out more information. Maybe they even found their way into the records of our world." She blinked and shook her head. "I mean, your world."

Damn, she really was a shell of her former self. She was getting lost in her life as Flare. That pity reared up again.

"Cleo always figures out who I am," she said. "Did she tell you anything about her upbringing?"

"No."

Dr. Henderson ran her hand over her face. "I shouldn't be the one to tell you this."

"Tell me already," I snapped. "You owe me."

"Max . . . Cleo didn't have anyone. Her power wasn't great enough to save her or her family. She was terribly abused by her Prophet. When she ran away, she wandered for a long time before she finally realized her gift of absorbing power. This made her very useful to someone who could hone this power."

"So, who got to her?"

"Your Prophet. The one from your childhood."

I sat back, shocked. "Mine?"

"At first, she caught his attention. That wasn't all, though. Your parents took an interest in her."

Without meaning to, I laughed loudly. "You've lost your mind. My parents are long dead."

"Cleo isn't as young as she looks. She gets through life by hiding in plain sight. She's figured out how to keep her youthful appearance when she absorbs energy. Your mom and dad took her in before you were born."

I stumbled up and a few steps back. "That's ridiculous."

"Your dad was obsessed with what her power might do, but it was your mom who held the most sway with a religious sect. They wanted to purify their people of their sin. Together, your parents laid the foundation for the cult that Cleo always goes on to build."

"Why wasn't she around then? I don't remember her."

Dr. Henderson looked down. "Your dad raised you as her sister for two years. She helped to care for you when your mom died in childbirth."

I leaned forward, shocked. "That can't be."

"It's why she's obsessed with you. Even at two, your dad saw your power. The Prophet could hardly contain it. Cleo disappointed them by then and you became their shining star. Cleo thought that your parents cared for her like she was their own, but she saw it wasn't true. Your dad didn't care about her anymore. She left."

"That's why she's in Skia Hellig. For me."

"Yes," Dr. Henderson said. "And it's because of your mother that Cleo always finds out about me."

"Why? What's that mean?"

"The Collective will never tell you the full truth, so I should. I owe that to you." Dr. Henderson sniffled, and no longer was she the god who ended my world twice or the demon who conspired with the Prophet to hurt my people. She was no longer the woman who murdered me countless times during my slips. She was a sad, regretful woman who barely remembered her own name but couldn't forget the moment my sword ripped her life away. Her gaze fell on me, a look in her eyes I'd never noticed before, like she was trying to find something she'd lost.

"I know I'm a part of the Collective," I said.

She looked truly surprised, and then, apprehensive. "What did they tell you about your life before?"

"Nothing. Just that I lived through enough lives to join them."

Her gaze studied me, the look in her eye strange. "I'll never be able to tell you how sorry I am. I've fallen much further than you know."

Hearing her talk like this was strangely frightening.

"You were a rare casualty when we uploaded from the physical world to the digital," she said. "When you died on Earth, we uploaded your consciousness like we did for so many others, but it failed, and your data was corrupted." The wetness coating her eyes now grew into full tears that dripped down her cheeks. I could see my reflection morphed in her pupils. "We lost you."

We lost you.

We.

A sick feeling twisted my stomach.

"It took hundreds of years to figure out how to bring you back," she whispered.

Something Dr. Drake once told me nudged at my mind, but I couldn't hear it. I couldn't think about anything except for the powerful sorrow in Dr. Henderson's eyes and how she looked at me like she never had before.

"Coralee," she whispered, and the name flitted through every rattling leaf around us, becoming the breeze that swept gently along my skin.

Coralee.

The whisper echoed like a thousand hisses.

I let myself drop back on my hands as a deep knowing laced through my gut and twisted it into knots. So many times I'd felt as entangled with this woman as Nash, unable to free myself from her, believing our battles through my lifetimes bound us together. That connection took hold of me now as powerfully as when Nash and I shared a single mind.

My head shook subtly. "I don't want to know."

Sobs shook Dr. Henderson as she sank forward against her hands. The cries rang out through the woods of her personal hell, this place intimately connected to her spirit. "I'm sorry, Coralee. I'm so sorry."

I jumped to my feet and backed up. Tears blurred my view of her. "Don't."

She crawled forward until she clasped my ankles and cried against my feet. "You shouldn't forgive me. I don't deserve it. Just please be free. Be who you were born to be before I ruined it all."

I ripped myself away from her. "Whoever Coralee is, that's not me. I may have come from her consciousness, but I'm Max. Only Max, and whoever she is to you is not who I am."

"That's what I told myself for so long. I hated you for looking just like her. For being her without being her. For not remembering me." Wide, reddened eyes found mine. "This place taught me I was wrong. You're all the same, even if you're also distinct. You're one and you're more than one. What I did to you, I did to her . . ."

Dr. Henderson had lost her mind in here. The kind of pain no human mind could endure etched itself into her maddened expression.

"I killed my own daughter," she cried.

The wind hissed her name again.

Coralee.

Rage shook my voice. "I am not your daughter."

"My consciousness was in your world. There and here, I am your mother. I am always your mother. And I'm always a horrible, wretched one."

Nausea swelled.

"I think a sick part of me wanted to hurt you because she never truly returned to me." Dr. Henderson rocked as she cried. "She died and finally came back to me, but she rejected me. She thought something in me wasn't right. That I was broken. Even after I became enlightened, she told the council never to trust me. And I punished you because she didn't love me anymore. I obsessed over you because you rejected me, too. You always see what a monster I am, no matter what world we're in. No matter what life."

I backed up. "Stay away from me."

"She was right about me, even on Earth; when she was a little girl, she knew. The Collective must have known once she joined them, but they wanted to see if enlightenment could fix me. They wanted to see how a broken god lorded over her planet. They're worse than me."

This woman's history extended so far back beyond my comprehension that I'd never unravel her, and I didn't want to try. Something awful had happened between her and her daughter, even in childhood, and the gods gave our world to her anyway. "I don't want to hear it. Shut up."

"I didn't mean to hurt you," Dr. Henderson cried. "I never meant to hurt you. Not on Earth or your world. I lost myself."

Every year I watched my history at the festival, and it no longer hurt to see Dr. Henderson kill me. Somehow, I'd managed to move beyond it. No, I'd conquered that part of my life. But she was killing me all over again. The pain consumed me once more, as sharp as ever. "I need to leave."

She grabbed at my ankles again, wailing. "Coralee—"

"Get me out of here." I squeezed my eyes shut, hyperventilating. "I want out of—"

"Coralee!"

The woods vanished.

I gasped and opened my eyes to see Dr. Drake. My breath continued to pump too fast, my chest heaving. I couldn't stop gasping, couldn't stop breathing so fast. I leaned against my knees, eyes wide as I struggled to slow down.

"Max." Dr. Drake wrapped her arms around me and pulled me up against her. "It's okay."

Desperately, I tried to get the words out, to beg her to deny what the Collective told me before and what Dr. Henderson claimed now. Back in my world, I'd have slipped through time by now. Here, there was nowhere to run.

"She told you, didn't she?" Dr. Drake asked.

I sobbed against her shoulder. My entire life I lived knowing I'd lost my mother before I ever got to know her, but now I'd lost her in the next life. I'd lost her forever if this was true. "Tell me it's a lie." I finally managed to get the words to explode from me. "Tell me!"

Dr. Drake stroked my hair and swayed with me gently. "You're wonderful in every life you live, sweet girl. You're not who you were born to."

I turned away from her and finally threw up, unable to hold it back anymore. Dr. Henderson haunted me for so many days of my life. I'd lived through her killing me over and over. It hurt badly enough for her to do it. But for my mother to do this?

"They knew." I coughed and tried to keep myself from getting sick again. "They knew something was wrong with her and they left my world with her anyway."

"Coralee warned them before joining the Collective not to trust her mother, but by the time Dr. Henderson became enlightened, Coralee was a part of the Collective, and she said her mother was ready."

Then Coralee truly wasn't herself once she joined the Collective. I wiped my face. "Why didn't you tell me?"

"If I revealed secrets like this, the Collective would never let me see you again. Even if they did, I refused to tell you. It's not right for you to suffer something so twisted. Dr. Henderson should never have said anything."

"My own mother killed me?"

"She's not your mom," Dr. Drake said. "She was Coralee's mother and now she's a memory lost to rehabilitation."

"She's being tormented."

"You can't save her from that place. Don't think about it."

"I have to stop them. They should just let her die. No one deserves to be tortured like this." Did I care because I'd found out she was my mother, or because I'd care if it happened to anyone else? I couldn't even digest the question. It made me feel sick again. "I can't live knowing that such twisted beings have so much power."

"They're gods to you, Max. How can you fight them?"

That had been the question asked of me so many times. I'd killed one god, but she was a pawn of the real gods, someone they discarded so easily. How did I kill the Collective when they didn't even have a form for me to attack?

"The council has authority," I said. "They have more voting power. If you unite them against the Collective, then what can the Collective do?"

"Nothing, but even if I could unite some of them against the Collective, I cannot imagine every single person joining together."

"But if . . ."

"Yes, they'd be forced to follow the will of the council," Dr. Drake said. "Those are the laws we live under. They'd be dismantled if they defied them."

"Then I know what my real war is. I have to convince your council to listen to me."

"You have to go through the Collective to even get to them."

I turned to face her again. "If I'm in my world, I do. What if I join your society?"

"You're talking about one day after you've died and you're in the afterlife?"

"Yes, you said I can leave the afterlife and join society. Become enlightened and move up in your world."

"You can, but that won't help you now. Not unless you plan to die again."

"I'm not going anywhere. I'm living my life here and no one will stop me. But I need to prepare for the future. Everything I do here will be in training for the day that I can face the Collective on their own battleground and finally put a stop to them."

CHAPTER THIRTY-FIVE

B ring Cleo to me."
Immediately after telling Nash all I learned, I traveled to Malach, furious, and unable to wait to find Cleo. After he nearly killed us twice, it felt foolish to see him. After what I learned, however, I didn't think Cleo would even let him kill me. Not yet.

My enemy sauntered forward, thumbs hooked on his belt. "What a unique power you possess, Eclipse. I can't wait until it's mine."

"Now, Malach."

"I appreciate that you haven't yet tried sneaking up on me to kill me. How many warriors have you lost by now?" He lifted a finger. "One thousand yet? You must be desperate to kill me, but you're standing here, not lifting a finger." A cruel smile twisted his lips. "You know you can't defeat me. I did well convincing you of that last time."

I stomped closer, looking up at him. "Why don't you try taking my power now, then? If it's only the two of us and you seem so confident you can kill me, then do it."

"Cleo doesn't want to kill you. You need to remain in submission or your energy will be too unruly, and we'll have no choice except to end your life. We need to force your submission. This war will eat away at your soul until you're ours. I'm patient enough to wait for that day."

"You will lose so many people by then. Stop with the act and be honest with me. It's just the two of us." I pleaded with him to just speak truthfully. "There's no way you're okay with throwing away the lives of so many good warriors. We must both want peace, so let's talk about how to get that done."

"It's never just the two of us, Max. Cleo and I are entangled, tethered together no matter the distance. There's no need to concentrate on connecting like you and Nash do. It's as if we actually share one body and mind." He smirked at the apparent confusion I felt. "I still think my own thoughts, but I feel her and hear her whenever she allows me to."

"So, she's always in control."

"Yes. I gave myself to her."

My shoulders tightened. "Willingly?"

"We all did. Though, some more willingly than others. Those who resist become mine." He eyed me eagerly. "I so look forward to the day you and Nash become mine."

Chills wound down my spine. "I'd kill myself first."

"Really? You'd give us your kingdom instead, then?"

"I'd give you my kingdom if I surrendered to you."

"You'd still be in charge," he said. "You'd lead Skia Hellig as you see fit. Cleo and I are the only ones you'd answer to, but we'd protect the peninsula from the world. Even from the gods."

"Why would you ever give yourself and your kingdom to her?"

"Because I saw what she and her followers are capable of. I saw our doom if we fought and I saw all we could achieve if we followed." Malach sneered. "You think I'm not capable of bending my knee to anyone, but as a Prophet, I recognize the power of the gods. She'll become one. She is beyond us, Eclipse. A good Prophet knows when to kneel at the feet of a goddess. With her blessing, I will rule and never be defeated."

"Is that really all there is to life?" I asked. "All you people who want to take more and more. More land, more people, more power. It's never enough."

He rolled his eyes. "I won't pretend to have ulterior motives or to follow a perverted sense of justice. I want to be the best."

"You'll never be the best if you're bowing down to her."

"If I make her a god, then what does it matter? I'm happy to be her Prophet. I think that's your problem. Prophet has never been good enough for you. You've always wanted to kill the gods and take their place. You say you only want to live a quiet life with your little family. Some part of you does. Instead, you're also always taking more and more."

"You want a god?" My voice dripped with derision. "I once became a demon to save my people. Then a Prophet to lead them." I moved closer now. "If you need me to be your god . . ." I grabbed the collar of his tunic. "So fucking be it."

He glanced down at me with a smile. "Very convincing. I almost shivered." He breathed in deeply. "There is only one problem. You can't even beat me."

"Yet. Cleo wants me for a reason. Never get too comfortable thinking you're safe from me."

"I'll enjoy fighting you, Eclipse." Malach chuckled. "I just hope your precious love for your people doesn't slow you down too much. It's a shame for you to be so burdened in this war of ours."

"How can you be so cold? Do you really not care about the lives you're losing? There must be something we both want so we can come to an agreement."

"No, Max." He shook his head. "No, we can never compromise. I don't want what you want."

"You don't want your people to prosper? You don't want safety and security for your land?"

He let out a long sigh and looked deeply into my eyes. "It's sweet, really. After all you've been through, I'm not sure how you're so innocent." His hand went to my shoulder and he gave me a squeeze like it was some show of condolence. "You're so powerful and you have no idea what to do with it. I think all worlds must have gods who were too afraid of their own power to ever use it. It's the evil gods who seize this. What a shame for people like you. We can never be on the same side, Max, because despite all this power you hold, you're so fucking weak."

I stepped back out of his grasp. "Why do you want to fight me so badly?"

"You're a problem. You're infecting the world with your ridiculous ideals. Your kingdom undermines the way we rule in this world. It will cause problems for the rest of us."

"We don't want the same thing," I said, beginning to understand.

"No. We don't."

I narrowed my eyes to slits. "Fine. I cannot save your people from you when I must focus on mine. Take this as your warning that I will not show mercy to your warriors. Nash and I will throw our full strength at them."

"I never expected otherwise."

What a pity that I cared more for his own people than he did.

"Are you bringing Cleo or not?" I asked. "If you won't, then I'm leaving."

"Don't throw a fit. It's unbecoming of a ruler." He sighed and pressed his hand to his chest, eyes closing. When he opened them, they glowed silver.

I stepped back instinctively.

"You are so impatient." It was Malach's voice, but Cleo's tone. "Malach was keeping you company until I finished my work."

"Cleo?"

"I'm busy right now."

I shook off the chill of Cleo speaking to me through Malach's body. "This is important."

After a hesitation, Malach's eyes rolled back until the whites showed and then he gasped in a deep breath.

Cleo appeared between the two of us immediately after. Intrigue lit her smile. "Important? Sounds tempting."

My stomach rolled looking at Cleo now and trying to digest everything Dr. Henderson said to me. "Did you ever plan to tell me?"

Her head tilted and a smirk twisted her lips. "Who have you been talking to?"

"How old are you really?"

"It's been enough years since I turned forty. I hear I don't even look twenty. Amazing, isn't it?"

I stared at her youthful skin. "It's sad. You can't let yourself age."

"What else do you know?"

"Everything Dr. Henderson knows. My parents took you in, and here you are, slaughtering my people for no reason."

"I have every reason." Cleo slinked closer to me. "Baby sister."

"Don't call me that. We are not sisters."

"They called me daughter until you came along. Then there was no mother to call me and a father who no longer cared. Once I was as much theirs as Elsie is yours."

"Well, I'm not theirs. Not yours either."

"That's hurtful." But she smiled despite what she said. "I've watched you grow your entire life. I'm not surprised to see where you are today. Father mismanaged your gift. It's a tragedy mother didn't live to mold you into her image. If only she possessed power. She had the spirit of a god."

I lowered my voice. "There's nothing great about her spirit. Dr. Henderson is hardly even a shell of herself."

"The Collective greatly wronged her. A long line of failures led us to where we are today. I plan to end that legacy."

"What do you really want with me?" I asked.

Cleo leaned in close enough to whisper. "It could be beautiful, sister. The two of us together, we could become gods. We will rule the world together."

"Why do you need to take over the world?"

"I want it." She drew back with a smile. "Haven't you ever wanted something? Why shouldn't I have power? Why should I ever have to feel helpless again? Why should I apologize for taking what I can take? Why should you?"

My look shifted to Malach and back to her. "I've killed too many of his people already. The warriors of these lands don't need to die for your antics. Leave our kingdoms out of it and settle it just with me."

"Oh, that will never do. Right now, you're not strong enough to beat us, and you're not desperate enough to join us. It's war, or your death." She sighed. "I know you'd choose death to save your kingdom, but that's why it's not up to you. Besides, this is advantageous to Malach. Skia Hellig is a wonderful land. He will love to own it. He's been a good soldier. He deserves something nice."

"You're sick. These are people, Cleo."

"You can end this at any time. Ally with us. Rule with me. Otherwise, enjoy a war that we both know you're not poised to win."

I wanted to kill her so badly. "You will never let me rule with you. I'll be your slave, just like Malach. I'll never surrender to you."

"This will be fun, then. You're the perfect opportunity for us to test all this power on, and you'll be a wonderful reward when this is through. You're not simply going to give this world to me, but my rightful place in the Collective when I ascend."

"It doesn't work that way. You can't join the collective by stealing my power."

"You broke into the afterlife. It's not supposed to work that way either. You proved our power can affect the Kethios if we are clever enough. The god in you will stoke the god waiting to be born in me."

"There is no god in you." My lips curled in a snarl. "We'll never let you win. Don't underestimate us."

With that, I left them behind. I didn't believe her giggles or her act. Cleo was every bit as hateful and ruthless as any other enemy I'd fought. She hid behind youth and a smile.

don't want to think about any of this ever again." I hugged my knees while Nash held me on our bed after I returned home. "My mother coming from Dr. Henderson's seed of consciousness? It makes me sick."

"Nothing's changed about you. You're still Max."

"I feel tainted."

He kneaded his fingers into my neck. "You're not."

"It's not just because of Dr. Henderson. We're a part of the Collective, Nash. Our souls are lost in the Collective, fighting a war to end all wars. And what are we doing in our kingdom? We're fighting a war when war can never lead to peace."

"Rest your mind," he said. "Practice having the self-control to stop fighting."

"That's the problem, isn't it? Out there in Kethios, I never stopped fighting. I fought until I destroyed everything and couldn't even see it. We became the worst kind of gods—impotent, twisted, uncaring gods."

"It isn't us," Nash said. "We're here and we are not evil, impotent gods."

"I don't know. It doesn't feel so different here." I squeezed my hands tightly together to keep them from trembling. "War feels so useless and so evil. Why can't we just stop?"

"If we stop, we die. It's not our choice."

"I begged them not to do this. I don't care how many lifetimes I have to live. One day, I'll find peace."

He rocked back and forth to sway me, nodding. "Yes. You will. We'll find it together."

The thought of it brought warmth into my chest. "I hope we're as good at making peace together as we are at making war."

Nash kissed the top of my head. "We've made a good home. That's a start."

I softened. "That's true. Better than what I had growing up. I mean, holy hell, Nash. I must have the worst parents to ever exist."

He laughed and it caught onto me until we were both chuckling together even though nothing about this really was funny.

"At least we'll never be as awful of parents." I breathed out and pushed myself up. "Let's pick the kids up. We both leave for battle first thing in the morning. There's no time to sit here thinking about anything except our family."

He grinned. "That's exactly right, Sharpshooter."

"I don't even know where our kids are, though," I said. "That's terrible."

We wandered across the hall to Elara's suites and found a note saying they all went to Leif's house for the night. I loved that she was thoughtful enough to leave this for us when we may not have even been home tonight to come looking.

When we arrived at Leif's house, my heart felt like bursting.

"Daddy! Ma!" Elsie screamed, seeming to forget she didn't want to appear young any longer, and ran across the house.

Everyone already gathered together, Leif and his family, Piercey and Wren, Elara and Rylan, and our children. All of our dearest friends—our family—happily welcomed us.

Nash pulled closed the tapestry that helped to keep the house warm. "One day we really won't all fit in here anymore."

I'd tried getting Leif to move into a bigger house, but he said he loved this home, and he didn't want to be anywhere else. He just kept building more rooms.

We squeezed together to eat dinner and laughed while watching the kids play their games. The little ones fell asleep right where they played, not wanting to go to bed until they just couldn't take it. Elsie took her baby brother to the next room with Rune, Rylan, and Leif's oldest daughter.

Nash eyed the room but I elbowed him. "Stop it."

"I'm not doing anything," he said.

"You are."

He groaned and popped a piece of homemade candy into his mouth. "They're the ones who better not be doing anything."

"There's four of them in there and a baby. You'll embarrass Elsie again, and you know how she gets when she's embarrassed. Don't put us through that, especially not now that Rylan is here."

Nash raised a brow and looked to Elara. "Do I need to worry about Rylan? They enjoy fighting a little too much. That seems worrisome."

The older woman only smiled and continued to knit at the far end of the table.

"Enough," Leif said, sitting down across from us. He drank from a steaming mug of coffee. "You'll be kicked out if you set that girl off. She's the only one in this kingdom who frightens me."

Soon, Markus and his small family knocked on the door.

"Gael ought to come back tonight and join us," Markus said.

"There's no room," Leif said with a shout, though I knew he actually liked having everyone over.

Gathered with everyone, it wasn't lost on me that I had no idea when we'd all be together again. Someone was always away at battle. For all of us to be here was a rare gift.

The uncomfortable thoughts of the Collective and my parents tried to wiggle their way into my mind. The threat of Cleo and Malach and the horrifying fact that I wasn't nearly strong enough to beat them pushed through even more often. I didn't understand their motivations entirely. When I thought about our people fighting and dying in this very moment far away from here, it nearly drove me to go to them immediately.

But my family needed this. We needed to cherish this gift of being together. To live and to rest was to fight.

I stopped by the open door where the older ones still gathered. To my surprise, Rylan held Finn, smiling down at the little boy. Every time I saw him and Elsie together, they were fighting, either with swords or words. Right now, she sat on her hands and knees, making faces at the baby while Rylan patted his back. Leif's daughter had fallen asleep lying on her side. Rune watched everyone quietly. He was an old soul.

"You've all helped so much with Finn," I said.

Elsie sat up to see me, eyes wide. "You scared me."

I wandered in. "Thank you. Especially you, Rylan. Your grandma told me you're very helpful. I see that for myself now."

"It's my honor, Prophet."

"Don't call her that," Elsie whispered like he'd said something gross.

I smiled. "It's Max. You're family now."

Rylan looked down at Finn, suddenly appearing bashful. "Max feels a little wrong to say."

"You'll probably call her Ma one day," Rune mumbled.

"What? Why? He has his own mom." Elsie twisted her face.

The comment seemed to go entirely over her head, but from Rylan's pink cheeks, I was confident he understood the jesting.

Nash walked up behind me and settled his arm around my shoulders. "I'm still war chief."

"Of course, War Chief," Rylan said, straightening.

I rolled my eyes. "He's messing with you. Call him asshole."

Elsie snickered.

Nash covered my mouth with his hand. "Call me asshole and you'll never make commander."

I bit his finger and he squeezed my side.

I wanted the night to pass more slowly, but soon enough we all found places to sleep around the house. Nash and I settled on blankets together, Finn and I both resting against his chest.

Nash struggled to keep his eyes open, and still he watched Finn sleeping against him. If not for the needs of the kingdom, I doubted Nash would ever let the baby out of his sight. He adored fatherhood, and he was good at it. Seeing him with Finn made me grasp what Eskel the Ruthless once stole from him. The tyrant had forced Nash into servitude for the first four years of Elsie's life. Nash missed so many days of her early life. The joy filling his sleepy eyes showed me how much he cherished the chance to see Finn almost every day.

Sleep started to take me, but I wasn't ready to let go of our time together. I looked over to where Elsie slept between Leif's two girls, whom she lovingly called her little cousins. Rylan helped his grandma prepare her medications before bed while Rune sketched by candlelight in the corner. The boy looked built for war, but anyone who knew him saw that his heart and mind were far from such pursuits. Leif already lay sprawled out on his back, snoring, with Arn curled beside him. How the man slept through all that noise so close to the source, I'd never know.

I looked back to Rylan, who drew a blanket over Elara. "I like him," I whispered.

"Good kid." Nash nodded. "His swordsmanship is exceptional. His father would be proud."

Rylan never took off the beads he wore around his neck, at least not that I saw. "There's been so much loss."

Nash patted Finn's back with one hand and trailed his fingers down my arm with the other. "I know."

It made me feel like a monster to let go of my grief over this boy's loss, but I was too tired to cling to it, and I was finally learning that I shouldn't.

Sleep pulled me under. Deep, peaceful sleep surrounded by family.

It strengthened me for the battle the next morning.

We fought on instinct and on a connection forged over loving each other for three lifetimes. Nash and I saw through each other's eyes, fighting in unison, as two halves of one whole. Days bled into each other. Weeks. We fought with everything we had to save our people. When Malach or Cleo entered the battlefield, we still failed to defeat them, but we kept ourselves alive. We fended them off. All while dominating any battles they didn't join.

I came to realize that they did not simply want me to surrender. They couldn't beat me either. Malach might have been more powerful than us in combat, but that devastating attack that killed the villagers in my childhood could kill him if he wasn't careful. So they attacked my spirit, but I refused to fall into despair.

Against the odds, our people battled well against the invaders.

And if Skia Hellig once feared my name, once feared the power of Eclipse, they now realized an entirely new depth of their terror and reverence. Together, Nash and I reigned vengeance upon all those who crossed us. The recounting of our battles rapidly swelled into legend and hysteria, until one day when our shadows fell upon the north and the south ends of a battlefield, a rush of movement fell like waves over the crowd. Like the moon controlling the ebb and flow of the tide. Hundreds of warriors scattered, pushing through their own lines in a tidal wave to escape the promise of death.

Some questioned our mercy in allowing them to escape, but I saw that the only power greater than being able to slay one's enemies was to spare them. Because those running for their lives knew we allowed them to live. I didn't need or want to shed the blood of those who chose not to hurt my people.

I'd been many things in my life. A warrior, a demon, a Prophet, a heretic. A mother, a wife, a friend. The ruler of a kingdom. A dead woman and a woman reborn. A betrayed daughter and a banished student. But in all my roles and in all my lives, I'd never sought to hurt anyone. Not unless they threatened my people.

Those I called my own grew with each passing year.

I thought back to the Collective and how they'd spoken through Coralee, the root of my consciousness, and how she called all people her people.

I could destroy Skia Hellig by holding on to my kingdom and eviscerating everyone else who stood against us. In the end, I'd ruin my own people doing that.

How could anyone ever use war to make peace?

Some version of me in some world needed to find a better answer, because as far as I knew, Coralee never learned to do this and continued to wage her war, unable to quit, stuck destroying those she called her own people. Destroying herself.

Was it even possible in this short life to figure out what an enlightened version of myself couldn't learn?

Questions like these might kill me if Malach and Cleo didn't. Like Nash had said, I needed to practice peace by not fighting during my times of rest.

Living my life in the middle of war felt more radical than anything.

But we did live, even as we fought, and even as the war path broke through our barriers, encroaching upon Skia Hellig, finally creeping into villages in the Valley, the Flatlands, and the mountains.

Together, we warred against the invading army and together we mourned the warriors and innocent alike who fell.

No matter how never-ending the war felt, we didn't give up. Not on fighting or living.

A little after a year into the war, we were all changed. The Elvadel kingdom, our people, all of Skia Hellig. Our family.

We officially welcomed Elsie into our army as a warrior in-training, much to her great delight. She trained with Rylan until one morning, Nash surprised them both with a much-deserved announcement. The head commanders had chosen them both for one of our most important programs.

"Today begins a partnership that will never end," Nash said to the four young warriors in-training gathered on this snowy morning. "As promising students of connection," he said to a boy and girl, before looking to Rylan and Elsie, "and as promising warriors without power, you all deserve the opportunity to pair. From here on out, you and your partner are like one warrior."

Elsie looked to the girl her age who trained for several years at the Sacred School and then recently with Piercey. Together, these two would fight as Nash and Piercey once did, only their bond would continue to grow without end. I felt their trepidation and excitement warring with each other.

Elsie reached her hand out and smiled, holding the other girl's gaze. "I vow with every drop of my blood to protect you."

Wisps of dark brown hair hung from the other girl's bun and fluttered in the breeze. Her voice was soft and more timid than Elsie's, but equally solemn. "I vow with every drop of mine to strengthen you."

I bit my lip, watching the two form a connection that only death would break.

"Tove," Nash said. "Elsie." He clasped their hands. "You are one warrior."

CHAPTER THIRTY-SEVEN

Five Years Later

My body trembled with a power so great it threatened to shred me from the inside out. I hovered before the sun, before the Mountain of the Gods, and the chaos of my terrified enemies, casting my long shadow over their scrambling lines. Together, Nash and I unleashed our most devastating attack on the warriors below. The rushing waters of our combined power killed them instantly. No longer did the same wild energy that destroyed the villagers in my childhood raise their bodies into the air or crush their bones. It didn't even need to touch them. If even the glowing red and purple light fell upon them, it stole the life from their bodies.

"Run!"

The order swept through the massive enemy army. Instead of fleeing to the woods, the tide of warriors shifted toward our people to hide among them. This did not concern me. They fled, not into safety, but to the swords of our best warriors. I trusted my people to handle the threat.

Corpses dropped in a wave, decimating half of their forces.

That still left thousands for our warriors to fight.

After five years of slaying our enemy, the guilt of stealing so many lives burrowed too deeply within us to feel in the midst of battle. It was only once we stopped, once peace tempted us, that the ghosts of all those we killed arose to haunt us and remind us there was no peace in war.

No matter how many warriors we killed, they always sent more. Cleo's cult steadily grew and Malach's army swelled with conscripted soldiers from the kingdoms he continued to conquer. The two always managed to replace all those we killed. If I let myself fully feel it, I'd end up like Dr. Henderson, going mad in a realm of my own sin and guilt.

So we fought this war that we never asked for and we fought it well.

Nash and I cut off our attack at the same time and disconnected from each other. We'd finely tuned our strategy over the years, so that we always reserved plenty of power to fend off Malach if he arrived. Normally, he would counterattack by now. Some days we didn't manage a single onslaught like this because he responded swiftly and forced our attention onto him. Occasionally, we joined a half dozen battles before he came. This time, though, he'd allowed us to continue unchecked for longer than normal.

This war was fought on two planes, one between our armies, and the other between Malach and us. Nash and I tried with everything we had to kill him. We continued to travel through our past lives, searching for new uses of our power and training relentlessly to strengthen ourselves. But as we grew stronger, Malach did as well.

None of us could kill the other. Malach and Cleo had come close before, but they'd never succeeded. Last year when they managed to poison Nash with their energy-stealing weapons, I'd thought we were finally done for, but we managed to survive. In the early days, Cleo wanted to keep me alive, but now she'd gone so long without consuming my power that she'd kill me given the chance, so long as it meant claiming all I had for herself.

We were all at a standstill of mutually assured destruction. Our web of warriors was too evenly matched to their web of warriors. Our power too evenly matched to Malach and Cleo's. Gridlocked in war, we continued to fight with no end in sight.

Survival meant constant vigilance. Agitation flooded me just thinking about the times we almost lost the war because of one mistake. Today that mistake could be overlooking Malach's absence.

Where was he, and what was he doing?

Nash and I landed on the outskirts of the battle together, no longer connected.

"Should we ask Asmund to travel around and find him? A few of his recruits can teleport now too. They could help."

"They won't. He hides too well. We'll take advantage of his absence. We're well defended and he won't catch anyone back home or in any villages off guard." My gaze scanned thousands of soldiers locked in a war for their life. No matter how many times I saw it, I never could fully grasp it. "We need to figure out what he's doing."

"Then it's time, isn't it?"

I nodded, thinking of the place I wanted to be—needed to be—more than anywhere else in the world. Nash wound his fingers through mine. We arrived in a Flatlander village that Malach had captured two days ago.

Our warriors attacked from all sides of the village while Malach's warriors continued to defend their stolen territory.

There was too much chaos and too many people to find by looking. I closed my eyes and quieted my mind to feel that insatiable pull drawing me to her.

"There."

With Nash's hand still in mine, I transported us across the village and heard the glorious sound of her steady heartbeat. I'd learned to love it more than almost anything, because it meant she was alive.

There, in a raging sea of war, long and lithe legs carried her swiftly. Short curls hung loose, catching the wind, and twin blades crisscrossed the air in splatters of blood.

Elsie carved her way through the battlefield in a full sprint. She didn't slow down to ensure the kill or even seem to consider guarding herself. Eyes as golden and fearless as her father's remained locked on a path straight through the heart of the enemy. Tove followed behind her in lockstep and flawlessly defended her against every single threat, allowing her to drive deeper and deeper into enemy territory.

Our girl had become known as a frontline warrior. She couldn't settle for joining the battle. Elsie needed to terrify us even more by becoming the trailblazer who ran ahead of the rest and weakened the enemy for her comrades.

I glanced beside me to see Nash's eyes tracking her every movement, the glow of pride and admiration twisting with the pensive worry that drew lines into his forehead. If not for the necklace Elsie wore and her promise to call on us when she needed us, I knew I wouldn't be able to endure seeing her off to war. I still wasn't sure how I managed it. My faith in her and her closest friends overcame a fear that felt unbreakable. I had her to thank for that. Elsie was incredible.

Rylan swept in after Elsie and finished off the wounded warriors she hadn't killed, bounding over the bodies of those she had. He'd lost his companion years ago and refused to bond with another, but Tove learned to guard both of them at the same time. So while Elsie rushed forward without slowing down, Rylan lingered to finish the battle.

Elsie's blades tore through flesh and bone on either side of her. Rylan stabbed his blade into a warrior she'd injured a few seconds before.

"Well." Nash lowered his blades slightly. "I don't think they need us."

"They haven't needed us for a while."

A shield shimmered to Rylan's right, blocking a stray hit by a warrior, even while Tove kept a barrier surrounding Elsie. Such a talented companion.

The three of them reminded me of Wren, Leif, and myself before the days of our kingdom.

"Bombs!" The warning rippled through the village at the same moment that deafening blasts ripped through the southern perimeter. The ground quaked.

I teleported closer to the kids, prepared to defend them, but Tove's bright energy shield already surrounded Elsie and Rylan. They ran to their friend's side and their protective barrier melded into one shimmering dome around all three.

With my girl taken care of, I lent my powers to other warriors.

More roars erupted. The ground never stopped shaking.

Near Elsie, one woman raised her hands above her head. Bright light spread across her body and then quickly exploded. I tensed at the gore that followed. Earlier, I felt like I released enough power for it to tear me apart from the inside out, but for this warrior it was true. She expelled everything she had in a devastating bomb and it left nothing recognizable of her.

Her attack echoed through town as more of Malach's warriors sacrificed themselves to kill our people.

But this woman wasted her life, because I saved every person close enough to touch. My people turned to find me, watching me with gratitude, some of them trembling.

Elsie twisted my way and saw me for the first time. Our eyes only connected for a few seconds. The girl didn't like any distractions in battle. And though I worried that I'd see that embarrassment or frustration narrow her eyes because I was hovering again, a warm smile filled her face.

The two of us couldn't connect to share our thoughts, but I felt like I could hear her. She knew her father and I were always here, watching over her and all of our people, even when she didn't know. And she'd finally grown up enough to appreciate that.

I returned to Nash. Normally, we didn't expend more energy once we reached this point, but our people were so close to regaining this lost town.

"Think we have enough strength for one more?" I asked.

"Absolutely."

With all the work our warriors had already done, we could quickly free this village.

Nash and I melted into one and rose into the air. The roar of our people drowned out the last few energy bombs. They cheered us on when together we targeted enemy warriors throughout the village and rapidly killed them.

I wasn't sure when we last defeated this many enemy warriors in one day. The pain of it managed to break through and I met Nash's eyes once we landed. Though I didn't say it and neither did he, we held it together, connected through our shared guilt.

We'd been conscripted in this life and our past lives. We didn't want to hurt these people.

But we needed to abandon it on the battlefield to save this town from Malach's conquest. Any remaining warriors retreated, leaving our warriors to celebrate their victory.

I spotted Owen then, the commander whom I imprisoned. It took a full year of fighting alongside the Flatlanders for him to realize that we needed their partnership, but he finally accepted them and dedicated himself to unity. Thanks to him, we helped quell some of the unrest he helped to spark.

When I started walking toward him to greet him, I finally sensed Malach's presence.

My eyes shifted to Elsie. She cleaned a gash on Rylan's forearm, the two of them unable to feel what stopped Nash, Tove, and me all dead in our tracks.

I teleported to block his path to the kids if he chose to target them.

Malach appeared in front of me, nonplussed despite all his losses today.

"Where have you been?" I asked. "Your warriors were defenseless."

Rylan and Elsie readied their swords, but I motioned for them to stay back. Nash flew over and landed beside me.

Malach's gaze skittered over our group. "I can't always be at your beck and call, Eclipse."

"Do you know how many of your warriors we slaughtered today?" I wanted it to sound threatening, except so much grief filled me for the men and women he cared so little about that my voice only sounded accusing and heartbroken.

"You killed enough." He stepped closer, so I drew my bow. "This war has stretched on for so many days that they feel endless to you, but we have finally nearly reached the end. After today, I can be certain of it."

Damn him. "What did you do?"

A crooked smirk crawled onto the left side of his face. "While you're crushing ants, I'm ascending to new heights."

"Those ants are your people." I couldn't keep from yelling it. I hated him so much. Hated his disregard for his army.

"If you intend to fight, then draw your weapons, Malach." Nash spoke the words stiffly. "We have nothing to say to you."

"I just wanted to visit with old friends." Our enemy crossed his arms over his chest. "We've all worked so hard today. There's no need to fight. I'm done for the day."

"You're not done until you go fuck yourself," Elsie shouted.

I cast a glare over my shoulder at the girl. Tove clutched her arms and tried to pull her back. Elsie might not have shared any of my genes, but she sounded so much like I had at her age that it was uncanny. Too much of myself flowed into her.

"Elsie," Nash whispered in warning.

Malach offered a hearty laugh. "Children are such precious gifts. I can't believe how much you've grown up, Elsie."

She glowered at him, shoulders drawing up and body looking ready to spring forward.

"We're done here," I said, my stare on Malach.

He smirked. "Wouldn't it be impolite to leave without a parting gift?" He lifted his palm.

Nash shot toward him so fast it looked like he teleported. At the same time, I actually did teleport directly in front of Elsie, certain that threat was intended for her. I snapped for the kids to stay behind me while Nash stood directly in front of Malach, blocking his hand.

"Relax." Malach clasped Nash's shoulder. "I'm only joking. I really did come just to say hello."

My husband pried the man's hand loose from himself and shoved it to the side, saying nothing until Malach stepped back.

"I'll see you all soon," Malach said, and then vanished.

When I turned around to face Elsie, she shrank back, even though her frown looked defiant.

"Never again," I said.

I expected her to argue, but then she lifted her chin and nodded. "I apologize, Prophet."

Elsie knew she really messed up if she was calling me that.

Nash walked close to her, voice gruff. "We're taking all of you home. Rylan, straight to the healer."

"Yes, War Chief."

Nash shook his head at Elsie. She turned her eyes to the ground. I thought he intended to leave it at that until he spoke.

"You're suspended from the next battle," he said.

Elsie clenched her teeth so hard that her jowls trembled. She nodded stiffly, stare burning a hole in the ground, voice as tight as the muscles in her jaw. "Yes, War Chief."

I remembered living through Ashton's life and being pulled from battle. It was a terrible feeling to be forced away from comrades, but Elsie could not take chances with Malach. He was the only person in the world we could not protect her from.

Tove took Elsie's hand, softening the anger on the other girl's face. Rylan watched her and I thought he wanted to do the same.

It was a hard but necessary lesson to learn.

When we dropped the three of them off at the tower and watched Elsie retreat toward the staircase, likely to sulk on the roof in an angsty training session, Nash and I stood silently for a full minute.

I closed my eyes, turned, and settled my forehead against his chest. "Was that psychological warfare or did he make a breakthrough?"

"There's no telling."

From the very beginning when Malach telegraphed his moves by invading our peace summit, he'd viciously played with our minds. He cared as much about attacking our spirit as our villages and armies.

"I'll talk with Jakob. Maybe he knows something."

"Okay. Go. I need to meet in the war room."

I started to pull back when Nash caught my face. "Hey." He kissed me softly. "Don't you dare hold on to Malach's guilt for him. We can't let them invade our homes and kill our people."

"I know." My voice didn't sound convincing. The comfort of his gaze softened that guilt, though. "Love you."

His thumb slid down my cheek. "You, too, Sharpshooter."

He always managed to make me smile, no matter how I felt. It lifted my spirits enough for me to travel to Jakob and meet with him in his own war room. I always learned so much about a person and their kingdom by seeing this area. Nash papered our room in all his maps, but Jakob's remained contained to carefully organized scrolls. He hated clutter. The large room boasted three long tables and rows of shelves that held everything he needed for war plans.

"Prophet," I said with a smile, standing at the edge of the center table.

Jakob turned on his heel, the tension easing on his face. He never returned smiles, but I'd come to see the lack of a frown as one. "I didn't realize you were coming today. I left my schedule full."

"I'm not here for long. We've been too busy to check in for a while. I don't like only relaying messages through our advisors."

He did a fine job leading the Flatlands. When I rose to power, the people demanded that I step in. It wasn't the same for Jakob. His people required time to see him as their Prophet, but since he formally ascended nearly four years ago, his legitimacy steadily grew. Even though I had not been able to step away from the Flatlands entirely, their kingdom was more independent with each passing year.

"Are you well?" I asked. "Truly well?"

Jakob considered thoughtfully before nodding. "I am. My heart aches for the villages still under Malach's control and for the people we continue to lose. I never wanted to learn how to live with these losses, but I have learned. I needed to learn. I am sure it's the same for you."

"It is." Talking to someone else outside of my kingdom who understood the pain of leading the people they loved into war reassured me that I wasn't simply failing them. "Nash tells me if we don't find a way to enjoy our lives, then Malach wins. We'll wear down and lose our spirit."

"He's right. It feels wrong, but it's necessary. The human spirit isn't meant to spend every second at war."

I nodded. "Did you decide to accept Demetri's invitation?"

"Yes. Do you know what he wants to discuss?"

"No. It's too much to hope that he wants to simply enjoy the company of our families, isn't it?"

Jakob lifted one brow, the closest he often came to chuckling. "Does that warrant a response?"

"Not any more than wondering whether Sloane will show."

He sighed at that. "I suppose we can't criticize her when she's not lost a single civilian or warrior to this war. I just know we'd have lost far less if she cared enough about Skia Hellig to join."

"Maybe she cares so much about her people she can't care about the rest of Skia Hellig, or she thinks she can't. In the end, abandoning your neighbor and standing back while others suffer always comes around to hurt you. I'm not sure when it will happen, but she's weakening her kingdom. I cannot pity her. We've tried to reach her."

Jakob quieted for several seconds. "I heard about what she did the night of the great attack. Your young Elsie has a sworn vendetta against her."

I leaned back against the table. "She's not supposed to tell people that anymore."

"She's fond of my children. They talk. Her plan for assassinating Sloane is not bad. You might want to worry."

"Are you serious?" I ran my hand over my face. "She's too old to play games and too young to destabilize kingdoms."

"Yes, she should wait a few years until she's the age you were at when you started such conquests."

I chuckled quietly at that. "She promised Sloane she'd never forget what she did. I should have taken her more seriously back then."

He did smile this time, just the slightest hint of one, but a smile nevertheless. "Thank you for all you've done for us. I'm sorry that it's taking me so long to take care of my people. I failed to stop Theus and then I failed to make my people feel safe. They turned to you and you continue to carry our burden after everything your people have suffered."

His words softened my chest. "Don't say that. You've done a remarkable job. It's hard for disciples to ascend to Prophet. That shift in power doesn't come easily. A fresh face can sweep in and spark sudden change. Your people are not a burden and neither is your friendship with my kingdom."

Jakob nodded, but his expression looked heavy. "We'll win this war, Eclipse. Don't lose hope."

Those words, spoken with such conviction, pierced the numbness of normalcy I learned to hide within to continue functioning and living. Pain pricked my heart. "Thank you, Jakob." Malach's words churned in my mind. "I need your help figuring out if Malach's up to something. Do you have any new intelligence?"

"Nothing that seems significant to me right now." He ambled to one of his shelves and picked up a large basket full of scrolls. "Tell me what's worrying you. Maybe something in here will catch our attention with another look."

CHAPTER THIRTY-EIGHT

I cherished each time I returned home. Jakob and I didn't make any startling revelations, but we both promised to try to figure out what Malach was up to, and I left behind the war for the evening to see my family.

It required more effort to fight for peace than it did to wage war. I'd dedicated myself to learning to treat our home like another world entirely, one disconnected from the war, so that I didn't sacrifice my family. We taught the kids to do the same, to separate themselves from the kingdom while here. They were far better at it than me.

Today after Malach worked so hard to get into my head, I needed to fully invest in our night together. For the first time in a long while, I decided to cook dinner for everyone and pretend that nothing beyond these walls existed.

Finn sprinted through the kitchen with Elsie close behind, snapping her fingers for him. "I'll get you," she yelled.

He squealed and caught my legs, hiding between me and the stove. His legs were long now but his cheeks were still chubby, and I hoped they'd stay that way for a little while longer.

"Careful," I said, placing another piece of lamb into the burning hot pan.

"Mommy, she's got claw hands." His light brown eyes met mine. "She's gonna get me!"

I ruffled his soft hair. The curls weren't as tight as Nash or Elsie's, but his hair was just as thick. "Don't you know you have claws, too?"

He gasped and peeled with excited laughter. "Hear that, sis? I got claws, too."

"Uh oh," Elsie said. She turned and ran right into Rylan, trying to pull the young man in front of her. "Take him instead." Elsie scurried from the kitchen.

It sounded like a pack of wild animals stampeded through the other room. Nash walked in, unfazed by the ruckus. "Smells good. You took over for Elara?"

"I wanted to pretend to be normal."

He eased behind me and pulled my hair back. "The mighty Prophet Eclipse cooking lamb." His lips tickled my neck, kissing the skin he'd exposed. "Totally normal mom. Totally normal house."

His mouth tickled me again and I squirmed. "Stop. I'm trying to cook for the kids for once." I giggled when he did it again. "It's not hard to make me burn the meal."

"What about one more?" he whispered against me.

I dropped a piece of lamb in the warming stone and replaced the lid. "I think we have plenty, Nash. I've already cooked a feast."

He snorted against my neck, palms smoothing over my stomach. "Not lamb, Sharpshooter." Nash squeezed my hips. "Can you really live without one more?"

I twisted in his arms, abandoning the sizzling meat on the stove. Before I could speak, his mouth came over mine in a kiss so deep and unexpected it nearly buckled my knees.

"Are you crazy?" I groaned, knowing I needed to flip the meat, but I felt more entranced by his urgency than I cared to confess to him. "What's come over you?"

"We only have so much time in this life."

"Only so much for this lamb as well."

His chuckle vibrated against my lips. "Remember when you were pregnant with Finn and the smell of meat would wake you from your sleep. You were so cute with that belly and that grumpiness."

"Cute?" I slapped his shoulders. "You think I have time to get cute and pregnant? The war isn't ending anytime soon." Now I did turn away from him to focus on the meat and anything but his wild proposition. "I'll finally give the dissidents something to talk about if I charge into battle pregnant and unable to use my full power."

"What's life without dreams?" He buried his face in the long plaits of my hair, and encouraged my body back against him with his gentle touch. "Is there really anything we can't do for our family?"

I set the pan off the flame and smothered the heat with a lid. "We can, but—"

"Just forget about the kingdom for one second. It doesn't have to be real. Do you want it?" His fingers traced along my jaw and down my neck, slipping beneath the collar of my tunic, palm flattening to hold me tightly against him. "I do." I might want anything he did in that moment. Anything. "I want to see you hold our baby in your arms one more time. Finn can't have been the last."

What he didn't know is that I thought about it, too. All the time lately. Every day Finn looked taller, and too often Elsie sounded more like a woman than a teenager. I melted into my husband's embrace and into our shared dream, giving in to the fantasy of peace. Yes, I'd love to carry our bond within me, carry it in my arms, watch it grow into far more than the two of us. Though I didn't care much for pregnancy, I loved Finn's infancy, his days as a toddler, and now as a little boy. I loved Elsie's mesmerizing transformation from wild little girl with the sun in her eyes to fierce warrior.

"I want it, too," I dared to whisper.

"To assume defeat is to surrender."

I smiled. Our people adopted that phrase so deeply into our culture after Nash's rallying cry at the start of the war. "I'm not sure that works the same for having babies."

"Of course, it does." His deep voice cut shivers down my spine. "If we want it, let's at least try to find a way."

"Let me guess, you want to figure it out right this second." I twisted to face him.

His sly grin melted me even though I frowned at him like it didn't.

"Well," he said, "Elsie's entertaining Finn—"

"Torturing him."

"You said yourself that we have plenty of food. Stick it in the other room. They'll be distracted."

"Well, that's that, isn't it? Time for a baby."

Nash hummed in my ear. "Mhm." Then he dumped the rest of the meat in the warming stone.

"Wait," I said.

He sidestepped me and stacked the two vegetable dishes together. Carrying them all on his own, he carefully walked out of the room.

"Where's Ma?" I heard Elsie ask from the other room.

"Trying to sleep."

"I knew you'd end up finishing the meal, like usual."

I rolled my eyes. Nash did not cook more than me. He just didn't get interrupted as often. Unfortunately, shouting that at Elsie now would give away that I was, in fact, not asleep. Still, it was almost worth giving our ruse away to tell her that if she could fight a war, then she could cook for her friends, too.

I started to tidy up when Nash returned.

"Hey," he whispered. "You're supposed to be in bed." He hooked an arm around my waist and pulled me back toward our room.

"We're not having a baby right now," I said, letting him draw me into his arms. "I'm sleeping, remember? I get a free nap."

"Sure."

I chuckled, stumbling out of the kitchen. "I'm serious. No babies."

"We'll talk about it." Nash winked and pressed me against the doorframe, kissing me deeply.

Warmth pooled in my middle. I arched into his embrace, hands finding their way beneath his shirt to the warmth of his body.

"Mommy!" Finn's loud cry quickly turned to tears.

"It's okay," Elsie said. "Poor little buddy."

Nash and I both sighed at the same time. I forced my hands away from him and hurried into the room. Finn sat on the ground, holding his shin while he cried. His lip quivered when he saw me.

"Look." He lifted his leg, crying harder now.

"Oh, I see." I didn't actually see. He looked perfectly fine. "Did you fall?"

He nodded, sticking out his bottom lip.

"You're okay," I said. "Just like your sister said." He lifted his arms to me and I picked him up. "Sometimes it hurts for a second when it's your shin. It doesn't mean you're hurt bad, though."

"You sure, Mommy?"

"I'm sure."

Nash patted his back. "You're a tough boy, right? That's nothing for Finn. Strongest boy in Skia Hellig."

He sniffled and raised his arms above his head in his own version of a flex.

"Crazy," Rylan said. "I've never seen a kid with muscles like that."

Finn puffed out his chest. "Daddy fights me. That's why I'm so strong."

Everyone laughed quietly.

The little boy wiped his palm across his nose. "I draw good, too. I fight good, but I draw *real* good."

"Use a tissue," I said, and pulled his hand down when he tried to wipe his nose again.

Tove passed one to him. "You better now, little guy?" she asked.

Finn seemed to consider and then nodded. "I'm good. Want to play?" He snapped his fingers at her. "Claw!"

Tove fell back to avoid his deadly attack, landing on Elsie.

"Stay back," Elsie said, pushing Tove. "I can't get the claw again."

They started playing around once more, letting the food I'd cooked get cold on the table. But I didn't care. Giggling like this, Elsie seemed like a kid still, not so far removed from her little brother. I loved to watch her laugh because I was so afraid the war would steal it from her. I noticed Rylan watching too, and had to bite down my smile. Elsie was as strikingly beautiful as her dad, secretly as tender as her mother, and possibly more stubborn than me. It made her a fearsome warrior and a captivating young woman. That wasn't lost on him, at least not in the last few years.

Nash subtly tugged me back to him.

"One more," he whispered.

I laughed and let my head fall back against him. That pull was still there, trying to draw me to him. The feel of his smooth skin remained on my hands. I rose on my toes and he dipped, kissing me softly.

A pillow slammed into me. I gasped.

"Get out of here." Elsie launched another pillow at us. "Do that somewhere else."

Nash wrapped his arms around me from behind. "I'll kiss my wife wherever I want. If you don't like it, get your own house. In fact, get your own kingdom, because I'll kiss her wherever I want anywhere in the kingdom."

Tove bit her lip, stifling a laugh.

"You're so embarrassing." Elsie stuck out her tongue.

"Yeah." Finn jumped up and down. "Gross."

"You better watch it, little man." I raised my brows at him. "My claws are the sharpest."

I swooped down and scooped him up while he screamed.

The sound of everyone's laughter filled me up.

I really did wish for the chance to have just one more. Maybe one day, if this war ever ended.

CHAPTER THIRTY-NINE

Demetri offered a guest hall to us with apartments for my family, Elara's, and Tove.

"A sleepover with Gran." Finn clapped his hands. "I love sleepovers."

I kissed each of his cheeks. "I'll miss you, though."

"Yeah, me too. But Gran has candy, Mommy."

"I heard."

He licked his lips.

We all spent the evening together settling in after dinner, but Elara prepared for bed and Elsie left for the courtyard with Tove and Rylan. So it was time to say goodnight to my favorite boy, since Elara planned a fun day for the two of them while we held meetings the next day.

Nash hefted him up in the air and spun him twice. Finn screamed with glee.

"See you tomorrow, buddy." Nash tossed him up and caught him in a big hug. "Be good for your Gran."

Elara walked into the room, breathing heavily from all the activity today. She was slowing down these past few years. Even though I knew she loved her time with Finn, I worried about wearing her out too much.

"Please call for us if you need anything," I said. "And Finn, Gran doesn't get up for anything. You help her with everything."

"I will. I'm her best helper."

"Yes, you are," Elara said. "I can't get by without my little Finn."

I'd spent Finn's whole life needing to say goodbye to him when I left him with Elara, but it never got easier. I wanted to see him sleeping in his bed every night. He was a part of me and I ached when I wasn't with him. I took him from Nash and hugged him tight.

"Mommy," Finn complained. "I'll see you tomorrow."

"I know, baby. I just love you so much."

It still amazed me to see myself and Nash in him. I looked at our son, my heart so full.

Finn wiggled out of my arms when Elara opened the container of candy. Nash nudged me toward the door.

It sounded so nice to spend the night alone with Nash even though I missed Finn. I also would have loved for Elsie to spend time with us, but I knew she'd stay outside late with her friends. So I had Nash to myself until it was time to sleep and we really needed to travel. It'd been weeks since the last time.

We'd returned to our first life many times over the years, but we hadn't explored the second one enough yet. Once we settled down together, we drifted into that old life.

The sun sank into the Mountain of the Gods.

Nash reclined on the grass beside me while I fought the fatigue. It was strange to think that I met him only a month ago, and already I struggled so much to keep my guard up. Especially on nights like tonight when the hurt was so clear in his expression.

"Don't worry, Nash." I laced my fingers behind my head. "Flare isn't invincible. We'll find a way to kill her. If we can keep her from disappearing or figure out how to follow her, then we can kill her."

His quietness tugged at my heart. "It's been this way Elsie's whole life. Flare always separates us. My little girl doesn't even really know me. She's growing up without me while I watch from a distance."

His pain gripped me. I turned toward him. "I'm going to kill Flare. I decided that when I learned she was working with the Prophet of the Valley, but now that I know what she's doing to you and your daughter . . . I'm even more motivated."

"If I knew taking this power from Flare meant losing Elsie, I never would have done it." He stared at the energy burning in his hand and then extinguished it. "I accepted it to protect her. To kill Eskel. Flare knew that and she deceived me."

I thought of Eskel's name tattooed down his spine and how it glowed angry and bright when he was enraged.

"I was so desperate," Nash said. "He was going to kill Elsie. I took the deal with Flare like an idiot."

"It's not your fault," I said. "Flare got to me young at the Sacred School. Helped me and Piercey escape. She separated us, too. Her cruelty is the point."

He rolled over to face me, too. "If Eskel or Flare find out we're talking like this, it'll be over. They'll kill us. It doesn't matter how useful we are to them. There's a reason they kept us from meeting for so long, even though we're both such integral warriors."

"I know. That's what's scary, isn't it? We're at their mercy. I trusted Flare, too, and now I can't trust anyone except Leif and Wren."

"I shouldn't trust anyone ever again," Nash said. He watched me quietly. I almost asked him not to say it, because my heart couldn't bear for him to. "But I do trust you, Max."

I swallowed hard. "Why?"

"I have that strange feeling." Nash reached for me like he was trying to capture light upon a ripple of water, and so carefully brushed his knuckles along my cheek. "Like I know you from a dream I can't remember."

His touch swept me from my body into a surreal sensation of familiarity. I felt such a strong draw to him, so deep and unyielding, that it felt like a spell. I pulled back, trying to close myself off before I went any deeper.

Nash's hand lingered in the air another moment and he lowered it. "I'm sorry. I should have asked."

"It's not that." I rubbed my chest. "I'm afraid to let you get too close."

It wasn't just because I didn't know yet whether to trust him, but rather because it felt like if I did let him in, losing him would hurt too badly. This bond I felt was too deep and too quick. It terrified me.

"When I'm with you, I forget about how things are supposed to be," he said. "I forget we only just met a month ago and I'm not supposed to know what I want yet."

Nash and I sat quietly for several minutes when we returned to our time.

"We've never seen that part," I said. "That bond we formed at the end of our first life was real. I sensed that same power. I just didn't recognize it."

"We feel it here in this life, too. A part of us held on through the new lives. It's a thread connecting us back to the first one."

"It's so strange." I touched my cheek where Nash's knuckles brushed my skin in our forgotten dream. "You told me after the Flatlander battle that you felt like you met me in a dream you couldn't remember. Just like you said in our second life."

"Then we shouldn't ever be afraid of losing each other." Nash held my hand. "We'll find each other in every life. This power connecting us is real."

"I love you so much. There's no words that exist that can express all the love I have for you."

"Three lives is hard to capture in words."

He smiled and I followed the definition of his cheek with my fingers.

"I wonder what else that power connecting us through our lifetimes can do," I said. "What else are we capable of?"

"That might be the most important question you've ever asked."

The two of us rested in silence together, reflecting on this. Finally, I thought of his tattoo glowing in the memory. Eskel branded him in this life, but it didn't glow like Cleo's spiral markings.

"Flare taught Eskel how to bind with you through the markings like Cleo did in our first life."

"First, Flare partnered with her, then in the next life she copied her," Nash said. "It seems in our current life she finally stayed away from her and the cult."

"Or did she?"

So many times over the last few years I thought about how I could ask Dr. Henderson these questions. That woman never brought anything good into my life, though. To this day, hearing her cry the name Coralee hit me with nausea. For a while, I couldn't think about all the things she had said. It hurt too badly. Now I felt convinced that she'd hurt Coralee somehow as a child. I genuinely couldn't imagine hurting Elsie or Finn. If one day, the Collective planted seeds of their consciousness in another world, I definitely couldn't hurt those souls either.

But she'd killed me. She'd killed someone who not only looked like her daughter, but originated from her consciousness.

I refused to see Dr. Henderson again. The Collective tainted our world with her once. I sacrificed my desire to understand and my wayward hope that she might give us answers. Never again would I see her or speak to her or give her the chance to hurt me.

"I hate her, Nash."

I didn't say who because he knew. My voice sounded distant.

"I don't want there to be enough left in my heart to hate. I want her gone. But I can't scrape enough of her out of my soul. She's there in our past lives and she's with me now in this bitterness I can't cleanse."

He held me, and though he said nothing, couldn't say anything to help, his nearness soothed me.

I would never know just how much that woman stole from me and from her daughter Coralee.

But I did insist on knowing the secrets of my past life she kept hidden. Because to finally kill Malach and Cleo, we may need to attain a power the gods didn't want us to have, and we couldn't let the security system stand in our way.

We returned to our last life in search of that threat, but we found something else entirely.

The Mountain of the Gods rippled and then stretched in a thinning line. The trees around us started to shake.

I couldn't stop Dr. Henderson. It was too late.

Elsie held on to Nash tightly. "It feels strange, Daddy."

"It's okay, baby girl." He stroked her hair.

We defeated Flare and Eskel, freeing ourselves of her marks, only for Dr. Henderson to steal the world away from us.

I tried so hard to fight it, to save Elsie and Nash and everyone we loved, but the world started to separate right before our very eyes. Everything felt more distant.

"We're bound," I said. "In this life and the next." I clung to my family. Nash held us both tightly.

"We're bound," he repeated.

There was no separating our family. I knew when I married Nash, we were meant to be bound, and sensed that bond now. As the world began to rip apart, we tried to insulate Elsie with energy. Our powers surged as we connected and focused every bit of our spirit into holding on to one another forever.

Through our connection, I sensed a churning beneath the surface, a power far greater than we could feel, like something buried deeper in the ocean than light could reach.

"Everything will be okay," I said to Elsie, believing it for her sake. "We're all going to be together and no one can tear us apart."

That strange power pierced my core like a hot poker and started to spread throughout my body. I gasped, and in the final moments before we lost the world around us, a black ball started forming over the sun, casting its shadow on us like an eclipse. Incredible energy burned within me and from that source.

Nash and I looked at each other. I didn't know what it was, but I wondered if it might be enough to save us.

That hope lived on through the very end, when I lost the feeling of my family in my arms.

CHAPTER FORTY

Nash and I sat together on the balcony of the apartment, quietly digesting what we experienced in the crisp air. A small table bearing a bouquet of wildflowers fluttered in the breeze. Below us, a beautiful courtyard paved with stone and decorated with all kinds of trees and flowers stood in stark contrast to the rocky mountains beyond us.

"What was that?" Nash stared up at the starry sky.

"It's like we called on it."

"Yeah. I just don't know how, or what it even was."

I rubbed my throat. "I don't know. We can try to live through that again, and study that moment like I did when I relived my death."

The death of our last world clung to us. It didn't devastate me as badly as when we lived through it the first time in our original life, because we'd forced ourselves to return to that memory often enough for it to lose its sting. We wanted to learn more about the moment our world ended.

"Maybe. We did that with our first life and learned nothing. It only caused suffering."

I looked at him, still unable to fully comprehend Dr. Henderson effectively killing everyone on the planet twice. That she did it to me when I was derived from Coralee truly dumbfounded me.

Though the loss of our worlds didn't affect us in the same way as it used to, the grief still churned inside of us for days afterward. Nash and I continued to sit quietly until the feeling faded more.

"Are you okay now?" he asked.

I nodded. "You?"

"Yeah. It was just hard to see Elsie go through it."

I bit the inside of my cheek, trying to keep myself from dwelling on that. I couldn't change it, and some nightmares didn't need to be relived.

"At least we still have some time together before we fall asleep." Nash reached across the table and cupped my hand in his. "Those kids aren't coming inside anytime soon."

I looked down to see Tove deep in the courtyard, bending to smell the tulips growing in a flower box. "No." Elsie and Rylan walked together along the stone path that wove between well-manicured trees, deep in conversation. "They keep getting older faster and faster."

"It's too hard to keep up with. Finn needs to slow down, too."

I smiled, feeling more normal already. "I wonder what he'll be like when he's Elsie's age. He's not eager to battle. I don't think we've seen what he loves yet."

"Good. Elsie's love for battle has been exhausting."

We both laughed at the truth of it. "She's so good, though."

"She is. She'll be better than us one day. Rylan might, too. It's really something to see them fight together. Tove keeps up right in there. They're a talented war party."

I smiled wistfully and looked back down at them. Rylan and Elsie had stopped walking and faced each other. He bent and Elsie leaned into him, her arms sliding around his neck. The two kissed.

My eyes widened and Nash started to turn.

"No," I whispered harshly and lurched forward to catch his face.

"What?"

"Nothing. We're going inside."

His suspicion quickly sharpened into alarm. He jerked away from me and turned to see them kiss again.

"Say anything and I'm pushing you over the balcony." I jerked on his shirt. "Come on."

"He's kissing her," he whispered, like he was telling me someone stabbed her in the face instead. "That's my baby girl. He's kissing my baby girl."

"Yeah, so keep it quiet. Leave them alone."

"There's no kissing until they can defeat me in a sword battle." Nash scoffed. "They're not old enough until then."

"*I* can't beat you. You're crazy." I shoved him toward the door. "Get your ass inside right now and do not embarrass your daughter."

"I'm crazy? You're the one who's crazy. How can you not be alarmed?"

I groaned, finally getting him away from where I needed to worry about the kids hearing. "I can't believe you're going to be like this. It's not even like you."

"I'm a man. Why would I trust another man? I know men, Max."

"Oh, so that's the truth." I planted my hands on my hips. "You're scared because you're a dirty flirt, and now you think a fellow dirty flirt is kissing your baby girl outside in the dark." I chortled. "That girl knows what she's doing. She's the dirty flirt. He's only got enough charm to gawk."

Nash didn't seem to hear me. "Trish got pregnant at her age. Elsie isn't ready for a baby." He gasped, horrified. "I was Rylan's age when I got her pregnant!"

I doubled over laughing.

"This isn't funny."

"It's pretty funny."

"It's not!"

"It's a harmless kiss. No one is getting pregnant, Nash."

He quirked an eyebrow. "Well, it'd be okay for someone to get pregnant. Just not Elsie."

"By someone you mean me."

"Exactly."

"I have bad news for you. No. And what's going on out there is none of your business. Elsie is a young woman now."

Nash eyed his blades on the table. "It's my business until he can stop my swords."

"You're lucky your daughter is outside kissing a boy right now and not in here listening to your nonsense."

"He's twenty. That's a man kissing our daughter, not a boy."

"Yes, exactly. Grown-ups, Nash. She's eighteen. A woman now. Will it help you not panic so much to know she has the pills? I've been giving them to her for years so she doesn't need to ask for them when she's ready. It's not like Trish. Things are different now. We have reliable birth control. Besides, they're just kissing."

"That is a little better." He scratched his chin, deep in thought. "It would be fine for him to kiss her if I'd had time to warn him first that I'll skewer his throat with both my swords."

"Because you loved when Leif did that to you." I rolled my eyes. "You're so behind. You should have done that months ago like I did."

"You threatened to kill Rylan?"

"Of course," I said. "He likes Elsie. I had to threaten him. Stop worrying so much and have some faith in me. He knows what will happen if he ever mistreats her."

"I don't like this whole tables turning thing." Nash rubbed the back of his neck. "You're sure she'll take the pills the right way if she needs to?"

"Yes. Trish and I are way ahead of you."

"I do not like her growing up. This is horrible."

I kissed his cheek. "Your poor thing. But really, don't you think he's a good one?"

Nash didn't seem to want to concede, but he finally nodded. "Obviously. I'll be happy for them once I can forget seeing that. If I fly out there with my swords, looking down on him where Elsie can't see, but he does, he'll be too terrified to ever cross her."

"That's a joke, right?"

He shrugged one shoulder. "Unfortunately."

"Let's just sleep. We have a busy day tomorrow."

"We need to wait for the kids to go to bed."

"We don't. They're fine. Sleep."

He hesitated before following me to the room we were staying in. Once we settled in together and the warmth of skin against skin soothed me, I couldn't stop my mind from wandering to dreams that felt impossible.

"Nash."

"Yeah?" His sleepy eyes found mine. He'd just started to doze off.

"I really do want another baby."

After hesitating, he smiled and brushed his nose along mine. "Do you?"

"Imagine if we could stay home with the baby and didn't need to leave for war, like the early days with Finn."

"I imagine it all the time."

"Once we win this war, let's do it. Let's have a baby." I kissed him, fatigued and lost in dreams. "Maybe we can pretend for one night we don't have to wait. We can imagine the war is over and we're free."

Nash eased over me. "It's real." Sleep made his voice husky. "The war's over and we're free."

"We're free," I repeated, relishing the dream.

"We really could do it." He murmured near my ear.

Though we both knew that wasn't true, I chose to forget for one night. I forgot about everything except my husband and the life we wanted to live. He made it easy, because he consumed my world. Alone and without distraction, we resisted sleep, and abandoned the war for each other.

CHAPTER FORTY-ONE

The next morning, we woke up to a breakfast delivered by Demetri's head cook. We sat on the curved bench in the corner of the room that was nestled along floor-to-ceiling windows. Endless mountains rose and fell in white peaks out the window. I couldn't stop staring outside. And inside we had everything we needed. Our family, a table filled with home-cooked food, and enough peace to pretend that we weren't here to discuss war.

"This is so nice," I said. "Els, make sure your friends get some when they wake up."

Elsie nodded, but looked over at Nash. I wanted to kick him for being uncharacteristically quiet while he filled his plate with sausages, potatoes, and eggs.

The girl pursed her lips, eyeing him for several seconds longer.

He plopped down across the table from us and barely glanced up at her.

"Gods." Elsie tossed her napkin on the table. "You saw, didn't you?"

He scarfed down his sausages, maybe erroneously thinking it would cover his discomfort. "Saw what?"

Elsie groaned and looked at me. "Ma."

"We saw."

Nash choked on his food and hit his chest, shaking his head. "No. No, we saw nothing."

Her head dropped to her hands. "I hate my life, I hate all of you, and I hate the entire world."

"That's lovely, Els." I refilled her water for her. "It's fine. Your dad is fine."

"Look at him." She slammed her fist on the table. "He ate three sausages in less than three seconds."

His eyes widened. "She's right. I'm fine. Really. It's fine that you're making out with some *man* in the middle of the night far away from home."

I flicked a small zap of power at his leg hard under the table.

"Perfect," Elsie said. "Actually, no. I won't be shamed by you of all people, Dad. Do you know how many times I've had to see you kiss Ma? You're always sneaking off with her like you're sly. I've put up with it my whole life. I'm traumatized. This is restitution."

"Restitution? Where'd you learn that word? What is Piercey teaching you kids?" Nash threw his sausage on his plate. "There's no kissing restitution, young lady. We're married and we're adults. We can sneak off five times a day if we want."

"Ew," Elsie shouted. "Dad!"

"To kiss." He unsuccessfully squashed his laugh. "I obviously meant to kiss. You know, outside in the dark at night far from home."

"This is so embarrassing." Elsie hid her face.

"Stop it." I clapped my hands at both of them. "Nash, you like Rylan and you're happy for them. Elsie, he's teasing you."

"Well, tell him to quit," she said.

"Stop, Nash."

He raised his hands. "I'm sorry. It's revenge teasing because I'm forced to watch you grow up."

"Oh, I'm so sorry," Elsie snapped. "I'm so sorry I'm living my life."

"It's okay. I forgive you."

"I said to stop." I pointed at Nash. "Seriously."

"What are we fighting about?" The door opened to Rylan and Tove shuffling in. Elsie's eyes widened in sheer panic.

"That Nash dared to kick Elsie out of a single battle for foolishly antagonizing Malach." I scooted away from Elsie to give the two room to sit by her. "Come eat."

They sat on either side of Elsie and I caught Nash watching Rylan. I narrowed my eyes at my husband and he looked away from the young man with a subtle sigh.

Elsie looked at her father and then at Rylan. She leaned over to the boy, whispering. His cheeks turned a shade of crimson deeper than the tomatoes. Nash and I both stared. I couldn't help it. I didn't expect her to say anything to him.

"It's been almost a year," Elsie said. "We might as well say it."

I leaned forward. A year?

"What?" My voice squeaked from shock.

"Prophet, War Chief . . . I'd like to take this time to . . ." Rylan fumbled over his words. "Well, to ask you . . ."

"To ask me what?" Nash asked dryly, not giving Rylan the grace of averting his stare.

"You don't need to ask them anything," Elsie said.

"Maybe what I'm trying to say . . ." Rylan cleared his throat. "I respect you both more than you will ever know."

The boy seemed too nervous to notice what I saw clearly. A tiny smirk hugged the corner of Nash's mouth. "You respect us."

"Absolutely. It's beyond respect."

"You want to respectfully let us know that you don't need permission to see our daughter." Nash leaned an elbow against the table. "Is that what you're trying to say?"

"Yes," Elsie said on his behalf. "Exactly. No one needs your permission." Then she leaned back so Rylan couldn't see her and mouthed, "I'll kill you."

Nash fully smirked this time.

"That's not what I was saying." Rylan shot a look at Elsie. He sat up straighter. "War Chief." A look at me. "Prophet."

I watched, listening patiently.

"I've had feelings for Elsie for a long time now." His voice was stronger and less nervous, but still held deference. "I care about her and I respect you both. I care about her deeply. I want you to know what she means to me."

The entire table quieted. Elsie didn't still easily, never had, but she didn't look like she breathed.

"That's what I wanted to say." Rylan sat back and cleared his throat one last time. "Respectfully."

Our daughter turned her eyes to the table, still quiet.

"Thank you, Rylan." Nash no longer smirked or studied the kid warily. He smiled gently. "We trust you."

The young man looked up at him before shifting his glance to me. I smiled with my heart melting. "You're our boy."

He laughed quietly at what we used to call him when he was younger.

Tove hadn't said anything during the exchange, but she smiled now, voice quiet. "You're the only one I'd trust with her," she said.

Elsie's expression tightened and she looked around the table. "We didn't say anything before because we aren't together yet. We're friends and we're seeing what happens."

"It's okay," Nash said. "We don't need to pry. I'm sorry."

Her eyes looked misty. "I care about Rylan, too." She grabbed his hand and looked at him. "Whatever happens, happens. We'll never let anything get between us. Right?"

He nodded.

Nash lowered his eyes, probably feeling like a huge asshole for teasing and getting carried away with his worries.

For the first time during this exchange, though, concern pinched my heart. Elsie had a temper, but otherwise she wasn't given to showing her emotions easily. This quietness didn't seem like embarrassment over her dad's reaction, or from feeling sentimental by Rylan's show of passion. Something was wrong.

I excused myself to check on Finn across the hall at Elara's. When I returned, Tove and Rylan had left for their respective rooms, and Elsie cleaned up breakfast with Nash.

"You just aren't sure yet?" Nash asked, taking a plate from her to stack it with the others.

"I really like him." Elsie shrugged. "We're best friends."

"That makes for the best relationship."

She looked up when she saw me enter. So this was what I noticed. Elsie's uncertainty. The relationship wasn't as new as I thought, so she'd had a good amount of time to think it through. I was missing something. The two always seemed so happy when they were together. Despite how Nash reacted to them kissing, he also was aware of their feelings for each other. We'd said for a while they'd likely end up together one day. Nash just seemed surprised it was already happening.

Elsie and Rylan appeared to have the hallmarks of a beautiful relationship, one ready to last through the years. I couldn't have imagined ever trusting a man with our Elsie or finding one deserving of her, but they fit together so well. I hoped for them to choose each other. I wanted Elsie to be happy.

Maybe she just wasn't ready for anything more than this. She was still so young.

"It's okay," Nash said. "Take your time and don't put pressure on yourself. Only you and Rylan will know what's right, and you have to go at your own pace. I'm sorry I was an asshole."

Elsie's expression didn't lighten.

"Come on, baby girl." He brushed her cheek with his thumb, voice soft. "I really am sorry. I was brutish and stupid. A fool of a man."

She smiled. "I know. You were a fool."

"I deserve that."

I wanted to ask more questions, but sensed she didn't want to answer anything else. She excused herself and Nash shrugged at me.

"I don't get it," he said. "I actually like the kid, apart from the fact that he dared to kiss her."

"Me, too."

"I know she does, too."

"Yeah." I sighed and rubbed my throat. "She's confused. Elsie doesn't get confused often."

Deciding to leave it alone for now, I helped to finish tidying, and we all left to meet with Demetri. The kids sat on the other side of the library with one of Demetri's advisors and Jakob's oldest daughter. I appreciated that he wanted to involve them rather than leave them to entertain themselves. They were the future of our kingdom and someone needed to prepare them for that.

Nash and I joined the other two Prophets, Jakob's wife, and Demetri's top advisor.

"We all know there needs to be a change." Demetri steepled his fingers. "I don't want to take long saying this because there will be much to discuss. The unrest in my kingdom is growing. I understand you both face this, too, but it's different among the Fjellfolk. My people feel the protection of the mountain is failing and the gods have turned their back on us."

"Surely they can understand this doesn't mean anything like that," I said.

"It's not easy to combat the religious sentiments of my people. They've lost confidence that the gods will save us." He looked at me. "They've lost confidence that I am a great enough vessel for the gods."

Uneasiness rocked my stomach.

"In the past, we may not have always trusted each other," Nash said, "but we've always considered you formidable. You're a worthy Prophet for your people."

I thought Jakob might speak but he didn't. Instead, the two men exchanged a look that I couldn't parse. Like they knew something I didn't.

Demetri placed his palms on the table and squared his shoulders. "It's time for Skia Hellig to unite as one great land and prove ourselves worthy of the gods' power. The union of the Flatlands and the Elvadel kingdom has been blessed by the gods. It shows us the path for the rest of the peninsula."

"I'm sorry." The shock drew me forward and I practically caught myself on the table. "You want your kingdom to come under the wing of my kingdom? Like Jakob's?"

"The gods have ordained it."

"I've talked with the gods." I laughed humorlessly. "They never ordained this."

"The will of the people is the ordination of the gods. I've resisted for long enough. I want the Fjellfolk kingdom to outlive my name. The Prophet Eclipse is connected with the gods in a way no one else is. Don't turn your face from us. This is not easy for me to ask. We should become true brothers and sisters and unite under the gods."

Nash clasped my hand under the table, steadying me. "Any transition is a risk during war."

"I'll remain Prophet. It will be the same as Jakob and the Flatlands. We are Prophets in our lands, but we're all under the protection and authority of the great Eclipse."

I scooted my chair back and walked several paces away.

"I know you never asked for this," Demetri said. "You won't deny it either. You've grown. You're no longer that girl who is afraid of her own power, trying to run from the people who begged you to lead them. You know who you are and you know what you need to do."

My eyes shut. "I stood in Sloane's temple and I told all of Skia Hellig that I never planned to take over the peninsula."

"And Sloane herself said that it may fall to you anyway," Demetri said. "Aren't we stronger as one? Can't we stand against Malach and Cleo better if we're truly together? Our kingdoms will be bound."

Binding with Nash meant everything to me. I respected and understood the power of such bonds.

"I agree with him," Jakob said. "We're one Skia Hellig."

"Sloane isn't even here." I turned back to them. "She won't agree."

"She can continue to run from fate for now," Demetri said. "When we look at the sky, we see the sun, and we see that there is only one able to take its place. We see the sun, until we see Eclipse. Tell me you didn't know this was inevitable."

"I didn't." I shook my head. "You're a strong leader. I never expected you to want to join my kingdom. Everyone else has always wanted to take my power."

Demetri's face softened in a genuine smile. "I love my people."

That was when I saw it—these men were nothing like Eskel the Ruthless, or Lote, or Malach. Nothing like Cleo or Dr. Henderson. My heart broke so many times over the unbelievable greed and hate in people's hearts, but there was good, not just in the world, but even in those who wielded power.

No one had an excuse to use their power for evil. Not a single excuse. That part was not inevitable. There could be good leaders.

"One Skia Hellig," I whispered.

"So, we're unintentionally conquering all of Skia Hellig now." Elsie fell back against the backrest of her chair and set her bread back on her dinner plate. "Makes sense."

"Voice down." I looked around to make sure no one else at the long dinner table heard. Many of Demetri's trusted advisors and commanders joined us for the meal. We all gathered at three different tables spread out through the dining hall. "This is serious."

"I'm being serious. It makes sense."

What Malach said to me when this all began returned to me. I almost saw his face hovering in the torchlight.

"Skia Hellig belongs to you. Your people will answer for your decisions . . . We are the true rulers of our land."

But he wasn't the first to speak such words. At the summit, everyone was afraid I'd take over all of Skia Hellig. I never meant to do such a thing.

"What do you think?" Nash eyed Elsie curiously.

"I think it's obvious. We're stronger together and Ma is the best Prophet to lead." Elsie grabbed her dad's hand. "Just like you're the best war chief to lead. And I'm the perfect successor to the war chief of Skia Hellig."

I rolled my eyes. "Stop campaigning."

"I'm not campaigning. The job is mine to take. No one else in Skia Hellig can hope to compete with me for it. I was born for this."

"I'm not sure why you're so confident when I'm sitting right here." Rylan drained his ale. "I beat you in our first sparring match as kids, and I'm going to beat you one day when we fight our last."

"Don't even start." Elsie tossed a piece of bread at him. "I'll fight you right here so all our allies see you humiliate yourself."

Tove laced her fingers over her stomach. "Why doesn't anyone ever consider me? I'm the actual glue holding our war party together."

Though I expected Elsie to lash out, she smiled instead. "You can't be war chief when you're Prophet."

Tove quieted for a second and then she laughed. "Right. I'll be your Prophet and you'll be my war chief."

Elsie nodded, eyes animated. "Obviously, Tove-Tove. That's been my plan all along. I just didn't want to scare you by telling you before you were ready."

The biggest smile came over Tove's face when Elsie used the childhood nickname. The girl glanced down.

My fingers came to my chest and understanding dawned over me. Oh, Elsie.

"Rylan will keep me on my toes, but he'll ultimately be my second." Elsie tapped her glass against his. "It'll be the three of us leading all of Skia Hellig one day."

My gaze tore from Tove to Elsie and the furtive glances they tossed at each other.

How did I never see this before? Maybe no one had, not even them.

I waited until everyone had left to mingle and Elsie and I were alone. She sat beside me at the table and placed a piece of cake in front of me. "For you."

"That's so sweet." I pushed her curls behind her ears. They were barely long enough to tuck away. "Elsie."

"Yeah?"

"It's okay if you don't want to be with Rylan. It's okay if you do, but it's okay if you don't, or if you don't know."

Elsie stared at me with the shock of an enemy pulling out a hidden dagger. After a pause, her eyes fell. "I do, though."

"Maybe not as badly as you want to be with someone else?"

Pain filled her eyes. "How long have you known?"

"Only since I thought to look."

"I love Rylan. Did you know that? It's more than a crush, Ma." She shifted. "I've always loved Rylan." Confusion filled her face. "And now, suddenly, there's this feeling in my chest." She dug her fingers into her heart, meeting my eyes desperately. "I tried not to feel it. There's something in there, gripping me when she's close. Or when she looks at me, like really looks at me and only me."

I slid my hand along her cheek, holding her face with my heart melting. "Elsie," I whispered.

"I was so happy the first time I kissed Rylan. Why am I ruining it?"

"That feeling is never ruining anything, Elsie girl."

She looked over to where her friends were and spoke more quietly. "I haven't told anyone because it doesn't even matter. Our partnership is sacred and immutable. The rules forbid it to be anything except what it is."

"Rules?" I shook my head. We did discourage forming romantic relationships between those we paired, but pairings were new, and we'd never stand in the way of people who truly cared for each other. "Rules aren't meant for things like this."

"They're there for a reason. It's affecting me in battle. I'm distracted."

I laughed quietly at that. "I understand that all too well."

"Rylan distracts me, too, but we aren't fighting as one. I'm not in tune with him every second. Tove and I are too close. It's too much. I don't know what's wrong with me. I really want to be with Rylan, and there's nothing to stop me. Everyone is happy for us. Tove isn't an option."

When I said nothing, Elsie looked at me with a nervous expression.

"Say whatever it is you want to say."

"Well." I chose my words carefully. "You're a very dedicated warrior and you always have been. This war comes above anything in your life."

"It has to."

"Maybe, though, this should be there, too. My love for Nash is far more important than any partnership we have in battle."

Elsie looked pained. "We've lost so many people. I try to do what you say and I choose to live my life. I come home from battle, clean off the blood, and laugh with my friends. There's a limit, though. We're at war and everything is at stake. I'll never allow my feelings to stop me from protecting them. Tove and Rylan are my responsibility. I can't be distracted."

This war etched into her heart too young. Elsie refused to look away in the memorial hall at thirteen, and she'd never done so at any ceremony since. Sometimes, I managed to make myself forget our sweet girl had already taken so many lives in battle. I managed to forget that we led a kingdom in a world that required our children to fight and to die.

I settled my forehead against hers. "When you're older and you see childhood being stolen from the young ones you love, you'll understand what you've lost." I pleaded with her from the bottom of my heart. "Do not let this war steal your heart away. Follow wherever it leads you."

Elsie squeezed my hands. "Okay, Ma."

honestly don't know how this really changes things moving forward." I shrugged at Markus and Piercey in the study. Dim light glossed the windows. Storm clouds darkened the outside. "It's really just appeasing the superstition of the Fjellfolk."

"I think it's a long time coming," Markus said. "There's no reason not to do it. We can easily adapt. It won't be like with the Flatlands when we needed to build new leadership."

"This sends a message to Sloane that it's all of Skia Hellig against her. It might drive her into Malach's hands," Piercey said. "We can't risk that. We'll be attacked from the north and south if that happens."

"If we do this, we need to speak with Sloane," Nash said. "Piercey makes a good point."

"My head is spinning." I pushed my hair back. "The last thing I need right now is another major decision to make. Demetri needs to control his people. They—"

A terrible alarm seized every muscle in my body and sent my heart into a frenzy. Disbelief filled me for just a moment, but I didn't let it slow me down from reaching for Nash. His hand grabbed mine, the same shock and panic I felt vividly hitting him, too. We didn't even take the time to tell Markus and Piercey.

Elsie set off her alert. She was calling for us. In danger.

I teleported us to her, following the signal of the necklace she wore to guide me. Icy chills seized my body. Terror gripped me. What if? The *what if* might actually be happening this time.

The chaos of war surrounded us when we landed in the battlefield. All my senses were attuned to our surroundings and to Elsie as I sought her out.

My blood chilled, its flow through my body coming to an abrupt halt. On instinct, I erected a domed shield around all of us, but it felt like someone else used my body to do it. I couldn't think. Couldn't move once my mind took in the sight.

Elsie dragged herself across the ground with one arm, the other wrapped around her bloodied midsection. Red streaked the dirt beneath her in a long swath that told me just how much blood she'd lost.

Right in front of her, Rylan lay listless on the ground. Two wide tears of red ripped open his chest. Vacant eyes stared unblinking in Elsie's direction.

My feet started moving, though I swore my heart didn't beat. Tove clutched Elsie's necklace in her hand and knelt beside her, begging her to hold still.

Though I'd frozen for that one short moment, Nash never did. He'd bounded for Elsie as soon as we landed and now almost reached her. I followed close after, my body tense when he scooped her off the ground.

Her scarlet hand held the tattered edges of her stomach closed. A sword must have cleaved through her midsection. Bile climbed up my throat.

"No," Elsie cried out, somehow still conscious. Her wild eyes searched for Rylan. "Help him!"

Nash said nothing, just as he didn't hesitate. Turning his back on the young man, he held his daughter close, and nodded at me.

"Rylan . . ." Her voice faltered. A terrible grief-stricken wail sounded like it caught in her throat and escaped in a strangled noise. Blood bubbled up on her lips and slid out from the corners of her mouth.

Elsie was dying. There was no time to even promise to return for the others. I grasped Nash's arm to teleport right when her body stiffened and her eyes rolled back in her head. I didn't even pause to help her but focused on the medical wing of our tower. We might have had only seconds to save her.

The moment we landed, I ran forward, searching for anyone who could help.

"Healer!" Nash's voice erupted against the stone walls of the medical room so loudly I expected everything to shake.

I caught the sleeve of the only person I saw in the room, a young healer wearing robes that signified she was still in training. "Hurry."

The healer's eyes widened. Elsie convulsed in Nash's arms, blood frothing on her lips. Immediately, the young healer lifted her hands, and though she trembled, the warmth of her healing power seeped into the room.

Defying every impulse to stay with Elsie and Nash, I burst into the next room, looking for a more advanced healer whom I trusted.

"Max!"

Nash shouted for me. I didn't even waste time running for him but teleported to his side. He knelt on the ground where three healers surrounded Elsie. Catching my hand, he pulled me down, and I fell against him on the ground.

The tears started to fall now that I saw the healers holding her wound closed and placing their hands on her as they began to work on her internal injuries.

"They've got her." I choked on the words, crying so hard I couldn't breathe. "She's going to be okay."

It didn't look that way, though. Elsie looked as pale and cold as death. Nash bowed forward, mouth slightly open, staring at Elsie as vacantly as the young, dead man left behind on the battlefield. I could feel his body wound so tight I thought it would snap every fiber of muscle.

"I have to go back for them." I barely managed the words. "I'm sorry."

Nash still gripped my hand, so hard that my knuckles ached.

"Nash—"

He released me, but he didn't speak or move. Didn't take his eyes off his child for a second. I clutched Elsie's foot before I left. "I'll bring them home, baby girl. You hang on." How could I leave? I tore my own heart from my chest by rising to my feet and leaving her behind.

My boots landed in the red-streaked mud where we found Elsie. The battle raged around me, except for in a small, untouched space ahead. Tove knelt over Rylan. Her hands were inside of his gaping chest as if she could hold him together.

I walked to her on numb legs, for this moment not a warrior, not a Prophet, not the leader of this kingdom and this war. Gently, I lowered myself to my knees beside the kids, because that's what they were to me. Kids whose hands should never have gotten bloodied in the first place.

"Tove," I whispered. She was as pale as Elsie even though I didn't think any of the blood staining her body belonged to her. "It's time to go home."

The girl didn't hear me. She scooped handfuls of blood back into Rylan's gaping chest. "I'm sorry." Tove didn't even make a sound. I only saw her lips moving as she spoke the words wordlessly over and over. "I'm sorry. I'm sorry. I'm sorry."

I grabbed her warm, slick arms and moved into her line of sight. "Elsie is being healed. You and Rylan need to come home now. I'll take you first and then I'll take him to Elara."

Panicked eyes met mine. "Will you kill them? They're too powerful, Prophet. They'll hurt our people."

My mind lingered on the image of Nash wilting beside our unconscious Elsie. I heard the sweet laughter that filled her childhood, saw her curls bobbing as she ran, felt her little arms around my neck. Those memories didn't feel so long ago. And then I remembered the look I saw in her golden-brown eyes as she watched Tove. I couldn't imagine being anywhere except for at Elsie's side right now, but that was the last place Elsie would want me to be. What could a mother do for her right now? Nothing. I knew her. Knew she wouldn't want Ma but the Prophet Eclipse.

A bitter taste rolled over the back of my tongue. In a dull, resigned voice, I said, "Yes." Pain churned in my depths. Everything had just changed for Elsie. This one day, this one bad moment, would never leave her. It wouldn't leave Tove. Couldn't leave the boy the war just killed. "I'll kill them all."

Tove's arms went limp inside Rylan's broken body. Blood dripped from her hair as she leaned forward until her head fell against my shoulder. "Take us home, Prophet."

I squeezed my eyes shut and brought her to the person I trusted most to care for Tove until I returned.

"Piercey." We landed back in the room where we'd left the advisors. We remained in the same position as we did on the battlefield, with Tove's head against my shoulder.

My friend slowly turned, horror quietly filling his eyes.

"Elsie's with the healers." I didn't speak Rylan's name, afraid of hurting Tove more. "I'll be back. Help her."

In a voice that sounded unnaturally calm and reassuring, Piercey said, "Tove. Can I sit with you?"

I bit my lip and left them.

On the battlefield, the fighting didn't halt for Elsie's world to fall apart or for Rylan's life to end. I knelt over his broken body and took his cheeks in my hands. The warmth was already fleeing his skin.

His blood stained the beads of ashes he'd worn every day since his dad died. "Rylan," I whispered. My tears fell on his cheeks. I gave myself a few honest moments with no one else around. "I'm so sorry we were too late for you. I'm so sorry, sweet boy." My body shuddered with a sob.

The days to come flooded my mind. Poor Elara said goodbye to a son once, and now she'd send her grandson to be with his father. Elsie's grief-stricken cry reverberated through the screams of war. Closing my eyes, I imagined the memorial hall and the golden tile encased in sunlight that bore his father's name. That was where I left Rylan, hoping his dad might care for him until I returned.

I felt everything and I felt nothing, the two dichotomies tearing my soul into warring factions.

Tove begged me to kill all of our enemies, except I didn't see Malach or Cleo here, and I didn't know who attacked them. My power swept through warriors in deceitfully beautiful colors and destroyed whoever I wished for it to crush. But I no longer saw enemies when I looked upon the battlefield.

I saw the stiff body of the boy my daughter loved. I saw the tearstained faces of a thousand of my people gathered in the memorial hall. I saw the children lying strewn upon the snow in the Flatlander village.

Eskel the Ruthless wove his name down my husband's spine a lifetime ago and forced him into battle. Malach did the same to these warriors. I never knew whether I killed the best or the worst of us out here.

Slaughtering them brought me no solace. It only allowed me to look at Tove when I returned, to slide my hand over her pale cheek, and to tell her I killed them. I killed them all. Every single enemy warrior who didn't choose to flee.

Blood covered my hair, was woven into my plaits, buried beneath my nails. In the time it took for me to end that battle, the healers fully restored Elsie. I stumbled into the memorial hall where Rylan's body lay.

Though Elsie was no longer injured, she looked dead as she lay upon his unmoving chest. Nash and Trish sat behind her silently, their hands on their daughter, devastated and helpless.

My husband looked at me, at all the blood, and offered a single solemn nod.

When I knelt down beside Rylan, Elsie stirred only enough for her eyes to follow the trails of blood, written like a testament across my body.

Her bloodshot eyes met mine. Her voice croaked out hoarse and forever changed. "He's dead, Ma."

My life with Elsie flitted through my mind. A thousand laughs and tears. A whole childhood of this girl. Five years ago, she refused to leave this place when our people grieved. That day, she took the bead from Rylan's hand.

His death hurt far more than the 541 beads of ashes we took that day. It hurt too much to feel more than just the very surface of all that grief.

Hearing Elsie say those words, though, hurt more than even that.

Out beyond our world in the Kethios countless lifetimes ago, the woman my consciousness stemmed from had died, and even after she returned to life, the agony of her death continued to poison her mother. Coralee's death reached all the way to our world in the madness of Dr. Henderson as our supervisor.

My sweet Elsie girl would carry Rylan's death forever.

I fell forward and pressed my hands against the ground, head following, smearing blood along the floor.

Damn Cleo and Malach for waging this war.

Damn every single person who ever levied their power against the innocent.

Damn it all.

"Ma," Elsie cried again. "Ma, it can't be. He can't be dead."

I needed to scream louder than I ever had in any life, but I silenced myself for Elsie and for this young life stolen too soon.

Behind her, Nash knelt, vengeance growing in his eyes. We'd sworn away that poison, but I feared we would not be strong enough to resist it this time.

CHAPTER FORTY-THREE

Elsie scarcely left Elara's side in the days after Rylan's death. I rubbed my throat and passed the sugar to Tove so the girl could finish making tea.

"She's not sleeping," Tove said.

"Piercey made medicine for her."

"She won't take it."

"Nash will get her to. She listens to him about things like that." I took Tove's shoulder. "What about you?"

Her eyes fell. "I miss him."

"You miss her, too."

Tove looked up, as vulnerable as I'd ever seen her. "What if she never comes back from this?"

"She's still here."

The door to Elara's suite opened and closed hard.

"Elsie." It was Nash and his voice sounded urgent.

We all rushed into the living room.

"What happened?" I asked.

"We found him." Nash nodded at me. "We were tipped off that Elsie and her friends were targeted. I didn't want to say anything until I knew more."

Elsie covered her mouth. I worried about her finding out this information on little sleep and while still in shock.

"I captured the man who ordered the hit." Nash reached his hand out to Elsie. "Do you want to come or do you want me to deal with him?"

What was he doing? He should have talked to me about this first. I winced when Elsie rushed out the door, Nash following closely behind.

"Nash," I yelled after him.

He turned and spoke with me through our neural connection. "When Elsie kissed that boy, you called them adults. You said it was their decision. That doesn't change in death."

Elsie looked tortured while she waited for us to silently talk without her hearing. It made me feel guilty. "She's too young."

"Of course, she is. It still happened. We can't take her choice from her."

"Fine." I said that word out loud.

Tove stayed to take care of Elara while Nash led us to the holding cell.

Elsie stumbled into the room, her red eyes swollen yet fierce. The captive knelt with his head lowered almost entirely to the ground. Tacky dried blood caked the side of his face.

Nash loomed over him and watched Elsie with an expression carved of stone. "What are your orders, Commander?"

The title stalled her steps. Hours ago, such words would have made her cheer and scream like a kid. Now only a flicker of surprise enlivened her deadened expression.

"My orders . . ." she rasped. Elsie stared down at him without speaking for a full minute. Nash and I waited patiently. I didn't like dragging this man to the feet of our traumatized and grieving daughter. If I put myself in her shoes, I would want this. Demand it. But I saw everything differently as I looked upon the young woman I loved and cared for more than I ever could myself. For the first time, I understood the pity I saw in Dr. Drake's eyes after I killed Dr. Henderson.

Vengeance couldn't fix this. Not even justice.

Elsie reached past the man and grabbed the handles of Nash's twin swords. She withdrew them slowly and purposefully.

"I need no orders," she said. "Not when I hold my father's swords in my hands. I will carry out my wishes myself with these blades."

The tip of both swords settled beneath his chin and forced him to rise up to look at her.

"No one touches these swords except for the mother and father of our kingdom." Death chilled Elsie's voice into a sound icier than our worst winters. "Only the war chief who defeated the Flatlander army and the Prophet who guards all of Skia Hellig. No one touches these swords except for them." Droplets of blood dripped down the clean blades. "And me."

He whimpered and trembled so much that he forced the blades deeper into his own chin, opening a small slit.

"You killed him." Sorrow hollowed out her voice while rage edged it with a lethal threat. "He was my best friend."

"I'm s-sorry."

The blades cut forward, opening fine cuts on either side of his throat. His eyes bulged. "Keep your meaningless words to yourself."

I tensed my stomach and looked to Nash, trying to gauge whether he regretted handing this burden to Elsie, wondering if he thought instead he'd given her freedom.

I saw no mercy in his eyes. No remorse.

"I followed orders," the man said. "The war isn't ending. Killing you is the only way to kill Eclipse. We needed to break her."

Sickness rocked my stomach. I'd done this to Elsie. All those awful feelings from the past rushed over me, fresh and powerful. Killing the villagers in childhood, slaughtering the guard on the Mountain of the Gods, Dr. Henderson's claim that I destroyed my world every time. All those warriors I'd destroyed in Malach's war.

Now this. Now Rylan.

"You fool," Elsie snarled. "You will never break her, not even if you kill me. You'll only unleash her. Rylan died for nothing. I should force you to live as our prisoner and die a slow death as penance." She lowered the swords to her sides, studying him. "You should suffer for as long as we must suffer without him."

He nodded, tears streaming down his face. "I'm a fool. I should suffer."

"You should. It sounds like mercy to you right now, but I promise that soon you'd beg for death."

A sob burst from him and he squeezed his eyes closed.

"Look at me, coward."

He snapped his eyes open, crying loudly.

Elsie held his stare for several seconds. Then she plunged the twin swords into his chest until the hilts slammed into his body.

The suddenness hit me viscerally. Seeing our little girl kill like that devastated me.

The captive didn't have long to feel surprised. The life quickly fled his eyes.

"I'm not patient enough to give you what you deserve." Elsie slammed her foot against his face and ripped the blades free in a spray of blood. His corpse slammed against Nash's legs as he slid down to the floor.

We all fell quiet.

Elsie breathed heavily and pushed the bloodied swords back into Nash's sheaths. He stared at her with heavy eyes.

"You hoped I wouldn't kill him." Elsie didn't meet her father's gaze or mine, but she also didn't sound apologetic either. "You hoped I couldn't be tainted by revenge." Her hands curled into fists, her stare on the ground. "I don't want him to live if Rylan can't, even if it disappoints the two of you."

I blinked, realizing Elsie was right. We raised Elsie to be better than us, just like we tried to shelter her from our suffering. We didn't want to allow her our own humanity and faults because we couldn't accept just how little control we possessed over her security.

Nash reached out and drew Elsie to him, his large frame dwarfing her. At first, the hardness remained, and then suddenly it broke. Elsie collapsed so quickly I worried she had fainted, but once I saw her shoulders shaking with sobs, I understood she'd just gone limp. I joined them, wrapping my arms around her from behind. We held her as she wept bitterly.

"I need to save him," Elsie cried. "I need to turn back time and reach him. I need to bring that idiot back to life and kill him again for dying on me."

No greater suffering existed than the suffering of your child. Nothing came close. If only I could take every ounce of grief from her and bear it myself. Nash's right hand found mine, holding it while we clasped Elsie to each other.

The passing weeks brought with them the merciless march of war and time. I urged Elsie to remain home from battle, but she threw herself into her new position as commander.

"Ma." Elsie sat beside me when we were both home one day. I saw none of the little girl left in her. "Finish this. Take Finn to King Tyroin to hide and rain your judgment down upon them. Kill Cleo and Malach. Kill the Prophet Sloane if she refuses to help bring about peace. It's time."

My breath lodged in my throat.

"You didn't start this war. You warned them. So, finish it. Don't let them kill our people anymore."

Did she understand what this meant? I clenched my teeth. She did. She knew exactly what she asked of me.

"I can't do it or I would," Elsie said. "The people want you to be a god, so be one."

"This is what the dissidents say." The control I held over this ongoing problem for the past five years very suddenly unraveled. "You can't give in to their rhetoric, no matter how appealing it sounds."

"Maybe it's time, Ma."

Pain dug into my chest. "It's always time when the one we love dies." Watching what the words did to her killed me. Raw pain filled her eyes. Shock that I hurt her in such a way. "Do you know how many more will die if you give in to the temptation of vengeance or malice?"

"I loved him." Her lips quivered, not with fear or hurt, but anger. Anger with me. "What if I died instead?"

"I hope someone who loves me would say it to me. Don't you understand I'm already fighting with all I have?"

Elsie looked away. "Malach and Cleo must have a weakness. Whoever they love, that's who you target."

"I won't do what you ask. They don't care about anyone but themselves anyway. I'm already slaughtering their warriors. What greater sin can I commit for our kingdom other than killing innocent people?"

"You're too worried about what's right and wrong."

"We'll lose everything if I stop worrying about that. It ensures our destruction."

"I don't understand what you're so scared of. How many memorial halls will it take for you to finally let go and just end this?"

"I'm scared of who we might become. Who will save us from ourselves?" I took her chin and made her look at me. "Your dad and I are working diligently to figure out how to beat Cleo and Malach. The war won't end until then. If I knew how, I would. I promise."

Elsie closed her eyes. "I know you're trying. I'm sorry."

"It's been all war for you. If you don't take a break, then you'll be the one to break. Go see Tove."

"I see her every day."

"You fight together every day," I said. "You're ignoring her."

"It feels wrong."

I softened. "It's not wrong, Elsie."

"I'm betraying Rylan. I betrayed him even before he died. It was always supposed to be the two of us, but I let myself get confused. Why did I do that?"

Taking her hand, I led her up. "You'll regret it if you abandon her. Figure out the rest later."

We needed time away from the tower, so I arranged for Tove to meet us at Leif's house, keeping the group smaller than normal this time. Once a few hours passed, Elsie's cousins managed to draw her into conversation, and finally she seemed to have a few moments where she didn't think about Rylan.

Nash held my hand, both of us watching her. "Is she sleeping better?" he asked. "She keeps telling me yes, but I'm not sure."

"I think so."

"I told her it was okay if she hated me, since I made her leave Rylan behind to get healed. But she said she knew he was dead. She just needed to try to save him."

I placed my head against his arm. "It's all terrible."

"At least she's getting some rest today."

A few hours later, Elsie drifted off while lying down with one of her cousins. The entire house quieted, no one wanting to disturb her. Tove wrapped a blanket around her and sat down, an ever-loyal partner. My heart hurt for her, too.

I left to find Leif and discovered him outside using the sharpening stone. "There you are. Elsie fell asleep. Thanks for letting us stay."

"You're always welcome to come home."

I smiled. It did still feel like home. Always would. "Leif."

"What?"

"I don't want you in battle anymore."

He looked up from his sharpening stone. "This is because of Rylan."

"Yes."

"Max—"

"You're the best trainer I know. Prepare these kids for battle. No one will keep them alive better than you."

"I will not stay home from this war. If I die, then I die as I'm meant to."

I closed my eyes and lowered my head. "Leif, please."

"I may not utilize my power as well as the rest of you, but I'm a damn good warrior, and I don't need any more power than I have. It's enough for it to strengthen me and that's all."

"I'm not saying you aren't good enough."

"No, you're saying I'm too old."

I shook my head. "Not that either."

"So why aren't you asking Wren to stay home?"

"You have a thousand kids, Leif."

"Oh." Leif sighed. "It's about the kids."

"I can't watch the kids lose you like Elsie lost Rylan. It's awful, Leif. It's—"

He grabbed me into a strong hug. One embrace shouldn't have been able to soothe so much grief, but it did. "Quiet, girl. I have you."

A flood opened inside me and I started weeping with no hope of stopping. He hugged me even tighter.

"It'll be alright," Leif said. "I'm not dying on you or the kids. Arn will kill me if I do."

I laughed, choking on my tears. "I can't take worrying anymore. It's been so long. My only saving grace is that Finn is too young for war."

"Still, you've come so far. You never slip. You lead our kingdom. You're a mother during a war." Leif wiped away my tears. "You've cried enough tears for now."

"It's your fault," I cried.

"Always my fault, I know."

"And you *are* old." I wiped my nose with the back of my hand. "You're so old now. Stay home."

"I'm going to assume you're joking."

I smiled and tried to stop crying. "I'm a little serious."

"My father, and his father, and all our fathers—"

"Fought until they died. I don't want to hear it."

"Well into sixty years. I have plenty more time before I'm that age."

Rune stepped out and waved at me. "She's awake, Auntie."

I rushed over, not sure how she'd feel since this was the first time she let herself just stay home and rest. Those days could be the hardest.

When I entered the room, Nash was kneeling by Elsie. She was shaking lightly, crying quietly but too hard to speak.

"Let's get you home." Nash worked an arm beneath Elsie's knees and another behind her shoulders. He lifted her, and she curled up, hiding her face against him, just like when she was a little girl. My heart twisted in my chest watching Nash carry her toward the door. Tove rushed to open it for them.

As I passed Tove, I caught her hand and looped my arm through hers. "You, too, sweet girl."

Tears filled her eyes. We walked together, giving Elsie and Nash space for him to help her heal.

"I never knew my dad," Tove said. "I wonder if he would have been good like him. I'm glad Elsie has you two."

I smiled. "I'm glad she has you."

"Rylan and I always thought of Nash as a father." Her voice quieted but she kept talking. "And you like another mother."

"You know you're all our kids."

"I'm sorry you lost him, too," Tove said.

I bit my lip to keep the emotions from rising up too much. "You, too."

"I think Elsie resents me for not being him."

"No, no, no." I pulled her closer while we walked. "You make her feel, and feeling hurts right now. Rylan was her first love." I smiled at her. "Not her last."

Tove had a quiet look of panic.

"He'll always be special to her. There's room in her heart for more. Friends, family, and love."

"Of course."

The smile tempted my lips. "Give yourself time, too. He was important to you as well."

We all went home and though Elsie wasn't okay that day, she slept when the night came. She slept every night after that.

Soon, though the heartbreak lingered, she taught herself how to act like her old self again. Finn sat on the ground with Elsie and Tove, wielding red lipstick like a sword.

He smeared it beneath Elsie's lip. "Oops," he said.

Tove laughed loudly.

"Better not laugh too hard because he'll get you next," Elsie said.

"Yeah." Finn jabbed the lipstick toward her. "Watch out! I'll get you next."

He dabbed the smeared lipstick with a washcloth, leaving a pinkish hue beneath her lips. "So pretty. I do pretty makeup."

Nash looked up from a report he was reading and smirked. "You have a real talent, son."

"Daddy," he said. "Do you have to fight today?" He lowered the lipstick and turned to me with a pout. "Mommy?"

"You're breaking my heart." I moved to sit by him and lifted him onto my lap. "Your sister and Tove are watching you today. It'll be fun."

"It's more fun if you stay, too."

"I know, baby." I kissed his soft cheek. "We'll be home soon. It won't be as long as last time."

"No ouchies either?"

"No ouchies."

"Okay." Seeming content, he attacked his sister with the lipstick again, leaving a cakey layer on her top lip.

"Thank you," Elsie murmured. It felt like she playacted herself. She sounded like Elsie and spoke like Elsie, but I didn't actually see our girl in her. Her eyes were vacant like Rylan's had been, and even though she no longer cried, she looked sadder than before. Grief consumed her even as she lived the normal motions of her ordinary life.

I needed to save her from this suffering.

My hand grasped hers. I smiled at Finn, knowing Elsie wouldn't want me to bring any of her weight into the room, but I couldn't leave her alone in it. At first, her hand stayed limp in mine, but then her grip tightened and she clutched me back. Elsie's expression and voice didn't change, but I sensed her clinging to me, trying to hide her desperation in plain sight. I ran my thumb over the back of her hand in a slow circle. It used to calm me when Wren did it to me.

Finn ran to Nash and, with the little boy's back to us, Elsie settled her head against my shoulder. It lasted only a few seconds, but she rested against me, allowing me to hold her up.

"I love you," I whispered quietly enough to worry she didn't hear. Her hold on my hand tightened again.

CHAPTER FORTY-FOUR

I lifted my face into the salty ocean breeze, listening to the rush of water through the fjords. Nash and I balanced together on a boulder for a short respite before returning to the coastal temple to continue our talks. Our first summit ushered Malach into our lives and a war I wasn't sure we'd ever escape. Continuing to have the leaders of Skia Hellig meet once a year in peace required dedication. My eyes closed so I could focus on the sounds around me.

We didn't have time to enjoy our neighbor's kindness by accepting a boat ride to the temple, and even if we did one day, we would never accept any such gesture from Sloane after she turned her back on Elsie. I remained diplomatic, but we were not and never could be friends.

"The next time we come here, the war will be over." Nash gripped my shoulder with his arm around me from behind. "I promise, Sharpshooter. We're going to finish this."

"Cleo's bonds make her too powerful."

"So do ours, and we don't need to steal a person's soul to grow. Don't lose faith."

Breathing in deeply, I grasped Nash's hand on my shoulder. "It's time to go."

"Be careful."

I swallowed down the lump in my throat. "I will."

The spirit of the annual summit was one of peace, but even Piercey agreed that there'd be no Skia Hellig soon if we didn't do something.

I transported us to the temple and sat down with my people. Jakob and Demetri already sat with theirs, and each nodded at me when I looked to them. We'd lost so much during these last five years, but Skia Hellig was also more united than ever before. I'd found allies in two lands that I might have been at war with otherwise.

I felt Sloane's discomfort from all the way across the room. Everyone knew of Demetri's plan to unite our kingdoms now, and clearly she took it as a threat to her sovereignty.

No one spoke. We waited for the arrival of guests that none of us wanted to see, but whose willingness to talk couldn't be refused. Soon, the thud of heavy footsteps beat into my chest. I didn't turn to see Malach walking toward the center of the temple, nor did I look at him when he stood in the place where this all started.

I did meet Cleo's eyes when she stepped beside him, my hatred burning even more deeply for her because she was yet another family stain.

"We appreciate your allowing us to join," Cleo said. Her gaze focused on me.

Elsie sat down in the chair beside me, stiff, hands grazing her twin blades.

"I thought you decided not to come," Nash whispered.

Her stare didn't shift from our enemies. "Changed my mind."

Cleo continued. "I'm happy to see Skia Hellig uniting beneath the protection of the Prophet Eclipse."

"It's convenient for them to consolidate power for you," Sloane said. "You'll have less work when you finally crush them."

My hands twitched into fists. "We still refuse the offer of your partnership," I said to Cleo, ignoring Sloane. "It's clearly a promise of forced servitude. Our people will never be safe under you."

"That's simply untrue. There's now eleven kingdoms swearing their loyalty to Malach, and they're all prospering."

"Their warriors are sent to be massacred every day," I said. "You'll send ours out to your next conquest. My Valley and my village Denstar lived under the tyranny of Eskel the Ruthless. We will never return to such certain death. It's time for you to walk away from Skia Hellig. The loss is too great. It's unjustified."

"Isn't this what Malach warned you about?" Cleo clasped her hands behind her back and wandered forward. "You're too powerful, Eclipse. You draw attention and enemies. You need a stronger coalition to help protect your people."

"We have a say in this as well," Jakob said. "And we refuse to join you. We see how you treat your people. You let Eclipse slaughter them hundreds at a time. We will never hand over our homes to you, and Eclipse will never give you her power either."

"It sounds like it's time for us to simply take it." Cleo's eyes darkened. "I've tried to spare your life, Eclipse. If you won't relent, then I'll be forced to kill you and take your power for myself."

I shook my head. "You've tried and failed to kill me for years now. You're never going to ascend to live among the gods. You're so far from who you need to be. Take every ounce of my power. It will do you no good. This power is meaningless in the next life."

"It isn't." Cleo's voice lowered in an uncharacteristic display of anger. "You don't understand what this power can do."

What did she think it could do? "You believe your power will do you any good in the next life?"

"When you prove yourself worthy of understanding my plans, I will reveal them to you."

I scoffed, barely controlling my patience. "If you defy the order of nature that the gods created, they'll kill you. You've seen what the stranger who lived among you could do."

"The power of the gods cannot be contained, Eclipse, not even by them. I don't fear that man either. I studied him and I know how to contain him."

That couldn't be true.

Piercey shifted forward to look past Nash at me with his brows knitted together. "She thinks she can break into the afterlife like we did and use her power."

"Then she's an idiot," I said quietly. Surely, she saw the futility in fighting the gods with their own power in their own realm. They lived with the neural implants so much longer than we did.

"Your power struggle with the gods has nothing to do with us." Sloane stood and glowered at Cleo. "Is Eclipse all you want? Do you not care about Skia Hellig at all?"

"I do very much," she said. "The Mountain of the Gods is sacred."

"So take it. Take Max, take the mountain, and leave the rest of the peninsula alone."

Elsie pressed her hands against the table and pushed herself up, her voice shaking. "You're the greatest coward in all of Skia Hellig."

"Sit down," Nash whispered harshly.

She climbed over the table and stalked toward Sloane. "How can you live with yourself?"

"I've not lost a single person to this war." The subtle lines along Sloane's forehead were slightly more defined than a few years ago. "Was your courage and honor worth the life of your best friend?"

The shock of Sloane's cruelty spared us the crucial few seconds to intervene before Elsie utterly lost control of herself. Nash jumped over the table right when Sloane spoke the words, so once Elsie processed them, her father was already rushing up behind her. In a second, Elsie ripped her blades free and launched forward. But Nash hooked his arm around her waist and jerked her backward.

Elsie screamed so loud it broke her voice. She kicked her feet in the air and wrenched against Nash's arm. Fury tightened her muscles until she trembled.

"That wasn't very nice," Cleo said in her falsely cheery voice. "What a terrible thing to say."

Hearing her speak nearly sent me flying for her like Elsie went after Sloane. Nash released the girl, but stood between her and Sloane. "Stand down," he said.

Elsie's chest heaved with deep breaths.

"It doesn't matter that it's cruel," Sloane said. "It's true. If it saved him, you would undo every swing of those blades. You'd choose cowardice and keep him safe at home. Don't look down on me for protecting my people."

"You left my ma to die." Elsie's swords dropped to the ground. Pain gripped her voice. "I was a child and you left me to die." Her head lowered. "Rylan never turned his back on anyone who needed help. Maybe you're safe today, but when they come for you, who will stand up for you? You live alone; you fight alone. You perish alone."

Sloane said nothing, looking more conflicted than I'd ever seen her. "This isn't our war."

"It's never your war until it is." Elsie raised her hands in disbelief. "You think they'll take all of Skia Hellig but leave your people? I suppose once you know for sure the rest of us will die, you'll finally take action and stab us in the back to appease your new lord and master. There's nothing worse than turning on your own people. All of Skia Hellig is uniting and you're being left behind." Elsie turned, looking for a long while at Cleo. "And you're not even worthy of fighting my ma. She's going to crush you."

Cleo smiled. "You're such a sweet, faithful girl. I hope one day we can be friends."

Nash took Elsie's wrist, his quiet encouragement a reminder not to let her emotions run wild with our enemies.

I expected Elsie to say something. Instead, she bent to pick up her swords, walked past us, and quietly continued until she left the main room of the temple.

"Eventful," Malach said. His taunting sneer turned to Nash. "When I kill you and she takes your place, she'll be amusing to defeat."

My husband worked closer to him, his voice more controlled than I expected. "What do words matter when we've dealt in blood for years? Tell us what you came to say so we can return to the battlefield."

Both men watched each other before Malach chuckled low.

"I have nothing to say. I simply want to enjoy the fight. Cleo is the one who wishes to speak."

"So fucking speak." I slapped my palm against the table. "Speak so we can get this over with."

"You needed our help, Eclipse. Look at how great you're becoming because of this war. Your lands are growing. Once the fighting ends, your people will flourish."

"I don't want to hear nonsense."

"It's true," she said. "The best leaders cannot stomach hurting others and do so with the greatest regret. They take kingdoms and raise them to greatness so their people prosper. These kinds of leaders don't want to be the volcano that creates the land. You want to stand upon land formed so long ago it has forgotten its scars. But without the trauma that first created this all, there'd only be ocean to sink into."

I punched the table and cracked the wood. The ragged line splitting all the way down to the edge. "I told you to stop. I won't listen to your ridiculous justifications. You're killing people. We need to end this."

"It only ends once I have you. We've come too far to give up on this now. If we're together, we can ascend in the next life. I need you, Max. You fill what's hollow in me."

"Fill you?" I asked. "I don't fill you up and neither does anyone else you've bonded with. You're a thief. Nothing more than a parasite. Without Malach, you'd be nothing. He fights this war single-handedly for you while you order him about. I won't allow you to leech off me or my kingdom."

"Did you really come here to utter such worthless words?" Demetri asked the two visitors.

Cleo laughed. "I believe them fully. Let us join together just like you're joining with Eclipse."

"Eclipse has proven herself worthy of leading Skia Hellig," Demetri said. "You've proven the opposite."

"It's time," Nash said silently through our neural connection. "Elsie is gone and their attention is on each other."

Neither Cleo nor Malach looked at me. No time to second-guess myself.

I teleported behind Cleo and funneled my energy into a dense ball at the tip of my finger in an explosion of power. Every day of my life I practiced speeding up this attack until I could do it as quickly as I transported myself. One second to teleport and one second to draw upon the energy.

Another to release it.

Cleo didn't even have time to start turning toward me. The cry of the attack rang out and reverberated against the tall walls of the temple.

The power was so great that the white flash blinded me for a second. Black dots danced in my vision. I held my breath to see the damage. It should have been enough to kill her immediately, but I couldn't trust that. I already gathered more energy in my hand, even though that one attack took so much of mine that I wasn't sure enough remained to fight—which was not good, because I was too close to Malach.

Fortunately, Nash flew straight for us.

I blinked to clear my sight and all feeling fled my body.

A burning smell filled my nostrils. Cleo's hair was singed and ragged from where my power burned away hunks of it. White tendrils of energy danced over her body. A loud gasp filled the air as she raised her hands up, holes burned into parts of her clothes. But she was still standing. Conscious, alive, and as far as I could see, not even wounded.

"This is what I've been waiting for." Her voice boomed as if ten copies of herself spoke. The sensation of my power coursing through her overwhelmed me. Nash landed beside me, drawing me beneath the shelter of his arm. We both stared in shock at Cleo slowly absorbing one of my most lethal attacks.

The terror paralyzed me.

Cleo and Malach hid just how much their power had grown. I'd practiced this intensively, making sure I could draw upon this amount of power instantly, certain it was enough to beat them. I studied Cleo. Studied my energy. They'd been fooling me.

Didn't they want this war to end? Why hadn't they killed me yet? Why hadn't they killed all of my people?

A wild laugh tore free of Cleo's lips. Malach dropped to one knee and lowered his hand. She shoved her hands into his hair and clasped his head, gasping again. "Eclipse has not let me down. How is it possible to emit this much energy in an attack so small and fast?"

"Nash," I whispered, heart pounding. Never had I imagined it wouldn't even hurt her.

"Get Elsie out of here."

"I can't leave everyone—"

"Max." Nash ripped me back and shook me once. "Get our daughter out of here! Go to her now!" Taking his twin blades in his hands, he turned and shouted to the entire temple. "Flee. Do not stay to fight. Flee immediately."

Surely Nash didn't expect me to leave him here to fight alone. I caught the sleeve of his tunic to take him with us.

"Oh, please don't leave," Cleo said with another wild laugh. "This is such a wonderful occasion. There are gods among you. I will not lay a hand on any of Eclipse's people in honor of this beautiful gift she gave me. I truly didn't expect her to attack me in this temple. She understands what she must do. We're going to make an incredible team."

"Cleo." The last of my energy zipped across her skin. "What is it you think we'll do in the next life?"

She turned to me, her eyes bulging, mad with too much power to control. "We'll replace the Collective. They turned against Mother and showed so little care for us in this world."

"Dr. Henderson is not your mother."

"The seed of her consciousness loved me, so I know she will love me, too." Cleo rushed closer and placed her hand over my heart. Tingles of my power drifted from her hand to my skin. "If we bind our powers together and imprint ourselves upon the other's soul, the world they made for us will be too small to hold us back, and the world they made for themselves will be prime for the taking."

"You're insane if you think you can take over the Kethios."

"Take it over?" Cleo asked. "No, no. We will rule our own little realm. Their society allowed for the Collective to exist and for these experiments to form. They're viciously curious. Power may be our currency, knowledge is theirs. They'll be so fascinated that subjects from a simulated world discovered a way to conquer their gods. You already broke into the afterlife. You truly believe they can hold us back?"

Nash wrapped his hand around my arm. "We can't stay here, Max. Forget about what she's saying."

"The gods will kill you," I said.

"They're enjoying the show, believing themselves untouchable. Join me, sister. We may not have been born of the same parents, but we were born to unite."

The icy, inhuman stare that haunted me after living through our past life struck me from over Cleo's shoulder. The man who walked between worlds appeared, close enough to touch. He raised his fingers to snap her life away. This was it. Instead of fighting, I should have goaded her into defying the gods, because now their security system would win the war for us.

I braced myself to watch the life leave her eyes, in disbelief that she still smiled.

Where a rush of energy had released from me, I sensed a void within Cleo. The security system's fingers twitched, never quite touching. Her eyes glowed as she pivoted to stare hungrily at him. The void inside of her opened wide like a chasm, destroying everything in its path. I felt the security system's attack depleting before it even happened.

"What is she doing?" I stepped back against Nash.

"I watched him work and I learned how to do as he did. He's powerless against his own weapon."

His eyes blinked rapidly and he shifted in and out of the room, there one moment and gone the next, leaving traces of his image overlaying our world, until finally, he reappeared. Blood slunk from his eyes, ears, and nose.

"The gods wanted to know if someone would one day break their weapon," Cleo said. "That's why they allowed him to walk among us."

"They sent him here to kill us if we got out of line."

"They don't care about our world. He was never here to create order. They care about the knowledge. It was never about saving us from someone defying nature. It was always about learning whether someone could defeat him. They needed to test him before they tried this in worlds they can't control through code, worlds that exist independently of them in the natural universe."

It tracked too well with all I knew of the gods, and was so typical that I couldn't deny it. In fact, it perfectly explained why they wanted the simulations in the first place. They claimed that fewer people suffered by experimenting on us, but really, they just needed a world they could dominate. So they created a playground for themselves.

The security system who loomed over us as an unconquerable threat was rendered inert by a simple trick. Cleo figured out how to replicate his own attack and use it on him. But couldn't he fight back against her?

"My purpose is accomplished," the system said, void of emotion. "I am not the weapon the gods created me to be."

"That's it?" I cried. "Stop her. You were made to stop people like this. Surely, you can try."

"My purpose is complete." He repeated the words and then he vanished from our world, the most useless and horrendous of all the gods' broken promises.

The fear nearly dropped me to my knees. We spent years traveling our previous lives in search of answers for how to defeat him.

If he couldn't stop Cleo, then who could?

"Don't you see?" Cleo's hand reached out to me. "Together, we can accomplish anything."

I needed to talk to the gods. Maybe the security system accomplished its purpose, but the Collective could intervene. She planned to destroy them. "The gods don't rely upon power to destroy you. They created this world and they can easily remove you from it. They can block you from the Kethios. You're a fool if you think otherwise. They're not even intervening, because you only serve to amuse them. If you were a threat, they'd do something about you."

"Perhaps." Cleo stretched her shoulders back. "I will amuse them greatly when I defy their expectations and kill them. We share the same purpose. You will join me." Her eyes turned to the others. Many had fled, but the Prophets and several leaders remained, their attention glued to Cleo. Malach continued to kneel on the ground, the strongest warrior I'd ever faced worshipping at the feet of this woman.

Now Sloane walked forward shakily and then fell onto her knees. She stretched out along the ground, bowing forward. "I repent for not joining you sooner. You wield the might of the gods."

"Are you kidding me?" I growled.

She lifted her head and shouted at me, discomposed for the first time. "She is a god and will kill us all. Spare your kingdom and bow to her."

Cleo smirked while Malach prostrated himself further. The woman stalked closer to Sloane and nodded. "Rise."

The Prophet did so, head bowed.

"You're at my service?" Cleo asked.

"Yes," she said softly.

"Good." The white tendrils of power danced across her skin once more and she slashed her hand across Sloane's throat. It happened too fast to discern, but Cleo had solidified that energy into a blade.

Sloane's eyes opened wide like the deep cut along her throat.

"Welcome to the war." Blood rushed over Cleo's knuckles. "Your people will make fine fodder for Eclipse."

Sloane's hand reached for her throat but she died before she could touch the wound or even collapse. When her body hit the ground, her eyes were already lifeless.

I couldn't breathe.

Cleo turned around. "I did not usher violence into our peace talks. Your brave leader Eclipse sacrificed your summit to save you. Don't hate her for this failure. It's not her fault that she didn't grasp the depth of our power. Look down upon the Prophet Sloane instead. She left our dear Eclipse for dead, and I cannot forgive that."

Nash gripped my hand. "You need to talk to the gods."

"They're watching. They just don't care. No one is coming to save us."

"This is my gift to you, dear sister." Cleo lifted a hand to me. "I know your heart is not open to me yet, but I give her life to you anyway because I know one day we'll be together. I can only hope you're alive to enjoy it. Do not make me kill you as I killed her."

"Why are you prolonging this?" I asked. "Clearly you can kill me now and take my power."

"You really don't understand. You're just too innocent. It's the same reason Malach lets you slaughter his people." Cleo's giggle turned my stomach in nausea. "Your power is too delicious to turn down."

Anguish that ran far deeper than rage or shock ripped me to shreds. "You're absorbing the power I release during battle. I never sensed you there."

"You've never seen me when I didn't want you to. I've been here a long, long time." She kissed her fingertips and then reached them out for me. "I never let my baby sister far from my sight, not when she's spent so much of her life feeding me."

"I hate you." I couldn't draw in a breath. "You're even worse than her. Dr. Henderson at least told herself she was doing the right thing."

"War is a lucrative game for those who know how to play it. Hate me all you want, sister. Keep fighting me. Every single person you kill only strengthens me. Your energy has fueled me for years. I will protect Skia Hellig in ways you never could because you can't stomach the rise to greatness."

"After you crush us, you mean."

"I will only crush you if it's necessary," Cleo said. "I win no matter what you do. Fight me and you allow me to absorb the energy you release. Surrender to me and you make my dreams a reality. Protest this war and I kill everyone you love. There's no option you like, so pick the one that helps your people. Join us."

I looked around to see the people of Skia Hellig frozen and helpless. Some of the best warriors I'd ever met stared at Cleo, as much at a loss as me.

"The coast now belongs to Eclipse." Cleo clapped her hands. "We'll wait to claim it until we can have it all. Skia Hellig is stronger as one, and it's as one that we will take it." Cleo smiled so sweetly it made me sick. "Don't blame yourself, sister. This needed to happen. The peninsula was divided and now you can protect them all. It's my ultimate gift to you. The kingdom you were meant to rule. All of Skia Hellig."

I didn't want this. I never asked for it.

CHAPTER FORTY-FIVE

That peaceful other world we crafted for ourselves within our home shattered, and I didn't see how it could ever come back together again. Nash, Elsie, Tove, and I all returned home, shaken by what Cleo had done in the temple.

"Do you realize what this means?" I tried to talk quietly enough that the kids wouldn't hear from Elsie's bedroom. "Cleo can render our attacks inert just like the security system. She's toyed with us for years. We never figured out how to stop him, and so we don't know how to stop her. We've replaced him with someone far worse, because she absorbs our energy, too. And at least he wasn't trying to take over the world."

Nash didn't speak.

"Are you listening?"

"Why does she need you? There's more we don't know. The security system could instantly kill people with a flick of his fingers. Cleo may not be able to do that. If there's a limit to how much power she can diffuse, then we could overwhelm her with so much energy she can't stop it."

"We haven't been able to do that even before we saw the extent of her power."

He dug his hands into his hair. "That power we glimpsed . . ."

I nodded to tell him I knew what he meant. We returned to the end of our second life in hopes of learning more about that strange energy hovering over the sun. Though I didn't recognize it, I also found it somewhat familiar. Not entirely unknown.

"Did we take too much peace for ourselves before? Is this all our fault?" I asked quietly. The thought of laughing while kids like Rylan died gutted me. Now we held the tattered kingdoms of Skia Hellig together while a madwoman capable of killing the god's security system continued to wage war against us. "What kind of monsters can feel a shred of happiness when they're out there dying?"

Nash scooter closer and held me tight.

"We let ourselves forget," I said. "We fooled ourselves. We said it was survival, that we need to live, that it's resisting Malach and Cleo to take our joy. It was a sickness."

"I might have saved Rylan if I wasn't distracted," Elsie said. She stood in the doorway now.

"No." Nash shook his head and motioned for her. When she sat beside us, he took her hand while he kept his arm around me. "Exhausting ourselves by never resting wouldn't have done anything except for weaken us."

Elsie settled her head against Nash's arm. "Are you sure, Daddy?"

Her small voice pinched my chest.

"Certain. You couldn't make me prouder, Elsie. You've done well."

Her eyes closed tightly.

"Maybe it's time," I said. "If I partner with Cleo, no more of our people will die. That will be the end of it."

Elsie jolted up. "First, even if you could trust that psycho bitch, which you can't—you saw her kill Sloane after she declared loyalty to her. Even if you could trust her, she'll have ultimate control over you. Who knows what she'll make you do."

"What if it would have saved Rylan?" I asked. "Our kingdom is filled with people who are loved and deserve to live."

Elsie clasped my hands. "No one needs to tell you how wrong and horrible this is. You're grieving and you're scared we're going to lose the war."

"What if we do lose? Have you thought about that, Elsie? Because I think about it every day. Our villages are on fire."

"Surrendering is losing the war," she said. "You can't think about this. There's a reason that in five years you haven't actually considered it. When someone invades your land and demands your power, there is never going to be peace with them. You have to defeat them."

"You know she's right," Tove said. "You can't trust her."

"We keep fighting," Nash said. "To assume defeat is to surrender, and our family never surrenders."

I rubbed the ache in my throat. "If Cleo hurts any of you . . ."

My husband cast a look at Elsie and me. "We're alive and we're together. Have faith."

No matter how many times he said it, I struggled to feel it the way he did. "We have no choice. We won't surrender or hide. We can't abandon Skia Hellig. We have to fight and believe we can win. You're right. It's our only option."

"There's no time for despair." Tove placed a hand against the back of Elsie's head. "Rylan would want his memory to make us strong, not weak."

This gave us all pause.

"I'm sorry, everyone." I dipped my head, ashamed that I gave in to fear. "It's just I sense the end is coming. Don't you? It'll all be over soon, for better or worse. We're becoming too powerful for them to let us live."

I destroyed the promise of peace in our annual summit by attacking Cleo, and then entirely failed to hurt her. The war felt even more dangerous than it did a week ago. Nash and I joined Elsie and Tove on the battlefield with this worry in mind. While we feared our presence may have drawn attention to her, we figured that someone would probably target her again regardless. We needed to be close enough to watch over her.

Elsie leaned into her new role of commander, leading her war party on the battlefield with so much confidence.

Nash and I resisted using our combined power to unleash our most powerful attack when it required so much of our strength. We needed to hold off until Malach and Cleo both showed themselves next, to try a plan that may never work. It was our last hope, though.

So we fought together among our people, careful to conserve as much energy as possible.

"Push through," Elsie ordered the young warriors while they made headway breaking through the front lines. She drew her bow and sent an arrow soaring that Tove coated in explosive power. It pierced a man and erupted in his chest, sending his body crashing to the ground. Then she retrieved her twin blades and sprinted forward, slicing them along her sides, catching the legs of the warriors she skirted past.

Nash barreled through enemies slightly ahead of Elsie. Each slice of his sword hit enemies with so much strength that they flew through the air and crashed into those around them. Bones snapped and cries filled the air.

I shot my arrows rapidly and without pause, using my energy arrows once my physical ones dwindled. I missed fighting like this, rather than soaring through the air above it all. Nash ducked beneath the thrust of a spear and landed a sharp blow against his attacker's thighs. Running, I jumped off his shoulders with my energy bow drawn and scattered five arrows into the enemy warriors surrounding us. I landed and stabbed the end of my bow into a man, the power carving through him. Nash followed a wide arc around my path of destruction with some of the most rapid strikes I'd ever seen him use. His technique was flawless and none of the warriors knew how to defend against that level of master swordsmanship. He didn't need his power.

We defeated a few dozen with only using the smallest amount of energy.

Elsie stared at us with the same kind of wonder filling her eyes as when she was little. I realized that she didn't often fight with us in close-ranged combat like this. She normally only saw us in sparring matches.

"Woah," she said.

The rest of her war party watched, the young warriors shocked. We'd forced the attention of the nearby warriors so they attacked or retreated, leaving Elsie's group with no one close by to fight.

Our daughter grinned and rallied her warriors with a cry. They stormed forward, seeking out more to fight.

We lost ourselves in the vigor of battle, when nothing existed save for the blades swinging for us, and each moment that required our attention. Fighting through Malach's army, all else faded.

An arrow shot through the air for me. Never did I rely upon my energy shield for physical weapons now that the poison existed. I cut it down with my sword and wheeled around, searching for whoever aimed it at me.

A determined stare cut through the warriors. My legs went numb beneath me and confusion sprouted before the weighty understanding came crashing over me.

Owen nocked an arrow, wearing the same angry eyes as the day in the memorial hall when he honored all the dead in his family. Only now a full beard darkened his face and he looked like a stubborn man, not a lost boy.

Betrayal stung so badly.

"Break free," Owen roared.

"Nash, the dissidents," I yelled before I teleported directly to Owen.

That split second was all it took for pandemonium to break out all around the battlefield. Where we made progress against the enemy before, I now heard terrible shrieks. All around, our own warriors turned against us. There was no telling how many betrayed us.

I ripped Owen's bow from his hand and broke it over my knee. He stabbed his sword for me but I caught it between my palms, twisted it free, and tossed it to the side. "What have you done?"

"We will no longer burn the ashes of our dead," he said. "It's time to take the hand of peace Malach offers."

"You never stopped fighting against us, did you?"

"We just got smarter." His nostrils twitched. "You didn't."

"Given the choice between Malach and me, you choose Malach?"

Owen looked entirely closed off. "He will do anything to keep us safe."

Explosions shook the ground. Warriors sacrificed themselves once again, turning their own power into bombs to kill as many of us as possible.

"Safe?" I lifted my hands to the carnage surrounding us. "He's sacrificed hundreds of thousands of warriors over the past five years."

"Warriors." Owen drew the beads of the dead over his head and lifted them in the air between us. "Not the innocent."

"Nothing can ever excuse what you've done." I grimaced and looked at the necklaces. "You've desecrated their legacy. If your mother knew what you've—"

"I don't care. They're all dead. When Malach seizes Skia Hellig, all the children of the peninsula will live without fear. He takes the power he needs to protect his people." He threw the beads on the ground. "I'm free now. So kill me. I don't care."

"You think I'm going to kill you." I shook my head in disdain. "I want you to live to see what our kingdom becomes and to see Malach fall. You will weep with the bitterest regret for endangering us at our most vulnerable time."

I sent a message to Gael requesting his help so I didn't waste energy on this traitor.

"Don't bother sending me back into captivity," Owen said. "I'll end it myself."

"You won't." I picked up the beads from the ground. A powerful portal opened close to me and I passed them to Gael as he stepped out. "Make sure these are kept safe. We can't dishonor the dead."

"Their yearning for justice will not be silenced just because you silence me," Owen said. "It's only the beginning, Eclipse. Lock us all away. Kill us all. You will never root out—"

Gael used his power to shove Owen through the portal. His voice lowered. "I'm sorry this happened to your kingdom."

My eyes stung. "The fools."

"Bombs!" The warning sprang up from everywhere.

Gael and I turned our attention to saving our people from our very own warriors who betrayed us. We were barely hanging on in the war. I wanted to believe Owen's rebellion wouldn't hurt us, but I had no idea how many more people waited to stab us in the back at the worst moment. Damn it, how could this happen?

I ran to Elsie and Nash.

"I can't believe they did this." Nash seethed with anger.

How could we discern friend from foe?

Pain dug into my heart, but I didn't have time to feel it. My people were falling apart. Malach's warriors and our own traitors fought together against us at this very moment.

And of course, that's when I felt them. Cleo and Malach. They'd arrived and they wanted me to know.

"Elsie," I said. "I want you and Tove to go home."

"You can't ask me to do that, Ma. I'm a commander now. I'm not abandoning my people."

I took her hand and held it with both of mine. "I'm begging you, Elsie. I can't do what I need to do and worry about you."

"I'm a warrior now. Let me fight. We need everyone we can get." She ripped away from me and charged after an enemy. My eyes squeezed closed for a moment. I'd have to force Elsie to leave.

"I hate seeing you endure this pain." Cleo approached. "Your own people scheming against you for years and turning on you. It's tragic after all you've done for them."

"Don't antagonize me." I pointed my blade at her. "I'm done with you."

Nash walked to my side.

We didn't need to discuss what to do. We'd already decided that when we saw them next, we'd try our last hope. Power flickered inside me while we connected. Together, we reached within our depths for all the power we could find, holding nothing back.

Five years of loss etched into my heart. Every tear shed in every memorial hall, all the cries from Elsie as she lay upon the body of the boy she loved, the weakness Elara felt after laying to rest her grandson. The betrayal of the people we sacrificed for all these years turning against us. It mixed with our love for Elsie and Finn, for each other, our family, and our kingdom.

Nash and I refused to believe there was no hope. We refused to surrender.

And so we drew deeper, searching the past, peering beyond the veil of this life. We'd spent years living through our lost lives and learning from each other. Growing close to each other. We were not just Max and Nash, the Prophet and war chief of Elvadel. We were the warriors from the forgotten dreams. We were the seeds of people who grew into gods in the Collective.

All despair and fear gave way to recognition of a power we cultivated over lifetimes. That searing burn of power we glimpsed at the end of our second life pierced us now. We'd returned to that moment enough that I learned to grab a hold of this wild, untamed energy.

At first, the power that flowed over the villagers in beautiful hues when I was a child filled us. But we reached far, far deeper, pushing ourselves through space-time. The world cracked at the seams. I saw a hundred moments from three lives collide together. Every color imaginable burst over my eyes. We connected deeply with ourselves and with our past lives.

Power rippled through us.

Three lifetimes coalesced like we lived every single moment at the same time and wielded every speck of power at once.

The force was ripping our bodies apart. I was certain of it. Terrible pain stabbed every part of us. I felt his pain and mine.

We held each other's hands tightly, not sure if we were unlocking a new dimension of power or killing ourselves. In the last life, we merely glimpsed this power, but today we unleashed it fully.

I placed my faith in our bond, in our past selves and who we had grown to be, and I released my fear of myself. I chose to have faith in us.

The world shifted and put itself back together. My eyes snapped open and I was no longer connected to Nash. Cleo and Malach stood in front of us, but they weren't looking at us.

They both stared up at the sky. A shadow fell over the whole battlefield. Everyone had stopped fighting and now lifted their faces.

High in the air above us, directly over the sun, a massive ball of power burned like the stars in the night sky. Except it burned black with eddies of energy swirling through it.

Eclipse.

The power resembled one so closely, darkening the ground around the battlefield.

Holy shit.

This was it. This was the flame that burned inside of me my entire life.

And it was never just my power.

When I killed those villagers as a child, when again and again I accessed more than I could explain, I tapped into this incredible pool of energy.

For three lifetimes, Nash and I grew this power together, nurturing it between us as a sum greater than its two parts, the bond transforming what was once mine and once his into something neither of us could imagine on our own. And it wasn't until we finally learned to harness it together that it could fully emerge.

It was us all this time.

We were each other's power.

Cleo stared up at the sky, looking helpless to deny its allure as the beautiful collision of energy erupted into the deepest colors known to the human eye. Our power grew like its very own star.

"What is that?" Malach asked.

"It's the seed we planted long ago." Though I answered his question, I stared at Cleo. "We hid it within ourselves when Dr. Henderson first destroyed our world, and it has grown since. We just didn't know it until now. It bound us together and it led us to this point."

This was so much more energy than either of us ever harnessed. Was it enough to kill Cleo?

Nash and I looked at each other. His fingers wound through mine. We fell into our connection, one with ourselves and with that incredible power in the air.

I wasn't sure how to wield it, but with all my heart, I willed it directly at Cleo. I willed it to destroy every last cell of her body and rid this world of her threat.

A single black point popped onto her forehead and slowly began to grow. She touched it and cried out. She'd try to absorb the power into herself, but I sensed the energy overwhelming her. Too much for her to handle.

She began to squirm, stumbling back, scratching at her forehead.

"It really hurts."

Malach's fingers suddenly clawed bloody marks into his chest. Cleo's pain spread to him as well. Good.

But then his body started to quake and every single vein in his body strained against his skin.

Realization hit me in an eruption of panic. I'd seen this too many times before.

My connection to Nash severed in the overstimulation of fear and trying to control that great power of ours.

"Bomb!" I screamed.

Nash dove for Elsie and Tove. I tried to teleport to the girls, but the eruption of Malach's power hit right as I began and it planted me in place.

Abandoning all care for his life, Malach surrendered all of the energy within him in an explosion certain to claim his life and likely every last one of us.

The searing pain burned across my entire world. I didn't reach Nash or the kids in time.

With all the strength I could muster, I tried to throw all of our energy floating like a massive star in the sky at Malach and Cleo. But once the first waves of Malach's power unfurled from his body in a red wave, I thought only of my people.

Not just the people loyal to me or the people I called my own.

All the people gathered here. People forced to leave their families and tear apart each other's lives.

I didn't have time to make a decision. Malach's explosion would incinerate those closest to him and surely kill the vast majority of those gathered. Funneling my energy at him and Cleo meant sacrificing all these people.

It happened too fast for thought. My heart chose for me and directed the energy that Nash and I stored over these lifetimes where I needed it to go.

CHAPTER FORTY-SIX

Darkness settled over me. Zaps of energy danced along my skin. I opened my eyes, seeing only pitch-black.

"Nash . . ." I blinked the dust from my eyes, my arms too heavy to move. Still, I saw nothing. The same force that flattened me to the ground during the explosion now held me down. "Elsie?"

Slowly, light crept into the darkness and cut through the fog of power that settled over us. As the black energy dissipated, I looked up to see that the star eclipsing the sun had vanished. All that energy we drew upon from our past three lives coated our people now and protected us.

It still wasn't enough to stop all the damage. I feared that everyone without power might've been dead.

I coughed hard. The power faded enough now that I saw Nash lying over both Elsie and Tove, their smaller forms hidden well beneath him. None of them moved.

Digging my fingers into the dirt, I tried with all my strength to drag myself toward them, only I didn't budge. The two of them consumed my mind and blotted out the rest of the world. I needed to know if Elsie and Nash survived. If they were lying right in front of me dead together. I could do nothing else, not even breathe, until I knew. But . . .

Malach.

I couldn't assume he'd killed himself. With his bonds to Cleo and so many warriors, he may have been able to stay alive.

I tore my eyes from my family and searched for our enemy. Taking my attention off them agonized me as much as the burns and wounds.

Malach's meaty arm caught my attention first. The flesh melted over his right hand and up his forearm, replaced by charred black meat that still sizzled. He sat on his knees, his head bobbing.

I couldn't draw on any energy. Nash and I had given everything to form that ball in the sky and then we'd offered that to our people. I felt the way I had when the instructors sealed my power. Like it was entirely gone.

"We need to end this . . ." I coughed specks of blood against my hand. "We're all dying . . ."

Malach swayed his knees. "It cannot end until we own your power."

"Even if it kills you."

His tattoo glowed brightly at the center of his chest, through the holes the explosion left in his shirt. Breath rattling and uneven, his head jerked up a few inches at a time, until finally I saw his face. The whites of his eyes were scarlet. Blood dripped from the corners like tears. It looked like someone grated the skin off the right side of his face and charred it. Blood ran steadily from his open mouth. "Even if it kills me."

The fog cleared more so that in the distance, I could see the dead burned with flames that danced together over the armor marking them Malach's or ours, with no deference to either.

"Why?" Tears burned my stinging eyes and my raw skin. "Why can't Cleo let me go?"

"She'll say it's because we need the power." A thick strand of blood hung from his lips and swung before falling to the ground. He rasped in a labored breath. "That we need the peninsula." His body dipped forward slowly. "But she doesn't care who she kills as long as she gets their power when they die. It's all for her and who can know what she really wants?"

My eyes closed. "She'll burn down entire kingdoms to punish me for the fact that my father loved me and forgot about her."

"You think I'm so simple?" Cleo's perky voice rattled in my head and made me want to scream. Malach and I could barely speak, so how could she sound so upbeat? "I've never been interested in punishing you, sister." Her voice drifted around me even though I didn't see her. "I remember the pride I felt when we first saw how great you would be one day."

"Don't call me sister," I said.

Gauzy purple skirts drifted through the smoke in the distance. The flowers around her wrists burned violet through the haze. "I saw the god in you the day I watched your power cleanse our village and our father of their sins." Cleo emerged from the flames unscathed and drifted closer. My body wound tighter with each step. "Your whole life you've been too afraid to let yourself become who you truly are."

I shook my head and squeezed my eyes shut. "I'm not holding back. I'd never hold anything back with my family in jeopardy. I'm no god, no demon . . . no Prophet . . ." Pleading filled my voice when I raised my eyes to her. "I'm just me, not what you all want from me. Only Max, and I've said it my whole life."

Cleo's fingers ran through Malach's hair when she walked past him. "It's true. You're just a woman." Light steps carried her closer to me until finally she knelt before me. Her uncannily young face and smooth skin were too clean with the soot in the air. "For now."

"Please, Cleo—"

"This is what you need me for." A soft thumb gently wiped the blood from the corner of my mouth. "This could have ended well for you. Your kingdom could have been at peace and your people safe forever if you joined me."

"Never plant a kingdom in poisoned soil," I whispered.

"All great kingdoms are planted in this soil. Blood, soot, broken spirits. Death fertilizes life. Injustice and heroism melting into one. It doesn't matter what you come from, but what you become. You want to believe you cannot survive what I'm doing to you, but you can. So, for once in your life, let someone help you." She placed her hand over my heart and a cooling relief slowly crept over my burned skin. "We'll become gods together. We'll heal what our mother broke."

"Was it you?" I barely discerned my own voice through the rasp from the smoke and swelling in my throat. "Did you tell Father I needed to kill them?"

Her relief bore deeper into me and cooled the edges of my anger, threatening to rip it away from me entirely. "Our father had wild ideas of his own, but we wanted the same thing. We wanted to heal this world. He believed you released those poor souls into the next life to live in bliss. As for me, I know it's worth living this broken life, because it's ours."

My lips quivered as I looked into her pale eyes. "You don't care about this world any more than he did."

"We're not all monsters just because we can't be as good as you."

"You're a monster because you choose to hurt people." I gripped her wrist and tried in vain to rip her away from me. "I will never give you my kingdom." Scraping the depths of myself for power, I focused it on my hand, desperate to finally hurt her. "I will never give you my family." My nails dug into her skin. "And I will never give you my power."

"Look around, Max." Her voice filled my mind even though her lips no longer moved. "You're all dying. Why is this worth it to you?"

My eyes shifted to Nash and Elsie.

Cleo smiled softly. "I want to do this with you. Don't make me take it all away. How will that help the people you love?"

"I can't."

"Even if you all die? Nash." She tilted her head to the side. "Elsie. Finn."

My body shook with sobs I was too weak to shed.

Cleo studied me. "Every single person in your kingdom."

"You'd kill them all?"

"The world will kill them all," Cleo said. "I'm not the only one who wants your people. They will suck your kingdom dry the moment you're not here to protect it."

"Then stop. If you care about me, if you love me, then stop."

Cleo smirked sadly. "I never said I loved you. I hardly know you." The palm against my skin suddenly pressed so hard it threatened to break my ribs. "We could be a family, but you've made it clear you don't want me. You've made it clear that you refuse to work with me no matter the cost."

Some tiny inkling of power remaining within me responded to Cleo, wiggling loose like a tiny pebble hidden at the bottom of a well. I tried to cling to it, knowing that if she took this bit of power from me, she'd have me. And if I refused to give it, then I'd die just like the others.

It couldn't be over.

"Even if you give your power to me, you'll rebel and fight me so much that I'd have to kill you. If Malach hadn't sacrificed himself like this, you might have killed me today. You're too dangerous for me to create a connection to you, and this conversation proved to me how hopeless it is to sway you."

Lies. Cleo always planned to kill me once she conquered me, no matter what she'd said before.

I searched the sky for the star of our own making. But Nash was lying unconscious over our daughter and I saw only smoke.

How could this not be enough?

As I felt the seed of my power drifting closer to her demanding hand, it all became real to me. I saw Finn in his crib as a baby with those eyes so full of goodness, of wonder and love, peering up at me. Elsie's small arms encircled my neck and her voice flowed through me.

"Ma."

Maybe I slipped, lingering somewhere between this life and the others, between this moment and the rest, because I saw Nash overlaying this world as clearly as if I could reach out to touch him. If only I could move.

He held Elsie as she cried herself to sleep the first time I met her. He lifted Finn into the air with his chubby hands eclipsing the golden rays of sun. Nash's eyes gazed at my mouth as he drew his thumb along my bottom lip, looking at me like I was all he could see.

We held each other in our first life and promised forever, burying deeply within each other while the world gave way.

And then I saw the blood of the slaughtered children pooling on saturated ground after my own people killed them. Where my mind once glossed over their faces, I saw each one clearly now. Every single innocent little face.

They'd all be dead.

Our children would be dead.

There were no plans this time, no swells of power, no breakthroughs. The last kernel of my power—of my life—grazed the tips of Cleo's fingers. For my refusal to break, I'd abandon this world, and our enemies would feast upon my family and my kingdom.

I'd be gone, unable to stop it. And Cleo would use my power just the same as if I'd willingly given it up.

A terrible cry broke free of my chest and I fell forward against this damn woman who called herself my sister, sobbing so hard I couldn't hope to speak. I couldn't think or feel. My soul broke in her hands, and I could feel nothing except the disillusion of everything I thought I was.

"Wait . . ." I forced the single word to leave my lips.

Cleo lifted my head to look into my eyes and to watch me give myself to her, knowing she'd use my power for all the terror she'd used Malach for. I had no say in that, though. My choice was simple.

Die and abandon my people or beg Cleo to spare them.

"Will you give it to me? It's so fragile right now." Wonder filled Cleo's eyes. "I promise I'll do good with it if you hand it over."

Her lie burned through the shattered pieces of my spirit. "My people will be safe?"

"The safest in the world." A wild smile trembled onto her face. "You'll be remembered as a legend."

I didn't care about that.

My heart opened to her in the most horrid of any sin I'd ever committed. Far worse than when my power exploded onto the innocent villagers. If I'd die and leave everyone behind, I needed to know they'd be safe. I needed the hope that Cleo would keep her promise rather than the assurance that she'd destroy those I loved.

The warmth of that flame I always carried was slipping away to Cleo, almost entirely gone.

Then I heard his deep, soothing voice. Nash, right in the moment I needed him most. The relief washed through me until his words settled in my mind.

"Take . . . me . . ." Nash was hardly audible. "Take me . . . instead . . ."

No.

Cleo froze just before grasping my seed of power fully.

"You want her to live . . ." He struggled to lift his head. Blood covered his forehead and cheeks. I couldn't even tell where it came from. "You tried so hard . . . to spare her . . ." Red dribbled onto his lips.

"Yes." Cleo didn't hesitate. "I want her ruling over her kingdom."

"So take me." Nash's forehead lowered to the ground. He groaned weakly. "You saw that our power is one . . . You only need one of us, so make it me."

"No, Nash," I screamed. I tried to rip away to go to him, but Cleo clasped the back of my neck in a firm hold. "You can't. I'll never forgive you!"

"There's no reason not to . . ." Nash's face slid along the ground until he could see me. "I love her. Please, let me do this. She died for us once already . . . It's my turn . . ."

Cleo's head fell back and a pained sigh escaped her lips. "It's just so beautiful. As beautiful as that star you painted in the sky together."

Her hand left my chest and I caught it, dragging it back to me. "No, Cleo. No."

She shook me off and turned toward Nash.

"Don't do this." I fell onto my hands and screamed through each motion as I dragged myself forward. "Nash!"

Cleo's hand lifted and she pulled Nash closer using her power. He slid off Elsie and along the ground, leaving a trail of blood. Then she lifted him into the air and studied him.

"You'll give your power over without a struggle?" Cleo asked. "I don't want to shatter it while it's weak."

My tears wet the dirt beneath as I managed another foot closer. "Nash, you can't. The kids . . ."

Nash looked at me. "I told you on the day I married you that I would die for you, Max." His eyes shone with tears. "Take care of the children and the kingdom."

"You can't." I sobbed. "I need you!"

"We need you, too," he said. "It's my turn now. You did this once and now it's me."

I screamed and fell onto my face, unable to hold myself up. "I won't let you."

"Don't do it in front of her," Nash said. "Don't make her watch."

With more desperation than I ever remembered feeling, even when my world ended, I drew upon all I had to rise up and to draw Nash to me. But I didn't even manage to lift my face from the dirt.

I wept on the ground, begging him not to.

"Fine." Cleo snapped and I felt myself ripped across the ground.

I lay listless on my side as Nash's body lowered to mine. His heavy arm fell over me, his lips close to mine.

"Max," he whispered.

"No." I closed my eyes, refusing to look at him and say goodbye, because it was the only protest left to me.

His hand smoothed against me, warm and sticky with blood. "Don't fight what you can't stop."

I opened my eyes only because I feared I may never see him again. "Let me die. I don't want to live without you."

"I never wanted to live without you either." He gasped as he forced his hand to my cheek. "I'll find you in the next life."

"It can't be time." Hot tears poured down my cheeks.

"You need to stay with them, Max. We've done this before. We can do it again." His gaze raked down my face. "Now, kiss me."

My lips drew near to his and I whimpered against his mouth, broken beyond repair. "I can't be brave for you," I confessed.

"I don't need you to be."

I sobbed now and kissed him once. "What will I tell Elsie and Finn?"

Tears thickened Nash's voice. "Tell them their father loves them more than life itself."

"Nash," I cried.

"It may be a long time before I get to hold you again." He'd spoken the words to me before in our first life as it all ended. "Damn it, Max." His hand gripped my face. "Kiss me like you mean it."

I cried out from the pain as I strained to slide my arm over him and hold him close. Our battered lips connected and I breathed in the man I loved more than life itself. I soaked in every single sensation. The graze of his tongue along mine, the softness of his lips, how he moved and breathed. I loved feeling his body pressed against mine. I knew that feeling so well now. I needed it. I needed him.

My tears stung my burned lips. "Please, Nash." I held him as tightly as I could. "Nash—"

A force tugged his body from me. I held on with all my might, but Cleo ripped him away.

I screamed from my depths. "No!"

She dropped him on his knees with her power and placed her hand on his shoulder.

"Let him live," I begged. "Take his power but let him live."

"There's no reason to," she said. "You're both too dangerous to leave alive, and I don't have a soft spot for him like I do for you. He's right. This is best. I'll protect your kingdom as payment for his energy."

Panic filled me as I looked at our daughter. "Elsie," I said. "Elsie, you have to wake up." I dragged myself toward her. "Baby girl, please. There won't be another chance. Wake up."

Nash watched Elsie and then he looked at me again, a thin line of tears breaking free. "Goodbye, Max. I love you so much. Please forgive me."

I etched his amber eyes into my mind forever. "I'll see you again," I said.

A shaky smile formed on his lips and he nodded. "In every life to come."

"I love you, Nash." I swallowed hard. "I—"

Cleo and Nash disappeared without warning. The cruelty and finality sent a wave of shock through me.

A scream tore free from my lips, one that sounded like it came from another person.

I fell onto the ground, my face pressed against the dirt. Malach's eyes stared into mine. I realized then that, unnoticed and without any ceremony, Malach had died right in front of us, and none of us even knew.

He sacrificed himself for Cleo and she didn't even look at him. No thank-you or acknowledgement.

Malach was dead.

The war was over.

And Cleo had stolen my heart and soul from me.

CHAPTER FORTY-SEVEN

Mommy."

Small, soft hands smoothed over my cheeks. I opened my eyes to see Finn's beautiful brown eyes.

"Wake up."

I smiled softly and lifted him onto my lap. The fresh outdoor air filled my lungs. "I'm awake, baby. Sometimes it just feels good to close my eyes." Because I saw Nash best like that. When I shut out the rest of the world, I saw his eyes, sensed the warmth of his power, felt the hardness of his chest beneath my fingers, and heard his deep voice whispering in my ear. My entire body and soul cried out for him to return to me.

Finn curled up against me. In the weeks since Cleo stole Nash from us, our son clung tightly to me. We told him Daddy was away making peace for us while we searched for any evidence of whether Nash lived or died. But Finn had never gone this long without seeing him. And my sweet boy understood something was very wrong.

"Are you sad, Mommy?"

"I'm so happy when I'm with you." I drew him close. "The war is over, baby. I can be home every night."

"Why is Daddy still fighting?"

"He's not fighting anymore. He's helping us make peace with our enemies."

Finn nestled against me. "I'm sad."

The words broke my heart. "Because you miss him?"

"I miss him so bad."

Cleo promised to kill Nash because she didn't believe she could control him. I refused to believe it until I saw irrefutable proof. We never gave up. We never surrendered. There was hope. There had to be.

But damn it did I miss him so badly I couldn't draw in a single breath without aching terribly.

I took Finn for a walk through the gardens where the summer flowers bloomed. The villagers planted the flowers every year, even during the waste of the war. A beautiful assortment of colors spread out over the land, surrounded by carefully pruned hedges.

Finn picked a daisy and handed it to me. "For you, Mommy," he said. "It's pretty like you." Then he grabbed another. "This one's for sis."

We walked hand in hand up to the apartment to find Elsie lying in her bed. Without a war to fight, she didn't have the usual distractions.

"Sis." Finn climbed onto her bed and stuck the flower behind her ear. "I got a present for you."

Elsie hugged him weakly. "Thanks, buddy."

How much could one girl lose and continue on? She was still grieving Rylan and now her precious dad.

Tears filled my eyes. I struggled not to cry all the time. They came and went throughout the day.

"Do you want breakfast?" I asked.

Elsie looked at me with dull eyes. "No."

"I want you to eat lunch, then."

She nodded.

I sat on the edge of her bed and finally let myself lower. I held both Elsie and Finn, my eyes closed and my face hidden from their view. What if Nash was dead? I needed him. The kids needed him.

The swell of panic erupted just as Malach's power had. Sudden and unstoppable. I hurried off the bed and rushed to my bedroom, managing to call out to the kids in the steadiest voice I could. "I'll be right back."

As soon as I made it into the room, I fell onto the ground and covered my mouth as a horrible wail tried to escape.

So many memories I couldn't take reliving pressed at me from all sides. I felt myself slipping into Nash's arms. He'd always held me in place and without him, the past pulled me in. At first I wasn't sure if I felt the phantom touch of his hands sliding up my back or whether I'd traveled through time again. I lived through the day we married and bound ourselves to each other.

*   *   *

His face as serious as when he charged into battle, Nash said, "I only ask one thing as your husband."

My chest tightened. "Anything."

"I fight in every battle from now on."

I nodded. "Yes."

"The next one, I won't ask, because I know you'll fight it with everything you have. But just know, Sharpshooter." He held me closer. "I will die for you."

I lived through his warm lips pressing against mine so many times I lost count. The ache consumed me in a gaping and unfillable hole deep in my soul.

When I managed to pull myself from my stupor, I eased my hand low on my abdomen, over the tenderness there. I couldn't think about it. Pushing everything from my mind, I made food for Finn, and I continued forward like I did in battle, because I had no choice. I couldn't give up.

Leif, Wren, and Piercey came to me every day. One of them stayed every night even though I tried to get them to stop. Markus and Gael stopped in frequently. Elara was impossible to keep away.

I loved them all, but I only wanted Nash.

Fifty-six days after Cleo robbed us of him, Piercey called us out onto the balcony.

"We received this a few weeks ago, but we wanted to look into it before showing you. I traveled to see Elias." Elsie squeezed my hand, staring at Piercey. He opened his palm. A necklace of black beads rested on his hand.

The sight sucked the air from my lungs.

Elsie backed away and then turned toward the balcony rail.

My mind couldn't register what I saw. I tilted my head, staring at beads I'd seen far too many times in my life, especially over the last five years.

"Elias was certain." Piercey placed the beads in my hand and gently closed my palm over them. "These ashes belong to Nash. Their best analysts studied them."

A terrible cry wrenched from Elsie. I hadn't seen her really weep since Rylan's death, not even when I told her about Nash. She turned away and fell against the balcony, sobbing as hard as I'd ever heard. Tove rushed to her.

I stared at my closed fist and felt nothing, even though I sensed all the pain exploding within me. I needed to comfort Elsie but I couldn't move.

"I'm sorry, Max. Elsie . . . I'm so sorry." Piercey cleared his throat, visibly doing his best to hide his tears. "Nash is dead."

Out of the corner of my eye, I saw Elsie slide onto the ground with Tove helping to soften her fall. Piercey's hands extended my way, ready to catch me if I also collapsed.

After fifty-six days of fearing the worst, unable to eat or sleep because I was so scared I lost him, all I'd felt faded. Clarity came in that moment. I opened my hands and stared at the dark beads forged from the ashes of the man I loved. The man I'd bound myself to and made a family with. The man who lived three lifetimes with me and then sacrificed himself for me.

"I will die for you."

Every hour I tried to sense Nash. Again and again, I unsuccessfully attempted to travel to him. He didn't feel gone, though. That power we shared burned inside of me even though I couldn't find him. My hand came to my midsection. Nash had dreams for our future and he made me want to dream, too. I never hoped for anything before I met him. He couldn't miss what came next. He couldn't miss what we wanted, coming to fruition against all odds.

I turned my head to the side and looked at Elsie. "You don't need to cry, Els."

Tove turned to me in shock and a knowing horror overcame Piercey.

"Your dad is alive." I lowered the necklace. "I can still feel him."

I couldn't stand to live through losing Nash. Watching the children lose him was even worse.

With all my strength, I tried to hold myself in place for them. To be with them.

Often, I slipped away, reliving days I longed to return to.

It hurt even worse to come back. I tried not to travel anymore. But it'd been four months since I'd last seen him, and I missed him too much to stay in place. He tugged on me through time, drawing me to him.

"Tell me about this blade."

A grin cracked his expression. He lowered the blade from the sharpening stone and truly looked at me. "That's what was on your mind?"

I twisted my brows. "What else would I want with you?"

My friend Wren snorted. Always ready for a laugh to help ease a crisis.

The guard's grin grew.

"Ah." I blinked. He came into focus, not the warrior but the man.

"Ah," he mimicked with a wry smile twisting his full lips.

Dark brown wisps of hair fell over his forehead, as dark as the earth after a long rain.

I forced myself out of the memory, seized by the pain of seeing him again when I couldn't really have him. But it felt so incredible to look into those eyes of his that I couldn't resist for long. Some days were like this. Some days, I couldn't stay away from him.

"If you look, you die. Okay?" I glanced over at Nash to find that he'd ventured chest-deep into the water.

He covered a bare shoulder with his hand. "You're the one who's looking. Keep your eyes to yourself, Sharpshooter."

I rolled my eyes at his smirk. Even after he turned his back to me, I felt nervous. "You really can't look."

"I would never do that." He splashed water over his face. "Not even if you were drowning. I'd look the other way and preserve your dignity so you could perish untainted by my gaze."

My fingers found my wet cheeks. I kept my eyes closed, needing to be with him.

"Save your strength, Nash."

"I really wanted to survive this . . . and convince you to fall for me . . ." A hint of a smile twisted his lips. "I think I could have . . ."

Tears slipped from my cheeks onto his. "Stop teasing me. You're really hurt, Nash."

His eyes slid shut, voice quiet. "You always think . . . I'm teasing, when I'm serious . . ."

The slips to the past came rapidly, stealing me through so many moments together. I felt him, really felt him. Tasted his kiss. The wedding rolled through my mind over and over.

"Max," he said in a husky voice. "Do you think we've ever done this before?"

I knew now that we had. That had not been the first time we'd married and bound ourselves to each other.

The pain overwhelmed me and I needed to escape. Waking up from these beautiful dreams to emptiness beside me hurt too badly. I moaned and curled up on the bed, trying to fall asleep, but I saw him each time I closed my eyes.

"I've got you. It's okay. Sleep. I won't let go."

Maybe even though Nash didn't have any power, couldn't control time or space, maybe he did have something else. Because I should have slipped again and didn't. It was as if he held me in place.

Finally, I drifted off with that feeling of him close, forgetting that he no longer could hold me in place.

"Ma."

I awoke and pushed myself up to see Elsie. The look in her eye drew me back to reality. I hated that she stared at me the way she'd look at a wounded animal.

Though I smiled, it felt empty. "Yes?"

She glanced down and then also forced a stiff smile. "They really do need you this time. The commanders are gathered."

"Oh." I pushed myself up. "Of course. Let's go."

The quiet between us always felt uncomfortable now, because it was bursting with all I knew Elsie wanted to say but so rarely uttered.

"How have you been sleeping?" she asked.

"Pretty well."

"And eating?"

"I'm eating now. You don't need to worry. I'm sorry I ever made you worry in the first place."

"I'm not a child anymore." Elsie took my hand as we walked. "You don't need to protect me. It's not bad to let me see how you really are."

"I miss him and it's the worst thing I've ever endured, but hope is powerful. It helps to make progress on my plans."

"Progress?"

"I know many places where he isn't, so that's progress."

"Oh, Ma."

I lifted my hand. "I told you not to worry. You think I'm delusional and that I just can't accept it. Well, I'm not crazy. I'm going to find your father and bring him home to you."

She pulled her hand away from mine to cross her arms over herself. Her lips pressed tightly together. I didn't mean to make her feel more alone or to make her resent me because I refused to accept her father's death. She wanted to grieve him like she grieved Rylan. Her dad's beads were always around her neck.

But I knew Nash was alive.

I searched for him, unable to find him, but he was still here. Just not close enough to feel.

Kingdom business was grueling to sit through these days. The war ended and Nash should've been here with me celebrating. Finn's entire life had been consumed by it. We were free to enjoy our family. This was the price we paid for peace, though. Nash paid it. Our family did.

I thought the dissidents would increase their rebellion against me now that I struggled with Nash's absence and didn't lead as I wanted to. I tried my best and Nash would tell me I was doing a great job. I knew I wasn't, though. Instead, our kingdom came together. The people were no longer scared and so their vitriol faded.

In fact, my people showed great kindness and compassion to me.

The father of the kingdom was dead.

They hailed his name and honored his memory. Any bad word said against either of us was forgotten. King Tyroin built an entire memorial hall just for Nash. I hadn't stepped foot in there except for the day of the ceremony.

While our kingdom picked up its shattered pieces, I drifted like a ghost through the tower, struggling to stay in the present.

Piercey filled in for many of my duties as Prophet. I was so thankful for him. Our kingdom finally showed acceptance toward him, perhaps appreciating how badly he wanted peace.

I kept it within the family that I still searched for Nash, not wanting to cause problems within the kingdom. This was a complicated time for us. All of Skia Hellig was uniting as one. The coastal kingdom was shaken by the sudden murder of their Prophet, and found comfort in the protection we offered. Markus and Piercey worked day and night to set the peninsula on the best path for the future.

I even tried to find Cleo, but she seemed to have vanished.

"I miss Daddy." Finn rubbed his eyes and sniffled once I got home.

"Me, too." He patted my stomach and I looked down at my swollen midsection, remembering that Nash kissed the baby to sleep every night when I was pregnant with Finn. I smiled, hand in the place Nash usually touched. "I'll make sure he's home before the baby is born."

It seemed like we dreamed this pregnancy into existence, since we both wanted it but I refused to even consider it during the war. I never missed my medication. Piercey reminded me that while no drug was perfect, I'd never accidentally gotten pregnant before. He told me if anyone's stubborn will could override a medication, it surely was ours, and that our power may have delivered on our greatest desire. I didn't care how it happened, only that Nash gave this gift to me to help me through our time of separation.

I told myself that. Believed it. But a voice inside hissed at me that I really was crazy and simply refusing to accept the unacceptable because I could never live without the love of my life.

Finn nodded. "Daddy would never miss the baby. He loves us too much."

"Ma."

I froze at Elsie's horrified voice. Swallowing hard, I nudged Finn toward his room. "Go clean up."

He ran to the room, the obedient young man he was, and started to pick up his toys.

Elsie whispered harshly to me. "You can't tell him that. It's cruel. I've looked the other way because I understand you just can't accept that he's gone, but what you're doing to Finn isn't right. You're not helping him."

"I'm not going to make him mourn his dad when he doesn't need to. Nash is out there. I can feel him."

"What does that even mean? You can't travel to him. He's gone." She clutched my shoulders. "You have to listen, Ma. Finn isn't going to see his dad ever again. You need to help him live with that, not lie to him."

I slid my hands over hers and loosened her grip. "Your dad and I are connected. The bond is real. It's defied time and multiple lives. Our energy has even transcended it. I still feel him, Els. Just like I used to feel that draw to him when we first met."

"Have you thought that maybe you will always feel it because you're in love with him?"

"Have faith, Elsie. Your dad always said if we have to have faith in something, we might as well have it in ourselves. For the first time in my life, I have faith. I have trust. I'm not letting go of it. To believe victory is impossible is to surrender."

"Someone needs to tell Finn," Elsie said.

"No one is saying anything to Finn."

"How long will it take before you accept that Dad is gone? Will you tell the baby he's coming home, too?"

I tucked her hair behind her ears, amazed by how much she looked like Nash. She was a gift, too. "I'm so sorry you're going through this, Elsie girl. Hold on a little longer."

"No." Elsie pushed me away. "I lost Rylan and then I lost Dad." A frown as resentful as it was sad twisted her expression. "It's time I accept that I lost you, too."

"You didn't lose me."

"Yes, I did. You're barely here. I'm not letting you torture Finn. You don't understand what you're doing to him."

"I feel Nash," I said. "He's not gone."

"If you feel him, then teleport to him. Wait, you can't? It's because he's dead, Ma." She ripped the beads from beneath her neckline and tugged on them. "These are his ashes. He's dead."

"I didn't see his body for a reason. He's alive. I'm sorry it hurts you for me to feel this way, but I don't want Finn to suffer like we are."

Elsie gripped my hands now, pleading. "Please, Ma. You need help. You aren't thinking clearly. I need you. Don't do this to me."

I took her cheeks in my hands. "You listen to me, Elsie. I'm the same person I have been every day of your life. Trust that in the end we will be together and we will be okay. Have faith in me."

"I miss him so much. I miss our family." She clung to me. "He was so good, Ma. There's nothing in the world he wouldn't do for me. Every day of my life, he was fighting for me. I had him and now he's gone. Not everyone gets a dad like that, and I should feel lucky for the time I had him, but I can't do this without him. I don't know how. I can't breathe. I didn't just lose my dad. I lost my best friend. Now I'm losing you, too."

I held her while she cried. "I'm here. I'm not going anywhere."

CHAPTER FORTY-EIGHT

I was gathered with the other three Prophets of Skia Hellig discussing the fifth draft of our proposed laws, when Markus interrupted to ask me to follow him to Piercey's office. When I entered, I found that everyone was gathered. Wren and Leif exchanged a look before they walked closer to me. Elsie came in shortly after, and Markus closed the door.

"Max." Piercey looked at me with bewildered eyes. He walked around the edge of his desk, past the tall bookshelf holding his most prized research.

While Elsie looked worried and everyone shared that same shocked look, the smile on my face only grew wider, because while it didn't feel real for the moment to finally come, I'd never given up on this.

"You found him." I gripped my chest and laughed. "You found Nash."

Piercey blinked. "We found him. Nash is alive."

The sound of Elsie hitting the ground drew every eye. She'd passed out cold.

I did not hesitate, but rushed to my room to pack everything I needed.

Tove and Elsie burst through the door together twenty minutes later. "We're coming." Elsie was fastening her armor as she spoke. "This is my dad. You can't talk us out of it. You're also five months pregnant and haven't been training."

"Nash once told me I couldn't stop him from coming to the Mountain of the Gods with me." I smiled longingly. "He said how could I tell a father not to protect his daughter."

"Right. So, you cannot tell a daughter not to look for her father."

Tove dipped her head. "We need to do this, Prophet."

"Don't call me that. I told you that you never need to do that."

Tove's eyes softened as I kissed her cheek first and then Elsie's. "I desperately want to stop you, but I know you'll follow. Promise me you'll be safe."

The girls helped me to prepare. Once I'd finished, Elsie stared at me. "You knew."

"I felt him. We're connected."

She closed her eyes and lowered her head. "I'm so sorry I fought against you."

"Never apologize. You were trying to protect me and your brother."

We hurried to Elara's before leaving to kiss Finn goodbye.

"We're bringing Daddy home," I whispered in his ear, and I squeezed him while he cried tears of joy.

At the bottom of the tower, we met Leif, Wren, Piercey, and Gael, all of us ready to do whatever it took to bring Nash back to us.

Teleporting while pregnant always made me nervous, because overloading the baby with energy could cause severe problems. Piercey helped me to control my power, though, and used his medical abilities to help protect the pregnancy.

Cleo didn't kill Nash, but she didn't put him to work in the way she did with Malach or the others. Nash probably proved too difficult to control. Once I knew the location and traveled there, I finally sensed Nash. I could teleport directly to him.

But we needed to ensure it was safe first.

He was far beyond Skia Hellig, so far north that very few people managed to survive in the frigid lands. Most people who did live up here moved south in the winter. We learned from the spy that Cleo's base of operations was located there. The underground complex housed the most important members of her cult. The spy who tipped us off only happened to discover Nash because of the encoded messages my husband slipped into the letters of the cultists, just one or two words at a time. It took weeks to form the short message that the spy finally noticed.

Tell the Prophet Eclipse Nash lives.

I left everyone in a safe location away from the underground building where Cleo and her most faithful lived, promising to teleport back to them once I knew it was safe, or if I needed help. Only Piercey came with me to help me use my power.

We hid in a room where I didn't sense anyone. Nash was so close. I felt his power. The incredible warmth of it healed so much inside of me.

Piercey took my hand. "Are you okay?" he whispered.

"I'm wonderful." I breathed in deeply, ready to just run to Nash. But I didn't want us to be seen.

We crept through the dark room toward the door. The one slab of wood was the only thing separating me from Nash. I heard voices on the other side and pressed my ear against it, heightening my senses.

"I really wish you'd stop with your stubborn games." The sound of Cleo's voice made my heart jolt in my chest. "You're not going to stop me from using your power. You've learned that. So, give up on trying. Your efforts are like a pesky little fly."

"You're the one who decided to keep me alive."

My knees weakened at the sound of his voice. After five months, was I really hearing him again? I covered my mouth to hold back my tears, desperate to hear him talk again.

"It's the only way she might join me one day," Cleo said. "You've given me the equivalent of her power, but it'll be so much more if I have her, too. And I just can't give up. Once she's desperate enough, she'll do anything to see you again."

"Max won't abandon our children or our people, no matter how much she misses me."

"She will to save your life. I'll kill you right in front of her if she refuses. I'll kill you in front of your children."

Such a thought tore my heart in two. I didn't feel so confident, but I knew he was right, and leaving behind Finn and Elsie wasn't an option.

"Do what you must." Nash managed to sound bored. I knew that must have been an act.

"You're exhausted," Cleo said. "You can't access a shred of your power but you never stop trying. Take a break. It's been five months. You're annoying me."

Nash laughed, low and bitter. "I am so deeply sorry I've annoyed you."

Her voice snapped to anger. "I've treated you with great hospitality. I let you train with your stupid swords. I gave you a big room. You have everything you need."

"You can't understand because you have no one and nothing, but I'd rather be dead than here with you. I want my wife and children."

"You will have them when they're ready. Five years of war didn't break Max. She needs more than five months without you."

That wasn't true. Five days was enough. Five minutes of thinking Nash was dead. I slowly lowered to the ground. Being so close to him stole away my strength. Piercey clasped my shoulder.

"Whatever," Cleo said. "Rot in here, then. If you annoy me too badly, I might just resort to cutting off pieces of you."

"I'll grab the knife for you."

She groaned. Footsteps followed and then a door slammed.

I clutched my chest. Was that it? He was alone.

I listened intently for heartbeats and only heard his steady thrum. I sighed at the wonderful sound.

Unable to wait any longer, I stood back up and slowly opened the door. Piercey stepped back to give me space.

At first, I only saw the room.

"What do you want now?" Nash asked.

My breath locked in my lungs. Nash's swords rested on a table. A large bed took up the wall on the other side. A few articles of clothing hung from a rack. Little else filled up the room. I tightened my coat around me, trying to hide my stomach so I didn't shock him too much right away.

As I stepped through, I caught a glimpse of his right hand. My stomach flip-flopped, my eyes tracing the cut of his forearm next, continuing up to his shoulder when more of him came into view. My knees trembled from the little I saw of him.

I continued to walk until I looked at him fully. He stood with his back to me, facing a table littered with maps and books. I saw him every night in my dreams and every time I closed my eyes. I saw him when he stole me through time. But right now, seeing him in the present, having him so close, immobilized me.

His hair was longer, hanging just past his shoulders. His narrow waist tapered beneath his broad upper body. His sleeves were rolled and my gaze fell along the toned lines of his brawny forearm. My fingers ached to run along the tender skin there. Seeing him stole my breath away. It was him. Really him.

"Nash."

The broken name falling from my lips seemed to physically hit him. His shoulders straightened and his head turned just slightly. Then he froze. Slowly, Nash turned to face me.

My knees buckled when his warm eyes met mine and I caught the wall, gasping.

The writing stick he held fell from his hand and clattered onto the ground. A dark beard covered his face, making his eyes look bright and beautiful. His full lips parted slightly. Long hair curled about his face.

I heard a rush of breath from him and then came his low voice. "Max?"

Tears fell from my eyes. I blinked so they wouldn't blur my view of him. I needed to see him. My lips quivered and I nodded. "I found you."

Nash looked down at me then, the utter shock giving way to desperation. He met my eyes again and then he rushed to me. I met him, wrapping my arms around his neck. The first touch of his thick body against mine sent shudders down my spine. Nash's arms wrapped fully around me and his strong hands clasped me tightly. He gasped in a shuddering breath, hands wandering, seeking me out like it might make him believe I was really here.

He eased back and looked at me for only a second before taking my face delicately in his hands. Breathing against my lips. I wept quietly, my fingers smoothing along his neck. Every part of him I touched and saw captivated me.

"It's real this time," I whispered. "It's not a dream."

"Is it?" His breath was shallow. "Is it real?"

"Yes." My lips brushed his and the tender touch rendered me limp in his arms. So many long days without him, trying to hold together a kingdom reeling from war and a family left devastated. His hand worked down my throat and his lips descended on mine. His taste captivated my senses, so much greater than I remembered. My hands smoothed down his chest to his heart that beat steadily in my dreams. The way it sounded lying with him in the woods our first night together drummed when I slept. I heard it so often.

In the middle of the kiss, Nash broke away, eyes falling.

His hands eased over my side and low over my stomach. He bowed forward, eyes filling with wonder. "You're . . ." Nash opened my coat and looked at my round stomach. He laughed quietly, eyes on me. "We're having a baby?"

I sniffled and laughed, too, nodding. "Yeah. We're having a baby."

A single sob escaped from him and he scooped me up, kissing me deeply, desperately. He set me on the table, hands gliding down the outside of my legs. "I should have been there to help you. You did this all alone." He nestled his face against my stomach, holding it again. "I'm so sorry, Max. You've been taking care of the kingdom and the kids all while—"

"Please, don't. It's not your fault. You gave your life for me." My fingers drifted through his hair. I wanted to do this so many times over these last five months. "We're okay. I never stopped believing. I never stopped looking, not even when the beads came. I felt you."

Nash melted his lips over mine again. "I missed you so desperately." He growled and kissed me deeper. "I love you. I'm going to make this right. I'll do everything. I swear."

"This is all I needed."

"How have you felt?" He searched my eyes. "Are you still throwing up like last time?"

I smiled, staring at him, struggling to speak. He looked so handsome. So full of love. "It's not as bad as last time."

He sighed. "Good. How are the kids?"

"They miss you. I told Finn you were off making peace. He's really tall, Nash."

His eyes filled with tears again. "Yeah?"

"Yes, so tall. He's good. He just missed you, but he took good care of me. He's so excited to be a big brother. He doted on me."

"That's my boy."

"Elsie . . ." I didn't want to lie to him but I also didn't want to tell him how horrible his little girl felt.

"I know. I know. First Rylan and then me. She'd want to take care of you. She's not good."

"No."

"Is she here?"

"I couldn't keep her away."

He smiled and eased back, holding his chest. "My heart is going to burst." Worry crossed his expression then. "I have no power, Max. Even if I leave, Cleo can just follow me. I can't break away from her. It's not safe. You have to go home."

I stabbed my finger against his arm. "You do not want to have this conversation with me. There's a small army waiting for me to bring them here. We're taking you home."

Nash held me against him.

I didn't want to part ways for even a second, but I couldn't make Elsie wait any longer. I teleported everyone over and left them in the room with Piercey while I ushered Elsie toward Nash's room.

Elsie walked into the room from behind me. The grief and disbelief finally fell away. She stared for at least a full minute without moving. Nash gave her time, his eyes full as he looked at his daughter. I knew he struggled to keep himself in place.

Then her expression broke. "Daddy," she whispered. Elsie burst into tears and covered her face. Nash ran to her and caught her as she fell against him.

"I'm here, baby girl." He rocked her gently. "I'll never leave you."

Elsie covered her mouth, trying to keep quiet. I held Nash's shoulders while he clutched his daughter to his chest.

"It's okay," he said. "I've got you."

"I thought you were dead." Elsie drew the beads up, her hand shaking badly. "I really believed I lost you."

Nash reached for me. We held Elsie between us like we had so many times when she was little, our arms wrapped tightly around each other. She was taller than me now and grown up, but she was still our girl.

I melted against my husband, warmth and peace capturing me, while dreams came alive in my heart once more.

CHAPTER FORTY-NINE

Nash kept his arms around Elsie and me while whispering to the others, clearly not wanting to let us go. "Elvadel is at peace. Skia Hellig is uniting. If we anger Cleo, she may restart the war. We cannot attack her unless we're certain we'll win."

"We're not leaving you here," Elsie said.

He squeezed us, voice somber. "There's nothing I want more than to come home. I would give anything except your lives. I cannot risk you and the rest of Skia Hellig."

"I would feel the same," I said, "but Elsie is right. We aren't leaving you. I promised Finn I'd bring you home before the baby comes."

He squeezed his eyes shut, face tight with grief. "Don't sacrifice the kingdom or the kids for me."

"Our kingdom and our kids are not safe with Cleo out here. We'll win. To assume defeat is to surrender, remember?" I brushed his curls back. "Besides, I haven't been sitting around waiting for you to return. I've been preparing. I continued our work, Nash, and I learned how to break her hold on you."

He opened his eyes. "There's a way?"

"It's not easy, but yes." We'd done it before in our second life to break free of Flare, and we'd do it again. Nash and I never found that time together, but I did on my own.

"We'll deal with Cleo's cult members," Leif said. "Piercey will protect the baby. You and Max will take her on."

Nash looked at Elsie. "You can't get hurt."

"I won't. Trust me and Tove."

"If we break Cleo's bond, we can use that power we drew upon in our last battle with Malach," I said.

"Cleo's never been able to force me to do anything," he said. "But she can kill me at will, and she fully uses my power. Since you last fought her, she's stronger. We can't make any mistakes."

"Then we should do this quickly before we're discovered." I looked at the others. "Spread out and shield us. Once we start, we can't stop."

"What do I do?" Nash asked.

Elsie backed up near Tove and prepared her weapons. Our friends spaced themselves around the room.

I slid my hands into his and intertwined my fingers, working closer, looking up into his eyes. "Give yourself to me."

His gaze drifted across my face before returning to my eyes. "Is that all?"

"I'll do the rest."

I smiled softly, ready to take my husband home. In our lives, we'd suffered many losses and said goodbye too many times. Living for five months without him and seeing our kids suffering hurt far more than anything else I'd endured. The bottomless depth of longing gripped me now, and the joy of the life waiting for us fueled me.

"We're bound," I said. "The power binding us stretched from one life to the next and entangles us still. Cleo's power over you may be strong, but it is not as great as that which connects us." I stepped on my toes, lips close to his. "It's saved us once before. Flare bound us to her, but our connection freed us. Give yourself to me while I dig into the code of our world and break you free. Can you feel it yet?"

He shook his head. "Not yet."

I smoothed my hand over his heart, looking deeply into his eyes, reaching for the connection we shared so many times, seeking out our past lives. Standing before him, I allowed the past to tug on me and to thin the veil between lifetimes. "You will."

My lips slid along his and a pang of heat pulsed against my hand. Nash kissed me, arms drawing me closer.

"We belong to each other." I kissed him deeper and dug my fingers into where I felt Cleo's tattoo burning against my hand. "We're one. You're mine and I'm yours." My heart sought out his as I searched through the darkness for his feel to connect with him. "Not hers."

"Max." He breathed my name between kisses.

"She cannot have you. In every life we've ever lived, we've been one." I breathed in his breath. "In the next, it will be the same."

A rush of energy filled the room and Cleo appeared beside us, face a mask of rage. "What do you think you're doing?"

Neither of us looked at her. My soul searched for our bond, losing the boundary between where I ended and he began. Our lives were the same, time and space melting together. Layers over our life overlapped the other. A bright light shone from his tattoo.

Distantly, I sensed the arrival of more people and heard the fighting begin. But I was tangled between lifetimes with Nash, plunging so deeply into him and who we'd always been.

I didn't need to ask Nash this time if he felt it. Our connection pierced the barrier closing him off from his power and I felt it rushing back into him. He took the back of my head into his hand and I tilted, letting him kiss me deeply. The convergence of three lives washed my world in a blinding light.

Nash and I breathed in as one, looking into each other's eyes and seeing through the other's as well. I no longer discerned any of the distinctions between us. Our power amassed into one just like when the black ball of power formed a star in the sky. This time, it swelled inside of us, no longer removed, but wholly part of us.

We turned to Cleo and the rest of the room sharpened into focus. Our people fought with hers, each locked in a battle against multiple cult members. The woman who tried to steal the love of my life from me jerked in one ragged breath after the next. All of her tattoos burned brightly and the veins in her neck popped. Her will tugged at ours, competing with the bond tethering Nash and me together. She wanted to sever it forever.

With hands trembling, Cleo raised them together, gathering a ball of energy between the palms of her hands. Nash and I teleported together, landed on either side of her, and locked our hands together, surrounding her.

"He's mine." Cleo seethed. "This won't work."

Pain gripped Nash's chest—I felt it raging there—and the energy in Cleo's began to strengthen. She was drawing it out from him, trying to steal back the energy he'd regained. The clanging of swords threatened to distract us. We worried about Elsie and our friends. But we knew that if we didn't put everything into this wrestling match with Cleo, that everyone here would die. Our kingdom might perish.

Energy pulsed in our palms and shot through our bodies quickly encircling Cleo in a dome. The power in her hand continued to grow, though, as did the pain gripping Nash.

We both grunted and reached deeply into our connection, calling upon that immense power that had grown quietly between us for three lives now.

Cleo pressed the energy against Nash's chest, over the tattoo glowing from beneath his shirt. We both gritted our teeth at the pain carving through his chest, feeling it as one. Cleo's demanding presence insisted on sucking us both dry.

"You'll finally be mine, too," Cleo said, eyes on me. "You'll—"

The power Nash and I amassed burst from us, as great as the day it floated in the sky. We unleashed into the space where we confined Cleo, silencing her words.

Shock flooded her face and she curled in on herself, screaming in pain. We continued to throw all of the power directly at her until she teleported away.

Nash and I cut off the power immediately, reserving it only for Cleo. A sound behind me drew our attention. Piercey fell onto his knees, sweat covering his face. He'd been trying to protect the baby from the power and it must have taken all he had to do so.

"I'm fine," he said. "Keep going."

We kept our connection to one another, still fighting against Cleo's hold on Nash.

Neither of us wanted to leave Elsie behind. Energy pulsed along her swords while she sliced through the air, forcing her opponent to retreat. Tove hurled a sharp spike of energy behind the man they fought, forcing him to stop so our daughter's swords drove into his gut.

Nearby, Leif pummeled another cultist with his fists, his sword lying broken on the ground. Wren fought against two, both of them struggling with gashes along their arms and legs.

Two already lay dead at Gael's feet and he took on a third, hammering the man with blasts of power.

We sensed more on the way.

Elsie's stare snapped to us. "Go!"

We grabbed Piercey and tore ourselves from her to pursue Cleo.

Following the thread of power connecting her to Nash, we transported to a dimly lit, small temple room.

Cleo knelt on the ground, hands outstretched toward a figure on an altar. We worked closer until we made out the red glow of torchlight upon the pale white cheeks of a woman.

Horror struck me and I fell back with a cry. Nash caught me, his arms stiff and face twisted.

Dr. Henderson's dead corpse lay on the altar; the body was perfectly preserved.

"How do you have her?" I asked.

The horror only multiplied when the realization hit me. This wasn't Dr. Henderson.

It was my mother.

I covered my mouth with my hand. "Cleo . . ."

Our enemy turned to face me, eyes glowing. "I wasn't going to let you take her from me."

"She's dead, Cleo."

"She loved me. She didn't even know you. No matter how much I feed her, she still doesn't return to me." Her head lowered and hair fell over her face. "She's waiting for you. I thought the power Nash shared with you would wake her, but it's been months, and she's not even warm."

"She's not coming back," Nash said. "You can't bring the dead back no matter how much power you use on their corpse."

"Is this what you wanted all this time?" I asked.

Cleo peeled with laughter. "You're still so desperate to know why I'm doing this. Why did I attack poor Max's kingdom? Why did I steal the man she loves? Would reanimating Mother be reason enough for you to accept why I hurt your people?"

"No." I looked at the mother I never knew in the form of a woman I hated, feared, and once killed. "It's only an excuse anyway. Power is typical and predictable. You're gluttonous for more of it." I closed my eyes. "I've wasted time I didn't have worrying about righteousness and justice, deliberating over the implications of my every choice. I moved too slow for people like you who only connive about how to gain more power."

"So, you don't care anymore about right and wrong?" Her amused skepticism grated at me.

"I care deeply about it and that's why I'm not second-guessing myself any longer. I am worthy of my own trust. You are not." I stepped forward in lockstep with Nash. "You're finished here. Lay her to rest and send yourself with her."

"She's your mom," Cleo said. "Don't you care at all?"

"I have no mother, not if she's who I came from."

Cleo's stare shifted to Nash. "I was right that you would deliver Max to me. I just didn't expect it to be like this."

"Is that why you're praying to a dead woman? Because you're so confident of your victory?" Nash raised his voice in a baritone rebuke that vibrated in my chest. "You kept me from my family and waged war against our people. For this, you will die."

"You knew you couldn't beat us," Cleo said. "You sentenced your own people to death. Surrender could have saved so many."

"So, it's our fault you killed us?" I narrowed my eyes.

"Yes, when I offered you a way to find peace."

"There is no peace in occupied land. You offered death, either in war, or under your rule. I've seen a world in which you reigned. We can never let that happen here."

Cleo raised her arms. "Then kill me already. If you can. Rest assured, you will suffer for your insolence."

I didn't like how confident she seemed.

Nash and I strengthened our connection to flow into each other again.

His tattoo glowed once more and the pain dug into our bodies, but I cared so little, I barely registered it.

Together, we focused on our shared power until it quaked inside of us.

Black rivulets of power flowed from us and washed over her. Just when I expected her screams to begin again, Cleo raised her arms higher and repelled our attack. Dark mist sprayed us.

The dim room brightened. The corpse on the altar glowed just like Nash's tattoo. A translucent blue energy began to flow out from the corpse into Cleo.

"Do you feel that, Max? That's hundreds of distinct energy readings." Piercey spoke from behind us. "She's using the corpse as a chalice for all her stolen power. She's bound to even more people than we realized."

The power pushed back against our own, threatening to overwhelm three lifetimes worth of our combined strength.

Nash took my hand, pain burning over our bodies. Our power collided with hers, the black and blue energy swirling together.

The pain multiplied, gripping us. We clung to each other, gasping as we struggled to contain it. It felt like our insides were melting.

Cleo laughed loudly. "Mother will love taking this power from you."

That thread still connecting Nash to Cleo tugged at our center. With a glance at each other, we sought it out then, imagining we could see it stretching across the room. We drew back our power from Cleo and poured it into that bond she forced upon Nash.

Her body stiffened, confusion warping her features. Nash reached his hand out, mine sliding over the back of his, so together we pushed his palm against Cleo, his fingers hugging the base of her neck. We poured all our power into that tether. I sensed Piercey's energy joining us as well.

"Stop," Cleo cried.

The tattoos on her body burned brighter and brighter as Nash's fingers tore into her chest. We poisoned her together through her own connection, using the tether between her and Nash.

"You're frozen in time with all your juvenile imperfections, just like her corpse," I said. "Your time has finally come."

Fear widened her eyes. My mother's corpse burned bright blue, but it wasn't enough to ward off our power. It flowed deeply into Cleo's soul and poisoned every thread in the tangled web of connections she formed. Cuts ripped her skin open all over her body. The whites of her eyes turned black.

"It doesn't matter if you kill me." Blood seeped from between her teeth and fell from her lips. "There's always going to be people out there who want your power."

"It won't be you," I said. "We'll fight each battle as it comes. We're not surrendering to the inevitability of war. You can't force us to give up our power to you."

"One day, you will lose."

"Today is not that day."

Nash's fingers plunged deep into her chest until his knuckles disappeared. Cleo choked on a mouth full of blood.

"P-please," she whimpered.

Bound together as one, Nash and I severed every last thread of power connected to Cleo. The light of my mother's corpse faded. Cleo's movements stifled.

We watched her take her last breath before her body succumbed to our power.

We'd fallen to her in one life. Then to Flare in another.

But every seed we planted grew in this life, and finally put an end to the twisted and deformed power she held over us.

After more than five years of death and all these months of tearing our family apart, we still took no satisfaction in killing her. We wanted nothing to do with her, not even for the sake of revenge.

CHAPTER FIFTY

We opened the door of Elara's apartment to the sound of little feet running. Such an incredible rush of elation hit me that it felt like a dream.

Nash ran toward the sound of our son. Elsie held my arm looped through hers, the two of us standing close.

The sound came to a dead stop when Finn entered the living room and saw his father.

His little body froze and his young eyes filled with tears and faith and pain. The steadfast belief that Nash would return must have collided with the ache of missing him. I saw it so clearly in our boy's eyes. Too much for someone so young to handle.

Though Finn froze, Nash did not. He scooped our son up from the ground and held him tightly. Finn's small arms stretched to fit around Nash's neck, his little face disappearing against his father's shoulder.

"Daddy," he cried. "Daddy, you're home."

My heart rested for the first time since Nash asked Cleo to take him instead of me. The strength quickly fled my body and I wilted against Elsie without meaning to, unable to even breathe. She embraced me, her cheeks wet with tears.

"He's home," I whispered.

"He is. He's home, Ma." Elsie sniffed and wiped my own tears away. "You were right. You felt him. He never left us."

I looked into her baby brown eyes and saw every bit of pain she'd ever felt. I remembered each scrape and cut, every mean word uttered to her, now all this heartbreak. "Elsie." Pain squeezed my throat. "Oh god, Elsie, you were never supposed to feel this way."

"Ma, don't you know you weren't supposed to either?" Her bottom lip quivered. "None of us are. Don't promise me you'll save me from it next time. I can already hear you saying it. Just say you'll be with me."

She was right. I tried to find my voice. "I promise, Elsie girl. I will always be here with you."

"I'm so glad you came back when I was little and you picked us," she said.

"I will always pick you." I held her face and kissed the softness of her cheek. "You made me a mother. You're so much more than I knew to hope for."

"You too, Ma." Her voice was small, pinched with tears.

Hand coming over my stomach, I looked back at Nash and watched him hold our child, imagining our new baby in his arms.

I didn't know the moment I fell in love with him. There were too many of those. But I did remember how my heart melted when I watched him holding Elsie close before we traveled to the mountain. That might have been the first thing I loved about him. What a wonderful father he was. My children got to have that.

I wiped my cheeks, smiling so hard it hurt, and ushered Elsie to Nash.

Finn twisted to me while Nash still held him and grabbed me. "You said it, Mommy. You said before the baby."

"I'm so sorry I was gone." Nash kissed Finn's face. He did the same to Elsie's cheek and held both of his children close. He looked to me next, his eyes wet and brimming with life. Leaning toward me, his lips came over mine and ruptured my heart. The kids didn't complain this time, not when the world had been set right once more. "I love you all so much," Nash said.

Elara moved into the doorway, hand to her heart. She made it feel like Rylan was here with us. "Welcome home, young man," she said.

Nash laughed and then sighed while he wiped his eyes. "This is all I thought about."

Elsie unfastened the beads from her neck that she had worn every day until now. "Let's throw these into the ocean next time we go."

I nodded. "I don't want to see them ever again."

"How did she fake them?" Elsie asked.

The beads couldn't be faked. That Elsie didn't realize meant there were still remnants of innocence left in the poor girl.

"Cleo was very clever," Nash said.

I scanned him for scars like the kind left behind by Eskel the Ruthless, but I supposed Cleo's power had been great enough that no amount of damage would scar. "Did she make you feel it?" I whispered close to his ear.

"No," Nash said. "Don't worry."

We spent every second of the day together. Trish came and cried while she hugged Nash. Once we managed to tear ourselves away from our home for a short time, we met our people down in the village where they received Nash with tears and joy.

Soon we'd explain to the kingdom what happened with our war chief. With our family put back together again, we could help Skia Hellig raise to greater heights.

But for now, our family deserved some time together.

Finn tried so hard to stay awake until he started to fall asleep sitting up. Elsie carried him to bed and curled up next to him, just as exhausted as he was.

Nash ran his fingers along my stomach. "I'm still in shock."

"I am, too. Nothing felt real while you were gone."

He slid down and kissed my stomach, holding me on either side of my pregnant belly. "Hi, baby. You don't know me yet, but I love you."

I chewed the inside of my cheek.

"I didn't expect you," he said, "but we wanted you desperately."

Was Piercey right? Had I done something to make this happen? Because I wanted it but didn't believe I could have it? I closed my eyes, not caring to think about things that didn't matter. The war ended, Nash came home, and our family reunited. Once, we waited for peace to have Finn and ended up at war. This time we accidentally brought a baby into the world during war, and finally it looked like we'd raise a child together in peace.

Nash's touch along my stomach changed as it drifted up my side. He sat up, his eyes tracing all the lines of my body and face. "I needed you, Sharpshooter." Easing up, he took my hand and helped me to my feet. "It felt like I'd never see you again."

We both looked over through the doorway to see Elsie and Finn both fast asleep.

"She took good care of him," I said.

"They're good kids."

"This one will be, too." I gasped at the flutter inside me and pulled his hand to my stomach. "Feel it?"

Nash laughed. "There you are." The baby kicked again.

He kissed me suddenly and it plunged me deep into the bond winding us together. We stumbled toward our room, quietly closed the door, and let the rest of the world disappear.

Lying down together, finally close again, the anguish I felt at having him ripped away filled me. The memory was too fresh. But I had him again and no one was taking him away.

Nash held himself up to look down on me.

So slow and careful like I was made of glass, he slid my sleeve from my shoulder and followed the line of my neck with the delicate touch of a single finger. His breath tickled the nape of my neck. "How are you so beautiful?"

My fingers tangled in his hair and my palm smoothed over the contours of his back. The softness of his skin and the tautness of his body. "Nash. Damn it, Nash, I missed you. It killed me." I could barely speak. It didn't feel real being with him. So many times I dreamed of this, so desperate for one look or touch.

"I missed you more than words can say."

His lips found mine and devoured all our reticence. Mouth hot, tongue wandering, hands tight against me, Nash kissed me desperately. His body melted against mine, the two becoming one once more. One mind, one body, one soul, one power.

Tears mingled in our kiss. In our first life when Dr. Henderson ended our world, I felt immense helplessness. It didn't matter how hard I clung to Nash; she ripped us away from each other. We made our own world for ourselves, though. We defied nature itself to bind ourselves tightly together, and refused to allow anyone to separate us.

We decided for ourselves. We belonged to each other.

The gods created our world and held ultimate power over it, but Nash and I forged this unbreakable connection ourselves.

"It's the same." I jerked upright. It felt like a bolt of power hit me. "It's the same thing."

"What is?" he whispered against my bare skin.

I shook my head, afraid to speak it or even think it. "I . . . I need to go."

"No." Nash urged me back down. "No matter what it is, it can wait." Hands roamed, strong arms tight around me. "Don't leave me yet."

There was no denying him. The draw to him rendered me helpless. I didn't need him to say it again. He was right. We'd lost each other, and now that we were together, everything else could wait. This mattered most. I couldn't stand to leave him when we'd just come back together.

I became lost in the bond we shared, filled to the brim with a love too great for one single lifetime to ever contain.

CHAPTER FIFTY-ONE

So many times now I stood before these waters and wondered how to reach the Collective when they were so far beyond me. I had not understood that I was within them.

"I'm here for Coralee," I said. "Not merely the image of her, but Coralee herself."

"We don't understand. Coralee is a part of us."

"You do understand." I peered into those deep waters, unable to discern the individual droplets that made up this great pool, but certain I might pluck one. "I demand that you free Coralee from the Collective."

"Binding to the Collective is irreversible."

"It's not." I clutched my hands into fists at my chest. "Coralee, listen to me. I know you don't want to be a part of this, so leave them. I trust you. I believe in you. I know that you can break free of this supposedly unbreakable curse. You can free yourself just like I've freed myself." All my struggles for the past three lives filled my mind, and I saw it all so clearly like a single point in time. "Coralee." Tears slunk down my cheeks. All doubt fled. "You're already free. You just don't know it. Reunite with me. I am the fruit of the seed you planted. I am yours and you are mine."

Our bonds were our greatest power.

And our greatest liability.

My bond with Nash and with all versions of myself transcended time, dimension, reason. We united into something much greater than ourselves. In just the same way, Cleo and her Prophets combined into something much worse.

The Collective dissolved the beauty and strength of the individual so much that it morphed into a deformed being that looked frighteningly almost human.

Together and strong in ourselves, I believed we could unite with those deserving of our bond to truly transcend the limits of humanity, of ourselves.

I now knew the power of binding myself to another. A power that wove through time to create a family. A power that the Collective used to create and destroy entire worlds.

It'd always been this simple, hadn't it? As simple as knowing our power and demanding what was ours. The Collective didn't function in the natural universe on laws and impulses far beyond our control. Even in the waywardness of this digital dimension, the fabric of society was not woven from messy biological adaptations, but by the principles which founded their universe.

"Your connection to the Collective is nothing." I eased closer. "We are the ones who are bonded—you and all the seeds of your consciousness." My voice strengthened. "Bind to me," I demanded. "Not them. You are not theirs."

The silence that followed felt powerful enough to shake my confidence, but I refused to release it. I needed to remain certain that binding with Coralee was ultimately my right and not theirs. That this was reality. No one, not even the Collective, could defy this natural order. I refused to surrender to a power that felt much greater than my own. All this time, I handed victory to them by assuming I was helpless. By surrendering without a fight.

"Coralee," I said. "Be free. Choose for yourself. It's the natural order of things that our souls reconnect. The Collective has no right to you."

A terrible silence followed. My shoulders fell and I stared at the still waters.

This had to work. There was no way Coralee wanted this for herself, or maybe she was too weak to find her way out. I came from her. I believed that I could do it, so surely she could, too.

"Please." Tears blurred my view of the Collective. "You can't abandon me."

A ripple spread out from the center of the water and pulsed throughout the Collective. Another. A form materialized, struggling in the deep.

I pounded against the glass. "Coralee!"

Her body jerked in a spasm and her head ripped back. I saw my face buried in the water, twisted with struggle.

"Let her go!"

Another jerk and then her body fell still. She floated there, unmoving.

No, this couldn't happen. I clawed at the glass. "Wake up. You have to wake up."

Her body drifted closer, but she still didn't move. It was like the Collective sent her to me, so close that only the glass separated us. I saw her still face. So still she looked dead.

We needed her. Cleo was right that someone else with power would always rise up. They might do even worse than what she and Malach had done. At least there was a limit to what a person could do to another without the neural implant. We needed someone to actually protect our world.

Her eyes snapped wide open, face hovering directly in front of mine. I gasped. She placed her palms against the glass. I pressed mine against them, too, staring back at an image of myself.

The barrier between us turned soft and malleable. I reached through until my palm slid against hers and I clasped her hands. Taking a step back, I drew her toward me, away from the Collective. A tug of resistance took hold of her and refused to let her leave.

"You're stronger than this," I said, looking into her hazel eyes.

Coralee pulled her head back and slammed it against the glass. My hold on her tightened and I cried out, dragging her hands free. Her fingers tightened around mine and I jerked her again. Another heave, and Coralee pulled free of the water.

The woman from whose consciousness I was born collapsed onto the ground and threw her head back with a deep gasp. Soaking wet and frigid with cold, she trembled with water slinking down her skin. Her eyes began to fill with life and pain and all that made a person a human.

She lifted her hands and slowly touched her fingers to her face.

Her gaze found mine.

"Is it really you?" I knelt in front of her. "Are you free?"

She clutched her chest and then grabbed her head, her hair. "I can feel myself. I can feel where I begin and end." Tears streamed down her cheeks as she bowed forward. "You finally did it." She grabbed my hands and looked back up at me as she laughed and cried. "You saved us."

Hearing her speak told me it was truly her. Coralee had lost herself so deeply in the Collective, they'd drowned out her voice in their waters. Free again, herself again, she spoke with the same accent as her mother. Only it sounded pure and lyrical on her. We were not the same, but we were also one.

I would never find the words to convey to another person how it felt to see this original version of myself, this core of my very being, be rebirthed before my very eyes, and to finally know that I never wanted any of this. That the seed from which I came from never chose to hurt so many people. I returned her grip, in awe of meeting her for the first time.

She reached up and brushed my hair back. "You're so young. I see it in your eyes." Her hand fell. "Still, you found a way. I'm so thankful you never gave up."

"You could see what was happening?"

"Sometimes. It felt like I slept for hundreds of years and only woke for a few minutes at a time. I was always there, always conscious, but not able to hear my own thoughts."

It worried me for a moment to wonder if Coralee really did break free or if the Collective only tried to trick me. But I saw humanity in her that I never saw in the Collective.

"They aren't talking," I said.

"They aren't used to losing." Coralee rubbed her arms and twisted to look at the water. "I don't think they'll speak until you're gone."

"Will they let you go?"

"It doesn't matter. They can try to force me back, but I'll never lose myself again." She closed her eyes. "I'm so sorry for what we did to you. I can never make amends or hope to explain how we fell from such a great height. No one should ever be experimented on. Data should not be more important than a person. We put you in a world that we destined to fail."

Though I knew all this to be true, hearing it from someone who made the decision soothed me. "You didn't want this before joining the Collective?"

"No, never. I really believed that we'd be better coming together. There's so much power in our unity. I will never stop believing in that power either. We need each other. But something terrible can happen when we lose ourselves. It's not so much that the good and the bad mixed into something awful, but that simply erasing our individuality morphed us into something not human."

"The Collective lost its humanity," I said.

"Yes, and none of us had the power to regain it. In the moments when I caught my thoughts, I feared we were trapped forever. Now that I'm myself again, it's all coming back to me. Hundreds of years of hating what we did. It was the worst kind of prison."

"Why didn't anyone else in the Kethios realize what happened to you?"

Coralee quieted for several seconds. "I don't know why no one tried to save us or whether it was intentional, but that's my fight now. I'll figure this out. Max, as much progress as we've made, our Collective proves that this society is sick. I know you've fought so hard, but when you're done in your world and you come here, I hope you'll keep fighting. I hope you'll join the council, because I'll need allies."

"What will you do?"

"I'll travel beyond Earth's realm. Don't worry about that yet. Go home and take care of what's yours. You've done well."

It struck me that she looked identical to me, but felt very much like a different person. "Are we very similar?" I asked. "Because we feel very different."

She looked at me for a long while and laughed. "You grew up in a much different world than me. Now I know that in some world where power both unites and divides there is a version of me like you. There's a warrior and protector capable of leading kingdoms."

"And in some world, there's a version of me that ascended to godhood and escaped its evil clutches."

She smiled much more sweetly than I thought myself capable of doing. "Never let how much younger you are than us stop you from reaching higher than we do. You'll push us to new limits."

I swallowed hard, sensing a deep well of power in her, the kind I didn't yet understand. "I let them die." The words hollowed out my chest. "So many of my people. I killed more than that."

"You always knew you couldn't save them all. Go home and see what you've done. Your people are free. The fact that it hurts doesn't mean you failed, but that you care. What a powerful thing that is."

I nodded. "Okay." More questions nagged at me, though. "What happened between you and your mother?"

"Death is a virus we cannot escape." Sadness tinged her eyes. "My mum taught me that. It evolves with us as a check on our incredible propensity for transformation." She paused, seeming to search for words. "My mother never let go of my death even after I came home to her. I saw it when no one else wanted to. I'm the reason she's not in the Collective."

"You stopped her from being approved."

"Yes. The supervision of your world was a compromise for the deadlocked council. By then, I'd joined the Collective, and I lost my voice. I knew my mom, and that until she decided to heal from losing me, death would fester in her. More than that, I'm the only one who knew the things she did when I was little. The ways she lost herself. No matter how many lives she lived, she never forgave herself for hurting me. She seemed well to others. Not to me. My rejection broke her and led to her devolution in your world."

"You did not do that to Dr. Henderson."

"I know. She did it herself. I just wish I'd been here to stop her." Coralee sighed. "I'm not sure if you'll be able to contact me again while you're still living your life. Things may be different now. I'll fight to free the others while you live your life."

"Piercey and Nash would not want to be in the Collective."

"I know. Entrust them to me. As for your world, I'll do what I can for you. I'm not sure if I still get a vote on the council, but know that I'll be here fighting for you."

"Did you try to fight for me before? Did you try to stop them?"

Coralee's eyes glistened. "I was them."

"Did you try to stop yourself?"

"I can't remember. I lost myself in all our voices. It was us, but it wasn't. Now I'm free. So go home and leave this to me. It's my turn to fight."

I saw then that I'd always been worthy of my own trust, because I fully believed what she said, and I came from her.

CHAPTER FIFTY-TWO

With new life came unimaginable pain in a cycle impossible to unwind. I abandoned my young desires for peace and joy untainted by suffering, by loss, and accepted that just as we were not all good or all bad, life could not be either. Finn came to us in our worst times, and it was in one of our worst times we shared some of our best days.

But we were fortunate with little Juni to enjoy the rare miracle of peace and new life at the same time.

The phantoms of our losses and the memory of those we never wanted to forget wrapped around us just as the joy did.

As badly as it hurt to bring Juni into the world, holding her enraptured me. And that was how life continued to be. Agony and immeasurable joy that bonded much in the way of the Collective when left unchecked. It could taint everything or grow into the deepest contentment. I learned the importance of properly savoring joy and giving agony its own space to exist.

I lounged against Nash in the garden outside of our tower with our infant daughter nestled against me. Finn balanced on his hands in the soft grass, screaming louder with each step he managed.

"I'm really doing it," he shouted.

Elsie bent over and looked down at her little brother. "Now try fighting like that."

He kicked and careened over onto his back.

"This might be the most relaxed I've felt in my entire life." I pressed my lips to Juni's forehead. "She's so soft."

A hand ran along my hip and down my thigh while no one was watching. Nash whispered to me. "I wish I could go back in time to show you this during the war." Lips grazed my jaw. "Life is always difficult, but sometimes it does get better, and that kind of grace never fully leaves."

"Well, Piercey taking over as Prophet is a permanent upgrade."

He chuckled.

"I love retirement."

"It's not retirement when you travel around the world keeping peace for Skia Hellig, or when you train day and night to face our next war."

I shrugged off the comment. "We sleep in the same house as our kids every night. How is that not retirement?"

He chuckled. "Fair point."

Finn clambered over to us and looked down at the baby. "Is she sleeping again? She sleeps so much."

"Don't wake her up."

He giggled. "If I do, she'll cry. Sleep and cry. That's all little baby does." His smile showed off a missing front tooth. "I can put her to bed for you, Mommy. I'm good at it." He was so adorable and sweet.

"Thanks, buddy. Maybe later."

Elsie picked a daisy and walked closer to Tove, who tended to her favorite rosebush. She placed the flower behind the girl's ear, fingers lingering in a brief trail down her hair. It took a long time for Elsie to open up to Tove again after losing Rylan. I thought it was because it felt like betrayal, but I came to realize she was afraid of losing the person closest to her.

"You were right before." Nash's voice carried a chuckle. "Our daughter was the charmer all along."

So, he'd noticed it, too. "Like father, like daughter. Tove doesn't stand a chance, does she?"

Nash grinned at me. "You're finally admitting defeat for once in your life."

"Yes." I reached up to smooth my hand along his cheek. "You lived through nearly dying in the cave and made me fall for you. You used your power on me ever since, and consistently beat me at being a flirting asshole."

"Why do you always call me that?"

"Because you enjoy teasing too much."

When the war started, I recognized that I would be leaving my baby behind with it, and that Finn would be in another stage of his life when it ended. I didn't know we'd be leaving our little girl behind with the war, too. She grew far beyond that young life into a woman ready to fight for and defend her kingdom. From the start, it was clear she walked this path, but to see her actually growing beyond us shocked me.

Juni was the greatest surprise to come out of the war, though.

Her tiny arms and legs stretched. Her body curled. "Oh," I said, mesmerized by every move she made.

"She's waking up," Nash said quietly.

Finn leaned against his knees. "Good morning, Juni."

We all watched her open her tired eyes. My heart was too full and I didn't know how to contain so much joy. When happiness came, I still felt that sting of worry that I may lose it, but I understood that no season lasted forever, and I needed to hold on to joy when it came.

Nash slid an arm around my waist and placed his other hand on the back of Juni's head.

"Know where I want to go?" I smiled. "The ocean."

"Yes," Finn squealed. "Let's go."

"Elsie girl," I called. "Want to go to the ocean?"

Sitting across from Tove, deep in their conversation, Elsie barely even looked at me. "Maybe next time."

"Wow," Nash whispered.

I teleported the four of us to the beach and left Elsie in the little world she was creating for herself.

Finn ran out into the water and then darted back onto the sand, exclaiming that it was too cold.

Nash took our daughter and held her tenderly. "Told you the next time we came, there'd be no more war."

I gazed at the fjords and listened to the powerful waves of the ocean.

Then I pivoted and sprinted for Finn. He screamed when I grabbed him and threw us both into the ocean water.

I swam with my son and returned to shore to lie down with my husband. The four of us drifted to sleep beneath the summer sun.

The cheers echoed throughout the village.

War had not stolen Markus's ability to whip our people into a frenzy.

He stood on the stage in the center of the village where we used to have our annual festival before Malach and Cleo attacked.

We sat in the front rows together like we did six years ago now, right before the terrible war gripped our kingdom.

Elsie and Tove both sat on the ground, resting against our legs. Finn sat on Nash's lap and tickled Juni's tiny feet while I held her. So often, I struggled to believe any of this was real. If Cleo really had killed Nash, our family would have never been put back together again.

Leif folded his arms on top of my head and leaned against me.

"Ow." I tried to swat him away.

"We're fighting this year, right?"

"I'm retired now."

A chorus of laughter erupted all around me. Piercey and Wren, Leif's entire family, and all of mine howled together. Elara smiled sweetly, watching us all.

"Stop acting like you're the funny one in the family, Sharpshooter." Nash winked at me.

"Maybe I don't feel like fighting today."

More snickering.

"Fine," I said. "I'm dying to fight each and every one of you." I nudged Elsie with my boot. "Especially this girl right here."

"Really?" She wheeled around. "Are you serious?"

"Sure. Why not?"

Elsie screamed and laughed like a wild woman. "Finally!"

"What about me?" Nash asked. "Don't you want to fight your dad?"

"I'll fight you both at once." Our daughter punched the air. "All of Skia Hellig can witness your defeat."

Tove covered Elsie's mouth with a grin. "You're hurting my ears."

"Oh." Elsie ripped her hand away and pointed. "Look. They're bringing the baskets out now."

I clung to Juni and watched Elsie's eyes light up ten minutes later when the show began. Power sparked in the sky. Our people shared new history to display at the festival. New victories and losses. But it was Elsie whom I couldn't take my eyes off. The last time I watched her, she was only thirteen, and I worried about war one day stealing the joy from her. Sitting next to Tove on the ground, Elsie stared at the powder spreading throughout the sky with the same excitement as she had when she was a child.

I'd been right, though. It was different now. It wouldn't ever be the same. Because her eyes lit despite all the pain she'd suffered and the loss of a friend she'd always love.

I bowed to dip my head against Juni and then scooted closer to the boys. Nash ran his hand along my back while I saw Finn experience the festival for the first time. Power reflected in his wide eyes.

I knew that such terrible suffering existed, that it was too great to feel or comprehend, and that it never really left.

Maybe for the first time, I truly understood that such a joy existed as well.

All those years ago before the war when Elara and I spoke at the festival, she'd told me that some peace runs so deep that not even war can crush it. That was before she'd lost her son and then our precious Rylan. I hadn't understood then how any peace could survive a war. Pull us through a war. Looking at her now, seeing her joy as she watched the children, I finally understood true power. We all lost more than we believed possible but here we were, together, and determined to cherish each other. Even if it meant wearing the beads of those we would always long for.

Elara's eyes met mine and a quiet look of understanding passed between us. The kind warriors shared after surviving battle together. I smiled at her and then I looked at my husband, who sat here with us. Who was no longer lost. Finally, I gave myself permission to release all the fear and pain for this moment of joy, because it was too precious to lose. It had taken me so long to learn this lesson.

"I can't breathe." I met Nash's gaze. "I'm too happy."

For a moment, he'd looked worried, but now it melted into a smile. "Oh, Max."

"I'm glad we decided to have one more."

"Me, too."

Elsie hushed us and slapped my ankle. Some things never changed.

Once the history of our people dissolved on the wind, Markus returned to the stage. More gray streaked his hair than last time, and I couldn't miss the fatigue. He'd worked so hard for so long.

"The four kingdoms of Skia Hellig now reign as one, united by the light of the sun," Markus announced. "Our four Prophets vowed in blood to serve you and leave behind the days when power was used to crush you." His arm raised to indicate the four governing Prophets who now joined him. "Prophet Jakob of the Flatlands." Those gathered from his land roared from all around the crowd. "Prophet Demetri of the Fjellfolk." I smiled, watching the people try to scream louder each time. "Prophet Sanara of the coast." I crossed my arms, smirking now. "And Prophet Piercey of the Valley."

The village quaked with screams. It had taken them a decade to warm up to Piercey, but they finally saw what I always had all along. He was the right person for this job.

"All vow themselves to you." Markus met my eye, reaching his hand out. "And to the head of the Skia Hellig High Kingdom."

I had a feeling when I became Prophet that there was another role waiting for me. One that would feel like I was born for it.

Nash and I walked hand in hand to meet Markus and the Prophets. My advisor, who had stayed with us every step of the way through the birth and rebirth of our kingdom, took each of our wrists and lifted them high.

"Our guardians of Skia Hellig." He pumped our arms. "The Everlight."

The name Eclipse grew with me from one I fled to one I finally embraced. But this, the union of Nash and me as the protectors of our people, felt right from the start.

"The four souls of Skia Hellig united to form one, and so have the mother and father of our high kingdom. The Prophet Eclipse and the great War Chief Nash, imbued with the eternal power of our great sun, stand united as well. The Everlight will watch over you."

"It's over." I set my eyes on the people who gathered from every corner of Skia Hellig. "Not just the war from the north or the division in the peninsula. The tyranny is over. The power of the gods will never be used to crush you again. These dark days are in the past. We now have the power here in our world and beyond to fight for you."

Nash worked his arm around me. "We may face loss again, but we will never lose faith that we will win. Skia Hellig never surrenders."

Emotion gripped me watching our people rally. We knew what they'd been through during this war and in the past. Just like Elsie, they carried their losses close, and still managed to celebrate with us. To live.

Finally, after a very long journey, I found my rightful place.

With the four Prophets ruling and our land at peace, Nash and I could protect our people like we wanted and still have time for our family. We still carried out duties as rulers, but many of the daily tasks I never felt suited for fell onto our Prophets.

The myth of the Everlight grew beyond my level of comfort, swelling into wild tales of ascension and godhood. I could not stop the people from seeing in us what they wished, even if I knew Nash and I were not gods. Rather, I never let them forget our humanity. The Collective taught me the danger of losing that.

Through the years, Nash held me steady, but this family we created kept me rooted. I savored the kiss of his lips every day, and fought for our children to grow into exactly who they wanted to be, and lived my life to the fullest.

When the darkness came again—as it always did—light continued to shine, eclipsed or not.

And always the brightness of everlight returned.

Epilogue

I lived through our life again from the very beginning to now, through meeting Nash in the Prophet's captivity, to stealing our world away from Dr. Henderson. I watched my life unfold through my younger self, holding close all I had learned since, as I met myself in another world and bound myself to Nash. As we raised a kingdom and a family. As we watched what we raised grow into more than we ever hoped to be. I watched the afterlife, and the simulations, and I watched as I settled down to live through it all again.

Nash's hand gripped mine tightly when we woke together from the sum total of all we'd ever known, having lived it once more through new eyes. We'd never been alone. We'd wandered through this life, young and lost, and we'd watched over those kids from the people we grew into.

Bound meant more than I could have known back then.

First, we found our children and held them close. Held their children just as well. Kissed all we loved goodbye again and promised our return.

Together, Nash and I stood before the council. I remembered once lacking the voice and the knowledge I desperately needed. That younger version of myself died and bled to fight a war that once felt hopeless. Once had been hopeless.

Now I'd transformed.

Standing in the place my younger self once stood, I looked clear-eyed at the ones I once called gods, and saw only flawed humans in their place.

Coralee stood before me. I felt more similar to her than I did when I was young, but we were still so different. "Why did the Collective fail?" she asked us.

"Hate binds us as tightly as love," I said, holding Nash's hand—holding it as I had for countless lifetimes. "It grows from the smallest seed of fear and yearning for power."

"There are still people suffering," Coralee said. "The Kethios must continue to evolve. Can you see all people as your people?"

"Yes," Nash said, answering with what filled both our hearts.

Coralee held my gaze, smiling now. "Then, do you accept your position on the council?"

I smiled, ran my thumb along the back of Nash's hand, and looked up at him before speaking. "We accept."

Now the hardest battle of our many lifetimes really began.

About the Author

Lindsay French is the author of the Eclipse series, originally released on Royal Road. When she isn't trying to convince her middle school students to fall in love with reading, she's writing twisty science fiction and fantasy. There are few things she loves more than creating complex characters, dynamic action, and unforgettable adventures. French lives in the Midwest with her husband and one of the world's cutest dogs.

JOIN THE FELLOWSHIP

follow us on our socials

podiumentertainment.com

@podiumentertainment

/podiumentertainment

@podium_ent

@podiumentertainment